THE BIRTHD

Zoë Miller was born in Dublin, where she now lives with her husband. She began writing stories at an early age. Her writing career has also included freelance journalism and prize-winning short fiction. She has three children.

www.zoemillerauthor.com
@zoemillerauthor
Facebook.com/zoemillerauthor

Previously by Zoë Miller
The House in the Woods
The Perfect Sister
The Visitor
A House Full of Secrets
Someone New
A Question of Betrayal
A Husband's Confession
The Compromise
A Family Scandal
Rival Passions
Sinful Deceptions
Guilty Secrets

ZOË MILLER

THE
BIRTHDAY
WEEKEND

HACHETTE
BOOKS
IRELAND

First published in Ireland in 2024 by
HACHETTE BOOKS IRELAND
First published in paperback in 2025

2

Cataloguing in Publication Data is available from the British Library

ISBN 9781399725644

Typeset in Sabon MT by Bookends Publishing Services, Dublin
Printed and bound in Great Britain by Clays Ltd, Elcograf S.p.A.

Hachette Books Ireland policy is to use papers that are natural, renewable and
recyclable products and made from wood grown in sustainable forests. The logging and
manufacturing processes are expected to conform to the environmental regulations of
the country of origin.

Hachette Books Ireland
8 Castlecourt Centre
Castleknock
Dublin 15, Ireland

A division of Hachette UK Ltd
Carmelite House, 50 Victoria Embankment, London EC4Y 0DZ

www.hachettebooksireland.ie

*Dedicated with love, always, to the
magnificent seven who bring so much joy –*

Cruz, Tom, Lexi, J.P., Sophia, Éabha and Holly

The Kerry Herald

Monday, 30 January 2023, 7 a.m.

BREAKING NEWS

A body has been discovered in suspicious circumstances in a property in west Kerry after a serious incident last night involving members of the Garda Emergency Response Unit, assisted by ambulance and emergency crews. Another person was found in a critical condition and has been transferred to University Hospital Kerry. The village of Wolf Cove and the immediate vicinity of Wolf Head have been sealed off by gardaí and the property is being preserved as a crime scene. An Garda Síochána is commencing a full investigation into the circumstances of the fatal incident under the direction of a senior investigating officer. The state pathologist and the Garda Technical Bureau are expected to arrive at the scene later this morning.

Investigating gardaí are appealing to anyone who has any information that might help the investigation, or who was in the area of Wolf Cove or Wolf Head between 1 p.m. yesterday afternoon and 1 a.m. this morning to contact them immediately.

Gardaí will not confirm if the incident is linked to a rescue operation mounted on Saturday afternoon at Wolf Head, in which a vehicle was recovered from the sea. The vehicle is confirmed to be registered to Dublin socialite Lucinda Oliver, who disappeared when her car plunged off the cliff in July 2022. Sources have indicated that the vehicle contained skeletal remains, which have been moved to University Hospital Kerry for formal identification. A technical examination of the vehicle is also taking place.

This is a breaking news story and will be updated.

FIVE DAYS EARLIER
WEDNESDAY, 25 JANUARY

CHAPTER ONE

Stella

The images are stalking her again, shredding her heart. Lucinda's car disappearing over the edge of Wolf Head on a stifling summer's evening, taking her with it. Her sister, trapped for ever in the coffin of her scarlet Mini Cooper, shrouded for eternity in her floaty yellow dress. The car hitting the water with force, and spinning around helplessly under shifting fathoms of steel-grey Atlantic waters, at the mercy of the deep ocean tides. Wolf Cove, The Lookout, Lucinda's birthday weekend, that last argument with her …

They speed in front of her vision like a disjointed video clip on fast forward, recklessly accelerating until it suddenly snaps.

Stella blinks. It takes her a moment to realise she's at home in her apartment in Portobello. The pages of a budgetary forecast she's been trying to study have slipped from her hand and are drifting down to the oak floor. She sits for a moment, breathing slowly.

It's painful to breathe. Painful to move around in a world without her sister. And six months after Lucinda's accident, nightmare images are tumbling in more frequently. She scoops up the report and goes over to the kitchen to get some wine. She's lifting a glass out of the press when her intercom chimes.

'Who's there?' she asks bluntly, unable to summon necessary politeness. She'd cast off her work clothes and pulled on a tracksuit as soon as she came home from the Women's Rescue office on Percy Place, glad to be discarding the brisk, efficient and relentlessly exhausting façade she'd hidden behind all day. She hasn't the energy for anyone right now.

'Stella?'

She freezes. She knows that voice. 'What is it?' she asks, hoping it's merely a form she hasn't filled in properly.

A mountain of red tape had accompanied Lucinda's accident. Bureaucratic officialdom and functionary forms holding boxes to fill and tick: a cold, clinical, crappy summary of her sister's life, a million miles away from the warm, rich, mercurial extravaganza of contradictions that once embodied the living and breathing Lucinda.

'Sorry for disturbing you but I need to talk to you,' he says.

She stays silent. She has nothing to say to this man. She can't bear to feel exposed to him again.

'It's urgent,' he says.

Her throat constricts. 'Come up,' she manages to say, pressing the entry button. She goes out into her hallway and leaves the door to her apartment ajar. No doubt he remembers to take the lift up to the third floor and that her penthouse apartment is the door on the right.

She wonders what else he remembers.

She goes back into the living room. Against the picture window, the softly lit room is reflected against the dark January night. She stands in the middle of it, like a bereft and broken survivor struggling to remain upright. She straightens her spine and wraps her arms around herself as a sort of shield against whatever is 'urgent'. From behind her, she hears the soft click of her door closing, the tread of his feet down the hallway and into the living room. A pause. The hairs on the back of her neck rise. She turns slowly to face him. Chief Superintendent Hugh Connell of An Garda Síochána, attached to Kevin Street Divisional Headquarters in the south inner city, is clad in a bulky navy jacket, his hair speckled with beads of mist, and he carries in the scent of damp January air along with his authority.

While the investigation of Lucinda's accident was coordinated from the office in Kenmare, Hugh is her liaison in Dublin. He phoned her regularly during those early weeks, checking in with her to see if she'd like any further support, then finding gentle ways to tell her that the investigation had stalled. She'd always found him to be kind, polite and considerate within the boundaries of officialdom. Until the night three weeks ago when he'd found her on Portobello Bridge, staring blankly down into the canal and he'd brought her home and stayed the night. They'd both agreed the following morning that it had been a big mistake.

'Sorry to intrude,' he says.

Even in the muted light, she sees the compassion in his eyes. Her scalp tightens.

'Maybe you'd best sit down,' he says.

'No,' she says, the empathy in his voice causing a spike of fear to shoot up inside her. Loss and fear go hand in hand, she's found out, nipping in unison at your heart. 'What's happened?'

'They've found something,' he says. 'In the sea off Wolf Head. It appears to be Lucinda's car.'

The inside of her head bursts into a long, silent scream. She's aware that she's about to slump, like a marionette whose strings have been cut. Hugh must have been expecting it, must have delivered plenty of alarming news in his time, because he catches her before she falls.

She sits on the sofa, her shaking legs hidden by a crimson throw. He hands her a glass of brandy, the mellow aroma drifting up to her nostrils.

'Medicinal,' he says. He knew where to find it. He'd brought it up from his car that fateful night, intending to drink it at home, alone, he'd said, because it was the anniversary of his wife's death from a brain tumour. Instead they'd shared most of it, as well as their darkest thoughts and deepest fears, before falling into bed and finding solace in each other's bodies. Before he'd left the following morning, he'd shoved the bottle into the back of the kitchen press, apologising for crossing his professional and ethical boundaries.

She hasn't touched it since.

He sits down at her table, his bulky winter jacket slung over the back of a chair. Hugh is forty-ish, of medium height and stocky, but his sense of self and his quietly confident bearing make him appear strong, invincible. His straight dark hair sticks up in clumps, like an upturned brush. 'Can I call a friend for you?' he asks.

She senses his unspoken words – *I don't want to find you on a bridge again staring down into the water*. She meets his gaze, forcing on the armour she's acquired to face the world. 'No, thanks. Just tell me what's happened.'

He sighs and rubs his face. 'I'm sorry,' he says, 'I know this is upsetting. Earlier today a car was spotted below the surface of the sea off Wolf Head by local fishermen, Eoin Fitzmaurice and his son, Tadhg.'

She takes a large gulp of brandy, relieved that it is already taking a tiny edge off her panic. 'Go on.'

'They were up on the head with a new drone when they saw something in the water, less than half a mile out. Eoin zoned in and realised he was looking at the underneath of a car a few metres deep. He zoned in further again at a different angle, and when the sea had calmed, he was able to make out a red car with a side stripe.'

A crump in her chest. The sense of something extinguishing inside her – the tiny flame of hope that a mistake of some kind had been made.

Hugh is talking: 'Current forecasts indicate that wind speeds are increasing over the next twenty-four hours and the sea will be too rough to attempt any kind of safe rescue, given the location of the car so close to submerged rocks.'

She gasps at the image of Lucinda's car being hurled against the rocks.

'Sorry,' Hugh says.

'Not something I haven't imagined a million times. What happens next?'

He gives her a look filled with concern before continuing. 'Garda divers are preparing to go down to Kerry and liaise with our colleagues, the Navy and the Coast Guard so that they can prepare for a multi-agency recovery mission as soon as conditions are favourable. That's likely to be Saturday. We're not yet releasing any specific information about the car but people, including the media, are bound to make the connection. Stella,' he pauses, 'I know this will be a traumatic time and you have my deepest condolences.'

'Thank you.' She puts down her glass on the low table and drops her face into her hands. Her skull feels like it's fracturing into a million pieces. When she eventually looks up, Hugh is regarding her with empathy in his eyes, but he has made no move towards her, conscious, she guesses, of what happened the last time he comforted her.

'How come the car wasn't spotted before now?' she asks, her voice flat.

'From what I know, the local fishermen have always kept an eye out. They're speculating that the car had been further out to sea in deeper waters. Then, over the months, it was shunted in by the shifting tides, but it was a combination of factors this afternoon. It was sunny in Kerry today, the sea was clear, and whatever way the current was running and dragging the water ...' He hesitates, wary, she guesses, of the picture his words are painting. 'It was unfortunate they were prevented from doing a full search at the time of the accident.'

She nods. A freak storm had surged in from the Atlantic that nightmare Saturday evening and settled in for a few days, making it too dangerous to undertake any rescue or recovery attempt in the seas around Wolf Head. It was almost a week after the accident by the time it was safe enough for the Coast Guard to search, and by then there had been no sign of the car. Or of Lucinda.

'The Kerry division won't release anything official until I confirm next of kin have been informed,' Hugh says. 'But something might leak out onto social media, I guess the division won't be able to contain it beyond tomorrow morning. Is there anyone you need to contact now or would like me to talk to?'

'No, thanks,' she says. Her parents are dead. There are relatives in England on her father's side, and a few far-flung cousins on her mother's, but nobody close enough to need advance notification, except Britt. 'I'll talk to Britt, my mother's cousin, although chances are, she already knows. She lives in Kerry, about twenty kilometres up the coast from Wolf Head. And Lucinda's friends who were at the party that weekend – I'll let them know.'

Hugh outlines the steps that will be involved in recovering the car.

'I'm going down,' she says. 'I want to be there when Lucinda's body is recovered.'

'I can arrange transport for you.'

'No, thanks. I'll be fine.' She looks at him defiantly, challenging him to suggest she's in no fit state to undertake the almost five-hour drive from Dublin to Wolf Cove.

'I'm sure you will,' he says. 'But don't try to be too much of a hero. Even our caped crusaders need a helping hand now and again.'

Their gazes meet. She remembers the feel of his hot skin against hers and looks away. She recalls the trail of their hastily discarded clothes running from the living room through to her bedroom. She thinks of the following morning, when he brought her coffee, and she had her duvet clutched up to her chin to cover her nakedness – hilarious in itself, given that he'd pretty much seen everything the night before.

A big mistake.

The mind loves playing tricks on us, she decides, if she can remember such contrary moments in the middle of the black news she's trying to absorb. Wanting him gone, she puts down her glass, shrugs away the throw and gets to her feet. 'Thanks for your help, but I won't hold you up any longer. I've calls to make.'

Hugh stands up and puts on his jacket, looking official all of a sudden. 'Text me when that's done so I know everything is covered before the news is released.'

'I will.'

He hesitates at the door. 'Are you sure you're okay?'

'I'm perfectly fine.' He seems at such a loss that she tacks on another fib for good measure. 'Honestly.'

'Let me know when you reach Kerry and where you're staying. I'll advise the team down there and have them liaise with you.'

In the stillness after he's gone, a sudden, visceral hunger for Lucinda swamps her, a craving to touch her skin and hug her, talk to her. She feels dizzy and untethered.

All along, Stella had clung to a faint hope that Lucinda's car hadn't gone over the edge after all, taking her with it. That the sighting had been a mistake. She'd staved off the worst of her bleak moments by imagining her sister out there in the world somewhere, getting her act together. Maybe on a retreat in a Tibetan monastery, or learning hula dancing on a Hawaiian island. Now that there's no hope Lucinda might be kicking her heels up in some far-flung, exotic part of the world, Stella is gripped by an urgent need to find out exactly what happened to cause Lucinda to drive off Wolf Head on a Saturday night.

She recalls the conversation she'd had with her sister two weeks before the party weekend.

'I went off the rails big-time. But I'm finally getting my life back on track.'

'What happened, Lucinda?' she'd asked anxiously.

Her quirky smile. 'Oh, you know me, Stella darling. The black sheep of the family, living a madcap life while my wonderful sister puts the country to rights. I don't deserve you, but I'm happy now that my past sins won't catch up with me, and I'm getting my act together.'

She can't help thinking about Lucinda's comment – *past sins*. Stella hadn't followed this up at the time, too caught up in her own problems, finding it convenient to go with the flow of Lucinda's carefree air. After the heartbreak of her sister's accident, she'd filtered those words out, too frozen with pain to go there.

Or, her deepest fear, could the accident have had anything to do with the argument they'd had that morning, the spiteful words Stella had hurled at Lucinda? Had Lucinda been more upset than she'd realised when Stella had threatened to cut short her weekend and go home to Dublin? Could it have made her too preoccupied to focus properly on the thin ribbon of road at the summit of Wolf Head? What if Stella's harsh words had driven Lucinda off the edge?

Or did Lucinda's friends know more than they were saying?

Caz, Maisie, Eddie, Janet and Aaron, Lucinda's closest mates. They had all been friends for years, some since school, others since college. Five years younger, Stella had felt a little apart from them and their love for high-octane partying. They'd always celebrated their various milestone occasions, including a week in Santorini around the time of their thirtieth birthdays. Stella had been invited on the trip, but had had to turn it down on account of a month-long residency at Boston College as part of her MPhil in Gender and Women's Studies.

Then early last July, Lucinda had asked Stella if she'd like to come to the party weekend in Wolf Cove. Caz, Eddie and

Janet had turned forty in the previous few months, Lucinda would be forty at the end of July. They hadn't all been together like that since the crazy week in Santorini, she'd said, and they were going to have a blast, all of them chipping in for the expense. Eddie's girlfriend Sasha was also coming, she'd said. The plan was that the weekend would culminate in a mega joint fortieth birthday gala celebration on the Saturday night, the eve of Lucinda's birthday, at which, she'd said, she had a special announcement to make.

It had never happened.

The days in The Lookout that surrounded the accident are still blurry in Stella's head, details eluding her. She has no idea what kind of announcement Lucinda had planned to make, but she remembers the charged feeling running through the weekend. Lucinda and her friends partied their way through Thursday and Friday, each day more frenzied than the one before. Stella mostly observed the madness, wondering how her patience and fake smile would last the wildly accelerating pace. Had something been simmering behind the scenes that she'd been unaware of?

She'd sensed something had gone amiss in Santorini, 'Totes savage,' Lucinda had said afterwards. Stella guessed by her widened eyes it had been a lot fiercer than savage, but Lucinda had refused to be drawn on it. 'What happened in Santorini stays in Santorini.' She smiled ruefully.

Still, after that, the group of friends hadn't all been away together until the weekend at The Lookout.

Stella picks up her glass of brandy and chucks the rest of it into the sink. She feels like she's waking up from a long sleep.

CHAPTER TWO

Stella

'Whatever you want me to do, just shout,' Britt Butler says. 'I'm always here for you, chicken.'

The term of endearment coming from practical, no-nononsense Britt rushes warmly through Stella's veins and floors her. 'God, Britt, is this really happening?' She has the urge to scream and howl and weep snotty tears, but that will have to wait. She has things to do. She tightens her grip on her mobile. Her call had been no surprise to Britt, who'd already heard the news from Eoin Fitzmaurice. He'd given her a quiet heads-up, Britt said, because Lucinda is family. Family in the spirit of the word, Stella privately acknowledges, even though she was no blood relative of Lucinda's.

One of Lucinda's demons.

'You were the planned baby,' she'd say to Stella. 'I was the dumped one. The foundling.'

'You were the chosen one,' Stella would reply. 'I'm so glad to have you for my sister.'

Stella pulls herself back from that twisty rabbit hole.

'It'll be tough, Stella,' Britt's voice is a mixture of pragmatism and concern, 'but I hope it won't be as shocking or painful for you as the days following the accident, and that it helps you get some sense of closure.'

'I'm coming down,' Stella says.

'I'll have the guest room ready, if that suits you.'

'Thanks for the offer.' Stella hesitates, an idea that has been churning away since Hugh left firming up. 'I thought I might stay in The Lookout,' she says, 'and ask you to join me there. If it's available.'

The name of the house scores painfully across her brain, like the point of a scalpel. The flamboyant, almost vulgar house overlooking the sea that Lucinda had rented for the party, situated on the laneway that leads up to Wolf Head.

A short pause. Britt says, 'The Lookout? Is that wise, Stella? I know it's convenient to Wolf Head and I'd be more than happy to join you there, but would it not be full of sad memories for you?'

Exactly. Being down there again might help Stella remember the chain of events that led to the accident. Does she know more than she realises? What else is hiding in the recesses of her mind, buried under months of frozen, compacted grief? But that was only the half of it. 'I'm also thinking of asking Lucinda's friends if any of them want to join me,' she says.

'Lucinda's friends?'

Stella can't blame Britt for the note of surprise in her voice. An invitation to the depths of Kerry at such short notice and in cold, grey January, for what was surely going to be a sad occasion, was a far remove from a lavish weekend celebration at the height of summer.

'I know how much I want to be there, and they might also want to be there, for Lucinda.'

'How are they all doing?'

'I haven't seen any of them since that weekend. I hadn't the energy to ...' She tails off. Lucinda's friends had sent texts in those early weeks, which fizzled out after Stella had barely engaged with them. She'd been so emotionally drained that she hadn't had the bandwidth to cope with smothering displays of sympathy, never mind to witness their grief or take it on board in addition to her own.

Then she'd also begun to wonder if one of them was trolling her.

'I can fully understand you needing your privacy, pet,' Britt says.

Stella's vision blurs from the tears in her eyes. She'd also kept Britt at arm's length, rebuffing her offers to come to Dublin to see her. Conscious of the wobble in her voice she says, 'I hardly spoke to Lucinda's friends after the accident. I was in shock. I'd like to give them the opportunity to be there, and it's a chance for me to talk to them properly. I was hoping you might check with the landlord and see if The Lookout is free.'

'Sure, pet,' Britt says, in calm tones, which Stella is grateful for. 'The landlord is in London but Tricia Dillon is the caretaker. I'll get on to her the minute I hang up. Once the news breaks, you can be sure the rooms in The Pier and any available beds in the area will be grabbed by media hounds and whoever else might be sniffing around.'

The small village of Wolf Cove, down below Wolf Head, doesn't boast a hotel, just The Pier, a few B&Bs and summer property lets scattered around the hinterland. Tricia was the owner of The Pier, a gastropub in Wolf Cove that also offers rooms on the first floor.

'Thanks, Britt, you're a star. I hope to be in Kerry early tomorrow afternoon. Send me a text when you know. I've other calls to make now.'

'Will you be travelling alone or coming with a friend?' Britt asks her.

Stella's three-year relationship with an actuary called Leo had been supposed to lead to marriage and babies but had come to an abrupt halt the previous spring when she'd found him in bed with Davina, one of her friends from college. She'd also allowed it to alienate her from their friendship group, Stella doing the withdrawing, lest they had to pick any sides. She had ignored social invitations in case they included Davina, and sent bland replies to their messages of concern in the aftermath of Lucinda's accident.

An image of Rex O'Neill tipping his glass to hers with his cheerful smile swims into her thoughts. Just friends, she knows he could be a help in shoring up the difficult days that lie waiting for her. Rex, with his breezy good humour and air of easy confidence, who always looks as though he can handle anything without bothering to sweat the small stuff, may be the right person for her to have at her side for support, a kind of relaxed buffer between her and Lucinda's friends.

'I'll be coming down by myself, Britt, but I might have a friend joining me later.'

After she's spoken to Britt, Stella makes short calls to her colleagues, explaining her absence. Everyone in the Women's Rescue office had gently and kindly put a supportive ring around her since Lucinda's disappearance, giving her a reason to get up every morning and put one foot in front of the other.

She goes into her bedroom to pack her bag for the weekend. From her chest of drawers, she picks up a framed collage of photos of herself and Lucinda, her heart splintering as she absorbs the images taken at various milestones in their childhood.

Five-year-old Lucinda, her wide smile showing two rows of perfect pearly teeth as she stands beside the crib where baby Stella is cocooned in pink softness.

A Christmas photo of them in matching red pyjamas, ten-year-old Lucinda's arm around her shoulders, Stella, round and chubby at five, her arm clutching Lucinda's waist.

Adolescence found Stella passing her sister in height, five feet six to Lucinda's five feet three. Lucinda kept her blonde hair at shoulder length, whereas Stella's mousy colour and flyaway style is now a choppy, dark-blonde bob. Just last year, Lucinda had heartily approved of the new look Stella was flaunting, saying it brought out her heart-shaped face and beautiful dark grey eyes.

Stella replaces the frame and subsides on the bed, her insides eviscerated.

After their childhoods, their lives had diverged.

Stella had chosen the academic route, a BA in Social Sciences at University College Dublin, followed by the MPhil in Gender and Women's Studies at Trinity. Having worked with various charities to help support and empower marginalised women over the years, she was now the CEO of Women's Rescue, a registered charity set up to support and improve the lives of women and children adversely impacted by drug abuse, whether by a family member or their own addiction. When her parents died, the proceeds of their estate had been split evenly between Lucinda and Stella. Stella used her inheritance to buy her apartment in Portobello, lured by its convenience to the city centre and the huge picture window overlooking the canal.

In contrast, Lucinda had always flitted on the edges of a precarious livelihood. After school, she studied Fashion Design with Styling at Greenfield College of Further Education in south city Dublin, surprising everyone when she dropped out just before the Easter term, heading to London for a few months with Caz. However, nothing daunted Lucinda, and in the months after her return, her interest in the world of fashion and styling had led her into a successful career as an underwear model at the height of the Celtic Tiger era, which then launched her into celebrity status just as social media was beginning to take off. She'd moved into the world of PR and event management, before returning to fashion. She'd used her inheritance to set herself up as a freelance fashion stylist and influencer, based in her rented apartment in Malahide, a lot of her work generated and supported through social-media platforms and regular engagement with her thousands of followers.

Amassing followers and increasing her traction had been Lucinda's bread and butter, so much so that sometimes Stella had found herself teasing her sister about dipping into Instagram to see what Lucinda was up to. The sisters hadn't met up on a regular basis, caught up in their totally different worlds, but they'd always spent Christmas together and made sure to take time out to treat each other for birthdays, weekends away, and any celebrations. Stella was happy that Lucinda was following her heart's desire, and she knew Lucinda was proud of her successes, bringing her out for a surprise meal when she'd been appointed to her CEO role early last year. And if Stella had sometimes worried that Lucinda was still renting in an increasingly volatile housing market, Lucinda had gently laughed off her concerns, telling her that she would always land on her feet.

Stella pulls her case out of the wardrobe, along with two pairs of jeans. From her chest of drawers, she plucks freshly laundered sweaters.

If it's anything like the news of her disappearance, her sister's adoring flock of social-media followers will be all over it as soon as the discovery off Wolf Head breaks, sparking a fresh outpouring of grief. After the accident, some of Lucinda's devotees had even made the long journey to Wolf Head, placing bouquets on the cliff top close to where her car had disappeared, calling it their pilgrimage, posing for selfies, smoothing beautiful hairstyles against the ravaging Atlantic gales.

Then about three months ago, one of her fans set up an Instagram page solely dedicated to Lucinda's memory, with a hashtag to be used by her followers: #leavealightonforLucinda. But interspersed with tributes to Lucinda, someone is using the page to troll Stella, blaming her for the accident. Composed to avoid a sanction, profiles continually changing and being deleted, the posts are always intimidating and cruel:

The sister knows exactly what happened to Lucinda – after all, she caused it with her ugly words.

How would it feel to know your sister is de*d because of you?

I'd hate to have my sister's death on my conscience – b**ch!

How can that sl*g sleep at night, knowing she kil*ed her sister?

Stella shoves clothes into her case, then goes through to her en-suite to fill a toiletry bag, scarcely heeding what she's throwing in. More troubling, and recently, similarly worded anonymous and untraceable texts have begun coming through to her personal mobile – the same person or a copycat? And who is doing this? One of Lucinda's friends? It has to be someone who'd been in The Lookout that weekend, had overheard her angry words and knows her personal mobile number. She should be reporting these, but what if her tormentor is right?

Back in her bedroom, she hears the ping of her mobile. Britt. The Lookout is available for as long as Stella needs it, and Britt will be there from midday tomorrow.

Stella throws some underwear and thick socks into her case. Time to face this head-on. The WhatsApp group formed for the party weekend is still on her phone – Caz, Maisie, Janet, Eddie, Lucinda and her, the Fizzy 40s. She composes a text, her fingers hovering over the words, her stomach churning. Once she presses send, she's going to propel shockwaves through their worlds. Her breath stops for a minute when she realises the message will also go to Lucinda's mobile, water-logged and ruined by now, trapped like her in a bright red car under dark grey seas. According to Hugh, her mobile had last been triangulated to Wolf Head, with no activity on it after the day of the accident.

He'd also told her that nothing out of the ordinary had been reported in the statements Lucinda's friends had made to the guards following the accident. Nobody had witnessed Lucinda driving off from The Lookout that Saturday evening, and in her shocked, numbed state, Stella had accepted Hugh's words at the time. But now, the more she thinks about it, the more she realises it's odd. For a house aptly named The Lookout, with windows and glass in every direction, and a woman as effervescent as Lucinda, leaving a trail of high spirits and mischief everywhere she went, somebody must have seen something, must have heard something, must know something.

She thinks of the charged atmosphere that had flared through the extravagant weekend.

Someone has to be lying.

CHAPTER THREE

Caz

Caz Costello is having great sex. *Amazing* sex. So she keeps telling herself as she grips the back of her chocolate velvet sofa, arches her spine and tightens herself around the man sitting spread-eagled beneath her.

She's come a long way from the terrified thirteen-year-old who'd cowered beneath the blankets wondering how best to protect herself from the next assault.

Yet in other ways she knows she hasn't moved on at all.

When she'd brought him back to her apartment, she hadn't paused long enough to turn on any lamps or draw the curtains against the night outside. Up here, on the eighth floor of a London apartment block, no one can see in, but the jewelled luminosity rising up from the city, like phosphorescence, casts the room in an intimate glow and enough light to see by. She hears his breath quicken as she rocks to and fro with increasing urgency, taking him deeper.

No use. Long before any slivers of pleasure manage to build inside her, he clamps both hands around her hips, his body shuddering as he comes. She gives a fake cry, as much for her benefit as his. She doesn't want him trying to force something that isn't there. Not tonight. Not any night lately.

Not since Lucinda's accident.

'Hey, nice one,' he says, lifting her off him and sliding out from beneath her, peeling off his condom carefully before he stands up. Her gaze flickers up and down his body, his toned abdomen and muscular bum hinting he'd be good in the sack. Not that she'd been satisfied. A black tide of emptiness and self-reproach sweeps over her. What had she expected? She'd known in advance it would be mechanical sex. That's what happens when you go alone, at nine o'clock in the evening, to a wine bar in Soho that is renowned as a pick-up spot and allow yourself to be escorted home after a few drinks.

She'd badly needed the distraction of a few hours whiled away.

'Where can I get rid of this?' He holds the used condom pinched between his fingers.

'There's a bin in the bathroom,' she says.

He grins. 'Right, but don't go searching for any of my little dudes afterwards.'

'*What?*'

'It happened to a mate of mine. A woman of a certain age helped herself to the contents of his spent shell.'

'A certain age?' *The fuck*.

'Last-chance saloon and all that … Nine months later he gets a request for maintenance.'

'You won't be hearing from me like that.'

She'd be forty-one in three months' time, but Caz knows she's begun to lose her youthful looks thanks to the stress, anxieties, lack of sleep and far too much booze consumed during the last six months. No prizes for guessing she's a card-carrying member of the last-chance saloon, but if she'd ever heard the ticking of a biological clock, she'd easily ignored it. Not for her the clarion call of motherhood. It was the one thing she'd had in common with Lucinda. Sort of.

'Where's the bathroom?'

'First left in the hallway.'

'Okay if I have a quick shower?'

'Sure.' Wiping any traces of her off him before he goes home to his wife. She suspects he's married. They give off different signals from those men who are still single at forty. They're also a safer bet for a one-night stand. At least he's house-trained. She picks up a soft grey throw and wraps it around herself as she plucks her clothes and underwear off the floor. Presently she hears the noise of the shower pump. She's glad they didn't make it as far as the privacy of her bedroom, glad he isn't invading the sanctuary of her luxury en-suite.

She knows she won't see Guy again.

Guy. She doesn't think for a moment it's his real name. She'd told him her name was Lucinda. She doesn't know why the name of her friend slipped out so easily, but it's not the first time that's happened. She doesn't know what that says about her, if she's secretly twisted in some macabre way, pretending to be Lucinda, or if it's a crazy struggle to keep her memory alive. Or some way of stemming the flutter of envy Lucinda had often provoked inside her. No doubt some therapist or grief counsellor would give it a label. If 'Guy' had snooped around her apartment long enough he would have spotted post addressed to Ms Catherine Costello. If he'd got his hands on her mobile, he would have seen her referred to by her friends as Caz.

As soon as he's gone, with a perfunctory kiss on the cheek and no mention of a further date, she pulls closed the thick drapes and switches on art-deco lamps. She tosses her clothes, the bathroom towels and the grey throw into the laundry basket. Then, shivering with goose pimples in spite of the under-floor heating, she goes into the en-suite and takes a hot shower, scouring every trace of him off her body.

Blanking her mind to the way she'd called herself Lucinda.

Clad in a cosy terry robe, she goes into the kitchen and pours a brandy and Baileys nightcap, dispensing some ice from the freezer into her glass. Only when she is sitting on the sofa, a late-night talk show flickering soundlessly on a muted, wall-mounted television screen, does she take out her mobile and re-read the WhatsApp message she'd received earlier that evening from Stella Oliver, a message that had driven her from her apartment in urgent search of a diversion of sorts, in search of conversation, movement, action, people, proof that she was still alive, anything to get away from the suffocating feel of her apartment, as though all the air had been sucked out, thanks to the reminder that Lucinda was gone.

Anything to get away from the gnawing of her conscience.

Stella had sent the message to the WhatsApp group that Lucinda had formed for the party weekend.

Sorry to bring you all upsetting news like this, I know it'll be a shock, and forgive me for the group message, but it's the best way to let you all know at once. A car has been spotted in the sea off Wolf Head that seems to be Lucinda's. The guards are hoping to recover it on Saturday when the weather improves. I'm going down to The Lookout tomorrow. I want to be there when Lucinda is brought ashore. I'm hoping to have a bit of a gathering, a sort of vigil, to honour Lucinda's memory. If any of you would like to join me, you're more than welcome. But no pressure at all, I know it's short notice and you're all busy people. Will keep you updated. Take care, Sx

Reading it again fills her with fresh shock. What the actual *f-u-c-k* ...

There are two replies to Stella's message, first up, Maisie:

Oh Stella, how terrible for you. It's so sad. Sending hugs. Let me know if you need anything, we're all here for you, I'll deffo make it down, stay strong, Maisie xxx.

This is followed by a string of emojis, including hearts, flowers and virtual hugs and kisses. She's not surprised Maisie says she'll be there – she doesn't like being left out of anything. But she's startled to see Janet has responded next. She'd expected Janet would have left the WhatsApp group and want nothing further to do with the gang after that wild weekend. Her marriage to Aaron must have survived because not only has she stayed in the group, she's responded to Stella's message:

OMG, how upsetting for you. This is desperate news but it might bring you closure. Bring all of us some closure. I hope to be there. Thinking of you, big hugs, Janet

The clue is in her message. Closure. It suggests that Janet hasn't reached that elusive state of mind any more than Stella has. Hence remaining in the group. Hungry to keep the connection, for crumbs of information of any kind even if it's an act of painful self-sabotage. Which in Janet's case it must be, given Aaron's stupid antics. Caz clicks into the menu and checks the participants: no one has exited even though little has been posted in recent months. Caz has the uneasy thought that, in keeping the group intact, they are like desperate people clinging to a sinking boat, frozen in time, unable to let go, even though the boat has already capsized and would surely drag them with it to the murky depths beneath.

No word from Eddie. She'd heard the unfortunate news about his business going bust a couple of months ago, and she suspected that he was probably in a bad place right now. He'd always been besotted with Lucinda. She'd found that out the hard way once upon a time in Santorini. She'd thought that holiday might have been a catalyst for her and Eddie to move their friendship to the next level. But no such luck – she'd never be Lucinda. Sometimes she feels, quite ridiculously, as though Lucinda has stolen a march on her by disappearing out of her life so dramatically, leaving her high and dry. She takes a generous slurp of her drink. Caz Costello is a right mixed-up bitch. She doesn't even know who she is any more. Or if she ever knew.

She silences notifications on her mobile before refilling her glass. She hasn't responded to Stella's message. A freelance hair and make-up artist, she has a lucrative bridal-party job booked in for that weekend in Paris. She could arrange cover, but The Lookout and Wolf Head are places she wants never to revisit, even in her mind. Images of that weekend will for ever have the power to haunt her and hold her in a tight grip, just like Lucinda always had.

She'd considered herself to be the yin to Lucinda's yang, in so far as Caz had seen herself as the ordinary one, the foil to Lucinda's sparkle and exuberance. Lucinda had always sent plenty of work her way and had helped her bring out the shiniest version of herself. In return, she'd always been the reliable one, the friend Lucinda counted on to keep her out of too much mischief and save her from herself, which she'd done on many occasions, much to Lucinda's subsequent gratitude. She'd looked out for Lucinda from the time they'd first become sozzled on cheap beer in a sand dune on a north Dublin beach at the age of fourteen, going on to squeeze the most fun out of their short-lived college days. Caz had even dropped out of college to support Lucinda, when they went off together, both of them not yet nineteen. And just last spring, Caz had extricated her from a row with a jealous rival outside a nightclub – whose friend was recording the proceedings for social-media posterity – bundling Lucinda into a taxi and making sure she got home safe.

Caz drops her head into her hands as an image floats into her mind: she and Lucinda having one of their long, boozy lunches, this time at the Merrion last April, to celebrate Caz's fortieth birthday.

'You sure you're okay waiting until July for the big bash?' Lucinda had said.

'Of course. This is lovely,' Caz had said, tilting her glass of champagne to Lucinda. Having her best friend all to herself was the big treat. Being there with Lucinda was balm to her soul, even if Lucinda had left her mobile on the table instead of putting it away, her eyes flickering to it occasionally. Afterwards Caz wondered why she hadn't taken a champagne shot to post on her socials, usually obligatory for Lucinda, especially with the chance to tag the Merrion. Had she not wanted to tag Caz? Sitting there, she'd been conscious that there had been times in the last year or so when Lucinda had gone off the radar for a few weeks at a time, largely ignoring her texts and calls – caught up in her career, she'd tossed lightly, certainly not a man, no one would pin her down – and it had made Caz aware that she needed Lucinda to add colour and sparkle to her life far more than Lucinda needed her. But even when she'd been out with Lucinda, her friend's effervescent energy had been more exuberant than usual, her hilarity more hysterical, and the scene outside the nightclub had alarmed Caz because Lucinda had seemed so uncontrollable, setting Caz on edge.

Then Caz recalls, with a tiny stab to her stomach, in the couple of months leading up to the party, Lucinda had disappeared off the scene again, leaving Caz to try to second-guess what arrangements had been finalised. With three weeks to go, Lucinda had swanned back into action, as though she'd never been out of it, smoothing over Caz's concerns, laughingly telling her not to be such a worrier, that chief party planner Lucinda had everything under control for the best weekend ever.

Caz lifts her head and stares unseeingly at the muted television screen. It was no surprise, was it, that she had finally run out of patience with her friend that awful weekend? Caz had seen that Lucinda was partying like a crazed woman. But this time, she didn't attempt to save her from self-destruction.

And the worst that could happen had actually happened.

CHAPTER FOUR

Eddie

In the small boxroom of a house share in Phibsborough, Eddie Hynes sits on the bed, his back resting into a pillow propped against the wooden headboard, legs sprawled along the top of the duvet, cradling a glass of strong whiskey in one hand, his mobile phone in the other. The minute the shock text had come through from Stella earlier that night, he'd sent Arianna packing, even though he'd enjoyed the sex. Ignoring the way she was flouncing out the door, telling him he was a right dick, he'd hurriedly pulled on some clothes. Since then, he's been unable to put down his phone, his head bursting with what this might mean, what horrors the weekend might bring, trying not to remember Lucinda – which was next to impossible – and watching for replies to come in from the rest of their group, refreshing his feed every so often, in case he's missed something.

He has only stayed sane these past few months by pretending the weekend never happened. During the nights he lies sleepless in rumpled sheets, trying to suck air into his squeezed lungs and calm his galloping heartbeat, he pretends Lucinda is still alive, still breathing, still laughing, that nothing bad has happened to her.

The first reply to Stella's message is from Maisie – who else? Always wanting to please. Then again, nothing wrong with that. He takes another mouthful of whiskey, surprised by this thought, considering he'd always seen her as a bit of a softie, a loser. Maybe now that he was a major loser himself, he could appreciate what it's like to be someone not so cool or popular, who tags along for the sake of appearances, for token friendship, even if it is soul-destroying.

But he'd discovered another side to Maisie that awful weekend, a side she tried to keep hidden from the group. Only now does he get that, more than likely, it sprang from some hidden resentment, and he wonders how long she had been feeling that way to cause her to do what she'd done.

Janet is next to reply. When he reads it, he groans. How could he face Janet again, after the stupid way he and Aaron had behaved that weekend, acting like they couldn't wait to give Lucinda one? *Jesus*. He runs through his usual litany of self-reproach. He's not surprised Sasha dropped him like a hot snot as soon as they returned to Dublin. He's not surprised Caz hasn't talked to him since. Apart from Sasha, and Stella, and maybe Caz, they'd all got ridiculously carried away. He didn't think he'd been knocking back *that* much booze.

Still, in a way it has been a huge relief that the group haven't spoken to him since that weekend.

He refreshes the page again. Nothing from Caz. *Feck it*.

How can he think of facing Caz? And how could he bear to witness everyone's pity now that his corporate leisure business, Theme to Team, had crashed and burned? And moving down the hierarchy of humiliation, how could he explain away the rust bucket he was driving, now that his precious sports car had been repossessed? *Driving?* Hah, more like coaxing a heap of shit on wheels. Or that he'd had to hand back the keys of his much-loved dockland apartment and was now lucky to be living in a house share with three plumbers, who command eye-watering call-out charges. And it all stemmed from Lucinda not delivering on her promise to him. Not that he'd ever admit that to anyone. No, that would remain his secret. His and Lucinda's.

He gets up off the bed and goes out to the shared bathroom to use the loo. Afterwards he glares at his face in the mirror, hating the sight of himself. If he could go back in time, he'd turn a different corner in the college campus all those years ago to make sure he never laid eyes on Lucinda Oliver, wearing skinny jeans and an oversized pink jumper in a shade only she could look sexy in. She'd been sticking up posters on the notice-board for a mad-sounding Halloween party. Of course, then he wouldn't have met Caz, but that had gone pear-shaped as well.

Back in his room, he pours another drink, despite his sore head. The whole idea of being there when Lucinda is brought ashore is torture. He wouldn't even be able to go on the lash and sink into some alcoholic oblivion. It wouldn't be that kind of weekend. But he knows it might be better to show his face rather than stay away, no matter how crap it would be. It would give him a chance to hear what others have to say, what they might remember. See if anyone has sussed that he's hiding something big.

For a brief moment he considers asking Arianna to come with him. She'd caught him at a bad moment when he was happy to drown his sorrows in the comfort of her willing body. That he had known Lucinda Oliver, and been there at the time she'd disappeared, had granted him instant elevated status with her, regardless of his personal circumstances. *Of course* she'd heard of Lucinda. She'd seen her tribute page on Instagram. It was heartbreaking. OMG, had he actually *known* her?

He'd told Arianna enough to elicit the right amount of sympathy and entice her into his bed. She turns up in his life at regular intervals, as if she senses he needs the consolation of sex, but she hasn't a clue who Eddie Hynes is or what he wants. And even if she'd been a handy distraction, a brief respite from the horrors of the weekend, he knows it would be a bad idea. He has to find the guts to face it alone. He needs to be alert to what everyone has to say, and what they might remember of that weekend.

Eddie gets back onto the bed and checks his mobile again. No updates. He sees that it's almost midnight. For once the house is quiet, the guys he shares with getting some kip before flying to Prague at the crack of dawn for a stag weekend. He drops his phone, picks up the remote and points it at the small telly on top of the chest of drawers, wondering if anything will distract him. A game show. A movie. Even a late-night news programme. But superimposed over the screen all he sees are images of the time he arrived at The Lookout that hot Thursday afternoon last July. That's the happy memory he goes back to whenever the dark terrors sweep over him.

He and Sasha were the first to arrive at The Lookout on that sunny July day. He felt as if he was in a lush, cinematic movie – driving in through the entrance to the ostentatious house with a flourish, swerving his white, open-topped BMW sports car to a stop, sounding the car horn to announce their arrival. He had never had any interest in going to the arsehole of Kerry before, and he was glad they were in for a bit of decent sun instead of lashing rain. With the huge mountains scraping the sky and the massive sprawl of the bay in the near distance, he could have been in the south of France. Good fodder for his Instagram, but Lucinda had specifically asked them not to post anything on social media that weekend – and what Lucinda wanted, Lucinda got. The woman who took every opportunity to flaunt the best of her carefully curated life in front of the salivating world wanted to have this celebration in private, away from prying eyes. Although he was probably the only one of the party guests to guess the real reason why.

She had promised to sort him out that weekend – the only reason he was there, because nothing else would have dragged him down to the arsehole of beyond. He held that thought until he actually saw Lucinda.

She appeared at the ornate-railed top-floor balcony wearing a gauzy white caftan over a white bikini and gold blingy sandals, her shoulder-length blonde hair caught to one side and secured in a big golden clasp so that it fell over one shoulder in a glossy, wavy plume. She raised a glass of something or other. He hoped it was non-alcoholic, whatever it was.

She looked like a goddess, a distant, unattainable star.

She disappeared from view, before throwing open the hall door and embracing them both, saying in her laughing voice that the blue skies and sunshine were exactly what she'd ordered from the weather gods, along with the two of them, her best friends. Eddie liked to think she meant only him. She didn't know Sasha at all. Eddie hadn't known Sasha that long either, to be honest, but he hadn't wanted to stay there solo. Sasha was a diversion for him against the beguiling Lucinda.

He remembered Lucinda giggling, laughing, bubbling over with happiness. Quite the opposite from the previous time he'd seen her when she'd been begging for his help.

He stepped through the door of The Lookout, with all its opulent and gaudy ostentation. The weekend had begun.

FOUR DAYS EARLIER
THURSDAY, 26 JANUARY

CHAPTER FIVE

Maisie

On Thursday morning, in the kitchen of her semi-detached home in the outskirts of Clonsilla, Maisie McKenna is persuading Finn, her nine-month-old son, to sit in his high chair, at the same time as reassuring two-year-old Freya, who's clinging to her legs, that her toast is almost ready. It's seven o'clock in the morning and they've been wide awake since before six.

'You know it's going to take you four hours thirty-five minutes?' her husband Keith says, looking up from his mobile between quick shovels of his Weetabix. 'I've google-mapped it.'

'Of course you have.' She can predict what he's going to say next.

'I'm concerned about you travelling to Kerry in the middle of winter,' he says, right on cue. 'Never mind what it's for. If you take the M8, there's a service station before you come to Cashel. You could stop there for coffee.'

She begins to feed Finn his porridge. She wants to tell Keith that if she stops off at any service station it'll be to pick up wine. Lots of it. Even though she knows that wouldn't be a great idea. Lots of wine had caused lots of problems the last time the gang had all been together. She should know.

What happens in The Lookout stays in The Lookout.

What happens in Santorini stays in Santorini.

She feels something cold slither down her back. 'I might check with Caz, see if she wants to come with me,' she says. 'It'll be company.'

'Caz.' Not a great fan of Caz, Keith falls silent for a moment, then, keeping his opinion to himself as he often did for the sake of peace, he says, 'You sure your mother is okay coming over to help mind the kids tomorrow?'

Maisie scoops a large dollop of porridge that's escaping down the front of Finn's plastic bib towards his pyjamas. He lets out a roar and she hurriedly feeds another spoonful into his open mouth with the several pearly teeth – trophies that had taken many fretful nights to break through – then peels Freya from her legs and dashes across the kitchen to rescue her toast.

'We can talk about this tonight,' she says, unable to mask her irritation, her fingers smarting as she throws the hot toast onto a plastic plate. 'I'm not going anywhere until tomorrow. And my mum is fine with it.'

'Okay.' Keith raises his hands in surrender. 'Just trying to help.' He gets up and rinses his bowl before placing it in the dishwasher. 'I'd better run. Can't miss the train this morning.'

She remembers that her loss-adjuster husband has an important meeting this morning with his boss. 'Best of luck,' she says, as Keith shrugs into his coat before going around his family with goodbye hugs and kisses and plenty of I-love-yous despite his hurry, ending up with porridge on the sleeve of his coat, which she wipes away.

She hears the door close behind him. She's full of relief that she's not in the office today. She'd recently returned to a three-day-week accounting-admin role in a builders' suppliers and she's off Thursdays and Fridays. She's also glad she's not heading to Kerry today. Most nights, one or other of her children disturbs her at intervals, but in a typical example of one of the vexatious Murphy's laws of parenthood, they'd both slept soundly last night while she hadn't had a wink.

Ever since Stella's heart-stopping message the evening before, she'd been trying and failing to blank her mind against a nightmare image: Lucinda's upside-down scarlet Mini Cooper being hauled up out of iron-grey seas, dangling in mid-air, water pouring from its innards, the bodywork scored, damaged and rusty here and there from its six-month submersion in the water.

Could she bear to witness this? Her heart stalls at the idea, but in the first flush of emotion, she'd replied to Stella, saying she hoped to be there, unable to say, 'No.'

Maisie sits down with a cup of coffee when her children have full tummies and there is respite from their demands. She wonders how soon she can call Caz. She bets Caz, caught up in her glam London career, isn't thinking about calling her. It would have to be Maisie doing the reaching-out. As always. No surprises that dependable, loyal Keith has never been too impressed with Caz.

Caz hasn't replied to Stella. On the WhatsApp group at least. She wonders if Caz has messaged Stella privately, maybe even spoken to her. It would be typical for Caz to try to set herself apart from the others, throwing herself into a more favourable light, just like she used to do with Lucinda. Maisie tries to squash her resentful thoughts. She fires off a text to Caz, asking her to call her when she's free, telling herself it doesn't matter if she feels she's doing the running this time, considering the tragic circumstances. As well as which, she dreads the thought of arriving at The Lookout by herself. She's terrified of coming face to face with a distraught Stella, fearful of being back there, and she's hoping Caz might be with her for support.

It's lunchtime before Caz calls her, which, for once, is perfect timing. Finn is in the middle of his two-hour daily nap and even Freya has gone back to her cot for an hour.

Caz is as shocked as Maisie at the discovery of Lucinda's car.

'I went into a panic,' she says, 'I had to get out of the apartment for a while – the walls were closing around me. I needed to be somewhere with noise and people.'

'I'm not surprised. You were a lot closer to Lucinda than I was.'

Maisie tries to keep the churlish note out of her voice. She's always been stupidly envious when it came to Lucinda because she's always felt outside the close bond that developed between Caz and Lucinda as soon as they met in secondary school. That this had happened after her sister Monica had produced unbeatable stellar results in her Leaving Certificate, much to the exaggerated jubilation of their parents, made it harder to accept.

Why is she remembering this now? At almost forty years of age? It proves there is something seriously wrong with her, some terrible flaw within her makeup. As if she needs any proof.

'I can't get it out of my head,' Caz says. 'I still can't believe Lucinda is gone.'

'Neither can I,' Maisie says.

'Sometimes it catches me by surprise. I see someone who reminds me of Lucinda, or I get a whiff of her favourite perfume somewhere, or I need to tell her something and I can't, and I want to scream the place down.'

'I can well imagine.'

Maisie realises that, since the party weekend, they've spoken little about the accident. Soon after they'd arrived back in Dublin, Caz had phoned to say she wouldn't be around for the foreseeable because she was renting out her Dublin apartment and moving to London. She'd have no trouble finding freelance work, she'd said, thanks to her connections in the television and entertainment world. It had always been the dream, she'd said, and unfortunately, they all knew now how short life could be. Besides, she couldn't bear to be moving around in a Dublin without Lucinda.

Even though Maisie had felt that Caz was abandoning her somewhat, she had been relieved. With Caz in London, and Janet and Eddie maintaining radio silence, it meant she didn't have to face anyone, which suited her fine. On top of the shock of losing Lucinda, she didn't want any reminders about that weekend.

Then Maisie asks, because she's bursting to find out, 'Are you coming over this weekend? I know it's a big ask for you, travelling from London.'

'I want to be there, and I don't want to be there,' Caz replies. 'But I got on to Stella before I phoned you. I had to see if I could get cover first for a super-glam job I had lined up for this weekend.'

Maisie knows she should ask her friend about the important-sounding job, but she's too anxious to know. 'So you're coming?'

'Yes, I have my flight booked. I'm arriving tomorrow.'

'It'll be good to see you, Caz, despite the occasion. I could collect you at the airport and we can go down together.'

'I'm actually flying straight into Cork,' Caz says. 'Arriving in around twelve. I'll hire a car from there to get to Wolf Cove. It shouldn't take more than two hours.'

'Let me pick you up,' Maisie says, relieved at the prospect that they'd arrive at The Lookout together. And maybe it would be best not to have too long a car journey with Caz. Things might come out that she didn't want to come out. Like how despicably she'd behaved that weekend, her old angst finally erupting and unleashing itself in a way she'd never anticipated. Why couldn't she fully rid herself of old hurts and jealousies?

'That could work, if it suits you,' Caz says.

'Yeah, sure.' Maisie would make it work. And no need to tell Keith that she'd be taking a detour, or why.

'Great. I'll text you my flight details and we'll touch base tomorrow. I'm surprised at Stella all the same,' Caz says.

'Surprised why?'

'Well ...' Caz falls silent for a moment. 'Let's face it, she was hardly talking to us even before Lucinda's accident, although I'm not surprised, considering the crazy shenanigans, but I didn't think she'd invite us down for what's going to be a tough weekend.'

Invite? Maisie suppresses a shiver. She can't say it's beginning to feel like a summons, thanks to her black conscience. A summons to some kind of court, a time of reckoning to be faced, finally, six months after the crime.

CHAPTER SIX

Janet

Janet Troy's soothing words echo around the yoga studio in Cabinteely, south County Dublin, on Thursday afternoon.

'Let your body become still,' she intones. 'Deepen the flow of your breathing and feel each breath filling your body down to your abdomen, hold it for the count of five or whatever is comfortable before breathing out … now, starting with your feet …'

Lying in front of her, ten supine bodies rest in shavasana pose on yoga mats spaced at intervals around the studio, most of them covered with blankets against the January chill. She's glad it's an early finish this afternoon and that this is her last class of the day. It's a wonder no one has asked for their money back, considering how stressful and distracted she's been all day, surely communicating her angst to each class, even subliminally.

She goes through the relaxation routine on auto-pilot, forcing her voice to be as calm as possible, badly wishing she could take some of her own advice. Anything to forget Aaron's angry face and words of fury that are still ricocheting around in her head since that morning.

'Jesus Christ,' he'd erupted, before he'd left for work, when she'd told him she'd be travelling to Kerry on Friday. 'I can't believe you're going back after everything that's happened.'

'I have to. For Lucinda's sake.'

They were barely communicating, these days, apart from what was strictly necessary, which included the alarming text from Stella last evening, but she'd waited until this morning to tell him of her plans, wanting to gauge his reaction in the clear light of day. It was exactly as she had feared.

'Bollocks,' he'd said. 'I know she was our friend but why put yourself through the stress of this weekend? Why resurrect everything?'

'What's wrong with you? Why shouldn't I be there to honour her memory?'

'What's wrong is that you'll be putting yourself through torture, chasing her ghost.'

'It's not a question of that.'

'Then why, Janet? Surely we've been through enough with all things Lucinda.'

'*We* have? I'm not sure about you, but I've certainly been dragged through the mill.'

'You know it was flirting that got out of hand, thanks to too much booze and the whole crazy party vibe. I wasn't the only one—'

'That's irrelevant,' she'd snapped, trying not to remember how suddenly aroused she'd felt at the sight of her husband giving it loads in the Jacuzzi.

'Then why are you beating yourself up by returning to the scene of the—'

'Crime? The guards are bound to be sniffing around, aren't they?' she'd said, putting it up to him. He'd immediately looked away, causing a quiver of fear in her belly.

Crime. The word explodes into her head, because that's how The Lookout seems to her. A crime scene. She loses her train of thought, only realising she's fallen silent when there is a gentle cough from someone in the front row. She forces her worries to the back of her head until she completes the relaxation session and the class is over. She says goodbye to everyone as they put on their trainers, roll up their mats and troop outside, half expecting a complaint or two. But, thankfully, no one comes to her with a gripe.

'See you next week,' a few chorus, and Janet feels a cold shiver going down her spine. She knows that by then everything will have changed, one way or another.

She rolls up her own mat and gathers her bags full of props, needing two trips to get everything out to her car. She squashes the final bag into the boot and snaps it closed, reminding herself to fill the tank on the way home, to have it ready for the morning. She's already cancelled her Friday classes, citing a family emergency. In the blowy afternoon, with the dark, lowering sky and biting breeze, she shivers. Is Aaron right? Is she nuts to be heading to a remote part of Kerry in the bleakness of January? Sliding into the driver's seat of her Renault, she glances at the photo attached to her keyring before she starts the engine – a headshot of her and Aaron taken on holidays two years ago, their faces close together against the background of blue skies and palm trees. She knows that if anything about this is nuts, it's the way she and Aaron are at loggerheads.

From the time they'd met in college they had bonded over their highly ambitious natures. Both of them coming from families where unemployment had been rife during their 1980s childhoods, they'd been determined to carve out successful lives. They'd worked hard to set themselves up as the beautiful people, the power couple: lean-machine Aaron at the top of his game in his personal-training career, perfectly complemented by toned, sleek Janet and her yoga-teaching practice. Their love is supposed to be special, strong and powerful enough to survive any knocks and enable them to rise effortlessly above the stupid crap of the world.

But they'd returned from that weekend in The Lookout a fractured couple. Utterly broken-hearted with what had happened to their friend, but both undone because of what had taken place before her accident. Thanks to Aaron's lewd behaviour with Lucinda, their six-year-old marriage had been badly bruised. Since then, they've kept up the façade of a united grieving pair in front of families and friends, but at home they've been sleeping in separate rooms, barely speaking when they pass each other in the house, both stubbornly refusing to admit to the huge scar the weekend inflicted on their hitherto ultra-perfect relationship.

But little does Aaron know that his stupid behaviour with Lucinda is the least of Janet's worries. It's convenient for her to lay the blame at his door for the rift between them, a handy excuse to distance herself from him and avoid talk of that weekend as much as possible. What Aaron doesn't know is that she had experienced a traumatic event in Santorini that Lucinda had helped her to cover up, and without her quiet support, there might not have been a wedding at all.

'My lips are sealed,' Lucinda had promised. 'What happened in Santorini stays in Santorini.'

Only it hadn't. For some reason Janet can't understand, it had landed in Wolf Cove that terrible weekend.

She turns out onto the dual carriageway, almost into the path of an oncoming car, the driver swerving and sounding his horn. She forces herself to concentrate on the road.

If Aaron had caught a whiff of what she and Lucinda had been hiding all these years, she knows how angry he'd have been with her, and how furious he'd have been with Lucinda for the part she'd played. He'd been hostile towards Janet since they'd come home, but – worst-case scenario and her deepest fears – was his behaviour towards her and his reluctance to talk about that weekend stemming from a guilty conscience? Sometimes, in the pitch dark of the night, the image of Lucinda's car dropping down into the ocean twists in her gut and screams in her head. And Aaron had been missing for a while that last evening, deliberately lying when the police had asked about his movements.

Why is he so annoyed she's going back to The Lookout? Why has he not even suggested he come with her? Still, she'd rather go alone. In the last few days, a new worry has crash-landed into her life, and she needs space from Aaron while she figures out what she's going to do. And no one will take any notice if she looks upset or over-emotional while she figures out a few things. It's going to be that kind of weekend. Space away from Aaron will give her a chance to work out how her life is going to look in the years to come, and whether or not Aaron will have a part to play.

If he'll be able to play a part, more like. It all depends on whether he'd had anything to do with Lucinda's accident. Why had he lied to the guards?

And why had she gone along with him and backed him up?

Because she'd been too scared to challenge him, in case other secrets came out.

She pulls off the dual carriageway into a garage. It starts to pelt rain as she gets out of the car. She fills the tank completely so she won't have to refuel on the way down to Kerry. Whether Aaron is guilty or not, hopefully this difficult weekend will give her some answers. If she can get through it without falling apart. The main thing she has to do is to pay tribute to her friend, keep her eyes and ears open, and all her fears to herself.

CHAPTER SEVEN

Stella

The further west Stella travels, the more sparsely populated this corner of Kerry is, and the higher the fold of mountains rises remorselessly against the sky, intimidating curves of dark purple and grey, sheep clinging to vertiginous slopes.

Just after lunchtime on Thursday, she sees it in the distance. There is a right-hand bend where the road turns at an acute angle around the perimeter of a long, narrow inlet. Straight across the inlet, beyond a stretch of heaving dark grey water mirroring the sky, she sees the high, jagged promontory jutting sharply out to a pewter grey ocean. It dominates the horizon, its brooding profile majestic, imperious and invincible.

Wolf Head.

Her chest squeezes with panic.

Down below the cliff face and to one side, she catches a glimpse of a small horseshoe harbour, a cluster of dwellings, a wooden jetty, all looking minuscule at this distance – Wolf Cove. There is a small shingle beach on the other side of the harbour, giving way to a succession of rocks and boulders by the base of the head. Then her view is interrupted by a thin line of stunted trees leaning drunkenly over a dry-stone wall. The narrow road twists and turns, hugging the perimeter of the inlet. She arrives at a junction where the road divides into a hairpin fork, a decrepit signpost lurching crookedly indicating that the road curving down an incline to the left leads to Wolf Cove. The right-hand fork leads up the hill to The Lookout, a mile ahead, with Wolf Head a mile further beyond and almost at the edge of the peninsula.

The house sits on a rising incline behind a dry-stone boundary wall, commanding a view of the sea and horizon. Britt has left the large wooden gate open. Stella slows down and turns between the pillars. Lucinda's laughing voice comes back to her, souring her stomach: 'It's the perfect find! Not too far from where your ancestors roamed. Hey, Stella, you'll be going back to your roots!'

In reality, The Lookout was about as far from the tiny cottage in Dunmullen where Mum had grown up as a bicycle is to a space rocket. Marie Ryan had left for a bedsit in Dublin and a job in the civil service at the age of sixteen, had met Bernard Oliver, and they'd settled in Lucan. The Lookout was also about as remote as possible to the glamorous, European location where Stella would have expected the stylish Lucinda to arrange a celebration. The ostentatious house, a major build completed five years ago, rises like a phoenix out of the ashes of an old, crumbling farmhouse. Three storeys high, there is a double-height window above the wooden hall door, and above that, the small balcony of the second-floor suite Lucinda had stayed in.

She can't stay here.

Then again, she can't *not* stay here. The vulgar pretentiousness of The Lookout draws her in, as though she and it are ready to face up to what happened to Lucinda in the course of that terrible weekend. As she parks her car in front of a row of wooden planters, wild and straggly now, their summer colour long died away, a spool of images grips her, making her nauseous. Painful memories she had blanked out surge through her head, savage and brutal.

Stella was the last to arrive at The Lookout for the party celebrations and all her senses were hijacked by the loud music blasting from the house as she attempted to park between the haphazardly abandoned cars belonging to Lucinda's friends. The music assaulted her as Fatboy Slim's 'Right Here, Right Now' thundered across the warm evening air, sending out sound waves to rival those of the heat.

Stella knew she wasn't in the right frame of mind for this party extravaganza. She still felt raw and shattered after seeing Leo and a heavily pregnant Davina in the city centre, coupled with a hectic time in the office, dealing with some harrowing cases. She told herself to go with the flow for Lucinda's sake. She followed the sound of the music around to the rear of the house, and saw that the party was already in full swing. Hot and dishevelled after her journey, she already felt out of sync.

Three women stood in the dazzling blue swimming pool, resting their forearms along the edge, their sleek heads dampened by the water, cocktail glasses lined up in front of them. On the patio, two men wearing swimming trunks and wraparound sunglasses were stretched out on sun-loungers, one wearing ear buds – surely an exercise in optimism, given the decibel levels. Bottles of beer chilled in a trough of ice on the ground between them, flip-flops and towels had been tossed carelessly nearby, a sound bar and mobiles placed on a small table.

A pathway led to three brightly painted beach huts at one side of the garden, but over on the other side, on a grassed area, Stella spotted Lucinda jumping on a trampoline. Barefoot, she wore a midi-length white gauzy caftan that floated around her hips as she bounced up and down. She was laughing, happy, and looking absolutely beautiful.

The music changed to Beyoncé and 'Halo' at the same time as Lucinda saw her. She hopped down from the trampoline, whipped off her sunglasses and hurried over to Stella, arms outstretched. She clasped her to her thin frame, then danced Stella around the patio, singing the chorus of 'Halo' at the top of her voice.

'I'm thrilled to see you, sis,' she said, her voice warm with happiness. 'I meant every word I was singing to you – you're my absolute saving grace, everything I want and more.'

'It's so great to see you too.' Stella returned the hug, warmed by Lucinda's enthusiastic words.

The music changed and 'Titanium' exploded across the air, the drum beat almost bouncing off the patio. With Stella's arrival, it enticed the three women out of the pool. Stella knew Maisie and Janet, of course, but it was her first time to meet Eddie's girlfriend, Sasha. After they had all welcomed her, they picked up their glasses and headed down to the wooden terrace bar, prettily lit with fairy lights. As they half skipped, half danced across the hot patio stones in their minuscule bikinis, Maisie tiptoed between the supine men, picked up a bottle and poured a stream of beer directly onto the men's crotches, rudely awakening them from their sunbathing.

'Maisie, you bitch,' Eddie said, sitting up, all pale, awkward legs, swiping beer off his shorts. 'I'll get you back for that.'

'Is that a promise?' She giggled as she tripped back to the bar. 'Whatever it is, I'm up for it this weekend,' she called.

Stella remembered that Maisie's new baby was only a few months old just as she noticed the slight swell of Maisie's post-natal tummy above her bikini bottoms. Fair play, she wasn't trying to hide anything. She had the sinking feeling that micro-bikinis were going to be the compulsory wear of the weekend. She had a one-piece swimsuit she'd thrown into her wheelie case at the last minute at Lucinda's urging that she pack her pool stuff along with her sun-cream.

Lucinda reintroduced Stella to Aaron and Eddie. Eddie had a mop of wavy dark hair, and a soft body. The first time Stella had met him, years ago, she'd thought there was an air of the carefree student about him, and he seemed the same now. Aaron pulled out his earphones and gave Stella a quick wave. Stella got the impression from his greeting that he was the least keen to be here. 'Welcome to the madhouse,' he said.

Maisie, Sasha and Janet lined up fresh cocktails along the edge of the pool before jumping in, prancing energetically around the shallow end. Lucinda had told Stella everyone was bringing a two-hour playlist of their favourite party anthem songs and she was welcome to bring hers. Stella hadn't told her she had barely enough favourite anthem songs to fill twenty minutes, let alone two hours.

Then, clad in a scarlet string bikini, with a matching slash of scarlet highlighting her mouth, Caz Costello was walking towards her. She plucked an emerald green sarong from a nearby sun-lounger, and wrapped it around her hips at the same time as she slipped her feet into jewelled flip-flops. Lucinda's oldest and closest friend, with whom Stella had never quite clicked.

As she looked at her, Stella got a funny sense of déjà vu. Caz's outfit was similar to one Lucinda had been flaunting on her Instagram page last summer, the image artfully captured as she walked along a sunset beach. But whereas Lucinda had oozed effortless chic, Caz looked as though she was wearing something mismatched.

'Stella, you made it,' she said. Her gushing voice sounded warm and friendly, but Stella observed that her thickly mascaraed green eyes were cool. She leaned in and kissed the air in front of Stella's face. Then, with a quick flick, she looked her up and down. 'Jump into your bikini and join us in the pool. I bet you can swim like a fish, not like us lazy animals.'

The tone of her voice caused Stella to take this as an insult. 'I can't actually.'

Caz shrugged. 'I'm sure you could do with a cool dip after your long drive.'

'I'll sort myself out when I get to my room.' What she needed was a big glass of iced water followed by a cool shower.

Lucinda clapped her hands. 'Stop the music!' she cried. Eddie looked up before reaching across and lifting his mobile to do so. Silence.

'Everybody!' Lucinda said, gazing around at the gathering. 'Now that we're all here ...' Her voice broke a little. She swallowed, smiled. 'Looking around, all I can see are my best friends and my wonderful sister. I want to say *thank you all so much* for being here. This is going to be the best weekend of my life. Of all our lives,' she added, throwing out her arms extravagantly. 'Everybody grab a fresh glass, time for bubbly.' Lucinda turned to Stella and smiled. 'I kept it on ice until you arrived.'

There was a bit of fussing around until the cork was popped on the chilled Taittinger, and everyone was handed a glass of fizz. Lucinda raised hers in a toast. 'Let's get the party started.' As if at an invisible cue, Eddie switched on the music.

Lucinda put down her glass. 'Someone else can have that,' she said, 'I just wanted it for the toast.'

'Are you not drinking?' Stella couldn't keep the surprise out of her voice.

'I'm off booze for now. I've told the gang I'm on a bit of a health kick but you're all to raid the bar as often as you like.'

'And what about you?'

'Don't worry, sis, I'm still well able to party to the max, you know me, and I've brought non-alco fizz and gin – they're so good it's hard to tell the difference.'

Lucinda took Stella's arm in hers. The touch of her skin felt warm and soft. Stella could smell her coconut sun-cream. 'Come on,' Lucinda said, 'I'll show you around. You need to see this fabulous house. We're going to have the party to beat all parties. And you're staying in the room beside me. The two of us are up on the second floor, queening it over everyone else. I didn't want anyone beside me except my little sis.'

Over the sound of Rihanna, Stella heard the whoop of laughter as Lucinda showed her through the patio doors into the back of the house. The party was certainly getting started.

Now, in the grey January afternoon, the remembered echo of that carefree laughter feels like a savage stab to Stella's heart.

CHAPTER EIGHT

Stella

Britt opens the hall door as soon as Stella nears it, a scattering of dried leaves and broken twigs whooshing into the hallway ahead of the stiff January breeze. Stella does a double-take at the sight of her. In her early sixties, with engaging green eyes and a crown of silvered hair shot through with a pink wash, Britt is wearing slim denim jeans tucked into black boots and a chunky, rainbow-coloured sweater. But her normally slender frame is thinner, so much so that her sweater seems two sizes too big. Her face is drawn, smutty black shadows curving beneath her eyes, hollows under her cheeks, a pinched look around her mouth. She looks like she's aged several years in the last six months.

She sweeps Stella into a hug. Stella feels her bones beneath her fingertips and she regrets not making more of an effort to see Britt since Lucinda's accident, fobbing her off when she'd offered to come to Dublin, too immersed in her own grief. Britt had clearly been grief-stricken too. They draw apart and then, bracing herself, Stella glances around the marble-floored hall with its floating staircase and double-height stairwell, lights sparking like shards of crystal against the January gloom.

No-nonsense Britt doesn't give her time to dwell on anything.

'Come on, I'm sure you're dying for a cuppa,' she says. 'Leave that case in the hall for now. Don't worry about the rooms – they were already made up with fresh sheets and towels when I got here. I turbo-charged the heating to make sure the house is warm.'

Stella follows her down to the large living space that runs from the front of the house to the rear. Most of the walls are comprised of large expanses of glass. A standalone centrepiece feature stove divides the kitchen from the huge squashy sofas in the living area. Britt passes the enormous slab of a kitchen island, and ushers Stella to the cosy seating area by the wood stove, where a low table is drawn up in front of a small emerald green sofa scattered with lemon and purple cushions. Britt throws another log from the basket into the heart of the orange fire, sending up a flicker of sparks. She brings over a tray with sandwiches and pastries, followed by a pot of tea.

'This is perfect, Britt, thank you.'

'I popped into the supermarket for a few essentials when I came through Dunmullen,' Britt says, 'but Tricia organised these for me. It was all The Pier had at such short notice.'

'It's food for the gods.' Stella sighs. 'I've been on the road since early this morning and I'm beginning to feel a bit hollow.'

'I thought you might fly down,' Britt says.

'Nah. I didn't want to have to talk to a single soul, much less make conversation about why I was travelling to Kerry. I switched my phone off and it was great to have a few hours of silence while I ...'

'Started getting your head around it?' Britt says gently.

'Exactly,' Stella says. 'Thanks for all this, and for being here.'

'Why wouldn't I be, chicken? I'm always here for you.'

'True.' For the first time since she'd spoken to Hugh, Stella feels a faint smile on her face.

Britt had moved back to her Kerry roots and a teaching role in Kenmare after a spell in America when Stella was a child. Living in a whitewashed cottage with mostly sheep for her neighbours, she'd spent a lot of her holidays travelling the world, sending exotic postcards and fun parcels that had duly arrived at Stella and Lucinda's childhood home. She'd always arrived back in time for the girls to spend a couple of weeks with her on holidays in Kerry, an arrangement that had lasted until Stella was in her mid-teens. Retired now, but still heavily involved with Kerry charities, Britt had dropped everything at the time of Lucinda's accident and stayed at The Lookout to look after Stella, throwing a safety net of care and attention around her as well as holding the braying press at arm's length during those first few nightmare days.

'How are you feeling now?' Britt asks, after Stella has had a cup of tea and some sandwiches.

'I don't know,' she says honestly. 'I've no idea what the weekend is going to bring.'

Britt's taut face is full of compassion. 'Anything at all you need me to do, let me know.'

'Thanks, Britt, but how are you?' Stella asks. Apart from her weight loss and her face that speaks of sleepless nights, in the short time she's been here she's noticed Britt is not as energetic or lively as she recalled. Usually the epitome of bustling efficiency, it seems as though a fire in her belly has gone out.

'I'm okay,' she says. Whichever way she looks at Stella, Stella knows she's doing her best to summon a brave face. She realises that Britt is as heartbroken as she is.

'Sorry I didn't make time to see you since ...'

Britt shakes her head. 'Och, it's been a tough few months ... It's been horrible, but far tougher on you,' she says, gathering herself, 'so I'm glad to be here to support you. Are many of Lucinda's friends coming down?'

'Most of them will be here. Caz, Maisie and Janet are arriving tomorrow. I'm not sure yet about Eddie. I'm not staying on the top floor this time,' Stella says. 'I don't even want to go up that far. It's the last place I saw Lucinda.' The last place she'd ever spoken to her sister or, rather, argued with her.

'I understand,' Britt says. 'I was talking to Tricia earlier. She can supply take-out food. We just have to order in advance. I know you've more important things to think about so I'm happy to coordinate with Tricia.'

'Thanks, Britt,' Stella says. 'So long as I foot the bill.'

'I don't mind covering some of it,' Britt says.

'Absolutely not,' Stella says. 'This is my call, but it'll scarcely be a repeat of the party weekend.'

Last July, Lucinda had arranged for Tricia and The Pier kitchen to cater for the party, paid for out of the Revolut fund set up for the weekend, everyone chipping in to cover the expenses. They'd been spoiled for choice with the array of buffet breakfast and lunch options, Tricia sending up staff to clean and tidy and help serve the meals each evening. Lucinda had also arranged for a generous quantity of Taittinger, wines and spirits to be delivered in advance, which were replenished from The Pier throughout their stay.

Stella is relieved Tricia can cater for this weekend. There are no supermarkets in Wolf Cove, just a small convenience store attached to the pub, and a couple of cafés that closed during the off-season. At this time of the year, trade would be quiet with few people passing through the village. Until now. Stella suppresses a shiver, thinking of the hordes of media and busybodies about to descend on the tiny village to feast lasciviously on Lucinda's tragedy.

'I guess word is out by now?'

Britt smiles sadly. 'It was on the midday news. Scant details, the bare facts.'

'I'd better take a look.' Stella rummages in her bag for her mobile. She powers it on, and ignoring the stream of notifications, WhatsApp messages and missed calls that have now appeared on her home page, she sends a message to Hugh, telling him she's arrived safely. He must have been waiting for her text because he replies immediately, letting her know that a local guard, Imelda, will be calling to see her on Friday morning with an update on the recovery attempt.

Then in a fog of cold fear, she scrolls through to a news site:

The Kerry Herald
Thursday, 26 January 2023, 12 p.m.

BREAKING NEWS

A submerged car has been sighted in Atlantic seas off Wolf Head. It was discovered by local fishermen and it is believed it may belong to Lucinda Oliver, the Dublin socialite who disappeared when her car allegedly plunged off the cliff six months ago. Despite exhaustive searches at the time, no trace of the car was found.

An Irish Coast Guard spokesperson said, 'An Garda Siochana and the Irish Coast Guard Rescue Team are investigating a report of a submerged vehicle in the sea off Wolf Head, Co. Kerry. A rescue mission will be under way as soon as weather permits.'

Seeing it in print is like a hammer blow to Stella. Morbid curiosity has her scrolling through to Lucinda's tribute page on Instagram, where the story has been repeated, only here it's accompanied by various comments.

@lisamag009 OMG this is so sad for Lucinda's family, my heart is melted for them. They must be devastated.

@kitticreme the worst news ever ... is it true its her sister who cause her death? thats wot I heard. wots her name anyone?

@DD40++ Stella, she's the little b*tchy sister who sent Lucinda over the edge with her cruel words

@lisamag009 it's vile to spread these rumours ... how do you think the family must be feeling?

@sallyluvxx Lucinda was so beautiful. I was hoping all along that a mistake had been made and she hadn't really died. I will always #LeavealightonforLucinda

@DD40++ Lucinda might have looked glamorous on the outside but she was a toxic cow who deserved her fate

@lisamag009 how can you be so disrespectful of the dead? How dare you!

@DD40++ f*&k Off you didn't know her like I did #sl*g #bi*ch #wag*n

@sallyluvxx reported and blocked. Lucinda was a beautiful and light-filled soul. Let's flood this page with nothing but love, kindness and positivity. Let's all #LeavealightonforLucinda

Thankfully Britt is not on social media, and Stella swiftly decides to say nothing to her about the abuse she's been getting online or the ugly anonymous texts she's received. No need to upset her. She can't help clicking into a fresh text on her mobile from an unknown number – she deletes it immediately but not before the words burn their way into her brain: What will it be like to see your sister's dead body, you revolting bitch-murderer? You should do us a favour and jump off Wolf Head yourself.

The pain comes again. Could her bitter words to Lucinda have caused her accident?

And, more to the point, who is sending these messages?

CHAPTER NINE

Stella

A bell chimes, the noise echoing through the house. Stella jumps and almost drops her phone.

'There's someone at the door,' Britt says unnecessarily. 'I'll go.'

There's no mistaking Tadhg Fitzmaurice as he comes into the living area, even though he is wearing a thick grey beanie hat that covers most of his head, a sturdy, hip-length waxed jacket designed to keep out rain and wind, and thick-soled boots. The last time Stella remembers seeing him, he was wearing a pair of cut-off shorts and a white vest. Of medium height, he is well built, with strong, sturdy shoulders from years of working on his family's fishing trawler. He is bearing a tinfoil-covered tray and talking to Britt.

'Tricia sent this up for this evening, on the house, like. It's shepherd's pie. It needs to be heated up and you're to ring if you need anything else. I'll be giving her a hand with the ferrying over the weekend because Seamus is laid up at the moment.' When he reaches the kitchen island, his voice trails away.

'Oh. Hi, Stella.' He sets the tray down clumsily on the countertop.

'Hi, Tadhg.'

He comes across and shakes her hand. 'Sorry for your troubles.'

'Thanks, Tadhg, appreciate it,' she says.

'Have some tea while you're here,' Britt says.

'Sure, why not?' Tadhg takes off his jacket and sits with his hands stretched out to the stove. When he has warmed them, he rests them on his jean-clad thighs. In his mid-thirties, Tadhg's around the same age as her. He lives in Dunmullen and when he's not out on the boat with his dad, he helps occasionally at The Pier, alongside Seamus Dillon, Tricia's father, who's in his early seventies. During the party weekend, Tadhg had taken a couple of groups of them out on a trip as far as the Skelligs.

'Let me know if there's anything I can do at all.' He darts a glance at Stella, his hazel-flecked eyes filled with discomfort.

Stella has faced this already – people frozen with awkwardness in front of her, unsure of what to say for the best. Afraid they might say something upsetting and make her cry, not realising that nothing they say or do could make the situation any worse.

'You've already helped,' she says, 'you and your father, by finding Lucinda's car.'

'I've always kept my eyes peeled, like, you know. The least I could do ...'

'Thanks, that was good of you,' Stella says.

'Tadhg is no stranger to grief, having lost Daithí in tragic circumstances,' Britt reminds Stella, bringing him a mug of tea.

'Ah, that was a long time ago now,' Tadhg says, a softness coming into his face. 'I'm sure 'tis the last thing Stella's interested in.'

Daithí, Stella recalls, was Tadhg's older brother, who'd been killed in a motorcycle crash on the road to Dunmullen ten years ago, around the same time Stella and Lucinda's father had died. During the years they'd visited Britt on holidays, they'd begun to hang around with a gang of the locals. Daithí, the natural leader and an attractive guy with dark hair and sexy green eyes, as her sister had gleefully described them, had been Lucinda's teenage summer romance, up to the time their holidays in Dunmullen had fizzled out. Lucinda had tearfully told Stella about his tragic death at the time, but Stella had been too wrapped up in the loss of her parents to be able to take on any further grief, her mum having died six months before her dad.

Silence stretches, Tadhg staring at the fire, fidgeting with his cup, and she realises that his discomfort is probably heightened because he knows from losing his brother how upset Stella must feel at the moment.

'How are your parents keeping?' Britt asks Tadhg.

'The usual,' he says, shrugging.

'They never got over losing Daithí like that.'

'No, to be sure. Never. It broke them.' He darts another glance at Stella, as though he's afraid he's said the wrong thing.

'Just as well they have you to lean on and step into your father's shoes,' Britt says.

'Sure, what else would I be doing?'

Even though the room they are in is spacious with a vaulted glass ceiling over the dining area, Stella feels suddenly suffocated. Cumulative grief and loss press down on her so that she can't breathe. In an effort to escape it, she gets to her feet.

'You've gone pale, Stella.' Britt looks at her anxiously. 'Are you okay?'

'I think I need …' Her voice is thin. She gulps. 'I need some fresh air. I'm going outside to stretch my legs – I've been cooped up in a car most of the morning.'

'Good idea,' Britt says. 'There are high-vis vests in the hall cloakroom. You might need one, a day like today.'

'I'm not going far, just around the garden.'

Outside, Stella gasps in the teeth of the buffeting wind, embracing the freshness of the sea air after the stuffiness of the house, but she is assaulted by the sight of the sea in the distance below, the restless surge of the waves, the wind whipping up the surface into an angry molten grey as it powers in from the horizon. After a few minutes she heads back inside, where Tadhg is in the hallway preparing to leave, Britt chatting to him about food arrangements. Then her phone rings.

Rex. She'd texted him that morning before she left for Kerry. She's had a couple of missed calls from him, so she accepts this one, slipping into the library to talk to him.

'Rex. Hi.'

'Stella! What's happening? I can't believe your message, and then I saw something on a news site. Have they really found Lucinda's car?'

'They think so,' she says.

'Oh, God, you poor thing, are you down in Kerry now?'

'Yes, I am. They hope to attempt a recovery on Saturday.'

'Who's with you?'

'Britt, my mother's cousin. Some of Lucinda's friends are coming down tomorrow, to be here when—' She finds she can't say the words.

'What a devastating time for you,' he says, his voice unexpectedly gentle. 'I'm coming down.'

'There's no need ...' she begins, not wanting to upset his weekend, and conscious that she's been holding him at arm's length since the night with Hugh.

'Oh, Stella, there's every need,' he says. 'Your friends and Britt are bound to be as cut up as you are, but I can be there just for you, to support you and look after you, help things run smoothly, whatever you need. Don't try to go it alone. I don't care if I have to sleep on the floor.'

'Honestly, Rex—'

'Let me do this, let me help, please. Let me be there for you. I can wash dishes, make tea, whatever. I've been floundering around in the face of what you've been going through and this will make me feel useful at least.'

'I have a friend coming down, after all,' Stella tells Britt later. The pitch black of the night presses against the windows, but they are cosy in the sitting area in front of the stove, sipping wine that Britt brought from Dunmullen.

Britt looks at her with interest. 'Oh, Stella, I'm glad to hear you've met someone.'

'Not that kind of a friend,' Stella says. 'Well, not yet, anyway. And certainly not this weekend. His name is Rex O'Neill and I met him about two months after Lucinda's accident when he came to my rescue after some scumbag mugged me by the canal on my way home from the office one evening. I've been seeing him since, except for recently ... something happened and I—' She blanks out an image of Hugh Connell shifting a little in her bed to make room for her head in the crook of his neck before he wrapped both arms around her. She blinks. Twirls the stem of her wineglass. 'Anyhow, Rex and I – I found it helpful that he didn't know about Lucinda at first, if that makes sense. I was able to be a normal person with him, not someone who was grieving and might break at any moment, or someone he had to walk on eggshells around. He wasn't watching every word out of his mouth in case it upset me. It gave me some space to be me.'

'That makes perfect sense,' Britt says.

'Some people seem to think that grief and tragedy are contagious,' Stella says, finding it easy to explain herself to Britt. 'They go out of their way to avoid me. Others piggyback on my grief and make it their own, which can be suffocating, but Rex is relaxing to be with. There were no preconceptions on his part, or complications. I was able to breathe normally with him, and practise getting out into the world again in a safe way.'

'I totally get that, chicken. Sometimes you need to distance yourself from too much sadness in case it swamps you completely.'

'I only told him about Lucinda recently, and by then our friendship had gelled.'

And then she'd gone and slept with Hugh, thanks to her messed-up head.

'So,' Stella pushes away the memory, 'Rex will be here tomorrow afternoon, and he'll do anything he can to help the weekend run smoothly, wash dishes, make tea, look after drinks, whatever. I'm going to put him into Lucinda's suite,' she says. 'No one else will want to stay there. Eddie, if he comes, he hasn't confirmed yet, can use the room beside it, which means two of Lucinda's friends will have to share one of the bigger rooms on the first floor. It's only for a couple of nights.'

'What are you thinking of, in terms of plans for the weekend?'

'Maybe a walk to Wolf Head tomorrow afternoon, if people arrive early enough. Then we'll go to the quayside on Saturday, when Lucinda's car is recovered. Just a way of honouring her, but no one needs to do anything they're not comfortable with. I'm hoping we can share some happy memories of her.' Stella takes a gulp of wine. 'You saw her that last day, Britt, what kind of mood was she in?'

'It was a quick visit,' Britt says. 'She came to invite me to the gala dinner that night. She was in good form.'

'Really? Before she went to see you, we'd had words ...' One way of describing their furious row. 'I thought she might have said she was angry with me.'

'Angry? On the contrary, she told me she was delighted you had come down for the weekend. She was saying how busy you always were, how important your career was, how dedicated you were to the women you were helping.'

'Did she?'

'Stella, we spoke about this in the days after the accident.'

'I don't remember. So much of that time is like a tangle of barbed wire in my head. She didn't have anything else to say that sounded off to you?'

'Like what?'

The ultra-casual tone of Britt's voice and the flicker of anxiety in her eyes gives Stella the strange sensation that Britt is keeping something from her. She tries to draw her out:

'Lucinda told me she had an announcement to make at the gala dinner. Did she mention it to you?'

'We had some chit-chat.' Britt shrugs. 'I don't think she mentioned anything about an announcement to me. She only stayed for half an hour.' Britt leans forward. 'Stella, please don't upset yourself by going back over the finer details looking for answers that aren't there. It's not going to change anything.'

'I'm trying to figure out how it all happened.'

Britt's face puckers. 'Look, pet, when a loved one dies, it's natural to want to find a reason, something to … almost justify the awfulness of it all, but accidents are simply that – fluky things that don't stand up to any examination and certainly don't lend themselves to any kind of rationale, no matter how much we want to find a meaning of sorts. Lucinda loved you. Please remember that. Life is cruel and unfair. Senseless things happen that cannot be accounted for, even terrible things like the horrific loss of our nearest and dearest.'

Stella stays silent. Lucinda's senseless death couldn't have been down to the fickle finger of Fate. Not her larger-than-life sister.

'I know the idea of recovering Lucinda's car is hugely upsetting,' Britt says, 'opening up all the wounds again, but please don't delve too deeply into motives or reasons. You probably won't find any and you'll only exhaust yourself. Sometimes, tough as it is, we have to accept there simply are no answers and let it be.'

Stella knows she's not prepared to accept this. There has to have been a reason for Lucinda's accident. A reason why someone is trolling her. Could the seeds of it all have been sown in the days before the tragedy? Or had it anything to do with those past sins Lucinda had mentioned? Thrown together over the next couple of days, Stella hopes Lucinda's friends will talk about her, about the party weekend, and that the truth behind her accident will emerge, however dark it might be.

THREE DAYS EARLIER
FRIDAY, 27 JANUARY

CHAPTER TEN

Maisie

Maisie pulls into the short-term car park in Cork airport knowing she has a full hour to spare before Caz's flight arrives. She left Dublin soon after her mother got to her house without even going through the children's checklist in detail, anxious to be on the road. Still, the prospect of a whole, uninterrupted hour to herself is a novelty. She'll pick up a couple of magazines in WHSmith and head to a coffee shop, enjoying the freedom to choose whatever she wants to nibble on without Finn hanging out of her arms, or having to bolt after a runaway Freya.

Who is she kidding? As she sips her coffee, picks at a sandwich, and turns the pages of the glossies she's pretending to read, everything is seething around in her head – Caz, Lucinda, Santorini and The Lookout. Why was she so anxious to arrive on time for Caz that she's miles too early? For once, couldn't she have worked it so that Caz was waiting for her?

But it had never been like that between them after Lucinda had arrived on the scene.

'Lucinda,' that's her name, she lives in one of those posh houses in Riverbank Manor, she's beautiful, and funny, and kind, and – oh my God, I can't believe it – she wants to be my friend.'

A year younger, Maisie had wanted to say to thirteen-year-old Caz, 'But I'm your best friend – we're almost sisters. I've known you for years, since long before this exotic-sounding Lucinda.'

She'd known Caz, or rather Catherine, since she was seven years of age. They'd lived three doors from each other on a council estate in Lucan, and Maisie's mother had encouraged her to be friendly with the eight-year-old Catherine whose adoptive parents didn't seem to care all that much about the little girl. Caught in the shadow of her perfect older sister Monica, Maisie had been pleased to feel superior to the girl in the hand-me-down clothes with the ugly haircut. She had quietly fed that one-upmanship over the years, annexing the quiet Catherine to herself and being the one who called all the shots – the one with the nicer home, the more loving parents, the better clothes, the annual holiday. Until Catherine had gone into secondary school a year ahead of Maisie, where she'd met Lucinda.

'She calls me Caz. I like it – it sounds cool. You can call me Caz from now on too, if you like.'

There was nothing wrong with 'Catherine', Maisie wanted to say. She bet Lucinda wouldn't allow Caz to shorten her lovely name to Lulu. Yet thus it had begun, Caz grateful to follow in the slipstream of the beautiful and funny Lucinda, Maisie always lagging behind them, hungry for scraps of friendship coming her way from the self-proclaimed besties.

She even managed to hang onto their coat-tails when Lucinda and Caz started college and the friendship group widened to include Eddie, Janet, Aaron, and whatever girlfriend Eddie happened to have at the time.

Until the holiday in Santorini, after which Maisie had avoided Lucinda as much as possible. Even though she'd hated herself for doing so, she just about kept on the right side of Caz and the gang, accepting occasional invitations to ensure she stayed in the loop and maintained some semblance of a friendship with them, because it was far preferable to being cast out in the cold. Then a few years later, her marriage to Keith, followed by two babies, had brought a convenient divide between her and the others.

Caz had urged her to come to the birthday celebrations down in The Lookout. She'd sensed Maisie had some kind of issue with Lucinda and had fallen out of the friendship loop over the years, but this would be a chance to put things right and catch up. Maisie had thought she'd moved on from Santorini until that unexpected meeting in town, a couple of weeks before Lucinda's party. One look at her ex-boyfriend and it had pulled the rug from under the life she'd papered together over the past ten years. Talking to him, trying to suck in her belly fat and make a rusty attempt at flirting with him, she'd realised she'd been merely drifting through the motions of life all along.

Maisie abandons her half-eaten sandwich, blindsided with memories of The Lookout – packing her case, fretting over the best tops and skirts to disguise her post-natal figure, assuring herself that only Lucinda knew the truth about the shameful and insulting way she'd treated Maisie in Santorini.

No one else knew about her scorching humiliation, which saved Maisie some face. Lucinda would scarcely have spoken of it to the others because it reflected so badly on herself and the ultra-sparkling, bubbly façade she showed to the world.

One of Maisie's magazines slithers to the floor but she ignores it. Because it had all been fine until the sweltering hot day she'd arrived at The Lookout, and the memory freshly assaults her – the surprise in her own voice, her unsophisticated, cringeworthy, gauche delight, as though she'd never been anywhere as exciting in her life.

'Holy shit, is this for real?' Maisie said, her voice echoing in the vastness of the marbled hallway. 'We're actually staying here?'

'Cool, isn't it?' Caz replied casually, stylish in her scarlet bikini and green wrap, compared to Maisie's sweaty stickiness.

'It's *amazing*!' Maisie couldn't keep the note of astonishment out of her voice as Caz brought her on a brief tour of the ground floor. Doors lining one side of the hallway opened onto a state-of-the-art media room with plush leather seating, a huge screen and, mindful of the surround-sound, complete with sound-proofing. Next to that, a games room with a full-sized pool table, a pinball machine, a treadmill, then a cute little library room, and last but not least, a well-stocked home bar that looked like a cosy snug. On the other side of the house, an enormous open-plan living, dining and kitchen area stretched from front to back, complete with sumptuous sofas, a twelve-seater glass dining-room table, and a cutting-edge, almost industrial-looking, kitchen area.

Through floor-to-ceiling bi-fold doors open beyond the dining area, she saw sunlight reflecting off a blue swimming pool, bunting fluttering against a sapphire sky, flowers spilling out of planters. Aaron and Eddie were lying supine on thickly padded loungers, and Lucinda, lean, lithe and magnificent in an ice-white bikini, was standing on the terrace at the edge of the pool chatting to Janet. As Maisie watched, unable to tear her eyes away, they caught hands and jumped into the sparkling water, sending up sheets of glittering spray along with laughter that she could barely hear above the thumping music.

'Am I the last to arrive?'

'No, Stella's not here yet. Lucinda said she was delayed in the office.'

She wasn't quite paddy last.

'It's great that you came, Maisie,' Caz said. 'I'll have a cocktail chilling for you on the terrace.'

Maisie felt as if she had been beamed onto a galaxy far away from her normal life. The clothes she'd packed were scarcely blingy enough for this extravaganza of a weekend, but she should have known. They'd all had to Revolut Caz with equal shares of the kitty, and it had been a far higher amount than Maisie had anticipated. Keith hadn't even asked her how much it was costing, telling her to enjoy herself, that she deserved a break.

She unpacked and had a quick, cooling shower. She ignored her tummy-tucking black one-piece and squeezed into her jade bikini, sucking in her stomach as much as she could. Then she pulled on a caftan and went downstairs, butterflies churning in her tummy. Ridiculous that old childhood jealousies can rise up and nip at you, even when you're a grown woman with children of your own. She knew exactly what to do to bolster her courage. She headed into the home bar, taking in the array of alcohol. She spied a bottle of Tequila Rose liqueur and poured some into a crystal glass, swiftly knocking it back.

Then she lifted her chin, threw back her shoulders, and sashayed through the dining area out to the terrace, delighted with the round of applause she got.

'Hey, no hubby?' Eddie asked.

'I'm off the leash for once,' Maisie quipped back, not bothering to explain that Keith had never had her on a leash. 'Watch this space.' She was encouraged with the whoops she got in reply. This was the way to play it, even if she felt out of step with everyone else.

'It's so good to have you here, Maisie, just like old times,' Lucinda said, after she had been introduced to Sasha and was sitting by the pool with a cocktail.

'I couldn't resist a few days away from nappies, baby goo, and a colicky three-month-old,' she said, immediately chiding herself for her reply. Why emphasise the difference between her life and Lucinda's? Hers being at the boring end of the spectrum, even her presence here tinged with a slice of guilt at leaving her small baby for the first time.

'Finn is so cute,' Lucinda said, surprising her. 'As is little Freya. Caz sent me on the photos. They're adorable. Lucky you.'

'Oh, thanks, Lucinda.' She took a long gulp of her cocktail, slowly starting to feel an ease in her stomach.

'It's a pity Keith couldn't come.'

'Yes,' Maisie said, not elaborating, concentrating on her cocktail. Even if Keith isn't very exciting as a husband, no way was she running the risk of him falling under Lucinda's spell.

And as the afternoon went on, the music became even louder and drinks were poured with increasing frequency. Stella arrived, and when she finally joined them by the pool she looked elegant in a cobalt blue swimsuit. Maisie was annoyed with herself for following the herd and squeezing into a tiny bikini instead of donning her one-piece. Later, the evening meal arrived from The Pier, and the weather was so lovely that they had it served out on the terrace. Maisie forced herself to get into the swing of things, even if she felt, deep down inside, that she was drowning. She glanced around the table after dessert was served and what seemed like the millionth bottle of wine was opened. These were the beautiful people: the glamorous Lucinda, always the sun around whom everyone else orbited; Caz, a complete reinvention, no longer the girl from the council estate, thanks to licking up some of the glitter cast in Lucinda's slipstream. Both had vowed they'd never have children. Janet and her husband Aaron, and their toned bodies, the epitome of smug, perfect coupledom – she couldn't see Janet ever ruining her slimline figure by getting pregnant. Then Eddie and Sasha, in the first flush of love, as they laughed and fed each other spoonfuls of a luscious brownie dessert, Eddie making wildly inappropriate comments to great hilarity.

Although Stella wasn't used to the dynamics of the whole gang together, Maisie could see it wasn't bothering her. She was full of ingrained self-possession, a relaxed kind of poise, thanks, no doubt, to her posh upbringing on Riverbank Manor and her accomplished career.

Maisie couldn't help envying all of them with their sense of entitlement and their careless self-assurance, evident in their conversations and the way they moved about the terrace as if they were taking the luxury of the break for granted. The way they all looked at home made her feel as if she was separated from them by a thick sheet of glass. None of them could understand the overwhelming changes parenthood brought, the new demands on your time, the total exhaustion that comes from the lack of decent sleep night after night, how bloody hard it is, much as you love these tiny babies. She knew she had lost sight of the person she once was, the woman behind the baby strapped to her boob, the woman she'd been before babies arrived. Before Keith, even. Her sister Monica had escaped marriage and motherhood, working in Wall Street as a financial analyst. The family WhatsApp was full of her photos of gala receptions, her plush apartment overlooking Central Park, luxury holidays in South America and the Caribbean, giving her mother plenty of fodder for the neighbours.

As the evening drifted on, and the Kerry sky swirled into a deep, fathomless blue, the fairy lights and coloured bulbs strung about the back garden looked magical, and Maisie couldn't help but recall images of Santorini. It was thanks to Lucinda's actions that she'd ended up in her dull cul-de-sac of a humdrum marriage compared to the exciting life she could have had. And how beautiful Lucinda looked, bubbly and sexy, prancing about the terrace without a care in the world, compared to the boring, still-carrying-pregnancy-weight Maisie.

When it was her turn to go to the bar, she chucked a shot of gin into Lucinda's mocktail, glad that Lucinda hadn't a clue about her sudden urge for some kind of retaliation. What did she think she was playing at, saying she was off the booze? Especially this weekend. There would be plenty more where this came from, Maisie decided. Anything to encourage Lucinda to make a fool of herself in front of them all.

Snapping out of her reverie, Maisie realises her coffee has gone cold. Now, six months later, she has come to regret her nasty vindictiveness. She shouldn't be here, in Cork airport. She shouldn't be heading to The Lookout. But it's too late, she's on the way, and the board is showing that Caz's flight landed ten minutes ago.

'You're too kind, Maisie,' Caz says, when she comes through, letting go of her wheelie case to enfold Maisie in a big hug. Caz needs to reach up because she is so petite compared to Maisie's average height. Maisie doesn't feel particularly kind. Seeing Caz reminds her that she's crazy to be facing everyone and the horrors of that weekend again. Out in the car, she inputs the code for Wolf Cove into her satnav.

'Two hours,' she says, concentrating on following the instructions as she negotiates unfamiliar roads before reaching the N22.

'I'll need a quick pit stop somewhere,' Caz says. 'I have to pick up some wine on the way.'

'Same here. I doubt alcohol is high on Stella's agenda.'

'I doubt if it's high on anyone's agenda after the party weekend,' Caz says, 'but I'll need plenty of it to get me through the next couple of days.'

'I totally get you. It's my wind-down treat as soon as Freya and Finn are in bed.' She finds herself giving Caz a run-down of her busy days.

Later, after a lull in the conversation, Caz says, 'I was surprised that Janet is coming.'

'But nothing about Aaron. I wonder what's happening there.'

'We'll find out soon, and we'll see what Stella's lined up in terms of a vigil.'

'It was good of you to drop everything and come at such short notice.'

'I couldn't stay away. I feel there's a lot of unfinished business with this whole tragedy.'

'What do you mean?' Maisie flicks Caz a glance. She's staring out through the windscreen, but Maisie knows by the expression in her eyes that, far from taking note of the murky January countryside, Caz is miles away and deep in thought.

'Dear God, I can't believe Lucinda's gone,' Caz says, not answering Maisie's question. 'I haven't even started to work through it.'

'You did scarper to London rather rapidly.'

'I had to get away, I couldn't live with my guilt in Dublin. London felt like a clean slate.'

'Guilt? What have you got to feel guilty about?'

There is silence from Caz until, after a while, she says, 'I mean in general. It seems wrong to me that Lucinda is gone yet I'm still alive. Survivor's guilt. I can't help thinking I could have done something to save her, to prevent the accident from happening. I keep going over it in my head, looking back at everything, trying to figure out where it all started to go wrong.'

'You don't think it would have had anything to do with … well, as far back as Santorini?' Maisie hopes she sounds casual enough. She'd love to know if any of them had found out how Lucinda had betrayed her, and how much Maisie had resented her. Her words have the effect of a pistol shot in the car.

Caz's head whips around and Maisie sees a flash of alarm in her light blue eyes before they close over in a guarded expression.

'Santorini? What made you bring that up?' Caz asks.

Maisie's heart skips a beat. 'Nothing really … Thinking out loud. It's the last time we were all away together as a group before The Lookout.'

'Jeez … I didn't mean that far back. That's ancient history,' Caz says. 'If anyone has moved on since then, you have.'

'I have, haven't I?' Maisie says lightly. 'Married, a mortgage, two kids.'

'See? About as far from Santorini as you can get.'

Maisie blinks and concentrates on the road in front of her.

After a while Caz sighs. 'It kills me that no matter how often I go over that weekend, I can't go back and change a single thing.'

Maisie knows that. No matter how many times she has regretted her behaviour that weekend, how often she hates herself because of it and allows it to feed her feelings of worthlessness, it won't make one iota of a difference. Lucinda is gone, out of their lives. Yet the hollow ache of guilt is still alive in her heart. As she stares ahead at the ribbon of road uncurling in front of her, drawing her inexorably to Wolf Head and The Lookout, she knows that, whatever happens this weekend, no one must find out what she did.

CHAPTER ELEVEN

Stella

Just after midday, Stella goes through the shopping list with Britt, who's heading to Dunmullen to pick up wine, spirits and essentials needed for the weekend, in addition to the food being supplied by The Pier.

'Could you see if they have some flowers?'

'Flowers?' Britt looks surprised.

'Any kind. I'd like to put some on the cliff top. I've never actually been there …'

'Of course.'

'And if you could get some tea lights?'

'Right,' Britt says, without batting an eyelid.

Stella has a vague notion of the group standing by the quayside, complete with saucers of flickering tea lights, to welcome Lucinda home. But that quickly fades when the guards call to The Lookout before Britt leaves and the painful reality of what's happening hits her like a juggernaut. Their rank floats over Stella's head, but she grasps that their names are Imelda and Brendan.

'No, thanks,' Brendan says, in response to Britt's offer of tea or coffee. 'This is a quick courtesy call to introduce ourselves.'

They sit rather awkwardly in the living area, the sumptuousness of the cushion-and-throw-bedecked sofas at odds with the grim reason for their visit. Stella guesses that big, ruddy-faced Brendan is in his fifties. He seems familiar, and she realises he was one of the local guards involved in the case at the time of the accident.

'I'll be the main liaison,' Imelda says. Late twenties, she exudes a friendly, youthful competence. 'I'll keep you updated on everything. Media are already arriving in Wolf Cove, but we'll be closing off the quayside to the public, apart from yourselves and members of the rescue team. They're going through tidal charts and weather reports today and, more than likely, it'll be tomorrow evening by the time ...'

Stella shakes her head and Imelda refrains from completing her sentence, placing a comforting hand on her arm.

Tomorrow evening.

No more pretending Lucinda is away somewhere, either for work or pleasure, and simply too busy to get in touch – the crutch she'd often used to cover the blindsiding and aching emptiness of her absence. Suddenly it all becomes real and she thinks the pain will slice her in two.

'We're the only family,' Britt says, sensing Stella is unable to talk under the weight of her distress. 'We might have three or four close friends with us. We're holding a vigil over the weekend to celebrate Lucinda's life. Some of her friends are joining us and they're due to arrive later today.'

'Let me know if I can help in any way,' Imelda says. 'We'll keep each other in the loop.'

When the guards and Britt have left, Britt bearing Stella's bank card to pay for the shopping at her insistence, Stella checks her mobile. No more updates, not even a word from her tormentor. Could that be because they are otherwise occupied, like, for instance, travelling down here? She shivers, even though The Lookout is warm.

Stella goes up the silent stairwell and has a quick look around, checking all is in order before Lucinda's friends arrive. To her, the empty rooms resemble an inanimate, elaborate stage set, holding its breath, waiting for the cast of characters to arrive, the drama to unfold.

How much will Lucinda's friends remember of that weekend? Whatever happens, she needs to keep a clear head to best organise this vigil. Now, down in the hall, she hears a car coming up the lane outside, passing the house, then a sudden squeal of brakes, the roar of the engine as it swiftly reverses. The growl of it splintering the surroundings outside as it comes up the driveway. The sudden silence as the engine quietens, then the slam of a door, footsteps outside. The peal of the doorbell.

Her heart sinks. She's not able for this after all. The idea of holding a vigil for Lucinda is so terrifying she feels a surge of sheer blind panic. Why is she gathering this assortment of people around her at such a tough time? The bell chimes again. She braces herself when she opens the door.

It's Rex.

Looking at him standing in the doorway, Stella feels a surge of relief, as though the cavalry has arrived to help her out of a tight spot.

She'd been walking home from the office one evening at the end of September, having returned to work two weeks previously, taking the track along by the Grand Canal at Wilton Terrace. It was past seven o'clock, the path mostly clear of the pedestrian commuters. Then a thump on her back that knocked her off-balance, her laptop bag wrenched roughly from her shoulder. A guy in dark clothes jogging off with it. She stood still, momentarily dazed, berating herself for drifting along in sleepwalking mode and not being vigilant enough. In the next moment, a man shot past her and chased after the mugger, catching up with him and recovering her bag while the mugger darted down a laneway.

The man approached her with the rescued laptop. He was tall with a friendly smile and an easy gait, wearing a casual jacket over his jeans. He had short hair that was fashionably dyed bright peroxide white, and a youthful early-forties face.

'One laptop returned to one lady owner,' he said, presenting it to her with a good-natured flourish. 'I hope you're okay and that little lowlife didn't give you too much of a fright.'

Stella swallowed hard and took a deep breath. All her limbs were shaking.

'Hey, you're not okay,' he said, concern in his eyes. 'Do you want to report the incident to the guards? I'll come with you. I witnessed what happened and can give them a description.'

'No – no, there's no need.' She didn't want to set foot inside a garda station ever again. She'd had enough dealings with them to last her a lifetime. 'I want to go home,' she said.

'Have you far to go?'

She couldn't place his accent – a mixture of Dublin and somewhere else?

'No, it's only ten minutes or so …' She stumbled over a knotted tree branch embedded in the track.

'Look, you're shaking,' he said. 'Let me at least buy you a coffee. It'll be my good deed of the day, and then I'll walk you home.'

She was too shaken not to agree. And it wasn't as if the four walls of her apartment guaranteed safety. Life could, and did, shatter in an instant. They were sitting in a café adjacent to the canal when he said with a rather juvenile grin, 'I have a confession to make.'

'What?' Stella couldn't compute this: her brain felt like jelly.

'I have an unfair advantage in that I know who you are. I thought you looked familiar but now I've twigged.'

Her heart plummeted. If this was about being the sister of 'that socialite who disappeared along with her car', she couldn't cope. She'd get to her feet and walk straight out the door. But he didn't have the look of someone about to speak of death and doom. He said, 'You were on *Prime Time* last week, weren't you?'

Stella breathed out. This she could manage. Work was safe. It was structured. She felt her professional mask slip into place. As the CEO of Women's Rescue, she'd participated in a panel discussion highlighting the range of supports available to women and children who were victims of drug addiction. 'You must have a great memory,' she said. 'I was only on it for about fifteen minutes or so.'

'You were very impressive with your level of commitment,' he said.

'It's part of my job,' she said, 'the ethos of our organisation.'

'Still, Stella, you came across as a warm and empathetic person. I'm sure any woman who was watching and needed help would have been encouraged to contact the helpline.

I couldn't believe how bad the drug problem in Dublin has become in the time I've been away.'

'Away where?'

'What am I thinking? I haven't even introduced myself – Rex O'Neill.' He leaned forward, his shoulders hunched, a mischievous smile on his face, as if he was happy to impart a secret. 'I came into some money from my uncle and I used it to fund a twelve-month career break so that I could go travelling. My girlfriend had broken up with me so it seemed like the right time.'

'Really? Apart from the break-up, which sucks, that's the kind of thing you can only dream of. Are you home long?' In other words, Stella thought, had he been around two months ago when the news about Lucinda broke?

'No, but it's as if I was never away, back to my apartment in Citywest and my job in cyber security. I'm usually to be found in one of those steel and glass buildings down in the docks – it could be any hour of the day or night depending on the number of infernos we have to put out.'

'It must be stressful.'

'It is for the firms who call on our services. We stay calm in the middle of their crisis, the better to sort it out.'

He chatted about his travels, and Stella relaxed, allowing the cup of coffee to be followed by a glass of wine, Rex's easy-going humour keeping her away from the silent apartment that screamed with emptiness. It was helpful that he had never known Lucinda, and he was a restful change from casual friends and acquaintances so stricken by her grief that they were embarrassed to talk to her in the aftermath in case they said the wrong thing, or, she suspected, in case tragedy was contagious.

There was another glass of wine, an exchange of mobile numbers, then a pleasant stroll to her apartment block. A week later he texted her: he had tickets for a show in Vicar Street the following evening. A few nights later, it was a movie in the Odeon in Point Square, then a play at the Civic in Tallaght, followed the next week by a movie in Dundrum, then drinks in a quirky new wine bar in Camden Street. By the end of the third week, she felt she'd known him a lot longer. She found herself looking forward to these date nights. Rex took her out of herself, chatting about movies and books, funny incidents from his various travels. Being with him was a welcome distraction from sitting at home alone, staring at the walls of her apartment, trying and failing to stem a flood of images of Lucinda. It also gave her an undemanding way back into the world of socialising.

By December she felt they were a steady item, although she hadn't yet brought him back to her apartment. She liked Rex, he was easy to be around, and while she was finding her way back into the dating game again after the painful loss of Lucinda, it didn't feel right to her to look for pleasure in bed with him. She was nervous about it too, the break-up with Leo having badly dented her confidence. She tried, haltingly, to tell Rex she wasn't ready just yet to take things further, but he'd hushed her by kissing her warmly, telling her to take all the time she needed.

He wasn't going to be around for Christmas, he said, making a sad face. He'd already made plans to get away from it all, a luxury one-off trip to the Maldives with some of his cousins, booked months ago.

'Poor you,' Stella had said, making an equally sad face and eliciting a laugh.

She'd already made plans to ignore the season completely, by volunteering to cover daily stints for the Women's Rescue freephone emergency helpline. Then a week into the new year, over after-dinner drinks in the comfy booth of a neighbourhood restaurant close to the canal, and one glass too many for Stella, she found herself pouring out her heart and telling Rex about Lucinda, including the guilt she was living with.

'I had a feeling there was something sad going on in your life,' he said, looking at her with kind compassion, 'but I didn't want to intrude.'

'Thanks,' she said. 'You were right not to. I needed that space and I won't talk about it again. I'd rather leave that side of me and my life behind when we're out. Otherwise, I think I'd ... stop breathing altogether.'

'I understand.'

But talking to Rex about Lucinda had opened a painful door and sent her into a black, downward spiral, which was how she'd found herself standing on the bridge looking down into the depths of the dark canal the night Hugh had rescued her. By sleeping with Hugh, she felt she'd cheated on Rex, and she'd refused his invitation to a concert a week later, knowing she needed to sort out her head once and for all.

And now, here he is, seemingly happy enough to be with her, sitting on a stool at the kitchen island, sipping coffee. He's wearing a dark grey jumper and jeans, which, set against his hair colour, lend him a certain glamour. Stella knows that letting Rex into her life like this is going to move things forward. She's not sure how ready she is for that, but here, this weekend, while everyone else will be caught up in mourning, Rex will have her back and be able to stay calm in the middle of the emotional charge of it all.

'It's kind of you to drop everything to be here,' she says.

'Only too glad to help out. Whatever I can do to ease things, tell me. I know what it's like to be missing a loved one.' His blue eyes are suddenly shadowed.

'Oh, gosh – sorry, I didn't know.'

Rex puts up his hands in a gesture of surrender and smiles warmly. 'I'm sorry, I didn't mean to bring that up. This weekend is all about you, not me, and whatever I can do to support you. I'm handy with a dishcloth, and can cook a mean spaghetti Bolognese.'

'The spaghetti might not be needed,' Stella says, going on to tell him of the arrangements for the weekend.

'Sounds like you have it all organised.'

'Don't worry, I'll find plenty for you to do.'

Their gazes meet, something in his eyes making Stella realise she needs to clarify something. 'I've put you in the room my sister had the last time we were here. It's a suite, on the top floor. No one else will want to stay there, including me. I hope that's okay?'

He smiles reassuringly at her. 'Perfectly fine with me. No need to worry about anything like that, Stella. Not this weekend.' A pause. 'I hope it's okay with you that I brought my laptop – I'll need to check in with the office from time to time. There are bound to be a couple of burning issues.'

'Of course, I understand that. I'm conscious I've taken you away from your work. Feel free to disappear whenever you need to.'

The bell rings. To Stella's immense surprise, she finds Eddie Hynes standing at the door, wrapped up in a thick dark ski jacket. A small grey Fiat – a car she'd never have associated with image-conscious Eddie – is parked alongside Rex's sleek black Mazda.

'Eddie! I didn't know whether to expect you or not,' Stella says.

Eddie gives her a look she can't exactly fathom. A mixture of sadness, embarrassment and apology. She sees immediately he's lost weight, if his angular face and slightly sunken cheeks are anything to go by. And no sign of Sasha.

'Sorry, Stella. I didn't tell you because I didn't know myself if I was coming or not,' he says. 'Then this morning I found myself getting into the car. I kept telling myself I could turn back at any time if it got too much – or if the car broke down, that would be my sign to go back home. But it kept going, I didn't turn back, so here I am.'

She'd never thought the swaggering Eddie would be the type to look for a 'sign'.

'You're welcome,' Stella says. He looks like he's about to bolt at any given moment. 'Did you bring a case?' she goes on. 'You are staying, I presume?'

'Yes, if that's okay?'

'Then what are we doing standing here? Grab your case and come in.'

'Sure,' he says, his gaze scanning the hallway behind her, his eyes stricken with something.

Fear, she realises.

CHAPTER TWELVE

Stella

Britt returns from Dunmullen and has been introduced to Rex when Tadhg arrives bearing trays of sandwiches and a covered tureen of vegetable soup from The Pier. They are having a late lunch as soon as everyone is here.

'That's all fab, thanks, Tadhg,' Stella says.

'Over here,' says Britt, directing him to the kitchen island. 'It's great you're around to do the ferrying.'

'Och, I might as well be useful. I can't take the trawler out for a couple of days,' he says, glancing at Stella awkwardly.

'Why don't you stay and have some food with us?' Britt suggests.

'Nah, I've to bring the ma to the doctor this afternoon, her nerves, like, you know ...'

Stella guesses the news from Wolf Head has upset Tadhg's mother. He isn't long gone when Janet arrives. Tall and sleek, wearing leggings and a zipped emerald green fleece, her dark hair pulled back into a severe pony-tail, she looks pale and distracted. She hugs Stella fiercely. 'Oh, Jesus, Stella, is this really happening?'

'I know, I know, it's a nightmare.' Stella hugs her back and tries to sound soothing.

'Totally. Sorry, I shouldn't be unloading on you.' Janet

straightens up. 'Aaron is sorry he couldn't come,' she says. 'Too many work commitments.'

'No problem, I'm glad to have you here, Janet.'

Caz and Maisie are last to arrive, coming into the hall suitably swaddled in thick scarves, boots and gloves, a long faux-fur coat on Caz, a thick quilted jacket on Maisie as befits the January weather – apart from the rather absurd fact that Caz is wearing oversized sunglasses in the middle of a grey January afternoon. When Caz slides up her sunglasses, Stella can see that her eyes are red-rimmed from crying.

Caz pulls Stella into a long hug, then stands back and takes her two hands in her gloved ones. 'Oh, Stella, this is desperately sad. I can't believe it's all happening. I wanted to come and I didn't want to come, if that makes sense.'

For once Stella is in agreement with Caz. 'It does, of course.'

They hang their coats and scarves in the cloakroom. Both women are wrapped up in comfy sweaters and dark jeans. Caz is another person who has lost weight. Always slim and diminutive, and with an air of busyness, now she seems muted somehow, her cheekbones more pronounced, her blonde hair scraped back into a messy chignon, and there are shadows under her eyes that she hasn't bothered to conceal. Her glance darts around the hall, slight panic in her eyes, and Stella guesses that like her, and Eddie before her, she half expects to see Lucinda appear, floating down the stairs. Caz covers her face with her hands, shaking her head before removing them, blinking rapidly, and visibly pulling herself together.

'Ah, Stella,' she says, 'it's a load of shite.' She looks as broken as Stella feels on the inside.

For the first time ever, in all the years she'd known her, Stella feels on the same wavelength as Caz.

Maisie is a lot more subdued than the last time she was here. Taller and more broad-boned, her long, blonde-highlighted hair loose around her shoulders and showing some roots, she tells Stella quietly she's glad to be here to lend her support, and will do anything at all to help.

'I hope you're both okay with sharing one of the larger bedrooms on the first floor,' Stella says, letting them know the situation as soon as they arrive, in case they want to make other arrangements. 'We have a full house.'

Caz frowns slightly before she smooths her expression. 'Who else is here? I thought it was only us and Janet.'

'Us, Britt, Janet, Eddie—'

'Eddie came?' Caz asks, suddenly alert.

'Yes, he did, and Rex is here, a friend of mine,' Stella says. 'Rex and Eddie are in the rooms on the top floor, leaving the first floor for us. Why don't I show you up and you can meet everyone over lunch?'

'Sure.'

The three of them troop up the stairs, and Stella shows them to a room across the corridor from hers, a larger room with two beds.

Stella slips into her own room for a minute and takes a few deep breaths, trying to relax her facial muscles, taut as they are under the strain of the mask she's been nailing to her face. From the time she goes down to lunch, it will be full-on. She finds it heartening, but also a little surprising, that all of Lucinda's close friends have managed to drop everything at such short notice – jobs, families, social appointments, weekend plans – to arrive down to this remote part of the country for her vigil. Downstairs the voices recede, as though someone has closed the door to the open-plan area. Everything quietens. She gathers the energy needed to go down and make sure everyone is comfortable after their long journeys, including Rex.

When she reaches the ground floor, Stella notices the cloakroom door has been left open, and a piece of material seems to be jammed under the door. Inside, along with the high-vis vests and an abandoned hoodie, the coat hooks are strung with puffy jackets and fur-trimmed winter coats. But it is the item trailing off a hook on the inside of the door and caught under it that makes her recoil in alarm. It's a silver-cream silk scarf, identical to the one she gave Lucinda the previous Christmas.

She stares at it in confusion, sudden dread forming a thick black cloud in her chest. She could swear it wasn't there earlier, when Caz and Maisie had hung up their coats. Looking closer, she sees it has been slashed in several places.

Someone has placed it here recently.

Leaving the door open for her to see when she comes downstairs.

Stella goes through to the open-plan area in time to see Britt disappearing into the utility room. Rex is at the table, laying out plates, cups and cutlery with the air of someone determined to make himself useful. Caz, Janet, Maisie and Eddie are standing around the kitchen island, looking rather sombre and awkward as though the occasion is getting to them.

'Who brought the scarf?' Stella asks bluntly, forgetting her hostess manners.

'Which scarf?' Caz asks. 'I think we all have one.'

Stella makes an effort to speak over the terrible constriction in her throat. 'I'm talking about the silk scarf, hanging on the cloakroom door.'

'Silk scarf? Not me,' says Janet.

'Or me,' says Caz.

Maisie shakes her head. 'It's not mine, but I hung it up. I was checking my jacket pocket for my car keys when I saw it on the floor beside some wellies.'

It hadn't been there before anyone arrived. Stella would have spotted it immediately.

'Is there a problem, Stella?' Caz asks.

Stella braces herself to go out to the cloakroom and pick up the scarf. She sees Lucinda's face in the light of a Christmas tree, opening the silvery wrapping and holding the delicate silk against her cheek. Sharp pain bursts across her stomach. 'I bought a scarf exactly like this for Lucinda,' she says, holding it up as she comes back into the room.

'That's hardly the same one, unless she left it here ...' Caz says, realising too late the inappropriateness of her words.

Stella shakes her head, unable to talk for a minute. Lucinda hadn't 'left' anything anywhere. One of the worst things Stella had ever had to do was to empty Lucinda's room in The Lookout and bring her belongings back to Dublin – dresses, tops and shorts, swimwear, cosmetics and perfume she'd selected for her party weekend. Britt had helped her. She'd packed them all into Lucinda's leopard-print case and matching vanity bag, which are still sitting, untouched, at the back of her storage press in the hall – untouched, that is, apart from the time she'd opened Lucinda's vanity bag to retrieve her hairbrush so that Forensics could take a sample of her DNA.

Stella swallows. 'She didn't leave it here. I know I packed everything. And it's damaged,' she says, opening it out.

'Bloody hell, what does that mean …?' Caz's voice falters.

Maisie's face whitens. 'I didn't notice that. It looked like it had slipped down off a peg so I hung it up.'

'Can you remember if you closed the cloakroom door?' Stella asks.

Maisie looks at Stella as though she's lost the plot. Stella realises she sounds like a mother about to reprimand a child. Then Britt comes through from the utility room, a smile on her face, bearing a bundle of napkins and an extra teapot.

'What's up?' she asks, her footsteps faltering when she senses something is amiss.

'This scarf,' Stella says. 'It was in the cloakroom. It's Lucinda's.'

Britt looks at the scarf and her face crumples. She puts a hand to her chest. 'Oh, God. She was wearing it that last day.'

'Was she?'

'Yes, she had it tied around her straw hat. When I admired it, she told me you had given it to her. But how come …' Her face creases with questions, the same questions, no doubt, that Stella has teeming through her head.

She tries to put them in sequence. If Lucinda had had it with her that weekend, then Stella must have put it into her case. If so, how did it get out? Or had it been mislaid at the time in The Lookout? Even if Stella had overlooked it, or if someone had taken it before Stella had left for Dublin, how come it was suddenly here now, and damaged so vindictively? If she had been wearing it when she visited Britt that last day, at what point had she taken it off? Which one of them had put it into the cloakroom? Her troll? The troll who has suddenly gone quiet. Why? Were they here now?

Stella's head starts to spin with anxiety, but her gut instinct is to hide her suspicions. 'I'm sure there's a perfectly ordinary explanation,' she says, making a huge effort to sound casual. 'Let's all have lunch. We've more important things to talk about right now. Like plans for the vigil.'

Plans, she hopes, that will help her uncover the truth.

CHAPTER THIRTEEN

Caz

Caz nips out to the downstairs bathroom before lunch is served, needing some space from everyone for a moment or two.

Images of Lucinda assault her from all directions and she feels so shredded inside that it's difficult to keep her grip on reality, never mind prevent herself from blurting something to Stella. She still sees Lucinda grabbing her hands in so tight a grip that all her bones and blue capillaries and tendons stood out, speaking in a ragged, begging, most un-Lucinda-like voice: 'Whatever you do, don't breathe a word to Stella. Ever. Promise me?'

But now the words are seething all over each other in the back of her head. On the journey over from London, the tangled web of them seemed to have mushroomed in size, ready to burst out of her. Does keeping a secret matter, though, now that Lucinda is dead? Do you have to keep a promise to the dead?

Yes, yes, yes, you certainly do. She'd sensed the ghost of Lucinda the minute she'd stepped inside The Lookout. But, of course, she is nowhere in The Lookout. Or anywhere else for that matter. The huge space she had occupied in Caz's heart since the age of thirteen echoes with a cold emptiness.

After the accident, the guards had spoken to all of them, trying to establish a picture of the events of that weekend. That was when she should have spoken up. But she'd hardly been able to talk with grief for her friend. Besides, she'd decided at the time, Stella had been upset almost to the point of being catatonic: why muddy the waters, make things worse for her? Maybe Stella was best left in blissful ignorance. After all, it was what Lucinda wanted. What she'd always wanted when it came to Stella.

Stella hasn't a clue how proud Lucinda had always been of her. Sometimes Caz had found herself resenting the way Lucinda had placed Stella on an elevated pedestal, admiring her for her intelligence, her diligence, her academic achievements, her ambition. Years ago, when she'd first known Lucinda, she and Stella had got off on the wrong foot, and although Stella was always perfectly gracious towards her on the sporadic times they'd met over the years, they'd never moved beyond a respectful politeness. That had been some creepy thing with the scarf. Stella had looked totally spooked and she'd felt for her.

Caz squeezes soap from the dispenser and takes her time washing her hands, glowering at her reflection in the ornate mirror over the washbasin. She looks haggard. No surprises there. In the months following the tragedy, she'd been full of remorse. She'd rescued Lucinda several times over the years, but she hadn't rescued her that weekend. At times Lucinda's behaviour had bordered on frenzied, as if she was high on booze. Yet she'd said she was off booze, and had even brought in some alcohol-free gin, prosecco and wine. Had she been trying too hard to persuade herself and everyone else that a sober Lucinda could still be crazy fun?

Maybe if Caz's patience hadn't begun to fray at the edges, thanks to the way Lucinda had been off her radar for a while and so offhand about it afterwards, Caz might have kept a closer eye on her. But then again, early on that weekend hadn't Lucinda cheekily laughed off her concerns? Caz rinses her hands and picks up a fluffy towel, the image of herself and Lucinda on the boat trip as fresh in her mind as if it were yesterday.

Caz will never forget the feeling of freedom on that warm, blue-skied Friday afternoon. She gripped the side rail of the boat as it dipped and swayed between glinting blue waves and the endless sky. They were on their way back from a trip around the Skelligs. 'What an experience!' Janet said to her dreamily. 'It was far more of a soulful experience than I expected. Aaron will be raging he missed it. We'll have to come back sometime and do a landing tour.'

'Yes,' Caz croaked beside her. The image of the Skelligs in the near distance had electrified the marrow of her bones, bringing every cell alive. But the return journey was making her feel more than a little queasy, and even the scent of Janet's sun-cream aggravated her.

Tadhg had suggested the trip when he'd arrived at The Lookout that mid-morning with a crate of beer from The Pier. Caz was making coffee; Maisie was pouring cereal into a bowl. They could hear Lucinda directing Tadhg to bring the beer into the home bar – there was more space in the fridge. There was no sign of Eddie and Sasha, or Stella, but out on the terrace, Janet and Aaron were doing sun salutations on their yoga mats.

Maisie winked at Caz. 'I'm going out there to horse into my Crunchy Nut cereal.'

'Maisie!'

Then Lucinda wafted into the room, in a wispy, cream-shaded ballerina-length sheath, Tadhg following in her wake.

'It's all sorted. Tadhg's bringing us women out early this afternoon. To the Skelligs.'

'Not on his smelly fishing boat!' Maisie squealed.

'No!' Lucinda squealed back. 'A proper boat, belonging to a friend of his. Wear your swim things. We're doing a circle around the island but we need to be down at the quayside for one o'clock. Eddie or Aaron can ferry us, before they go off for their game of golf.'

'Golf?' Caz said. 'This is the first I've heard of it.'

'They were hatching plans last night,' Lucinda said. 'But there's no way they'll last the course after yesterday's booze intake. I predict they'll come crawling home after nine holes.'

'I'll take charge of the drinks,' Maisie offered. 'I presume we're bringing fizz.'

'Of course,' Lucinda said, 'including a bottle of my own special concoction.' She made it sound as if her alcohol-free prosecco was a lot more exciting than it was.

Now, on the return trip, Caz realised she shouldn't have had even one glass of fizz, never mind the two or three that Maisie had insisting on pouring. Tadhg, with his back to them, was wearing khaki shorts and a white vest stretched across his broad shoulders under his lifejacket. Barefoot at the wheel, he manoeuvred the boat out of a wide semi-circle. Lucinda, Maisie, Sasha and Stella were sitting further up in the stern.

Lucinda drained her glass. 'I'll top that up,' Maisie

offered, as she opened the cool bag packed with the chilled bottles.

'Mine is the cream label.' Lucinda handed Maisie her glass and headed over to Tadhg, which caused the boat to rock wildly, much to Caz's horror. Lucinda ran a hand across the muscles of his back and down his arms. He didn't respond.

'Tadhg, you really are a full-throttled tiger, aren't you?'

The sound of a throaty purr … then the silvery cascade of Lucinda's laughter as she plucked the keys out of the engine. She dropped them along with her sunglasses on the deck, pulled off her lifejacket and walked over to the side, bending down to hold the rail as she lifted herself over and slipped down into the water, disappearing under the surface for a moment. Then her head and shoulders emerged and she pushed back sopping wet hair so that it trailed down her back. She paddled about for a minute or two before she reached up a tanned, sea-spattered hand to Tadhg.

'Hey, the water's freezing, give us a whoosh up.'

He duly obliged and she rocked against him slightly as she regained her balance. Her white string bikini, almost transparent, clung to every curve of her body.

'Oh dear,' she said, a mischievous smile on her face. 'I'm soaking.'

She unhooked her bikini top, letting it drop to the deck. Quick as a flash, Maisie was up beside her, laughing as she untied one of the ties to her bikini bottoms, saying something about getting her out of her wet things. Lucinda happily allowed her bottoms to fall away so that everyone was treated to a view of her Brazilian wax, including Tadhg who looked around at the crucial moment as if he sensed something in the air. His face flushed as far as the tips of his ears.

Caz tossed a towel towards her. 'Lucinda! Stop acting the eejit and cover yourself.'

Lucinda threw the towel back at her. 'What's got into you? Spoilsport! Can't you see I'm having fuuuun!' Lucinda flaunted her perfect golden body before she finally picked up a towel and wrapped it around herself. Tadhg silently handed her the lifejacket. He only started the boat once she had it fastened.

'Here.' Maisie proffered her a fizzing glass. 'I've topped up your special concoction.'

Lucinda wasn't even knocking back the booze, Caz thought blackly. Not that that would be any excuse for her ridiculous behaviour. But it wasn't up to her to be Lucinda's minder. Not any more. Spoilsport – after all the times she'd looked out for Lucinda, that hurt.

Caz straightens the towel on the rack and takes a deep breath before she rejoins the others, determined to put the painful memories of the boat trip to the back of her mind. Everyone is settling themselves at the table, Britt passing around sandwiches, Rex taking charge of ladling the soup into bowls.

Now he's a surprise. She hadn't expected Stella to bring a boyfriend although she gathers they're not sharing a room. He doesn't look at all Stella's type. On first impression, he seems too relaxed and easy-going for the intelligent, ambitious Stella. Although maybe that's exactly what she needs right now, someone calm and laid-back. There's a spare seat at the table opposite Stella and she sits there.

Rex moves along, offering bowls of soup. When he reaches Stella, he gives her a friendly smile, the warm kind of smile

Caz wouldn't mind getting from a man like Rex. She can't help envying her a little as he puts his hand lightly on Stella's shoulder and bends his head to hers. Stop. It had been bad enough living in Lucinda's shadow when it came to the men in their lives. One thing for sure: Stella wouldn't have got a look-in with Rex had Lucinda been around. Caz watches as Stella listens to him quietly, her face giving nothing away.

Stella's face has clearly borne the toll of the last six months. There are violet shadows under her eyes and they have the tense, flinty look of someone who is operating from a hard place on the inside. Her roots need treating, her skin is dry. Caz swears at her professional self for noticing this. Stella's bereaved, for Heaven's sake. In a moment of empathy, she wonders how she will cope with the inevitable tsunami of emotion that's bound to be unleashed over the next thirty-six hours.

The downside of Rex's presence is that it means sharing a room with Maisie, so she can't leave the en-suite light on all night – her plan to prevent frightening images of Lucinda looming towards her in the pitch black. She'll have to knock back enough alcohol to make sure she conks out. Beside her, Maisie is talking to Janet, and snippets of the conversation drift over to her: '... you've no idea how tough it is, the exhaustion, the endless washing and cleaning ... you don't know how bloody lucky you are, Janet.'

Janet murmurs something noncommittal.

Caz tunes out. Uncomplicated Maisie, who has no stain on her conscience, whose busy life is safely shrink-wrapped into a constant juggle of looking after babies, crèches, her job, her days full to capacity, her evenings punctuated by regular wine o'clock wind-downs, and all accomplished on far less than the minimum recommended hours of sleep. She'd heard all about it on the road from Cork. From the sound of it, Maisie has simply no time to think about Lucinda, no room in her brain to allow any thoughts of that tragic weekend to infiltrate. Her life is too packed with managing the logistics of her daily manoeuvres. Caz envies her for this, but not as much as she always envied Lucinda.

Breathe, Caz, slowly, in and out. That part of your life is over. This is now.

She'd been surprised to see Janet here – Caz had been sure she'd cry off at the last minute. What on earth had possessed her to come back to the place where her husband had flirted with Lucinda so blatantly? What had happened to her sassy, confident friend that she was such a sucker for punishment?

She looks around the table, her gaze sliding down to Eddie, sitting at the end.

Eddie! She hadn't expected him to show his face. They'd all witnessed the rubbish way he'd treated Sasha during the party weekend. Eddie had been off his head, and Lucinda had been fizzing like a firecracker set to self-destruct. She wonders what Eddie is trying to prove by being here, having stepped over an invisible boundary that weekend.

Just as well she's over him. Isn't she? Long over him by now, Caz corrects herself, having wrenched off the rose-tinted glasses with which she'd viewed Eddie Hynes during that holiday in Santorini, when he'd finally cut his feelings for her stone dead. But what had happened between them in Santorini hadn't stayed there, Caz knows. In her case it still resonates to this day.

CHAPTER FOURTEEN

Stella

The atmosphere is subdued, most people picking at their food, but at least Lucinda's friends are here, making an effort in the face of the challenging days ahead.

On the one hand, Stella is grateful that friends have shown up in Lucinda's memory, despite what had happened the last time they'd been gathered here, Lucinda carving a trail of destruction through some relationships, even, on the day of the boat trip, that sharp put-down to Caz. Could it be that in one, maybe two cases, they're afraid *not* to be here?

One of Lucinda's friends was probably behind the Instagram page. And there's a possibility they are the same person who's sending her anonymous texts, because the wording on some of the messages is so similar. Or has her anonymous texter been copying Instagram comments to throw her off the scent? Caz needed to be here so much she'd flown from London at short notice, no doubt incurring an expensive flight and having to cancel work in the process. But, Stella acknowledges, as Lucinda's closest friend she might have set up the tribute page, but she looks far too broken right now to be able to conduct a campaign of vitriol against her.

'Do I have you to thank for setting up the Instagram page?' she asks Caz.

Caz looks at her blankly.

'Hashtag leavealightonforLucinda?' Stella prompts.

'No, I haven't even seen it.'

Stella's head starts to throb. Is she telling the truth? No more wine for her this weekend, no matter how much she needs to numb the jagged edges of her pain. She can't afford to have her critical faculties hijacked by an alcoholic fog.

'I'm on Instagram myself,' Caz says. 'I must check it out.' She casts around for her handbag, which is dangling off the back of her chair.

'I'm sure it's flooded with messages,' Stella says. 'But I have to warn you some comments are less than savoury for both me and Lucinda. And that's an understatement.'

'*What?*' Caz looks aghast. She drops her bag. 'I know how vile some keyboard warriors can be. Don't tell me you and Lucinda have been targeted.'

'We have.'

'But that's appalling, Stella. Some people are bloody monsters. I hope you've reported it.'

'Not yet.'

'Stella, you should. Don't put up with that shite on top of everything else. I'm not driving up their engagement by liking their posts or viewing stories. I'm not interested in looking at things that will make me feel even worse than I already do. Social media can be a toxic cesspit. I wonder is that why ...' Caz's voice trails away.

'Why what?'

'Just a thought, Stella, but I've sometimes wondered why

Lucinda asked for a total social-media blackout that weekend? Remember? No posts, no pics.'

'She said at the time she wanted us all to be in the moment,' Stella says.

Caz doesn't look convinced. 'Another thing, and I shouldn't even be saying this, but she did pick a fairly remote place. You can't get much further west than here.'

'My mum was from around here, and we spent loads of summers with Britt.'

'Oh, of course, I remember that now,' Caz says, giving her a half-smile. 'I used to be so jealous of you both getting out of Dublin. But, Stella, make sure to report those posts. It must be upsetting. Let me know if there's anything at all I can do to help.'

Maybe, Stella thinks, it's time for her to revise her opinion of Lucinda's oldest friend. 'I appreciate you being here, thanks so much.' Stella's unused to thanking her for anything and she hopes she doesn't sound too stiff.

'I'm glad to be here to support you,' Caz says. 'The least I can do. I know how important you were to Lucinda, and always have been. You've no idea how much she admired you and looked up to you.'

She gives Stella a sad little smile.

Stella feels gutted. Someone else telling her how much Lucinda had looked up to her and she'd thrown it back in Lucinda's face. She thinks of the undercurrent of dislike that had lingered between her and Caz for years, ever since Caz had pulled the rug from under Lucinda's secure existence and altered the course of her life.

It was time to let it go once and for all.

The first Stella had known of Lucinda's true start in life was when she'd arrived home from a friend's eighth birthday party one Saturday afternoon. The minute Mum opened the hall door, Stella heard the noise coming from upstairs – Lucinda sobbing her heart out in her bedroom. It echoed around the house, so raw and convulsive it frightened her.

She sometimes thought afterwards that Lucinda's distress that day had seeped into the walls, floors and ceilings of their home, reverberating throughout the years, colouring all of their family events, imbuing her mum and dad with a sadness they could never completely shake off. They spent the rest of their lives tiptoeing around Lucinda as though they were negotiating a dangerous minefield.

They sat Stella down that evening and told her Lucinda was upset because she'd found out they'd adopted her as a baby when there was no sign of a child of their own. Although they had assured Lucinda they loved her and would always love her as if she were their own biological child, she was upset because they'd kept the truth from her. As these things sometimes happen, Stella had come along five years later. They'd decided to keep the truth of her origins from Lucinda, lest she felt in any way different from Stella or excluded from the immediate family fold.

Lucinda had a different slant on the story, which she'd told Stella angrily afterwards when she eventually unlocked her bedroom door, her face raw from sobbing.

She'd been *abandoned* as a baby. Her *real* mum and dad had *never* wanted her. She'd been dumped in – *of all places*

– a crummy telephone box in inner-city Dublin. Her cries had been heard by a passer-by, who'd brought her to the nearest hospital. They estimated she'd been less than a week old.

What really upset her was the difference between this crude beginning and the story Stella's dad used to come out with every birthday when they were young, telling them the tale of how he and Mum had picked them both out from all the hundreds of baby girls in the world, chosen them for themselves. They had been beautiful babies, he'd say, lying in beautiful white and pink lace cribs, cooing softly, with delicate pink cheeks and perfect minuscule eyelashes and cute button noses, Lucinda chosen first, and then Stella, five years later, when it was time for her to have a sister. Up to that day, Lucinda had still clung to the image of herself as a pristine baby, nestling in folds of lace in that pretty crib.

But secrets have a habit of rising up from the swamp when they are least expected. When she was thirteen, Lucinda had become friends with Catherine Costello.

After all the talk about the new friend she'd made, Stella had been taken aback when she'd brought her friend home for the first time. The girl, who was three months older than Lucinda, was almost colourless compared to exuberant Lucinda. Stella fancied her eyes held a tinge of resentment towards her when Lucinda showed her around their home, glowering when Lucinda showed her into Stella's fairy-tale-themed bedroom, as though she had no right to such a lovely room. Lucinda's bedroom was bigger than Stella's and had recently been redecorated by their dad to suit her newly acquired teenage status, including a study desk that turned out to be an exercise in supreme optimism on his part.

Lucinda told her afterwards that Catherine was finding it hard to fit into the new school. Lucinda felt she had so much going for her, that the least she could do was to take Catherine under her wing. She found the way Catherine looked up to her all the time made her feel good about herself. Sometimes it was them against the class, half of whom were looking down their noses at Catherine, the other half resenting Lucinda for her careless confidence and easy good looks.

Catherine called in two or three times a week after school, both girls hurrying up to Lucinda's bedroom, her sullen resentment of Stella softening a little the more her friendship with Lucinda developed. She was to be called Caz from now on, Lucinda said on one occasion. It sounded tougher than the soft 'Catherine'.

Two months after Stella had first met her, during a make-up session in Lucinda's bedroom, Caz was experimenting on her friend with cheap and cheerful cosmetics, chatting about hair colour and eyes. Then Caz had mentioned casually that Lucinda must have been adopted, because she looked so different from the rest of her family. Stella had grey eyes, like her father, and her mother's were brown, but Lucinda's were a deep, sparkling blue. She was a natural blonde, while Stella and her father had mid-brown hair, her mother a deep chestnut mahogany.

Caz knew how to recognise these things, she'd told Lucinda, because she, too, had been adopted but her home was unhappy. She was forever caught in the crossfire of alcohol-fuelled arguments. Lucinda was one of the lucky ones, she'd said, with her lovely adoptive parents. Lucinda had laughingly said it to Mum when they went downstairs, expecting Caz's words to be dismissed, but Mum's sudden silence and the look of frozen alarm on her face had told Lucinda all she needed to know.

'It's not as if I can even attempt to trace them,' Lucinda cried. 'Not that I ever want to. I was dumped in a dirty telephone box. That's how little my birth-mother cared.'

'Does it really matter?' Stella had asked. 'We all love you. Who cares what happened years ago?'

Stella had only prompted a fresh storm of weeping from her hormonal sister, the dramatic stakes now raised considerably.

Lucinda had never come to terms with her 'dirty, smelly' start in life, and it changed her. A bright student with lots of potential, she used her tawdry beginnings as a badge of dishonour, and an excuse for all sorts of wild behaviour. Stella became anxious with her outbursts, her screaming matches with Mum, the times she stayed out late into the night coming home with the smell of alcohol on her breath, or sometimes not coming home at all. She was barely hanging on to her place in school. For her parents' sake, Stella over-compensated by sticking to the straight and narrow, being diligent and dutiful about school and homework, not daring to step out of line.

She came to resent Lucinda's devil-may-care attitude. But she became even more resentful towards Caz, and the part she'd played in disrupting their family. She didn't call to the house much after that infamous afternoon, only dropping in when Mum and Dad were away, Stella's thinly veiled hostility clashing with the defensive way Caz looked at her, as though she had been perfectly right to crack open Lucinda's past.

When Stella was fourteen, Lucinda dropped out of college and went off to London with Caz. She'd had a long talk with a weeping Stella before she left, telling her she would always be her sister, bequeathing to Stella her best pieces of jewellery, her Discman and CDs. She'd surprised Stella by coming home a few months later, but she moved into a cheap and cheerful apartment, putting the best of her energy into a rickety career in fashion modelling and her friendships with her former college mates. She didn't come home to Lucan that often, and when she did, she was at least civil to Mum and Dad, but the damage had been done. Old resentments are hard to get over, and the chill that had existed from the start between Stella and Caz had never really dissolved.

CHAPTER FIFTEEN

Eddie

Stella is on her feet. 'Thanks so much to you all for turning up,' she says. 'I appreciate you're here for Lucinda, and for me. And special thanks to Caz for flying in from London.'

Eddie's gaze drifts to Caz. So far, she hasn't made proper contact with him. Or asked him how he is. He doesn't need to ask how she is, he can see it in her face, but he lost the right to comfort her long ago.

'There are plenty of basic supplies in the house,' Stella says. 'Help yourself to whatever you need.'

Eddie is relieved when Stella goes on to say they're to help themselves to the supply of wine and spirits in the house. At least it won't be a dry weekend. He's trying to cut back, though, isn't he? Just not this weekend.

'If anybody needs anything we don't have, I can do a run to Dunmullen,' Rex offers. 'I'm sure you all want to be here as much as possible for Stella.'

Pompous eejit. Eddie has taken an instant dislike to him. Rex has helped Britt to set out the lunch but, Eddie thinks, in a patronising way as though he's in charge, ambling around The Lookout, directing operations as though he's the host. Stella smiles at Rex, and in return he inclines his head, looking too self-satisfied for Eddie's liking. He never even knew Lucinda, and he's staying on the top floor, in the splendour of her old suite, right next to him, for fuck's sake. Why isn't he sharing with Stella? Giving her the best of his support this weekend? For all Eddie's gripes about him, Rex exudes a careless power, the ability to take relaxed control of everything. Maybe that's why Eddie instinctively resents him. Rex makes him all too aware of his own failings.

Maisie is sitting beside Janet, banging on about her terrible children. A handy smokescreen to hide behind, he thinks, considering what he knows about her and how stupidly she'd behaved that weekend. She looks up and sees his eyes on her, and something in his baleful stare has alerted her, because she turns immediately to Janet and launches into yet another grumble about sleepless nights.

Aye, I'd say you have those all right, he thinks.

Stella is talking. 'Now, this is the difficult part,' she says, taking a sip of water. 'Bear with me, please.'

'Take your time, Stella.' That twit Rex, of course.

Stella – she must be in bits but she's rising above it for the sake of Lucinda. She has always been made of stern stuff. A bit too prim and proper for him, but he knew how much Lucinda loved her, how proud she was of her, which had granted Stella a certain status in his eyes. Yet when Lucinda needed serious help, she had turned to Eddie, not Stella. Too afraid of upsetting her sister. Too nervous of causing her any kind of angst. Too fearful of casting a big shadow on her sister's esteemed CEO career.

With the result that it was his career that had crashed and burned.

Stella gives everyone a tight smile. 'There are two – no, three things I'd like to do over the weekend. First up, as soon as everyone is ready and before it gets dark, I'd like us to go up to Wolf Head and spend a few minutes paying our respects to Lucinda ... I have some flowers ...' She pauses, her eyes searching the group. 'Has anyone been there since ...?'

Eddie's gaze flickers around the table. Stella is being met with blank looks, shrugs, silence.

'Even in the days immediately after the accident? I seem ...' Stella pauses again, gives a half-laugh. 'I seem to have forgotten a lot about what actually happened then.'

Another silence that seems to swell until Eddie has a prickly, uncomfortable feeling, although he doesn't know why. Stella seems all alone as she stands there, as though she's separate from the main body of them. It impels Caz to speak.

'The guards didn't allow us access to that area straight after the accident, Stella,' she says, as gently as possible. 'Most of us had left by the time it was opened again, and I don't think any of us had the heart to return.' Caz glances around the table as if looking for confirmation and he nods in agreement, along with Maisie and Janet.

Caz, the person he most wants to gravitate towards when the empty place inside him needs to be seen and heard. He knows he's wrecked whatever special thing they had somewhere along the line. On the face of it a friendship going back years, but behind that the one woman who'd always been there for him and made him feel safe, who'd always made it feel okay for him to drop his gung-ho, happy-clappy guard and be just him, in all his messiness, in front of her. Trouble is he can't pinpoint what he did wrong. He has a vague memory of going into a Santorini bedroom one alcohol-crazed afternoon, but everything is a blank after that.

Come on, admit it, Eddie. He'd been stupid enough to do a line of coke with Lucinda beforehand. Caz had been giving him the eye and he'd felt unaccountably nervous. He'd soon weaned himself off the coke – unfortunately he couldn't say the same for Lucinda. Since that holiday, Caz has blanked him at every opportunity. Not overtly. On the surface she's still perfectly pleasant with him, but there have been no more private chats, and she's gone out of her way to avoid being alone with him whenever they've been out with the gang. Invitations to coffee or lunch have been turned down. She's not available. She's busy with something else. She's up to her tonsils in work.

A couple of years after that holiday, he'd plucked up the courage to ask her what had gone wrong between them, and she'd laughed. 'Nothing that I know of, Eddie,' she'd said. 'We've just drifted apart, haven't we?'

'Did I fall out of line that time in Santorini?'

She'd shrugged. 'What time? I don't remember.'

'And what happened to … you know …' it had been an effort to get the words out in the face of her nonchalant look '… if we're still single by the time we hit thirty, we'll take on the world, us, together …'

'We hit that milestone a couple of years ago,' she'd said. 'Jeez, you hardly think that was for real.' And she'd laughed into his face in a most un-Caz-like way.

I thought you were for real, in my life. I thought it was us against the world.

It was only as time went on that he realised how arrogant he'd been, thinking it was okay for him to be attracted to Lucinda and under her spell, yet in love with Caz. How unfair he'd been to Caz, expecting her to be on standby, ready to soothe him, steady enough to anchor him and quench his deep-down loneliness.

He'd blown it. He's nothing but a sad bastard.

Bringing Sasha to the party weekend had been a prop for him. But arriving in The Lookout, he'd hated himself for falling under Lucinda's spell as soon as he'd seen her, hated himself for the way she'd played him for an absolute mug, and coupled with Caz's deliberate coolness, it had filled him with enough crazy contrariness to throw caution to the wind, drink like a shark, and to hell with the consequences.

Then Lucinda's light had gone out of his life and he didn't even have the comfort of the loyal support and warm friendship that Caz used to lavish on him.

He'd have liked to confide in her. *Lucinda was in trouble, a few months before the party,* he'd have told her. *She had a problem she needed to sort out and she came to me for help.*

Then again, that would mean admitting Eddie Hynes had been soft putty in her hands. Admitting that sad bastard Eddie had been delighted she'd chosen him to turn to when she was at an all-time low, trusted him enough to confide in him, instead of her prestigious sister or her best mate Caz. That had to mean something.

But I don't think it had anything to do with her accident, he'd have said to Caz, needing her reassuring agreement. *Before that weekend, she told me it was all sorted.*

After the accident, he hadn't the guts to tell anyone, his friends, or the guards, about it. How could he admit how stupid he'd been? And, anyway, he'd had Lucinda's word that it was all sorted. Eddie forces himself to follow the conversation and come back into the room. They are still talking about Stella's plan for a walk to Wolf Head.

'You know I've been there already,' Britt says. 'I brought flowers at the time of the month's mind.'

'Yes, thank you, Britt,' Stella says quietly. 'Can we leave as soon as everyone is ready? I'd like us all to be back before it gets too dark.' She gives a half-laugh that sounds like a sob and his heart wrenches. 'We can't be wandering around the cliff tops in Kerry at night. It's windy but not raining, so if we stick together we should be okay. There are high-vis vests and torches in the cloakroom … wellies if anyone wants them. It'll be Lucinda's last night out there, in the ocean …'

Eddie takes a sharp breath and tries to blank his mind.

'Which brings me to the next thing,' Stella continues. 'According to the guards, they expect the car to be recovered sometime tomorrow evening. Access to the quayside will be restricted to the rescue team, and us. I hope we can form some kind of a vigil along there. We have tea lights, and hopefully they won't blow out in the breeze. It should have died down by then.'

'We'll be there, when … like, when the car is actually taken out of the water?'

Janet. Eddie could have throttled her. They are all on edge, but no need for Janet to make it worse. She looks in bits, pale-faced and ill-at-ease. What the hell is she doing here anyway? And why hadn't she had the balls to leave Aaron after his alcohol-fuelled performance? It's a mystery to him, and out of character for cool, self-assured Janet.

There's something niggling him about Aaron, something odd about that last afternoon, but it slides away from him.

'It's a great idea.' Caz speaks up. 'And the lights will be a nice touch, guiding Lucinda home, so to speak.'

'Guiding her home is exactly what I'm thinking,' Stella says. 'Not that it'll make any difference to her. But, please,' Stella goes on smoothly, 'nobody is to feel under any pressure to come to the cliff or the quayside. It's more than enough that you took the trouble to be here. Taking part in anything … it's entirely an individual decision. Do whatever you're comfortable with. But I'm hoping we can talk about Lucinda over the weekend, our good memories, maybe remember the last time we saw her alive and well …'

Oh, Jaysus – he shouldn't have come.

'And it will help us celebrate her life,' Stella is saying, 'rather than fixate too much on how or why it came to an end. I don't know if we'll ever find out the why.'

A thick silence descends. He can feel the tension in the room.

'I think that's an excellent idea, everyone sharing their memories,' Rex says warmly, directing his glance around the table, lingering for a moment on Eddie as though he senses his hostility and is slightly amused by it.

The fucker.

He feels a wave of anxiety spiral within him and prays he won't say the wrong thing. Nothing will bring Lucinda back, least of all a revelation from him, and it would only make everything so much worse.

CHAPTER SIXTEEN

Caz

They're all moving around the hall, pulling on scarves, coats and gloves. Caz doesn't know if she's imagining it but there were moments during lunch when she'd sensed something running under the atmosphere, a frisson of unease, hidden agendas that people might have, maybe drawn here more by morbid curiosity than a desire to support Stella. She can't unsee the way Janet's jaw dropped in alarm when Stella mentioned the cliff-top walk, or forget the electric silence when Stella had asked if anyone had been back there.

'Right, then, are we off?' Britt asks, in a solicitous tone. There are murmurs of assent from everyone. She has flowers, bunches of white chrysanthemums, which she has separated into individual blooms to hand around for everyone to throw down the cliff.

Rex opens the door and a blast of wind rushes into the hall with the scuttle of dried winter leaves, propelled by the breeze. The heavily bundled group troop down the driveway. The cold realisation that she is visiting the awful spot where Lucinda's car went over the edge blooms in Caz's head. Stella, Britt and Caz are leading the short procession, Janet and Maisie behind, Rex and Eddie taking up the rear. That suits

Caz fine. No matter how tortured she feels, she's keeping her distance from Eddie. Even now, when she longs to throw herself into his arms and cry for her friend. He would know exactly how she felt.

It was no secret that Eddie adored Lucinda. They all did, almost from the start of those college days when their group had come together. Greenfield College of Further Education was a stepping stone to good career options and an alternative route into university if you failed to make the grade or got unlucky with the random allocation of university places. She and Lucinda were studying Fashion and Styling and, moving through the corridors and the canteen, they had instantly gelled with Janet, Aaron and Eddie, who were studying Fitness Instruction and Health Studies. Even though she and Lucinda had left college before the end of the first year – Caz later studying Make-up Artistry – they remained firm friends. When they socialised, the group made room to include Maisie, a year behind them in school, whom Caz had invited in. Caz knew all about Lucinda's unhappy home life, but it was as though she shrugged that off when she left the house, and turned into a bright, fun-loving, brilliant, dazzling butterfly that glittered lightly above them all. Out with the gang, Lucinda had spoken so often about never being captured or pinned down by a man that even Eddie couldn't have failed to get the message.

Caz had asked Lucinda early on if she had feelings for Eddie, and had that been the case, Caz would have backed off instantly and nipped her growing attraction to him in the bud, knowing she'd be no match for the vivacious Lucinda.

'Of course I have feelings for him,' Lucinda had said. 'I love Eddie to bits, but as a friend, like, say, a decent enough brother, but that's all. That's all it'll ever be.' Lucinda had looked at her closely. 'Why – don't tell me you ...?'

Caz had shrugged. She had shared lots of personal things with Lucinda, intimate things she hadn't shared with anyone else, but she couldn't bring herself to admit that she was desperate enough to be in love with a man who, although he considered her a good friend, had clearly put Lucinda on a pedestal. Caz had waited for most of her twenties for Eddie to see her for who she really was and what she offered – a woman who had fallen in love with the friendly, caring-looking guy soon after she'd met him, who wanted only the best for him, who'd look out for him through thick and thin, and who couldn't wait for him to return her passion and devotion. What was more, since their mid-twenties, it had been a regular quip between her and Eddie that if they both reached their thirties single and unattached, it meant they were destined to be together and would gladly take on each other.

'You're like my best friend,' Eddie had told her, bringing up the subject again around the time of her twenty-fifth birthday at a party that had gone on until five in the morning. They were sitting out on a balcony in a Sandyford apartment block, watching the sun rise in the distance over Dublin Bay, in the way they had often found themselves taking a private breather in the middle of a frenetic party, time simply to be themselves without having to pin on a smiley, happy face. She knew all about Eddie's demons: his father had done a runner when he was six, and his alcoholic mother had blamed Eddie, neglecting him, flitting from boyfriend to boyfriend, each more antagonistic to Eddie than the last. Until he'd been old enough to fend for himself, he'd turned up at school in unwashed uniforms, homework not done, and nothing decent for his lunch. In turn, he knew a lot about Caz's unhappy family life also, but not everything about her – only Lucinda knew that.

'I can tell you anything,' he'd said, 'and I feel we have loads in common.'

'And Lucinda? Where does she come in your life?' she'd asked, with a hammering heart.

He'd shaken his head and given her a warm smile. 'Lucinda is like … I dunno, a witch. She casts a spell on you but you know it's only an illusion. She's fun, great for a laugh, for a bit of magic, but you, Caz, you're for real. You're my grounding force, my safety net in this crappy world.' The vulnerability in his eyes as they fastened on hers had resonated with her. 'It's … well, we're still so young,' he'd said. 'Just another few years to the big three-oh. Remember what we agreed?'

She'd readily gone along with him. Again. Anything to hold on to a bit of hope. Anything to stay within his orbit. Even if being labelled a safety net didn't sound anything like the passion or magic she'd hope to arouse. Even when she began to wonder if the quip between them had been in earnest on her side, but half joking on his. Even when she knew, deep down inside, that she should be walking away with her head held high instead of hanging around him, waiting to see if any leftover crumbs would fall to her from the table of Eddie Hynes.

It had been difficult to blow out even a tiny ray of hope. Easier to cling to familiar patterns rather than face the trauma of cutting them out of her life.

Santorini was to celebrate the thirtieth-birthday milestone. Caz and Eddie had already reached that, celebrating with a joint birthday party in Galaxy, at that time one of the coolest clubs in Dublin – it had been Caz's idea, to link them together in some way by having a shared party. But Eddie had got hopelessly drunk after a huge row with his mother, arriving at the party already tanked up. Santorini would be different, seven full days of hot sunshine, sand, sea and hopefully sex. They were both thirty now. Both still unattached. She packed her case with a sprinkling of optimism along with expensive bikini sets, frothy undies, slinky evening wear. She spent hours in a beauty salon beforehand, having her hair highlighted, getting de-fuzzed, and indulging in a manicure and a pedicure. She felt like a warrior going into battle, using all her resources to claim what should be hers.

But other people had different agendas that changed the dynamic of the week. Two days into the holiday, Janet and Aaron became engaged, twisting the knife in her stomach with their cringe-worthy celebrations, their loved-up coupledom so saccharine-sweet they got on everyone's nerves. Four days into the holiday, Maisie had a huge row with her then boyfriend, Dean, who had tagged along on the holiday. None of them had witnessed the argument, and the first they knew about it was when Maisie, incandescent with fury, told them he'd packed his bags and gone home. And not that any of them were surprised: Dean was trouble, loud and overbearing. Caz had sensed something rough about him and was relieved to hear he'd left. After that, Maisie had refused to talk to anyone, and privately, Caz was glad she elected to spend the rest of the week on the seclusion of her balcony, saying she was unwilling to face anyone and didn't want her rage to spoil the party vibe. Then Lucinda got busy hooking up with one of the local bar staff, asking Caz, whom she was sharing with, if she could bring him back to their room. In other words, could Caz make herself scarce.

It left her free to seduce Eddie at last.

Which she managed to do on the penultimate afternoon, having waited patiently for years. Wanting to savour every moment as she finally led him back to his room after a mega-strength liquidy lunch, and locked the door, in case Janet and Aaron decided to burst in with yet more celebratory champagne.

She felt like someone else as she undid the ties of her black, floaty caftan and let it drop to the ground. She thought she was in a dream sequence as she slithered out of her bikini and stood in her full glory in front of him. He hardly looked at her before he pulled her to him and buried his face in her neck, holding her tightly as he kicked off his flip-flops and shimmied out of his shorts. They sank down on the bed, Eddie nudging her legs apart, Caz hardly able to believe this was happening at last as she lifted her hips and felt him thrust inside her, then move deeper and harder. His hot face was so close to hers that she could taste his booze-laden breath and was beginning to wonder if the liquidy lunch had been such a good idea. Then came the moment that killed everything.

At first, when she heard it, she thought she was mistaken. But then he said it again, breathing it into her ear. 'Lucinda …'

Ten years on, it's a moment that still sits like a dagger in her heart.

CHAPTER SEVENTEEN

Stella

Tucked up in her padded coat, a scarf wound around her neck, thick mittens on her hands, Stella feels numb. The light is already fading, the bruised skies low and glowering. For most of the twenty-minute journey to Wolf Head, the potholed route rises in an upward incline between verges of wild grasses and tussocks of wiry, untamed gorse, the heaving sea an unrelenting grey surge below. Then the laneway rounds a bend and plateaus out into a wide, rectangular tarmacked viewing area in need of resurfacing, bounded by a low stone wall, which has collapsed in one place. An area of scuffed grass leads down to the serrated edge of the charcoal cliff face on a slightly sloping gradient. The cliff face at Wolf Head is almost two hundred metres above sea level.

The sight of it wrenches Stella's stomach. It seems inconceivable that Lucinda's car is somewhere out there, and has been floating in these waters for six months.

Wolf Head is about a third of a mile in diameter, a desolate, remote, inhospitable place of wild beauty, with rough grasses stunted by the wind, hillocks of scree and shale, and clusters of boulders, said to be burial stones dating back to Celtic days.

She's glad she can't see anything of the recovery operation beyond a few pinpricks of light on the horizon. Most of the crews will be going in as soon as conditions improve.

Now that she is here, though, looking at the cliff top, it seems odd to her that Lucinda's accident could be classified as a fluke. The only way to go over the edge is to come up the potholed track that runs by The Lookout, then through the small gap where the low wall has collapsed, and down the slight gradient of the grassed area. No car could go through that gap unless it was deliberately lined up in the right position. Neither was a car going to slip down the incline and over the edge unless the handbrake had been released, on purpose, in advance. Even allowing for those two possibilities, if a car went through the gap and began to move down the slight slope, there would surely be time to pull on the handbrake to stop it toppling over the edge into the ocean far below, or jerk the wheel around to move the car into a safe position.

So for all Britt's gentle talk about the cruel vagaries of life, and the ease with which dreadful things can come knocking on doors, her attempt to cast Lucinda's accident in the light of a particularly callous hand of Fate is way off the mark. Stella recalls the look in Hugh's eyes when they'd spoken about the accident, the empathetic way he'd tried to soothe her heartache that night – before they'd even got to bed – the kind solicitude in his voice when he'd said that from his experience some catastrophes in life simply defied any logic, that bad things happened to good people all the time.

He would have seen the police reports, the photographs on file, the investigation that remained open but hadn't gone anywhere because there was nowhere for it to go. And remembering his kindness, along with Britt's compassionate smiles, in a flash of sudden understanding she knows what they've been thinking behind their concerned faces.

Along with Britt, Hugh Connell has clearly taken an educated guess as to what happened to Lucinda. That it couldn't have been an accident. It was something far crueller than broken-hearted Stella can face up to, and will surely place the blame on herself. Britt and Hugh have come to the conclusion that Lucinda took her own life and they have tried to spare her this knowledge.

No way – not her effervescent, laughing sister. The kind-hearted sister who'd brought her to London for a weekend to celebrate Stella's Leaving Certificate results. Who'd stayed in her apartment and sat up with her for nights on end after her parents had died.

From what Stella can see of the lie of the land, this couldn't have been a careless accident precipitated by any row, because for a car to slip over the cliff at Wolf Head, it would have to be manoeuvred into position on purpose. And from what she recalls of Lucinda's plans for the weekend, her excitement over her party, and the announcement she had yet to make, she had no intention of doing herself any injury. Her car going over the edge of this cliff could only have happened if someone had deliberately and cold-bloodedly engineered it by lining it up in the right spot.

A terrible suspicion slams into Stella. Her sister was murdered.

❖

'Are you ready, Stella?' Britt's voice, raised above the whine of the wind, breaks into her thoughts, pulling her back from the abyss.

Stella turns to face her, this shocking new reality flooding her veins like thick shards of pain. She sees the warm bath of Britt's concern reaching out to her. Britt has been here already, laying flowers. She must have figured out that the chances of an accident having occurred were slim to the point of negligible. Was everyone aware of this, and afraid to breathe a word in front of her? Even Lucinda's social-media followers? The countless strangers who'd trekked here as if on pilgrimage?

Totally your fault, you bitch, that Lucinda's dead.

Is that what they meant – that she had driven Lucinda to this? Far from having a careless moment at the wheel because she'd been upset after their argument, she'd actually done it on purpose? Stella refuses to believe that. Also, according to Britt, Lucinda had been in good humour when she'd seen her, just hours beforehand.

Unless Britt is feeding her lies.

'Stella?' Britt's voice again.

She blinks and looks around. Her plan to release flowers off the cliff as a tribute had been a sort of fantasy, fuelled by her shock at Hugh's news, as well as softly lit television images she'd seen of other flower-filled vigils for victims of crime and misadventure. But Wolf Head is no quiet, reverent scene. Getting anywhere close to the edge given the incline is out of the question. Any one of them could be whipped off their feet, with that battering wind. Lucinda's friends are huddled into bulky coats, bundled together against the buffeting breeze, under a dark, lowering sky. Caz is huddled between Maisie and Janet – just as well: she's so slight the wind could easily lift her off her legs.

Eddie stands apart, a brooding look on his face, his dark hair tossed in the gale.

'Stella? Are you okay?' Rex's voice. He's standing right behind her and puts his hands on her shoulders. Can he feel the tremor in her body? She's shaking, not from the cold, but from her new realisation about Lucinda. Britt is looking at her anxiously, aware no doubt of the impractical nature of Stella's plan, given the boiling sea below and hurling gale-force breeze.

She knows then what to do.

'Let's throw these up into the sky,' she says to Britt.

'Good idea,' Britt says, opening the carrier bag with the flowers.

'Come on, everyone,' Stella says, picking up a few blooms, tossing them as high as she can into the slate-grey heavens. Right now, somewhere up above the blanket of cloud, a yellow sun gleams in a pearly blue sky. That, she tells herself, is Lucinda's happy place, where she rests. To Stella's relief, everyone gathers around and joins in, picking out flowers and flinging them high into the air. Some blooms fall back to the ground immediately, but the breeze picks them up and sends them scudding down the incline. Others are whipped up onto a wind thermal, floating out between the earth and the sky, until they dip and eddy and fall down to the white-capped, angry surface of the sea. There is a moment of anticlimax after Britt hands her the final bloom and she throws it as high as she can.

'Let's go,' she says, turning away from the water, not waiting to see where it lands, telling herself that Lucinda's spirit was long gone from this raw, cold, albeit beautiful, landscape.

Britt and Stella keep pace together, leading the way as they hike back to The Lookout.

Throughout that afternoon, as Lucinda's friends had arrived and mingled, Stella had been glad to hear from snippets of conversation that being in The Lookout was jogging some memories and stirring old ghosts. This is what Stella wants – recollections coming back and being aired, bits of information surfacing that might have slipped under her radar that crazy weekend. Maybe also a guilty conscience or two awakening. Even in the short time she has been back, images of that weekend are filtering with renewed sharpness through her head, sense impressions of Lucinda, snatched fragments of conversation, and she's become more and more convinced that something dark was running under the frenetic party atmosphere.

But now Stella has something new and more frightening to think of. Something icy rushes through her chest, freezing her heart. If, as she suspects, Lucinda has been deliberately killed, her accident engineered, is there any chance that one of the party group was involved and they now have a murderer in their midst?

CHAPTER EIGHTEEN

Janet

As soon as they arrive back at The Lookout, Janet pulls off her coat, scarf and gloves and kicks off her muddy boots, placing them in the cloakroom before she heads for the staircase in her stockinged feet. She sees Eddie making straight for the home bar. All of a sudden, she's longing for a drink, for the blurry ease of alcohol. But it's out of the question. There will be plenty of drinks flying around, no doubt, but she's telling everyone she's doing a dry January, a good excuse for opting out.

Upstairs, her room is next to the one she'd shared with Aaron that wretched weekend, thankful then for the extra bed after Friday night – Caz and Maisie are in there now. She makes sure her door is locked before she takes the chemist's bag out of her case. In the bathroom, she studies the instructions on the test kit, the words jumping up and down in front of her, forcing her to focus. But afterwards, there is no mistaking the result on the stick.

She's pregnant, after years of trying, and nothing happening, after opening the conversation on IVF, then abandoning it after the rift between them. But there had been that one night, recently, when she and Aaron had slept together at a friend's wedding in Galway, both of them hammered by wine and champagne. They'd shared a bed that night, keeping up the sham of love and togetherness they'd donned for the reception. It hadn't been love, though, it had been pure sex, noisy sex, urgent sex, as if the seductive wedding vibes had got to them and they needed to prove they still had it, both of them parched after months of inactivity.

She'd sensed the change in her body almost immediately. She'd stuck her head into the sand, putting off having it confirmed, but at least this weekend is giving her the opportunity to absorb the positive result without Aaron being around.

Janet goes through to the bedroom. Feeling a sudden wave of exhaustion, she lies on the bed, resting her hands lightly on her abdomen. It's crazy to think that she's here to honour Lucinda's life, senselessly over, yet life for her is going on in the strangest way possible, and something she's wanted for years has finally arrived, but at the worst ever time.

If only Eddie and Aaron had cut short their golf that afternoon.

If only they'd been back at The Lookout when the women had returned from the boat trip.

If only the women hadn't decided to go to The Pier ...

'Hey, it looks like nobody's home,' Sasha said, her little-girl voice grating on Janet's ears. 'Eddie's car is missing. He must be still out golfing with Aaron. I thought they were going to cut it short.'

'Aww, Sasha,' Lucinda said, mimicking her voice. 'Don't worry about Eddie. He'll be back soon – he hasn't abandoned you. We'll mind you, won't we, girls?'

They were in Seamus Dillon's minibus as it swung to a halt outside The Lookout. Used to pick up supplies from wholesalers in Kenmare, it also ferried tourists from The Pier to the nearest public transport, and Tadhg had arranged with Seamus to drop the women back up the hill to the house after the boat trip. It was sweltering hot, the air-con hardly had a chance to get going on the short journey, and they were all a bit dishevelled after spending the guts of two and a half hours on the boat.

Janet was sitting in the rear seat between Caz and Stella. She sensed a new reserve about Caz, annoyed no doubt by Lucinda's public snub of her on the boat. She couldn't work out what Stella thought about everything. Janet guessed she was just about putting up with them for the sake of Lucinda's celebrations. At least she came, give her her due. The whole gang, at a high-octane weekend celebration, could be too full-on for most people. But more so that weekend.

She couldn't understand how Lucinda seemed to be a bit drunk that afternoon, given her alcohol abstinence. Was the whole party vibe fuelling her with over-the-top adrenaline?

It gave Janet a worry she could have done without – if Lucinda got too carried away she would be liable to let slip some carefully guarded secrets.

'I have an idea,' Maisie said.

Lucinda laughed. 'Jeez, Maisie, you've been full of ideas this weekend. Even I can't keep up with you.'

'Instead of us waiting patiently on the men to come home, like good little women,' Maisie said, 'why don't we feck off back down to The Pier? Let them wonder where we've got to instead.'

'You're so funny, Maisie. When have we ever been good little women?' Lucinda asked. 'Seamus, can you give us ten minutes to change out of our bikinis and bring us back down to The Pier?'

'I suppose I could,' Seamus agreed. 'Though this set-up is a lot classier than The Pier.'

'I think I'd rather stay here and stretch out on a sun-lounger under an umbrella,' Caz said.

'So would I,' agreed Stella.

Lucinda turned around and widened her eyes at them. 'Nope. Not allowed. What kind of party poopers are ye?'

Less than half an hour later, they were sitting on wooden benches under an awning to the side of The Pier, and Maisie had gone into the bar to order drinks.

'On the Revolut account,' Lucinda reminded her.

Maisie presently returned, a barman following in her wake, carrying a heavy tray of drinks, mostly chilled white wine, a bottle of beer for Janet, and an exotic-looking drink that Maisie instructed him to place in front of Lucinda.

'What's this?' Lucinda asked. 'I hope it's a mocktail.'

'Something to help you see your thirties out in style,' Maisie said, winking at her.

Lucinda picked off the flower petal floating on top and popped it into her mouth. 'I like your style, missus. To me, being forty means you're not one but two twenty-year-olds at once. So cheers.' She took a long sip of her drink.

Even though the hum of conversation was light and jokey, and enticing scents of beer and food wafted from inside the pub, Janet knew she could have done without this. Caz's idea had sounded far more enticing. An hour or so dozing on a sun-lounger with an eye mask, after a pint of chilled cucumber water, then a long cool shower was what Janet craved. It wasn't yet five o'clock. They still had the evening and night to get through. Lucinda had mentioned something about trying out the Jacuzzi later on.

But no one wants to be labelled a party pooper. They are *the* gang. For ever young. Invincible as opposed to invisible. Most of them might be hitting forty, but the unspoken rule was that they were still the same careless, carefree, up-for-fun girls they were at twenty, with the same capacity for hard and fast partying. Apart from Maisie, who had been at pains in the beginning to boast about how crazy busy she was, with her two small demon children. Thankfully she'd moved on from that particularly painful soapbox.

They were on their second drink when Janet sensed she was being watched. She looked around, then through the open door into the bar, the interior dimmed compared to the blinding light outside, she saw him standing in the shadows at the far side of the counter. She blinked. Blinked again. She then made the fatal mistake of taking off her sunglasses so that their eyes met and he knew she had spotted him.

It was the way he was leering at her that caused the horrific memory from her past to crash back again, jolting all her senses. The flower-filled garden in Santorini. The lecherous look in his eyes flicking down her body, mentally stripping her naked. The shock of him bearing down on her. Boring into her. Squeezing her. Crushing her. Hot skin. Panic. Pain. Sickening humiliation.

In spite of the warmth of the Kerry evening, every cell in her body froze, just as it had back then. What the hell was he doing at The Pier?

In the next moment he was gone, no sign of him at all.

Janet knew she hadn't imagined it. He had been staring at her in the same way he'd stared at her ten years ago. What was he doing here? She forced herself to shift her gaze, to disengage from her shock, to look up the alleyway to where Tadhg was rolling barrels of beer into position, then back towards the front of the quayside, out to the rim of a far horizon melting into a clear blue sky.

She felt a touch on her arm and she jumped as though burned.

'Sorry, Janet, you were miles away.'

Caz. Janet didn't know if she could speak, but somehow words came out. 'I'm going back to The Lookout.'

'Yes, good idea,' Caz said. 'That sun-lounger is calling me.'

'Me too,' Janet heard herself say.

'Oh, can we go now?' asked Sasha. 'Eddie and Aaron are back. In fact they've been back awhile. I messaged Eddie when we got here, I thought it was only fair to let him know where I was.'

'You did *what*?' said Lucinda, hearing the drift of conversation.

'Leave it, Lucinda,' Caz said. 'It's time we went back.'

'So you're all ganging up on me?' Lucinda said, with a laugh.

'Lucinda,' Stella said quietly, 'it's time we went back. And you don't want to take the chance of someone recognising you, do you? Remember, no pics, no posts.'

Lucinda turned to Stella. 'Ooh, so that's what you're worried about. I might be spotted on TikTok letting my hair down and it wouldn't look well for your do-gooder, corporate image.'

Stella stared at her. Lucinda laughed before demolishing the last of her drink. 'I thought of that already.' She shrugged. 'No one would recognise me with my hair in bits and without my make-up. Still, the majority rules. Seamus said he'd bring us back up when we're ready.'

Back at The Lookout, Aaron and Eddie were necking beer out on the terrace, joking about going straight from the fifth hole to the nineteenth, boasting that they'd had to leave Eddie's car at the golf club and get a lift back. It had been a long time since health-conscious Aaron had had so much to drink and it made Janet uneasy. She went upstairs, stood under the shower, and watched as copious amounts of suds sluiced away from her body.

Would she ever feel safe again? She straightened up, telling herself the show must go on. She had far too much to lose.

Hopefully she was seeing things, imagining it.

CHAPTER NINETEEN

Stella

Now that she is back in the warmth and bright lights of The Lookout, Stella's fears about Lucinda's friends seem inconceivable. Does she seriously think that any of them could have it within themselves to cause harm to Lucinda?

'Thanks everyone for braving the wind and the cold,' she says. 'It was a lovely way to pay tribute to Lucinda. Please relax and make yourselves at home. There are plenty of drinks, and tea and coffee. Tadhg will be bringing hot food from The Pier at seven o'clock and we'll lay it out buffet style. After that I thought we might have a few drinks and chat about Lucinda. Not for too long, because I'm sure most of you want an early night, especially after travelling down here today.'

'That sounds perfect, Stella,' Rex says, squeezing her arm. 'Well done on the cliff walk too. It was a lovely tribute.'

Stella gulps. 'It was my first time to be there. I'm still finding it all so hard to believe. It's ...' She shakes her head, bowing it, suddenly overcome.

He pulls her into a gentle hug. 'You're doing great. It's a difficult time and you're holding everyone together, as well as yourself.'

She's glad to have Rex here, on her side, especially when most of the group are on her radar as a potential suspect.

Suspected of what exactly, though? Maybe of being her social-media tormentor, which is bad enough in itself, but it's terrifying to carry her thoughts any further into dangerous territory.

'You'll have to excuse me for an hour, if that's okay,' Rex says. 'I have a bit of work to do. It's urgent. But call me if you need me for anything. Otherwise I'll be down in plenty of time to help with the food.'

'No problem at all, Rex. I'm going to grab a coffee and disappear myself for a while, a little recharge before we all come together again.'

She's already seen Janet heading upstairs, and everyone must have had the same idea because there's no one in the living area and it has an eerie, deserted feel when Stella goes across to the kitchen to make some coffee. By now it's pitch-black outside, save for rectangles of light spilling across the garden from various rooms in the house, light fizzing from the bi-fold doors illuminating the terrace in a pale, ghostly wash.

When Stella comes out of the kitchen with a coffee to take up to her room, she hears voices coming from the home bar, the door slightly ajar, and she pauses, a sudden shard of memory catching her breath. Other voices had been coming from this room six months earlier, on the Friday evening they had been in The Pier and Stella had come downstairs after her shower.

Lucinda's voice: 'Hey, chill. I've never told a soul about Santorini. Hand on heart. Why?'

'Oh, nothing, nothing at all to worry about.' Janet's voice.

'Good, hon. It's our second last night, time to ramp up the party.'

'Absolutely.'

Stella swallows hard as the memory fades. All she had focused on at the time was Lucinda's need to ramp up some-thing that was already galloping recklessly out of hand, thanks to the constant flow of booze and Lucinda's exasperating antics. But something had clearly gone wrong in Santorini.

This time it's Eddie and Maisie in the home bar. Their voices are low, but they float out into the echoey hall where she listens quietly.

'What do you want?' Eddie's voice.

'A drink, same as you,' Maisie says. 'Pour me one while you're at it.'

'Or did you follow me in here to effect some damage limitation?'

'*Damage* limitation?' Maisie laughs, but it sounds strained to Stella.

'Yes. You copped the way I was looking at you during lunch.'

'What way?' Maisie, sounding defensive.

'See, I know, Maisie. I know what you were up to that weekend. I'm still trying to figure out why.'

'I haven't a clue what you're talking about.'

'You hadn't a fucking clue what you were doing, that's for sure. Otherwise, you wouldn't have dreamed of doing what you did. At least I hope not.'

'Don't talk to me in riddles,' Maisie says.

'Did you not stop, for one minute, to think of the consequences?'

Maisie is silent.

'Even the state *I* was in ...' Eddie says. 'I can't blame Sasha for dumping me on account of that mess with Lucinda, but ...' His voice breaks.

'I still don't know what you're on about.'

A pause. Then Eddie says, 'Relax, Maisie, I'm not going to spill the beans. What's the point? It won't make any difference to Lucinda now.'

Another brief silence. Then, in a suddenly steely voice, 'A word of warning, Eddie. If I were you, I'd be careful about whatever beans you want to spill. Some are more dangerous than others.'

'*What?*'

Without thinking, and still holding her cup of coffee, Stella walks into the home bar. 'Hi there,' she says, forcing a casual note. 'I was wondering who was in here. Is everything all right?'

She intercepts the quick warning glance Eddie and Maisie exchange.

'Everything's fine, Stella,' Eddie says smoothly.

'What was that about Lucinda?' she asks.

'We were ... you know, reminiscing,' Maisie says. 'The Lookout – it's full of memories of her.'

'I look forward to hearing about them this evening so,' Stella says, sensing she isn't going to get anywhere right now.

Eddie nods to the bottle of wine sitting on the counter. 'I'm going to open this, if that's okay?'

'Work away,' Stella says. Hopefully a few glasses will help loosen his tongue. 'How about you, Maisie?'

'I'm okay, Stella,' Maisie says, sounding subdued. 'Tough times, but it's good to be here. With everyone. I need to call home and see how the little monsters are before I unpack.'

'I'll leave you to it,' Stella says, walking out, aware of the thick silence behind her.

Up in her bedroom, she closes the door and goes over to the small table to put down her coffee. She's heading into her en-suite when she sees it – something propped on her pillow. It's a photograph of Wolf Head, and with a red Sharpie, someone has crudely sketched a car falling over the cliff. There are words on the other side of the photograph – also in red Sharpie, block capitals: 'YOUR FAULT.'

CHAPTER TWENTY

Maisie

'I hadn't a clue what I was signing up for,' Maisie says, unable to keep a note of petulance out of her voice as she marches into the room she's sharing with Caz, and lifts her wheelie case onto a luggage rack. 'I was expecting a weekend wallowing in alcohol and fuggy memories. Not military-style cliff walks in the freezing cold and a whore of a breeze. I hope it lashes rain tomorrow evening and our trip to the quayside gets called off.'

'Maisie!' Caz says. 'I know you don't mean that.'

'I do,' Maisie insists, zipping her case open.

They are finally unpacking, having had little or no time between their arrival, a late lunch and the walk to Wolf Head. Caz has insisted Maisie take the king-size bed; she's happy with the single.

Maisie doesn't care either way. She feels shaken after those words in the bar with Eddie. What had he seen that weekend? She knows it will take every ounce of composure to carry on as if Eddie was mistaken and she doesn't know what the hell he's talking about. Still, she has an ace card up her sleeve if he tries anything.

'Not only was I freezing, but that hike scared the absolute shit out of me. I kept imagining Lucinda ...' Maisie pulls out a bottle of extra-proof vodka from her case. 'Just as well I brought this from home, some decent ammunition, but it's not for sharing downstairs. It's staying in the room for our benefit.' She pulls out a bottle of tonic and pours two generous measures into the glasses set out beside the bottled water, handing one to Caz.

'I dread tomorrow evening,' she says, taking a slurp. 'What is Stella thinking of?'

'Hey, relax,' Caz says. 'Whatever about Stella, we owe Lucinda this.'

'Jesus, Caz, it's the other way around if you ask me. Lucinda owed you big-time. You did more than enough for her when she was alive – you let her sidetrack your life.'

'No, I didn't. Don't speak of her like that. Besides, it doesn't matter any more.'

'It does when I think of the life you could have had. Even now you dropped everything and came from London at short notice. What big job did you have lined up?'

'What do you mean?'

'You said on the phone that you had to arrange cover for a big job to be here.'

'Did I? It was the hair and make-up for an event.'

'Come on, tell us. Let me bask in the glory of your glamorous London life for a moment.'

'I was booked to fly to Paris tomorrow morning, hair and make-up for a celebrity wedding.'

'Jesus! You can't have given that up to be here?'

Silence. Caz unpacks her phone charger and puts it on the locker.

'But that's huge, Caz, you mad thing.'

'Something similar will come around.'

'Here's hoping. That unfinished business … about Lucinda, you mentioned it in the car. Is that huge as well?' However Caz had said it, it had registered with Maisie as something to be followed up.

Caz frowns. She lifts out a pair of rolled-up jeans and straightens them on the bed. 'Look, Maisie, I owe it to Stella to be here.'

She hasn't answered Maisie's question. 'I don't know why you feel you owe Stella something,' she says, leaving it for now. 'I don't think we owe her anything at all, unless you know something I don't. Did you hear about the rumours?'

'What rumours?' Caz asks sharply.

'They were all on Instagram, sickening comments, a lot of them blaming Stella for the accident, that Lucinda was in tatters after their row, blah, blah, blah.'

'That's disgusting, vile rubbish. I haven't seen them, thank God.'

Maisie sloshes more vodka into her glass. 'So you don't think there's any truth in them?'

'Are you for real? How could there be?'

'Still, there's no smoke without fire, is there?'

Caz drops a cosmetic bag so that it falls back into her case. 'Where's all this coming from, Maisie?'

Maisie takes a deep breath. 'The creepy part is, and Stella must have copped this also, whoever posted about their row obviously knows about it. And who knew about it? Only all of us. The party gang.'

'Christ. I'm not going to even think about that,' Caz says.

'Other posts are claiming that Lucinda was a toxic cow who deserved her fate.'

'Maisie! For fuck's sake! I can't believe you actually read that revolting rubbish, let alone think it's worth repeating to me.'

All of a sudden, Maisie doesn't like the way Caz is looking at her, a hard glint in her eye.

'It's still there, isn't it?' Caz says. 'That resentment.'

'What resentment?'

'I've always sensed you had a bit of a grudge against Lucinda. I felt it because I was sometimes caught in the middle, but then it got worse … after Santorini, I think. I know you were upset that time about your boyfriend going home and leaving you in the lurch, but that had nothing to do with Lucinda.'

Maisie's stomach clenches. 'Did Lucinda ever talk to you about that?'

'No, never. Was there something to tell me?'

Maisie turns back to her unpacking.

'Soon after that I thought you made more of an effort to avoid her,' Caz says, 'even drifting away from the gang over the years.'

'Hello! I happen to be married with two small kids and a busy career. That's enough to bring even the crummiest of social lives to an abrupt halt. Anyway, I'm not the only one who might have had an issue with Lucinda. I don't like speaking of her like this, I think what happened to her is devastating, but being honest with you, Caz, after her tomfoolery that party weekend, it's a wonder she had any friends left at all. You know that as well as I do.'

'I didn't think your fuzzy alcoholic brain remembered much about the party.'

'Apart from insulting you and Stella, Lucinda was behind Eddie's break-up with Sasha.'

'Who told you that?'

'Sasha was scarcely talking to him that last day after his carry-on with Lucinda. She told me she couldn't wait to get back to Dublin and dump him, when we were sitting by the pool. *And* Janet's here without Aaron – a couple who were always glued at the hip. No prizes for guessing what's happened there.'

'Anything else?' Caz's voice is brittle.

She obviously doesn't want any reminders of that weekend, or the way Lucinda had snubbed her, which had given Maisie a tiny thrill at the time, but Maisie's not quite finished. 'Just something else … About what you said the day after the accident …'

'What did I say?'

'That you needed to talk to Stella … but you didn't want to break a confidence.'

'Did I say that?'

'You did.' Maisie holds her gaze.

'I can't remember,' Caz says, lifting the last of her clothes out of her case. 'I only know we were all in bits. I don't think I knew what I was saying. We all got far too wasted that weekend, thinking we were twenty-one again. Then afterwards we were all over the place, in total shock. But look …' she pauses, a pair of woolly socks in her hand '… whatever you're thinking about anyone, or that bloody Instagram page, please keep it to yourself. There's no point in upsetting Stella or anyone else any further. It's going to be a tough enough couple of days as it is.'

Maisie sighs. 'Isn't it just … Here, let's have a refill before we go down and face whatever demons we have to face.'

'Thought you were glad to get away from your small demons this weekend.'

'Oh, these are big ones.' Maisie splashes vodka into a glass. 'Don't you feel it too, Caz, the tension in the air? Because I certainly do.'

CHAPTER TWENTY-ONE

Caz

A short while later, Maisie heads downstairs, Caz making the excuse of having to call London so that she can stay behind. She needs a few minutes of alone time to have a breather from Maisie, and a respite from the group before the evening meal. The visit to Wolf Head had been more painful than she'd expected, looking at the dark, turbulent sea, coming face to face with the reality that the remains of Lucinda, her beautiful, vivacious friend, were still out there somewhere, six months on from the tragedy.

The stuff of nightmares.

Even Eddie had looked shaken to the core when they came back from the cliff walk, and she'd barely managed to resist the urge to comfort him.

But she's not looking forward to the chat Stella was talking about, everyone sharing memories of Lucinda's last day. She can't think of anything more traumatic. Sometimes, going about her day in grey wintry London, she'll hear a song from that hot, sunny weekend, and memories she'd tried to blank out unroll at will, and the pain grabs her in the gut, squeezing so hard she can't breathe. One weekend she'd actually pulled out of a lucrative booking for a wedding in

Sussex at the last minute when Alphaville and their haunting version of 'Forever Young' came pouring out of the radio that morning.

Enough.

Caz draws a shaky breath. She can't stay here all night. She has to go downstairs at some stage. She tries to remember what she'd said to Maisie about breaking a confidence. Had she said it to anyone else? Like Stella? She didn't think so but, still, she'll have to be careful.

She has left the bedroom and is walking down the corridor when she hears footsteps overhead, then someone coming down the stairwell from the second floor. She recognises the dark jeans through the glass. Rex. She feels too wiped out to make conversation with him so before he spots her, she shrinks back and slips through the next open door, to wait until he's gone.

A mistake. It was the room she'd been determined to avoid at all costs this weekend. The big, gleaming bathroom, with the big, equally gleaming eight-seater Jacuzzi, fraught with memories of that Friday night and the carnage that ensued.

When the meal had arrived up from The Pier that evening everyone was out on the terrace, where the Kerry sky was turning a pale blue, the sun slanting a trail towards the west, the water of the swimming pool in shadow, the deep blue surface ruffled by a slight breeze. For once the music was in the background, something Spanish-y. Aaron and Eddie were still cracking jokes about their afternoon on an alternative golf course, Janet insisting they missed out on some spectacular sights.

'The Skelligs are a totally spiritual experience,' she said, as she sat up on the sun-lounger, arms clasped around her drawn-up legs, a pint of chilled water on the low table beside her.

'There's only one spiritual experience I'm interested in,' Eddie said, 'and it begins with W and not S.'

'So it's not me.' Sasha pouted. Caz thought she'd been asleep on her sun-lounger, but the young woman sat up, using an arm to shield her eyes from rays of sunlight. 'I guess it's not you, Stella, either,' she said to Stella, who was relaxing on the lounger beside her.

Stella reached for her sunglasses. 'Sorry, I missed that, what is it?'

'Eddie doesn't want me any more,' Sasha whined.

'Believe me, you're not missing much, Sasha,' Lucinda said, without moving.

'And you'd know?' Sasha asked.

Lucinda pretended she hadn't heard. After The Pier, she'd changed into a fresh white bikini under an emerald green jewelled caftan. The other women, including Caz, had changed for dinner and were wearing tops and either shorts or wrap skirts.

'Don't worry, Eddie, I hear you and I will obey,' Maisie said, and headed down to the terrace bar. She quickly returned with a glass of liquid of indeterminate colour, handing it to him. 'Whiskey – your favourite spiritual experience, right?'

'Top of the class, Maisie,' Eddie said.

'Teacher's pet,' Sasha said.

'Don't worry, Sasha, you're my favourite carnal experience.' He took a sip and made a face. 'What the fuck, Maisie?'

'It's a whiskey cocktail, a Maisie special.'

'I'm afraid to ask what's in it.'

'Don't, then. Anyone else want one?'

'Not whiskey, no thanks,' Lucinda said. 'Do me a virgin margarita special.'

Caz didn't know if she was simply tired after a late night and all the partying, or a little deflated at the way Lucinda had put her down that afternoon, but she felt out of synch with the rest of the gang. Janet looked a little out of sorts too, Caz noticed, the other woman staring into space a couple of times before plastering on a happy smile, as if remembering where she was. Caz knew she had better get her party act together to get through the rest of the evening. But she decided she would look after her own booze intake, as she eyed the concoction Maisie had put in front of Eddie. To judge by the way some of them were knocking back their drinks, the night was not going to end well.

Everyone was happy to have the meal served out on the terrace, Tadhg readying bottles of chilled white wine while Aisling and Ruth from The Pier moved around with seafood starters and a grilled-peach vegan dish for Janet and Aaron, telling them they might as well take advantage of the sunny evening because there was talk of the weather changing the next day.

'It can't change before tomorrow evening,' Lucinda said, as she speared some crabmeat and popped it into her mouth. 'That's our big gala celebration night.'

'I thought the plan was to get all glammed up and eat inside at the dining table,' Caz said, beginning to wonder when they'd move on from the terrace. Much as she enjoyed the warm sultry evenings and atmospheric lighting, combined with the pumping music, being outdoors seemed to give some of them permission to lose the run of themselves.

'Caz! What's got into you? That's too stuffy,' Lucinda said. It sounded like a joke but, to Caz, it grated. She wanted to ask Lucinda what had got into her, why she was being so antagonistic towards her.

'The plan is to get all glammed up and eat out here,' Lucinda said. 'And then, after the cake, I'm going to make a speech.'

Caz noticed several of the group glancing at Lucinda in surprise.

'And after that, it'll be party time,' Lucinda continued.

Later, after the dessert had been cleared and Tadhg and the waitresses had left, the sun had gone down behind the mountains and the evening folded into a soft twilight. The sound of 'Forever Young' echoed across the cobalt-blue sky.

Caz watched as Lucinda kicked off her heels, climbed onto the table and, using it as a stage, sang along to the lyrics, moving gracefully in time to the music, her caftan glittering and sparkling where it caught the light from the strings of tiny bulbs. Eddie plucked a rose from one of the planters and handed it up to her, and Lucinda held it like a microphone. He was about to climb onto the table when Sasha grabbed him, pulling him into an embrace, Janet and Aaron following suit. Maisie scooted around the table and sat between Caz and Stella, grabbing their hands and holding them in the air, singing and swaying in time to the music.

Caz knew she would always remember that spine-tingling moment with a fierce intensity. The haunting sounds shimmering across the sultry evening, the softly lit candles, glimmering fairy lights, the floral scents infusing the air, everyone singing, Lucinda dancing barefoot on the table.

Later, someone reminded Lucinda about the Jacuzzi and she felt her heart dip. Not this, and not now.

'I'll bring the music,' Eddie offered.

'I'll organise the fizz,' Maisie said.

'Quick change for whoever is not in her bikini!' Lucinda whooped, 'But, of course, clothing is optional!'

'I'll give this a miss if you don't mind,' Stella said.

Lucinda widened her eyes. 'Stella! Of course I mind, but if you want to abandon us then go ahead.'

Caz hadn't the guts to say she'd rather go to bed too. Her vivacious, sparkling, sometimes maddening friend was on fire.

Still, she was annoyed with herself when she was dutifully sitting in the Jacuzzi some fifteen minutes later. All of them were there, bar Stella, their limbs almost tangling in the chest-high, foamy water. Maisie handed Lucinda a glass of something before passing around glasses of Taittinger to the others, a couple of bottles stuck in buckets on the tiled floor close to where she was sitting.

Caz noticed that Lucinda was topless, the water bubbling around her breasts.

The door opened and Stella popped her head in.

'Hey, come in, Stella. We can shove up and make room for you,' Lucinda said, getting up, and Caz realised that Lucinda was completely naked. She picked up some foam and lobbed it in Stella's direction, 'Come on, don't be a wuss. It's okay to let your hair down once in a while. What happens in The Lookout stays in The Lookout.'

Stella shook her head.

Someone hooked an arm around Lucinda's waist and hauled her back into the water.

'No, thanks,' Stella said, backing out of the room.

There was a hoot of laughter in her wake. Then the music changed to Frankie Goes to Hollywood, 'Relax'. Lucinda jumped up again, gyrating on the spot.

Eddie got up. He was wearing swimming shorts but his arousal was clearly straining against the wet material. He stood behind Lucinda and grabbed her hands, raising them up with his as he moved in close behind her and pushed his crotch against her bum in time to the music. Then Aaron jumped up and stood in front of Lucinda. Cupping her breasts, he thrust his pelvis against her. Lucinda reached down and opened the zip of his shorts, slipping her hand inside. Aaron's eyes closed and he let out a small groan.

The door opened. 'I wanted to say …' It was Stella, walking back into the room again, halting abruptly as she registered what was happening, before quickly turning on her heel and marching out.

Caz watched the scene unfold, frozen in stunned disbelief. Janet must have been equally stunned because it took her a minute to react. She stood up, slapped her husband across the back, and gave him an almighty push so that he collided into Lucinda and Eddie and the three of them collapsed in a heap of limbs and spilling water, sending up a wave that flowed out across the tiled floor. Janet climbed out of the Jacuzzi and stormed across the floor, slamming the door behind her.

Sasha followed suit, but not before she had chucked Eddie's sound bar into the foamy water.

CHAPTER TWENTY-TWO

Stella

Stella swallows her panic as people start to drift downstairs for the evening meal.

Your fault.

The words in red lettering are emblazoned across Stella's brain. She'd torn the offending photograph into smithereens, throwing the pieces into the bin in her room. Whoever had placed it is here, in this house, and that's enough to send alarm bells shrieking through her head. It could have been put on her pillow either before or after the cliff walk, and it could have been any one of them. Whoever it is, they must know she's seen it by now. She forces herself to act as though nothing is amiss, determined not to let the perpetrator know they'd upset her. She would flush out whoever it was sooner or later.

Maisie and Janet arrive downstairs first, followed shortly by Rex. Although the heating is on full blast, all of them are wrapped up in thick jumpers or fleeces, still warming up after the cliff walk.

'I hope you're bearing up,' Rex says, tipping her on the shoulder.

'I am, thanks,' Stella says, wanting to lean into him but knowing this isn't the time.

'Hey, Britt, I'll do that,' he says, going across to where she's emptying the dishwasher.

No sign yet of Caz. Eddie is in the bar – Stella saw him when she passed by – sitting on a high stool, his elbows on the wooden counter, his head in his hands, a figure of dejection, a glass of wine in front of him. Presently Caz comes downstairs, her pale face showing the strain of the evening. Rex organises pre-dinner drinks as Eddie comes in from the bar, and everyone gravitates towards the big sofas in the seating area, Caz and Maisie making inroads on the bottle of gin. She hears Maisie teasing Rex for producing such huge balloon glasses with mini-avalanches of ice, never mind the generous measures of gin. Janet and Britt are sipping fruit juice, as is Stella, who's determined to keep a clear head.

'Thanks for your support this evening,' Stella says, keeping her voice as neutral as possible. 'I appreciate it. Food will be here shortly and after that I'm hoping we'll have a bit of a chat so I can find out more about Lucinda's last day.'

'You mean the actual Saturday itself?' Caz asks.

'Yes. I saw her here at midday and she was with Britt at one o'clock, but that's as much as I know. I'm trying to fill in the gaps after that.'

'I remember that Saturday was a quiet day for me.' Maisie jumps in, as if she wants to get it over with. 'I had a massive hangover after the night before, and when I eventually got up, it was after lunchtime. I spent the rest of the day outside on a sun-lounger, with iced water and painkillers, trying to recover before the gala night. Sasha was much the same as me.'

Stella can't miss the glare she gives Eddie, and neither does he because he raises his hands in some kind of supplication.

'The guards asked each of us about our movements that day,' Caz says. 'We even went to the station in Kenmare to make formal statements. I don't think they found anything amiss, Stella,' she says quietly, looking around Lucinda's friends for agreement.

Stella nods. 'So I believe, Caz. At the time I was too shocked to talk to you but now I'd like to know as much as I can about Lucinda that afternoon. I wasn't here.' Her gaze scans the group. She's uncomfortably aware that they all know why she wasn't here, why she'd left The Lookout in a child-like tantrum. The open-plan area is not the cosiest space in the world on a dark winter's night where floor-to-ceiling glass faces into the black void outside and Stella sees ghostly versions of them reflected in it. Who resents her so much? Do they believe those rotten messages they're sending? Or are they trying to muddy the waters and confuse her in an effort to prevent her from thinking clearly and figuring out that one of Lucinda's friends had borne a huge amount of animosity towards her, enough to engineer her fatal accident? It seems inconceivable, all the same.

The doorbell peals, Britt answering it, and Tadhg comes into the kitchen area bearing an industrial-sized steel tray carrying food containers.

'I'm a little early ... The Pier is jammers tonight and everyone is rushed off their feet. Tricia said the food can be kept warm if you're not ready to eat ...'

'We're all ready now,' Britt says.

Rex and Eddie help set it out – Stella hears Rex commenting that his waistline will be ruined. Dishes are spread, buffet style, along the top of the vast kitchen island – slow roast beef, vegan curry, an array of steaming winter vegetables, rice, pasta, to be followed by freshly baked apple pies, with jugs of custard and cream, or strawberries and balsamic reduction.

Stella picks up a plate although she's not hungry. Above the murmur of conversation around her, she becomes aware of the wind outside, like someone tuning to a different wavelength. It keens like a mad witch, buffeting the glass, rattling a shed door, sending something rolling to and fro across the patio – a bottle, slamming into the legs of a patio table, then rolling down to clink against the planters. Stella realises she's heard that exact noise before in the exact same place. It's a noise she can't bear: it cleaves open a memory of sickening terror, a dark, lurking monster, so that she is being sucked down, down, down to a dark place inside her, back to that fateful last day.

Twenty-four more hours, Stella reminded herself as she went downstairs at ten o'clock on Saturday morning. She could swallow her annoyance and stay calm for that length of time, couldn't she? Cool, calm and detached.

It was quiet in The Lookout. The morning sunshine poured through the glass, fizzing along the walls, throwing spangles of light across the floors. Stella guessed everyone was still in bed as she moved through the empty spaces on the silent ground floor, some of them no doubt too mortified to show their faces the morning after last night's show.

She'd been unable to sleep for hours, Lucinda's antics churning like tickertape in her head, stoking her anger, lending it energy, from the boat trip onwards and culminating in the Jacuzzi. Still, the wild, untrammelled weekend that unfolded around her only served to remind her how desperately empty her personal life was, compared to the effervescent Lucinda's.

Her love life had come to a juddering halt after the painful break-up with Leo.

'You're too buttoned up,' he'd said to her, when she'd discovered his infidelity. 'Even in bed, you can't seem to let go properly.'

They'd been together for three full years. His words had stung her to the quick.

And while she was appalled at Lucinda's bawdy behaviour, she was ridiculously envious of the way she was able to let rip and behave with no inhibitions in front of her circle of friends.

She had been lying awake at two o'clock in the morning when she heard something outside – a noise, a raised voice suddenly cut off. She went to the window and looked down into the darkness of the garden, barely able to discern the glint of the swimming pool. Then to the side of the garden she saw something – a tiny blue-white light emitting from a mobile phone, throwing into grey relief the doorway of a changing hut, the shape of a figure standing in it, before emerging as the pinprick of light went out. The figure blended into the shadows and disappeared. Stella listened hard, her ears straining, her heart beating fast. She didn't know if she was imagining it, but it seemed to her there was a soft click from downstairs and an occasional creak on the staircase, as if someone had come in from outside and was now creeping up the stairs as quietly as possible. Up as far as Lucinda's room. Eventually, she had slept.

Now Stella's thoughts were interrupted when she heard a car coming up the driveway. Aisling and Ruth from The Pier. She let the young women in. They had brought fresh supplies for breakfast and lunch, sourdough, soda bread, croissants, bowls of creamy yogurt and chopped-up fruit, a selection of smoked salmon, cheeses, hams, pastas, quinoa, sauces and dips that went straight into the fridge. They moved around the ground floor and the terrace outside, sweeping and tidying, collecting dirty glasses, replenishing gaps in the terrace and home bars with fresh glasses from a large wire basket.

'We'll be up with the cake this afternoon,' Aisling said. 'It's absolutely fabulous. Tricia is storing it in one of the fridges. And we'll make sure to be here early tonight. It's the big one, isn't it? The gala night.'

'Yes, it is,' Stella said, marvelling at their enthusiasm. She couldn't think of anything more stressful – she felt this party had already careened way out of control and it didn't need a grand finale. Just as Aisling and Ruth were leaving, Caz came down the stairs in a silk dressing-gown, her hair askew, her face shiny.

'Just ignore me,' she said to Stella. 'I'm in bits. I had to come down for fresh water, then it's straight back to bed. I need to recharge the batteries before the main event tonight.'

She couldn't believe Caz was talking as though nothing untoward had happened the night before, not even acknowledging it, when Stella had been unable to stop the vision of Lucinda eating away inside her. 'After that warmer-upper last night, God help us with whatever is next on the agenda,' she said, unable to keep the acerbic note out of her voice.

'What warmer-upper?' Caz's face was guarded.

'Eddie and Lucinda *and* Aaron getting it on in the Jacuzzi.'

Caz shrugged dismissively as though it was no big deal.

'Come on, Caz, even you must agree that practically having sex in front of your friends goes beyond a boundary.'

'*Even* me? What's that supposed to mean, Stella?'

'As Lucinda's friend—'

'Exactly. I'm Lucinda's friend. I'm not listening to any more of this. Now, if you'll excuse me.' Caz headed into the kitchen and Stella heard the sound of chilled water being poured from the dispenser in the fridge.

Stella stalked out onto the terrace, envy curdling in her stomach. She'd never had a close woman friend as staunchly loyal to her as Caz was to Lucinda, or a friendship that lasted from the early teenage years. Another stick to beat herself with. By midday, she was still alone downstairs. She had coffee, fruit, yogurt and croissants, her irritation further compounded by the amount of food jammed into the fridge, since no one seemed to be bothering with breakfast. What a waste.

She went up to Lucinda's bedroom and walked in without knocking.

Bad idea. Lucinda was propped up against the pillows, checking her mobile, a strappy, midi sundress in a shade of bright yellow hanging on the door of the wardrobe, ready and waiting. She smiled at Stella as though nothing was wrong. 'Hi, sis, how's the head? I've been on to The Pier to order more booze. They'll have it sent up shortly.'

'*More* booze?' Stella was almost trembling with indignation, everything coming together and surging up inside her – Leo and Davina's duplicity, her envy of Lucinda's devil-may-care attitude, her inhibition-free close circle of friends who were not afraid to push at the edges in search of high-octane fun. Not that she was remotely interested in joining in their tomfoolery, but she envied them their shameless confidence. After Leo, hers had crashed to the floor.

She knew she should have left then, got away from Lucinda until she felt calmer.

Lucinda laughed. 'You were always the sensible one, Stella.'

Sensible. It was a red rag to Stella. 'What do you think you're playing at?'

Lucinda's face changed. 'What do you mean?'

'This whole ... set-up, this weekend, your drunken friends, and you, acting the eejit big-time.' Stella couldn't stop the shake in her voice. 'If I'd known it was an excuse to spend the weekend getting down and dirty, I'd never have come.'

Lucinda put down her phone. 'Hey, Stella, what brought this on?'

'You did, with your behaviour.'

'What behaviour?'

'Hello? What do you call flashing your butt and your boobs and groping your friend's husband? Sorry, Lucinda, but you're more than this. You're more than a pathetic forty-year-old getting some teenage kicks.'

Lucinda sat up straighter in bed. 'Is that what you think of me? Pathetic?'

'You should have seen yourself yesterday evening.'

'Okay, look, I didn't expect to get as carried away as I did,' Lucinda admitted. 'I don't know what happened.'

'Yeah, right. You looked sloshed to me.'

'Sloshed?' Lucinda looked thoughtful. 'No way, Stella. You know I'm not drinking, but from the start of the weekend I was determined to show everyone that I haven't turned into a boring soberista. I'm still the same party animal and well able to have a fun time.'

'Fun time? God knows what hedonistic delights you have lined up for tonight for everyone's titillation.'

'Hey, don't be such a prig.'

'Prig? It so happens that pretending to screw other people's partners is not my scene.'

'I did *not* pretend to screw Eddie.'

'You as good as. And what about Aaron?'

Lucinda shrugged. 'Yeah, well, maybe it wasn't a great idea but it was just a bit of messing around. It didn't last long.'

'So that made it all right? Jesus, Lucinda, you're even more of a slapper than I thought.'

'Hey, chill. I told you I don't know how I went over the top. Honestly.'

Lucinda frowned and bit her lip but Stella was in full flow. 'Have you any idea how mortified I am with your clowning around? Why do you feel the need to flaunt yourself like this? It started on Thursday night, then Tadhg on the boat, then last night—'

'Jeez. I didn't know you were keeping count so conscientiously. Don't be such a killjoy. Relax, calm down. Okay, it all went a bit crazy, but it's a *parteeee*.' Lucinda put a big bright smile on her face as though that was enough to appease Stella.

Her words infuriated Stella further. She was supposed to be clever, intelligent and successful. Instead she felt boring, dutiful and all over dull. 'I've a good mind to go home,' she said. 'I can't sit by any more and watch you make a fool of yourself in front of your friends.'

'Hey, we haven't even had the cake yet or—'

'Sung happy birthday?'

'No, actually, I have an announcement to make tonight.'

'If it's all that great, tell me now,' Stella said.

'I can't, not yet.' Lucinda shook her head. 'There's something I need to do first, someone I need to talk to.'

'Someone more important than me? Caz, I suppose.'

'Please, Stella, go along with me for now,' Lucinda begged. 'I'll talk to you this evening. Promise.'

'I've a feeling tonight will be another excuse for you to act the eejit, make a pathetic fool of yourself. How can I sit around and watch that?'

'Hey, come on, I agree that last night got a little out of hand, I still don't know how, but it was fun and games. Why can't you for once lose the run of yourself?'

'Are you joking?'

'Look, Stella, you know I've always been so proud of you, and I admire you to bits, but I'd love you to be a bit more spontaneous, to loosen your shackles. Move on from being so self-controlled. Sometimes you still go on like the dutiful schoolgirl you once were.'

Lucinda's words stung. Echoes of what Leo had said to her when she'd tackled him about his infidelity.

'If I can't cut loose it's your fault,' Stella snapped.

'*What?*'

Pent-up words tumbled out of Stella. 'I always tried so hard to be the good daughter,' her voice shook, 'the daughter who didn't cause any trouble, or turn our parents' hair grey, or put worry grooves on their faces, or give them sleepless nights, or cause their hearts to sink with disappointment. I never rebelled, never ran amok with myself, I squashed myself into a safe little box so as not to rock any boats, so as to keep my parents – *our* parents, Lucinda – happy, after the way you treated them so horribly.'

'Jesus, it's all coming out now – how much you resent me.'

'Not half as much as you must have resented me for being the natural daughter. Proud of me, my arse.'

'I never bore you a grudge, Stella. How could I? I admire you so much. You're the one decent thing in my life.'

'Is that what gives you permission to go off the rails? Look at all the times you laughed at Mum and called her your pretend mum. Have you any idea how much that hurt her? Then the way you rejected Mum and Dad and caused endless trouble. Staying out, getting drunk, bunking off school … It was like you were thumbing your nose at the three of us.'

'Have you any idea how much it hurt me when the truth of my birth came out?' Lucinda countered defensively. 'That the people I thought loved me most in the world had been lying to me for years?'

'For fuck's sake, grow up, Lucinda. They *were* your parents in the real sense of the word. They *chose* you. They fibbed to make life easier for you. They loved you to bits and lavished whatever they could on you, on both of us, and you threw it all back in their faces. Then you bummed off to London and hardly bothered to keep in touch when you came home. They were always worried sick about you. No wonder Mum got cancer and they both went to an early grave.'

Lucinda recoiled. Stella faltered momentarily. She'd never lashed out at Lucinda like that before, never mind suggesting Lucinda had had something to do with Mum's illness and untimely death. She felt dizzy. Had she truly thought this, deep down inside? Some kind of ingrained belief that coloured her perception of Lucinda?

'You can't mean that,' Lucinda said, a flash of alarm in her eyes. 'Look, sis ...' She got out of bed and put a hand on Stella's arm.

Her thoughts spinning in confusion, Stella pushed her away. 'How dare you call me that!' she said. 'I'm not your sis. I never was.' She knew it was one of the worst things she could have said to Lucinda as she stalked out the door and slammed it behind her.

CHAPTER TWENTY-THREE

Stella

Stella picks at the food on her plate, not knowing how it got there. Sitting beside Rex at the dining table, she's relieved he's busy chatting to Eddie. She knows she's incapable of joining in any conversation right now. Outside the wind is still howling around and all her nerve endings feel raw and exposed. She is gripped by a painful cascade of memories from that last day. She sees herself stalking back to her room after the angry exchange with Lucinda, their sharp words resounding in her head.

Stella's scalp prickled with tension as she stripped off her clothes and stepped into the shower, turning the dial down. The shock of cold jets bouncing off her warm skin jolted her into rude reality.

How could she have spoken to Lucinda like that? Attaching blame to her for their parents' untimely deaths? Her mum's cancer diagnosis and death within a year had stunned all of them, so much so that Dad had died six months later from a sudden heart attack. It had been a deeply harrowing time, and it had been totally unfair of Stella to lash out at Lucinda in the way she had. Then she had finished it off nicely by shooting that hurtful sister barb. She increased the temperature of the water so that it was a more pleasant lukewarm, adjusting it to a rainforest flow, and stood under the stream for as long as she could, determined to sluice away all her annoyance.

Afterwards she got dressed, and could hear the faint chime of the doorbell from two floors below. Someone else could get it, she decided. She dried her hair and applied her make-up, staring at her image in the mirror, remembering Lucinda's alarmed expression. She knew that she owed Lucinda an apology for her harsh words. She left her bedroom, and crossing the corridor, she stood outside Lucinda's room, taking a deep breath.

And then she heard it: a series of rapid, high-pitched cries, accompanied by grunts, followed by a long-drawn-out guttural groan. The unmistakable sound of two people having sex.

Reality slammed into Stella's head. Whatever she had said to Lucinda, it hadn't fazed her in the least. She returned to her room to grab her bag and car keys before marching out of The Lookout, hardly able to see where she was going in the heat of her anger, needing to stop the car and take a steadying breath as she turned out onto the lane. She headed off for the afternoon, needing to put as much space as possible between herself and everyone else.

Lunch in Caherdaniel and a long walk on the beach in Derrynane helped to clear her head and calm her frayed temper somewhat. Just get through this evening, she decided.

She'd sort out her shredded confidence when she was in Dublin. She arrived back at The Lookout after five o'clock and headed straight to her room, determined to avoid everyone until it was almost time for the gala meal. They were having pre-dinner drinks at eight o'clock, followed by the meal at nine.

When Stella went downstairs, wearing a black Zara shift dress, everyone except Caz and Lucinda was gathered in the seating area, all glammed up and swigging champagne, ready to party even if Janet and Sasha were pointedly avoiding Aaron and Eddie. A watchful hush at her appearance told her that word had gone around about her row with Lucinda.

Then Eddie handed her a glass of champagne and conversations cranked up again.

Aisling and Ruth, with Deirdre from The Pier, were in the kitchen area putting the finishing touches to the meal prep. The champagne birthday cake, a frothy concoction embellished with pink fondant and fresh cream, and studded with sparklers, was sitting on a side table. Lucinda planned to cut it on the stroke of midnight. Aisling and Ruth had already set the long table with crystal glassware and gleaming cutlery in the dining room, because eating outside was not an option that evening. The blue skies had vanished, replaced with thick, scudding grey clouds, and strong winds had whipped up out of nowhere, the bunting outside whirling wildly, twisting and turning, pulling on its moorings, a strand of fairy lights spinning free. Beer bottles left on the terrace after late-afternoon drinks were rolling around on the tiles, clinking against each other every so often.

Britt arrived from Dunmullen just after eight. Then Caz came downstairs to join them. She was wearing a shocking pink mini dress, similar to but not half as stylish as the one Lucinda had modelled on a TikTok clip earlier in the summer.

'I can't get hold of Lucinda,' she said baldly. 'Has anyone else heard from her?'

A sudden silence descended, broken only by the sounds coming from the kitchen area, the rattle of a tray being slid out of the oven.

'What do you mean?' Eddie asked, wheeling around to face her. He scrubbed up well, Stella had to admit, in a crisp white shirt and black chinos.

'She's not in her room, or answering her mobile,' Caz said, looking puzzled. 'I was supposed to have her hair and make-up done by now. Even her car is gone.'

Eddie looked perplexed. 'Her *car*? Where could she be at this hour?'

Stella privately decided that Lucinda had taken herself off somewhere else to get beautified and was going to make a dazzling entrance any minute now. But the minutes ticked past, more champagne was opened, conversation stalled, and all the while Stella heard the bottles rolling around outside, crashing into each other as though they were having a crazy dance. Aisling came in and asked Stella if it was okay to serve the starters: the celeriac salad with quinoa and pomegranate, and prawns with mango salsa were already plated, the Albariño perfectly chilled.

Then the doorbell rang and Stella felt the general sigh of relief rippling around. But it wasn't Lucinda. Eddie had gone out to open the door and now he arrived back, leading a man and a woman across to the seating area. Stella noticed their garda uniforms and for a moment she thought Lucinda had hired strippers to kick-start the night's entertainment.

But they could have been speaking in a foreign language. They asked about Lucinda. They spoke of a car being spotted, going over the edge of the cliff at Wolf Head. The same make and colour as Lucinda's. They mentioned Seamus Dillon, Tricia's father, who witnessed it. He was walking his dog as he did most evenings, down past the harbour and along the stony seashore trail that twists around the peninsula from Wolf Cove to the base of the head. He recognised the distinctive stripes on the side of the car and remembered it as being Lucinda's from his trips up to The Lookout. By the time he hurried back and raised the alarm, the wind had risen further, the tide had turned. By the time a rescue team was scrambled, there was no sign of the car. It had disappeared beneath the heavy Atlantic swell. Unfortunately, the rescue attempt had to be aborted due to deteriorating weather conditions. They would recommence the operation at first light the next morning, weather permitting.

Stella heard all this through a fuzz of white noise. She had shooting pains in her head and her chest. She couldn't grasp why Caz and Maisie were hugging each other, their faces blanched, or why Eddie was sitting with his head bowed, his shoulders shaking. Was he crying? Janet and Aaron sat immobile on the sofa, Janet with her hand clamped to her mouth as though she was holding back vomit. After the guards had gone, Britt swooped on Stella, arms outstretched, but Stella shrugged her off and stood by the window staring out, wondering how empty beer bottles were still rolling around freely when the life of her sister had shuddered to a full stop.

The following morning Seamus called up, twisting his hat in his hands, saying that if he'd had his mobile with him, he could have called for help sooner. He always left it behind on his walks. 'Just me and the dog,' he said.

The guards called again. Weather conditions were making it impossible for any search-and-rescue operation. They explained that even if Seamus had had his mobile, the extremely high swell of the sea and the dangerous rip tide off Wolf Head could have dragged the car miles out by the time help arrived. Stella was glad that their words flowed over her head because they were meaningless. She was aware that on some level an enormous reservoir of self-hate was building up inside her, a monster waiting to attack her for arguing with Lucinda in the first place and for not trying to make peace with her as soon as she came back to The Lookout the previous afternoon. Britt had already told her that Lucinda had been visiting her at one o'clock, so it couldn't have been Lucinda having sex in her bedroom before Stella had gone off for the afternoon. But Stella couldn't make sense of anything, because she was falling into a terrifying black vault inside her from which there was no escape.

CHAPTER TWENTY-FOUR

Maisie

'It was half past one by the time I was up and out on the terrace,' Maisie says. 'I remember Lucinda drifting out at about two o'clock. She sat on the edge of a lounger with a cup of coffee.'

'She must have come straight back here after she left me,' Britt says.

'The problem I have,' Stella says, 'and Rex, you don't know this, but I'm sure the rest of ye do. Unfortunately I had a row with Lucinda around midday,' Stella's voice wobbles, 'and after that, I went off for most of the afternoon. I'm trying to piece together how Lucinda spent it.'

The meal is over and they are all gathered in the seating area. Rex has organised fresh drinks, bringing wine and spirits through from the home bar to the kitchen island before sitting down beside Stella and holding her hand. Of them all, he looks the most relaxed. Maisie can't shake off the idea that this is some kind of inquisition, but she knows that's her guilty conscience speaking. It's creeping her out that the wind is howling around the house much like that terrible Saturday evening, the only difference being that it's pitch black outside now. Her chat with Eddie earlier is also freaking her out. She's

189

not sure exactly what he knows. She should have left well enough alone instead of following him into the home bar. Still, if he'd been all that concerned, why hadn't he spoken up six months ago? She hopes he doesn't speak up now, despite his assurances that it wouldn't make any difference. God knows what she might say in reply. She hopes Stella doesn't sense how closely she's watching every word out of her mouth.

'Janet and Sasha arrived out onto the terrace before Lucinda,' Maisie continues. 'Soon after that I conked out. I was lucky Janet covered me with a sun umbrella,' she says. 'Otherwise I could have got sunstroke.' Too late, she realises how silly this sounds in the context of their conversation. Stella is not here to talk about what might have happened to Maisie. 'But, Stella,' Maisie quietens her voice and leans forward to where Stella is sitting on a sofa at right angles to her, along with Rex and Britt, 'that was the last time I saw Lucinda. There was me, Janet and Sasha out on the terrace at that time, and soon afterwards, I conked out.'

'But Lucinda could have come back later when you were asleep?' Stella asks.

'She could have,' Maisie says. 'Janet and Sasha might know. Then around five o'clock I had a couple of drinks with Sasha – we were sitting on the stools at the terrace bar.'

'I don't remember seeing Lucinda after two o'clock,' Janet says, 'but, like Maisie, I was hung-over and there were times that afternoon when I nodded off. She could have popped back and I didn't see her.'

'How about you, Caz?' Stella asks.

'I let in a delivery of drinks from The Pier in the early afternoon,' Caz says.

'What time was this at?' Stella asks.

'Jeez, I don't know exactly, maybe before one o'clock? There seemed to be no one around,' Caz says. 'I thought everyone was sleeping off a hangover.'

Maisie can't help darting Caz a glance. She'd been well and truly woken up soon after twelve by the sounds of raised voices coming from Lucinda's bedroom followed by the slamming of the door. It had probably disturbed the whole house.

'I went back to bed,' Caz says. 'I came down to the pool about three o'clock. There was no sign of Lucinda then, but neither was there any sign of Aaron or Eddie.'

Maisie sees the mocking glance Caz throws at Eddie.

'I thought you pair were keeping a low profile after the previous evening,' Caz says.

'No, we were gone off in the boat with Tadhg,' Eddie says, giving her a look that Maisie can't fathom.

'Were you?' Stella asks. 'I don't remember that.'

'He brought us out to see the Skelligs,' Eddie says. 'We were jealous you guys had been there. We were half cut, though, because we had a pint or two before we left and Aaron had brought a bottle of rum along for the boat.'

'What time did you get back?' Stella asks.

'It was about half past five,' Eddie says.

Stella leans forward. 'So you would have been coming up from Wolf Cove around then? Did you see Lucinda at any point? Even later in The Lookout?'

'No,' Eddie says. Something about his face makes Maisie feels he's hiding something. She wonders if anyone else has noticed.

'Are you sure about that?'

'Hang on a minute,' Janet interrupts. 'Lucinda went down, didn't she, to get more paracetamol in the village? I kind of remember you complaining that you were running short, Maisie, but she said it was no problem to swing down, that she needed something from the mini-market anyway.'

'That was earlier in the afternoon,' Eddie says, 'when she gave us a lift down.'

'What time was that?' Stella asks.

'Just before half two, I think.'

'So she came back from Britt's place,' Stella says, 'had coffee on the terrace, then brought you two down to Wolf Cove at half past two?'

'Yeah. Our boat trip was arranged for three o'clock,' Eddie says, 'but we dropped into The Pier first for a couple of scoops beforehand. Hair of the dog and all that.'

'How did Lucinda seem to you?' Stella asks. 'What kind of a mood was she in?'

'She was fine,' he says. 'She was her usual self, saying how much she was looking forward to the gala dinner.'

'So that was the last time you saw Lucinda?' Stella presses. 'Half past two?'

He hesitates.

'Eddie? This is important to me.'

'I can't remember for sure if I saw her after that,' he says, sounding cagey to Maisie's ears. 'I was sick and queasy and more than a bit blathered by the time we were coming back on the boat. Tadhg had given us some poitín shots as well.'

'Poitín?' Janet interjects.

'I think Aaron spat his out, it was so strong,' Eddie says. 'I barely remember us getting back to the quayside. It must have been about half past five. Tadhg offered us a lift back up here, but I decided to walk. I needed the fresh air and I couldn't bear the thought of swinging up the hill and around the sharp bend in his smelly fish van. Aaron said he'd take the lift but I'm not sure ...' Eddie stops suddenly.

'Not sure about what?' Stella asks.

'I'm not sure ... if I saw Lucinda any time after I came back,' Eddie says.

Maisie sees Eddie giving Stella an apologetic look. She was full sure he'd been about to say something else, but changed his mind at the last minute.

'Look, I'm not proud of being sloshed to that extent,' Eddie continues. 'I went up to my room for some kip and I passed out on the bed. Sasha wasn't impressed.'

'Sasha was in your room then?' Stella says. 'When you came back from your boat trip?'

'No, she was still outside by the pool. She said she came up afterwards and couldn't rouse me for ages. I don't remember because I was conked out, and snoring like a hippo.'

'So that was the noise we heard through the walls?' Janet says.

Eddie glares at her.

'If you walked back up to The Lookout from the quays,' Stella says, 'it must have been soon after six o'clock by the time you got here. Did you see Lucinda's car in the garden?'

'Her car?' Eddie sighs. 'I'm sorry, Stella, I can't say one way or the other.'

'What about you, Janet?' Stella asks. 'Do you remember Aaron coming back?'

'Yeah,' Janet says smoothly. 'He took a lift off Tadhg and was back before six. I remember because he said we had plenty of time to use the Jacuzzi, just us, like, together. He took a quick shower and we went straight in.'

'I'm impressed with your ability to forgive and forget,' Maisie can't help saying. 'I would have had his balls after his antics the night before.'

Janet shrugs. 'Maybe I ate them for breakfast.' Turning to Stella she says, 'I don't think we came out until after seven to get ready for dinner.'

Maisie can't help noticing that Eddie is staring at Janet, looking puzzled, as if he's still trying to plumb the depths of his alcohol-ridden memory. He sees Maisie looking at him and freezes for a moment, like a rabbit caught in the headlights, before his expression clears.

Even Stella is looking at Eddie thoughtfully, as though she's trying to work out something. 'Does anyone remember Lucinda coming back with the paracetamol? Or seeing her any time after she dropped Eddie and Aaron to Wolf Cove? Or even seeing her car in the garden?'

Silence stretches uncomfortably, which Rex eventually breaks.

'Time to top up drinks,' he says. 'More of the same?' He picks up Maisie and Caz's balloon glasses, heading across to the kitchen counter. Then, casually, on his way back, almost as an afterthought, he says, his gaze sweeping around, 'Look, one of you must have been the last to see Lucinda alive. I think Stella deserves to know which of you it was, and when. This is her sister we're talking about.'

'It's also Lucinda we're talking about,' Caz says quickly. 'She was …' Caz puts her hand to her mouth and shakes her head as though she's sorry she's spoken.

'She was?' Rex asks.

'She was … a great friend, but hard to pin down lately. Sometimes she chopped and changed plans at the last minute. We had …' She gulps.

'What is it, Caz?' Stella asks gently.

'We had planned a pampering hair and make-up session in her room for seven o'clock, getting her beautified for the gala dinner,' Caz says, her voice becoming thinner and thinner. 'I had nothing to drink all afternoon to make sure I did the best job possible. I got myself ready and was in her room waiting for her, thinking she'd come in at any moment, but she never turned up and I – I remember feeling so annoyed with her. I didn't know …' Her voice chokes. 'Sorry, Stella.'

'I'm the one who's sorry, Caz,' Stella says. 'This is the last thing I intended, upsetting you like this.'

'It's okay.' Caz gives Stella a shaky smile. 'It's a tough weekend for all of us, but especially you, Stella.'

Stella looks around at the group. 'If anyone remembers seeing Lucinda anytime after half past two, please let me know. It's important to me. One more thing, and then I'm heading upstairs for an early night.'

Stella pauses and everyone waits expectantly. 'Does anyone know anything about an announcement Lucinda had planned to make? She talked about making a speech after the cake-cutting. Has anyone any idea what that might have been about?'

Maisie glances around. To her mind, everyone looks uncomfortable, except Rex, Britt and Stella.

'No, Stella, 'fraid not,' Eddie says nonchalantly.

Caz shrugs. 'I've no idea either.'

'Nor me,' Janet adds hurriedly.

'Maisie,' Stella turns to her, 'she didn't mention anything to you, did she?'

Maisie feels a nervous laugh coming on. She wants to say she's way down in the pecking order, and Lucinda would scarcely have told her before the others. 'No, Stella, sorry.'

Stella looks exhausted. 'Never mind. It can't have been that important.'

Maisie picks up her fresh drink, taking a long gulp. It can't have escaped Stella that a significant amount of time would have elapsed from half past two until the guards arrived at The Lookout that evening. Surely the tension in the air, the feeling that people are being economical with the truth, is not escaping her either.

CHAPTER TWENTY-FIVE

Eddie

Eddie can't sleep. Everything about that evening and Lucinda's last day is churning around in his head. He'd felt it for Stella, trying to piece things together, things that didn't add up. Everyone, he'd sensed, had something to hide from her when it came to the beautiful, vivacious, totally mercurial Lucinda.

There is a crashing noise from the patio outside, a chair toppled by the gust, he guesses. Above the keening of the wind, he hears something else, coming from inside the house. He checks the time on his mobile, blinking in the light of the screen. Two in the morning. The time he hates most, when the deepest dark hours are still ahead and dawn seems far away.

He hears the noise again. It sounds like someone singing eerily and hairs rise on the back of his neck. Caz and Maisie could be having a private party in their room. Except Caz wouldn't – not this weekend. The wind gives a particularly vengeful roar and there is another crash from the back garden before the gust abates. And in the sudden quiet the noise becomes clearer. It's coming from downstairs, a voice echoing

197

up the stairwell, the volume rising and falling. It sounds ghostly in the dark of the night.

It sounds like Lucinda. Is he dreaming this?

Fucking hell. He gets out of bed, and using his mobile for a flicker of light, he pads out onto the landing. At the top of the stairwell, he leans over the glass balustrade and looks down at the curving depth of it, past the first-floor landing, at the shadowy hall far below, at the way the polished, wooden stair treads seem to be floating in thin air.

Floating like Lucinda in her yellow dress. Oh, Jesus.

He sees a flicker of pale light moving over his head and he freezes, chilled to the bone, before realising it's the reflection of his mobile bouncing off the Velux windows.

Out here, her voice is louder. Lucinda's voice. He tries to keep a grip on himself. Everything is plunged into darkness, save for pale light coming from his open bedroom door and a faint white glow filtering up from the ground floor. He flicks the light switches at the top of the staircase but neither the upper stairwell nor the hallway chandelier is working.

Movement from the corridor beneath him, a door opening, Caz's voice.

He nips back into his room to pull on his jeans and goes down to the first floor, almost slipping on the stairs in his haste, the pinpoint torchlight flashing around in all directions. He sees Caz, shrinking back.

'It's me. Eddie.'

'Oh, Eddie!' She's wearing a long, turquoise tiger-print cardigan over her pyjamas and looks on the brink of launching herself into his arms. He can't think of anything he'd welcome more.

Then she steps back, keeping a distance between them. 'What's going on?' she hisses urgently. 'Isn't that Lucinda's voice?'

Maisie appears behind her. 'Jesus. What the fuck?' Maisie has pulled the quilt off the bed and is clutching it to her chest so that it fans around her, like a huge cloak. She inches her way up the corridor, her gaze darting about apprehensively. 'I knew this house was haunted,' she says. 'Didn't you feel it too?'

A bedroom door opens and Maisie jumps. Stella emerges, hastily pulling on a jumper over her pyjamas, her face tense. Eddie doesn't think she's slept a wink either.

'What's happening?' she asks.

'I'm not sure, but we're going to find out.'

From down below, the wailing sound of Lucinda's voice rises to an eerie crescendo. They reach the landing and Maisie squeals, looking up. 'What's that?'

Eddie sees a dark figure on the upper landing. Silhouetted against a small white beam, it's staring down at them. Maisie shrinks behind him.

'It's Rex,' Eddie says.

Rex comes down the stairs with a brisk, assured movement, wearing a black T-shirt and black leisure pants. The ghostly sound is still coming at them, echoing up from the shadows below, dark except for a wash of white light shimmering from an open door.

'Are you okay, Stella?' he asks, putting an arm around her.

'I need to know what this is,' she says.

'Someone thinks they're being very funny,' Rex says.

He leads the way down the stairs, pressing light switches in the hallway, to no avail. 'They've been messing with the fuses as well.' Then he stops outside the media room from where the light and the sound are coming. It's Lucinda's voice, but it sounds like a mad version of Kate Bush's 'Wuthering Heights'. Her voice is distorted, the recording slowed down, the volume engineered so that it rises and falls with the rhythm of the music.

'Who the hell is messing us about?' Eddie asks heatedly. The white light spilling into the hallway is coming from the large screen. It shows a video of Lucinda singing and swaying in a karaoke session at a party somewhere. She's wearing a short white sequined dress that glints in the light. All of them are transfixed at this sudden image of a singing, swaying, living, breathing Lucinda.

'For fuck's sake,' he says, striding into the room and breaking the spell. 'Someone stop this infernal thing.' Caz tries the switch for the main light and they all blink in the sudden brightness.

'How come that works?' Eddie asks.

'This room is on a different circuit,' she says.

He looks around for a remote control, remembering that everything in the room can be controlled from small consoles embedded discreetly in the arm of each chair, but Caz gets there first, picking up the main console off the cabinet running under the screen. Seconds later, Lucinda disappears. Gone, vanished, just like her life. He feels for Stella, who has wrapped her arms tightly round herself, looking shattered.

Rex curves an arm around her. 'Whose idea of a sick joke is this?' he asks.

'Don't look at me,' Maisie says. 'I'm shitting bricks as it is.'

'Does anyone know anything about that clip?' Eddie asks.

'It was a Christmas party, a couple of years ago,' Caz says. 'It was put up on YouTube at the time – and before you ask me, this sick joke wasn't my idea,' she says, giving Rex a challenging look. 'I can't imagine Britt or Janet engineering this either.' She turns to Stella. 'I hope you're okay. You must have got a terrible shock. Can I get you a nightcap or anything?'

'No, thanks, I'm going back to bed,' Stella says.

'We'll all go up together,' Rex says, clicking off the light in the media room as they leave.

They are plunged into semi-darkness, a column of faint light coming from the open bedroom doors illuminating the first-floor landing. The shadowy vault of the hallway and stairwell look eerie to Eddie, coming on top of the malicious prank. 'I need a shot of something,' he says, going into the home bar in search of whiskey. It's clear someone in the house has to have set up that video. It was designed to rattle and upset, and it was particularly venomous. But it's not as if anyone is deliberately threatening them, is it?

TWO DAYS EARLIER
SATURDAY, 28 JANUARY

CHAPTER TWENTY-SIX

Stella

Stella leans against the kitchen island and gulps down two cups of coffee in quick succession. The gale of the night before has died down, and from outside, the staccato whirr of a helicopter flying in loops over the sea cuts ribbons through her heart. Tension is running like an electric eel through the house this Saturday morning, and there are moments when she feels she can't breathe.

She has no idea yet as to the identity of the person mercilessly trolling her.

After dinner last night, when she'd been asking everyone about Lucinda's last day, she'd had the gut feeling that it was them against her, that somehow Lucinda's friends had closed ranks, shutting her firmly out. She felt instinctively that they each knew something they weren't about to tell her. For such good friends, someone must have known about the announcement Lucinda was planning to make.

And other things didn't add up. Janet and Aaron had been staying in one of the larger first-floor bedrooms adjoining Eddie and Sasha. But from what Janet had said, she'd been in the Jacuzzi with Aaron during the time Eddie had been sleeping off the effects of his afternoon. So how did she hear him snoring? One of them is telling lies, perhaps both. Or covering up for someone. And who had been having sex in Lucinda's bedroom, when she was at Britt's, inadvertently preventing Stella from making an attempt to talk to her?

Stella forces herself back to the moment. Sitting in front of the stove, Eddie is in full flow with Britt and Janet about last night's incident.

'Someone copied Lucinda's original YouTube clip and doctored it,' he is saying. 'It was set up to play on repeat.'

'Mother of God, that's appalling,' Britt says. 'I'm used to sleeping through the noise of the wind, so it takes a lot to disturb me, but I can't believe I slept through that, and I can't believe someone stooped to do such a thing.'

She darts a worried glance at Stella, who shrugs her shoulders in reply.

'It's insane,' Janet says. 'I'm glad I missed it all. I was exhausted after everything and conked out the minute my head hit the pillow.'

Stella wonders if Janet is telling the truth. She knows none of Lucinda's friends are going to admit to hooking up the video, but they all know it has to have been one of them. A macabre joke, in vile taste. Surely the work of her troll. However, this morning she has more urgent things on her mind. Imelda has confirmed she'll be calling in to update Stella on the recovery operation, and that is adding to the general air of unease.

Rex comes over, looking apologetic. She'd had breakfast with him earlier. He'd made her toast and scrambled eggs and she'd forced herself to eat some although she wasn't hungry.

She's finding it a bit unreal, seeing him in this place that was so full of Lucinda, and out of their usual Dublin context, but she's so glad he's here, the one person she can trust. The one person who is there for her and not caught up in the vigil. He'd had to go up to his room to send some emails, and now he's back down again, dropping a kiss on the top of her head.

'Hey, I've to leave you for a while. I've to pop to Dunmullen to pick up a couple of essentials I forgot to bring. Do you need anything?'

'Not that I can think of, except – maybe see if anyone wants to go with you. You could cut the tension with a knife and it's doing my head in.'

'I'm sure it is, and last night didn't help. I'll take some of them out of your hair. We could get lunch out, but only if you're okay with that? It'll give you some breathing space. Unless you need me around?'

'No, go ahead,' she says.

With the exception of Britt, they all want to escape the strained and sad atmosphere, so shortly before midday they pile into Rex's car, Eddie in front, Caz, Maisie and Janet in the rear. Stella has only a short while to absorb the relative peace when she gets a text from Imelda to say they're on the way. She's sitting in the cosy area beside the stove when Britt lets them in.

Imelda and, looking at Stella with a thoughtful gaze, Hugh Connell.

The sight of him is like a deluge of icy cold water rushing through her veins.

'What are you doing here?' She bristles.

He shrugs. 'All part of the job.'

'I wasn't expecting you,' she says ungraciously.

Britt glances at Hugh with interest, before throwing a quizzical glance at Stella. 'Can I get tea or coffee for anyone?' she asks.

Their answers are simultaneous.

'Yes, tea would be lovely, please,' says Imelda.

'No, thanks,' says Hugh.

'Right, so. One tea coming up. How about you, Stella?'

Stella wants to tell her to shut up about tea. She wants to scream that the sight of Hugh Connell standing there is shredding the last of her fragile composure. She sees herself leading him into her bedroom, wanting him with a ferocity that flayed every cell in her body, wanting to lose herself in the sweet pleasure of his, finding instead that Hugh awakened a new, uninhibited, sensual version of Stella Oliver that scared her. Where is Rex when she needs him? He is a far safer option, and would paper over the hot embarrassment of that night.

A mistake.

'No, thanks,' she says.

'We won't hold you up for too long,' Imelda says, loosening her jacket and sitting on the opposite sofa. 'We know it's a difficult time for you.' She looks around the room. 'Have your friends arrived?'

'Yes, four of them who were here that weekend.'

'They've gone across to Dunmullen,' Britt says.

This might be an opportunity, Stella thinks, to mention last night's disturbance. Which, added to the other incidents, suggests one of them is hell bent on tormenting her. And what about her fears that Lucinda's tragedy couldn't have been an unfortunate accident? Yet what evidence has she? Nothing but gut feelings and a couple of unsavoury incidents. Hugh would have examined Lucinda's file and the investigation has stalled. Who knows? Her tormentor could be right, and Stella, with her harsh words, was to blame for Lucinda going over the edge.

Imelda takes out a notebook. 'Please bear with me, Stella, while I update you with what's happening.'

Stella forces everything else out of her head. The plans for this evening take priority. Everything else can wait.

'Thankfully the weather is favourable this afternoon,' Imelda says, 'and the recovery will be proceeding. The platform will be in place later.'

'Platform?' Stella echoes, a prism of terror slicing down through her chest.

'With the crane,' she says gently. 'It's a delicate operation, and will be a slow manoeuvre, but we expect the, ah, recovery to be reaching the quayside around half past five this evening.'

The full significance of her words is a punch in the gut. Stella is afraid to meet Hugh's gaze in case he sees the terror reflected in hers.

'The quayside is already cordoned off from the general public,' Imelda says softly. 'Only certain personnel are allowed through, same with the area around the recovery site. There are patrols out on surveillance ensuring it's being kept clear.'

'Is that the reason for the helicopter we keep hearing outside?' Britt asks.

'Yes, among other things … It's a multi-agency effort between the gardaí and the Navy. We're taking all necessary precautions to ensure the operation flows as smoothly as possible, and with due dignity to Lucinda, her family and friends. The car will be completely covered as soon as it's lifted onto the platform before it's conveyed to the quayside.'

'What happens then?' asks Britt.

Stella braces herself. Hugh had quietly gone through the process with her on Wednesday evening so that she'd be fully aware of it. 'Better to hear in the privacy of your own home,' he'd said. 'Give you a chance to get your head around it.'

'Once the recovery operation reaches the quayside, the car will be removed to the safety of a garda compound for full examination and investigation,' Imelda says, more or less repeating what Hugh had already told her. 'That will take several days. In the meantime, any human remains found inside the car will be brought to the University Hospital for examination and forensic DNA identification. Stella, you might have to—'

'That's all covered,' Hugh says gruffly.

Stella has already handed in one of Lucinda's hairbrushes.

'We'll arrange a car to bring you down to the quayside this evening,' Hugh says.

'That won't be necessary,' Stella says.

'Hugh has it all arranged,' Imelda checks her notes, 'and he's one of the powers-that-be.'

'It's for your own safety,' Hugh says. 'The area will be busy. We'll get you through the cordon and find a suitable and safe place for you away from any media.'

Something else she had forgotten about: they'll have to brave any curious throngs gathered outside the cordon.

'How many are in your party altogether?' Hugh asks.

Britt answers, 'Me, Stella, and there are five more.'

'All part of the group who were here originally?'

'No, four are part of that group. Another friend, Rex O'Neill, is here.'

Britt's glance drifts to Stella as she mentions Rex's name. Hugh picks up on it immediately, turning to her with a bland look on his face, 'A friend of yours or Lucinda's?'

'A friend of mine.'

Hugh says, 'Right,' in a bored tone.

Stella flicks him another glance and finds him studying her. He looks away immediately. 'So that's seven altogether,' he says smoothly. 'We'll send up two cars. We'll let you know when to expect us, but it'll be sometime after five o'clock.'

A fresh wave of panic slams into Stella. It's finally happening. Her sister is being returned to her, her beautiful, effervescent, golden Lucinda. Under cover of darkness, and shrouded in heavy-duty tarpaulin, a technical operation and part of the job for strangers who never knew her, a morbid object of curiosity for the salacious, dopamine-fix masses, hungry for their social-media hits. She's not ready for this. She jumps to her feet and makes it to the downstairs bathroom in the nick of time, watching her breakfast propel into the toilet bowl. When she eventually emerges, having cleaned her face as best she could, Britt is waiting outside, a roll of kitchen paper in her hands. 'Thanks,' Stella says, shivering in the aftermath.

'I'll get you some hot tea,' she says. 'The guards are leaving.'

'I'll say goodbye to them first.' With as much dignity as she can muster, she goes back to the living area, where Imelda and Hugh are already on their feet.

'You okay, Stella?' Imelda asks.

She nods. 'It happens occasionally if I get very stressed or panicky.'

'It's a difficult day,' Imelda says. 'Call me at any time if you want to talk. I mean that, Stella. Anyhow, we'll see you this evening. I'll give you a text when we're on our way over to you.'

'Thanks.'

They head up the hall, Hugh hanging back when he reaches the door. He touches her arm. 'It'll be fine, Stella,' he says gently. 'You can trust the team. And it's good that Lucinda's car has been found. In time it'll help you accept what has happened and gain some form of closure. I hope you've moved beyond beating yourself up with a pile of regrets.'

It's a direct reference to the night they spent together and it floors her.

They'd been awake into the small hours, as though dazed by what had flared between them, neither of them wanting to sleep or bring the night to an end. Lying beside him, Stella finally unburdened herself of the ever-present, all-powerful black monster that lived in her soul, those last few moments with her sister and the terrible words she'd flung at her.

Hugh didn't try to fix it, but he said things to help her look beyond the darkness and find an easier way of living with it.

'What does five minutes of anger count, in the hours and hours of a lifetime of looking out for your sister?' he'd said. 'Do you think Lucinda would want you to be beating yourself up over this on top of grieving for her? If, God forbid, the situation was reversed, what would you say to Lucinda if she was carrying the weight of this regret?'

'I'd hate to see her unhappy,' Stella had said. 'I'd tell her to live every day of her life to the absolute max and I'd send out waves of love, enough, I'd hope, to dissolve every scrap of her sadness.'

'That's a beautiful thought, Stella,' he'd said. 'Whenever you feel trapped in a dark cave – of your own making, I have to add – I'd like you to imagine Lucinda sending out those same thoughts to you.'

She wishes Hugh hadn't referenced that night. Because now she feels raw to her very bones as she stands at the door of The Lookout watching him walk out into the grey January day.

CHAPTER TWENTY-SEVEN

Stella

A mood of impending gloom deepens in The Lookout as the afternoon wears on. The group had returned from Dunmullen, becoming subdued when Stella brought them up to date with the recovery plan. Now Maisie and Caz are drinking endless coffee at the kitchen island, glancing out the windows every so often into the shadows settling around the misty afternoon. From the front windows, pinpricks of light indicate a steady stream of traffic coming around the bend in the peninsula before they disappear, swallowed by the folds in the landscape. Rex, Eddie and Janet are on the sofas talking quietly among themselves. Britt has already set out tea lights, matches and torches, ready and waiting on the hall table.

Someone's mobile shrills – Rex's. He disappears into the hall to take the call and comes back in presently, beckoning for Stella to join him, a flustered look on his face.

'What's up?' she asks, alarmed at his expression.

He puts his hands on her shoulders. 'I feel terrible about this, but I'm sorry, I can't join you on the quays this evening.'

She almost slumps against him. 'Is that all? I thought from your face something was seriously wrong.'

'It is, in so far as there's been a messy security breach in the Passport Office's IT system and I have been called up to help sort it out. That means I have to put in a few hours' work. But, look, if you really need me, I'll try to get someone else on my team to step in and lead it.'

'No, it's fine. You'll be here when I get back. I'll have Britt, and Lucinda's friends with me.' Even if one of them is her troll, they couldn't get up to much down at the quays this evening.

Britt heats a large pot of vegetable soup at half past four, Rex dishing it out before he heads back upstairs to work. Tadhg has already delivered a large cottage pie and a vegan lasagne to be reheated when they arrive back from the quayside. At five o'clock the text from Imelda comes through, and at half past five, Stella's legs almost buckle beneath her when two cars draw up outside the house.

Hugh arrives into the hall, where they are in various stages of donning coats, hats and scarves.

'Everybody ready?' he asks. Stella senses he is directing the question at her.

She nods, even though she feels outside her body, which is a mess of painful nerve endings inside.

'Is this it?' he asks, scanning the group.

'Yep,' she says. 'Rex can't come. He has to work.'

He lifts an eyebrow. 'Right then, Stella, you're in the car with me, and we'll take two more.'

'Britt,' she says. 'And Caz?'

Caz takes a breath and Stella senses she, too, is feeling the dreadful enormity of it all. 'Sure,' she says, stepping forward.

'The rest of ye can travel in the next car with Imelda,' Hugh says. 'When you're on the quays, please stay together at all times. I'll show you where to go. There are a few people around. Best not to pay them any attention.'

Then Hugh is leading her towards a dark saloon car, piercing blue lights flickering above the headlights slicing through the shadows in the dark Kerry evening. Despite her legs feeling like water, she manages to get into the back of the car, sitting behind the driver, Britt clutching a bag with candles and torches beside her and Caz next to her. Hugh is in the front passenger seat, and after throwing her a quick concerned glance, he stares out the windscreen, his face set, his expression remote.

As they approach the end of the lane, before taking the hairpin fork that leads down to the cove, a man dressed in high-vis gear appears out of the murk. He lifts a red and white traffic cone that is sitting in the centre of the laneway and waves them on.

'What was that in aid of?' Britt asks.

'Just keeping prying eyes away from Wolf Head and making sure you have no unwelcome visitors,' Hugh says matter-of-factly.

'Thank you,' Britt says. 'If these were your orders, Hugh, we appreciate it.'

'Just part of the job.'

Then they are rolling down the hill that leads to the cove, where two further officers in high-vis are on patrol by the side of the road. Stella catches a glimpse of the cove below before they veer around the final bend.

The crescent-shaped area is all lit up. Normally, the night-time darkness is broken only by the lights from The Pier, a few running along by the quayside, and those shining from the scatter of houses. Now, lit by arc lamps, the area is a hive of activity, figures in yellow and orange fluorescent overalls moving about with an air of purpose. A boat pulls in and figures dressed in diving equipment disembark. Over to one side, there is a slew of garda vans and cars, a fire engine, blue strobe lights flashing, and closest to the quays, a large flatbed truck, the sight of which turns Stella's blood to ice. Around another bend, and they are on the final descent down into the cove, before the road levels out in its run along the quays.

They are here.

Hugh disappears along with the cars. They form a tight group, standing to one side, directed by a man in a bright orange jacket. Caz and Maisie on one side of Stella, Britt, Eddie and Janet on the other.

Stella senses a slight disturbance running through the small crowd of locals gathered outside The Pier, like a breeze riffling the top of tall grass. A murmuring that stops as suddenly as it started. She shudders. Who might be in the crowd outside The Pier or up on the road behind them, armed with mobiles ready for a photo opportunity?

She sees something coming around by the harbour wall, moving in a small arc before it straightens and sets course for the quayside. It moves slowly, looming through the dark evening, lights in front of it and behind. More than one vessel, she realises, as it clears the harbour wall. A small flotilla. Some kind of naval boat hauling a platform in its wake, and behind that, another boat with a heavy-duty crane. There are three fishing trawlers rigged with lighting in the small cavalcade, one in front and one to each side of the boat hauling the platform. Tadhg Fitzmaurice, she guesses, and others, forming some sort of guard of honour, as a mark of respect. Three more boats follow in their wake.

The group is silent, the wind has calmed, the mist has settled and their tea lights flicker on saucers. Then the activity intensifies. As the small procession of boats approaches, Stella makes out a dark, covered shape sitting on the platform and a chill runs through her. Lucinda, her beautiful sister, coming home in the most devastating way possible.

A new energy seems to ripple around the quayside, figures hauling ropes, the flatbed truck edging closer to the pier, another crane appearing out of the night. Britt hands around more tea lights and they watch as the minutes tick by and the boat carrying Stella's precious cargo gradually comes closer and closer until, finally, it reaches the quayside. Several figures dart about, securing it to its moorings. In a daze, she watches the preparations for the last part of the recovery, figures scurrying around with ropes and cables, preparing for the winching of the covered car from the platform up onto the flatbed truck. Pain shoots through her head and she feels dizzy. No matter how well the gardaí have kept the crowd back from the scene, a lot of them can't fail to see the covered car being hoisted slowly into the air, swaying gently for a moment, water dripping from gaps in the underbelly of the tarpaulin, before it's placed in position on the back of the truck. A further tarpaulin is laid over this; ropes and cables are pulled fast to secure it.

Out of the gloom and the teams of people moving purposefully about the scene, others getting into garda vans and cars, Hugh appears. 'It might be best if you all move back a little,' he says.

They are standing on the road the truck will have to take out of the cove. Stella senses the others falling back and rearranging themselves. She doesn't think she can do it, that she can even move, but Britt has her arm around her and begins to guide her across to the path. Hugh is on her other side. Stella stumbles, and he puts his hand on her arm to steady her.

'How are you doing?' he asks, not releasing his hold.

'So-so,' she says, her teeth chattering. Then she asks him the question that has been burning in her brain all day. 'Is Lucinda – did they – is she …?'

Hugh bows his head. 'I'm so sorry, Stella, but, yes, it appears so. They have confirmed there are human remains in the car, although that won't be made public yet.'

He seems to hold her arm for a long time while her limbs shake at the impact of the news, even though she'd been expecting it. The last ray of a tiny flame of hope flickers out.

In the dark of the night, another of her fantasies had been that, maybe, Lucinda had somehow jumped clear of the car and was hiding for now, acutely embarrassed at all the trouble she had caused, waiting for the right moment to come back into their lives. But her rational self knew that Lucinda didn't do embarrassment. Had she been in that situation, she would have been proud of her narrow escape.

Hugh waits with Stella while another sad cavalcade forms, this time on the quayside. The flatbed truck has moved away from the edge and into position on the road, a garda car in front of it, and another taking up the rear. She has to brace herself and not scream aloud as it advances slowly towards her. She keeps her gaze fixed on the ground and can only see the reflection of the blue strobe lights on the damp tarmac and the spray shooting from the big wheels of the truck as it hisses past. A smothered gasp from behind her – Caz most likely. Then the sad convoy is gone, picking up a little speed as soon as it clears the quays, up the incline out of Wolf Cove, around the bend, and out of her sight.

She is the last one holding a flickering tea light and then she blows it out.

Cars are moving off now, including the fire engine, a van full of divers. Personnel are hauling equipment off another boat. Onlookers begin to move away, the spectacle over.

'I'll get the cars to bring you back,' Hugh says.

'Thank you,' she says. 'And thanks for all your help.'

'No bother.' He pauses, his face filled with kindness, looking at her as though he's going to say something, then continuing, 'I'm back up to Dublin tonight but don't hesitate to call me if you need to. As soon as there's any news, I'll let you know.'

'Thanks.'

'You're welcome, Stella.'

A final light pressure on her arm, a half-smile. Then the look of tenderness is gone, replaced by a focused, purposeful mask – his work face – and she wonders if she has imagined his empathy because she needs it so badly.

CHAPTER TWENTY-EIGHT

Caz

Back in The Lookout, Rex is ready and waiting to welcome them, fussing around Stella, pouring drinks for those who want them. Everyone seems subdued, drifting aimlessly around downstairs, and Caz is happy to hold off on a drink for now, slipping up to her room for a short respite before the evening meal is served. She steps into the shower, hoping to feel she is washing away some traces of that depressing quayside vigil, but she still feels it clinging to her, like a cloak of sadness. It lingers afterwards, when she changes into a cosy, soft-knit leisure top and leggings, donning her black-framed glasses in place of her contacts. With her face free of make-up, her blonde hair scraped back in a small bun, she couldn't look any less like Caz Costello, celebrity make-up artist and hair stylist to the stars.

And who cares?

Lucinda's not around any more to encourage her to put on her sparkle or up her game. Missing her is like a constant knife in Caz's heart.

And Eddie?

He doesn't care either.

God – she'd been so furious with how much she'd longed to fall into his arms on the corridor last night when that spooky noise had disturbed them. He's not interested in her. Hadn't that been a lesson hard-learned? She's only here this weekend to get closure as far as Lucinda's accident is concerned, she reminds herself. And find out if anyone suspected the secret Lucinda had shared with Caz. But she hadn't expected to see the ghost of Lucinda rattling her everywhere she looked. And she hadn't expected to feel a fresh stab in her gut when she'd stepped into the bathroom last evening and remembered Eddie's antics in the Jacuzzi.

She straightens her spine and goes downstairs. The worst is over. She has braved the quayside and done her duty by Lucinda. She's kept her secrets. Tomorrow night she'll be back in the bright city lights of London. She decides there and then that she's never coming back to Ireland.

After the evening meal, everyone gravitates to the seating area. The side lamps throw out a soft glow and Britt has put out tea lights, placing them safely wherever she can, in the centre of the island counter, on low tables, on the sideboard that runs behind the sofas, so that small plumes of dancing light are reflected in the dark expanse of the glass. While Rex is fixing after-dinner drinks, Britt excuses herself. 'I'm a bit flattened,' she says. 'I'm going to call it a day.'

Flattened? Britt looks totally wiped out, Caz realises, giving her a hug goodnight. Her face looks sunken. The last few months have clearly taken a toll on her, not helped, she guesses, by living up the coast from Wolf Head.

'I'm hoping we might talk of Lucinda again tonight,' Stella says tentatively. 'Just for an hour or two. In the middle of all this … sadness, I'd love us all to remember our best moment with her, when we were the happiest with her.'

Caz bites her lip. Nobody seems to want to be the first to respond. Rex is sitting beside Stella and Caz sees him reaching for her hand, squeezing it gently. She gives him a grateful smile.

'We're all leaving tomorrow,' Stella goes on, her voice a bit stronger. 'It's probably the last time we'll be together like this, and I'm grateful you dropped everything to be here and share this difficult time with me … It would be good to end the weekend on a positive note, remembering a happy time with Lucinda, rather than being sad over this evening's events.'

'You mean like a sort of wake?' Caz says.

'Kind of. But I don't expect anyone to stay up past midnight. We all have to travel in the morning.'

'Great idea, Stella,' Rex says. 'Good memories of Lucinda instead of being preoccupied by the circumstances of her tragedy. I'll keep the drinks flowing.'

'I think I'll have a whiskey,' Eddie says, getting up and going over to the bottles of wine and spirits on the kitchen island. He comes back with a generous measure. 'Sounds like I'm going to need this.' He tilts his glass and smiles across at Caz, a sad little we're-all-in-this-together kind of smile that immediately gets her back up.

'I think we all know your happiest moment with Lucinda,' she can't help saying to him. 'We were all there to witness it. Even Stella got an eyeful.'

Too late, she realises she shouldn't have spoken about Stella like that, as though she was somehow an outsider, set apart from the circle of Lucinda's friends. 'Sorry, Stella, I didn't mean that to come out the way it did.'

Stella blinks, as though she's miles away. She shakes her head. 'No worries.'

'Just what did you mean?' Eddie asks, his eyes flinty.

'You know full well,' Caz says, unable to prevent an image of Eddie and Lucinda churning freshly in her head. 'We were all there to witness you getting almost naked and simulating sex in front of everybody, including your girlfriend. Great fun altogether.'

Eddie stares down into his glass before looking across at Caz with a humbled expression on his face. 'Believe me, I'm not proud of that moment,' he admits. 'I don't know how it happened, or what devil got into me. I don't blame Sasha for dumping me.'

'Aw, Eddie, you must have been furious with Lucinda for causing that break-up,' Maisie says.

Caz almost chokes on her gin. What does Maisie think she's playing at? Making Eddie out to be angry with Lucinda? Still, she had started this, Caz realises. No matter how much her heart had twisted, it was wrong of her to put Eddie on the spot, never mind selecting a rather tawdry memory of Lucinda to pull out in front of Stella.

'I apologise, Stella,' she says. 'I didn't mean to be insensitive, bringing up this particular memory.'

'Look, Caz, everyone,' Stella sighs, 'if you have anything you'd like to share about Lucinda, even if you think it's less than flattering, I'm happy to hear it, especially if it's giving you any kind of difficulty or grief. She was my sister and I know she wasn't perfect. None of us is. I know how guilty I've been feeling since our row, and I wouldn't wish it on anyone. It's no secret that the booze was flying that weekend. Even if Lucinda wasn't drinking, she got a bit carried away, to say the least. I had words with her myself about it, and who knows? Maybe the same silly devil got into you, Eddie, as got into Lucinda, whatever it was.'

Caz doesn't like the way Eddie is suddenly staring at Stella, as though he's looking at a ghost. She feels goose pimples on her neck.

'D'you know, Stella, I think you have something there,' he says slowly. He turns to Maisie, his face dark. 'Were you messing with my drinks as well?'

CHAPTER TWENTY-NINE

Maisie

What the fuck, Eddie? Why did you go there?

Maisie looks around at the sea of faces. Even laid-back Rex is sitting up straighter. How could she explain herself? Start by saying how different she'd felt from all of them that weekend? That the more they'd lounged around the pool that Thursday evening, all of them looking like beautiful, entitled people, the sadder her own life appeared, and the more the image of Lucinda's golden arms wrapped around her then boyfriend in a secluded part of a Santorini beach had burned into her brain?

She'd been nine months short of her fortieth birthday, that weekend in The Lookout, but never in a million years had Maisie thought that an edgy teenage angst could unleash itself as powerful and destructive as ever as she approached that supposedly mature birthday. A shot of alcohol now and again into those mocktail concoctions for Lucinda, to make her a little careless – it was ridiculous that she wasn't drinking on her birthday weekend.

The result had been more spectacular than she'd expected, a naked Lucinda prancing around, all inhibitions cast away. Then it had been easy to take it all one step further, by making sure Eddie and Aaron were sufficiently hammered to join in with the act – let some of the others see how it felt to have their man up close and personal with Lucinda.

But they are right in what they say about revenge – it might seem sweet at the time, and it certainly had, but the aftertaste is bitter, and now she knows all about that.

She'd been hoping no one had spotted what she'd been up to that weekend, but she'd sensed from the speculative way Eddie had been looking at her yesterday at lunch that he knew all about her spiteful behaviour. Now the mean and vindictive side to her nature has been exposed in front of them all.

'You were messing with drinks? Were you *spiking* Lucinda's mocktails?' Stella asks, her face taut.

'Jesus Christ, Maisie, did that really happen?' Caz says.

'Not as such,' Maisie says, trying to row back a bit. 'But I might have given Lucinda a shot of something now and again.'

'Oh, Jesus.' Caz shakes her head. 'No wonder Lucinda seemed wired some of the time.'

'Lucinda told me she hadn't been drinking at all,' Stella said quietly, almost to herself. 'I couldn't understand how she seemed to be sloshed.'

'It was just to make sure the party went in the right direction,' Maisie says.

'And what direction was that?' Stella asks.

'I wanted to make sure Lucinda was enjoying herself to the full.'

'By making sure she was wasted?' Caz asks furiously. 'I knew you resented her for years, but this – Christ, Maisie, there was no need for that.'

'You've no idea the harm you were doing, Maisie,' Eddie says. 'Sasha told me, when we weren't shouting at each other on the way back to Dublin, that she'd seen you chucking a shot into Lucinda's mocktails a few times. How often did you do that? Were you messing with my drinks as well?'

Maisie shrugs, unable to meet his eyes.

'Even Aaron?' Janet says, her face pale.

Maisie stays silent.

'You didn't mind that Lucinda was enjoying herself with my husband, did you?' Janet says, her voice shaking. 'What was that all about? Had it anything to do with Santorini?'

'Why should it have anything to do with Santorini?' Maisie asks, feeling icy inside. She'd hoped that Lucinda had kept that torrid little secret to herself.

Janet doesn't get a chance to reply before Caz jumps in, rounding on Maisie. 'Don't tell me that was why Lucinda was all over Eddie and Aaron like a rash. You messed with her drinks and it made her act the fool? And the same with the guys?'

Maisie stares at her. Jesus, it sounds awful. If anything, she's proved to them all how stupid and silly she was.

'Holy shit, Maisie, why?' Caz presses.

Maisie shrugs. 'It seemed a good idea at the time ...'

'Not if Lucinda was so wasted she went over Wolf Head by mistake,' Eddie says.

Maisie drops her head into her hands.

'Hang on. Let's not jump to conclusions,' Stella says. 'Lucinda seemed fine on Saturday, unless—'

'Unless what?' Caz says.

'She came back here after dropping the guys to the quays and someone interfered with her drinks again,' Stella says.

'I didn't,' Maisie says.

'Look, Maisie,' Stella says, 'anything I can find out about Lucinda's last days is absolutely crucial to me. But I don't understand why you felt the need to mess with anyone's drink. The party seemed lively enough without anyone having to fuel it further.'

Maisie feels trapped, all the eyes in the room upon her. Eddie started this, even though he'd said he wasn't going to spill the beans. And she knows exactly how to take the heat off herself.

'There is something, Stella,' she says. 'I'm not sure if you know. But you could start by asking Eddie how much money Lucinda owed him. I gather it was rather a lot.'

There is an eerie, ringing silence before a wave of tension reverberates around the space they're sitting in, so thick it almost suffocates Maisie.

Eddie is on his feet. 'You fucking bitch.'

CHAPTER THIRTY

Janet

Janet's head feels as if it's going to burst. From the time Maisie admitted she'd spiked Aaron's drinks, she's been making a huge effort to focus on her breathing. Inhale through her nose, fill her belly as deeply as possible, before a long, slow exhale. She is sitting on the sofa at right angles to Stella and Rex, and directly opposite where Caz and Maisie are sitting. From here she can see the flickering tea lights Britt arranged on the sideboard that divides the seating area from the dining table. She tries to focus on the tiny plumes of dancing light, rather than the implications of Maisie's words. Or the way Caz had said that Maisie had resented Lucinda for years. Something is snaking through the back of her head that she can't quite grasp.

But Eddie has jumped to his feet and called Maisie a bitch in a hard tone she's never heard him use before, and the angry vibes coming off him are zinging around in the air.

Caz and Stella speak at once.

'What money?'

'What do you mean?'

Eddie slowly shakes his head. His face is shadowy whichever way the soft light falls on him, his mouth set in a grim line. Then, all of a sudden, it's as if whatever has been holding him upright has snapped. He collapses back onto the sofa.

'Who told you?' he asks Maisie, his voice hoarse.

So it's true. Despite the tense circumstances, Janet can't help feeling a spike of adrenaline land in her chest.

'What's this all about?' Stella asks.

Eddie ignores her. He is staring at Maisie as if she's the only person in the room.

'Your lovely, indiscreet ex-girlfriend told me,' Maisie says, in a small, victorious voice.

'Sasha?'

'Yes, that last evening when the two of us were sitting out by the terrace bar,' Maisie says. 'She was furious with you after the carry-on in the Jacuzzi. She was only too happy to drop you in it with me. You told her about it one night shortly before the party weekend. She didn't know if you remembered afterwards, because you were pretty sozzled. You said it was the only reason you were coming down to The Lookout, to make sure you got your money back.'

'And you've known all this time.'

'Yes.'

'You kept information tucked away in case it proved useful to you. You're a right piece of work.'

Maisie looks stung. Then she shrugs. 'No more than yourself, Eddie.'

'All right, everyone,' Stella says. 'Let's calm down for a moment. I hope nobody is deliberately keeping anything from me that might shed light on Lucinda's accident, but ...' she pauses '... maybe you know something important without

231

realising it. Maisie, if you had a particular grudge against Lucinda, maybe we could talk privately.'

Janet feels she's standing on the edge of a chasm. The reason why Maisie could have resented Lucinda is beginning to clamour in her ear, making her feel faint. Had she seen anything, that evening in Santorini? What did she know?

Stella is still talking. 'Eddie, the same goes for you. I need to talk to you about this, to know what kind of money problems Lucinda had and if they were significant. Don't feel the need to spare me anything. I'd rather know.'

'In fairness to Stella,' Rex says, 'whatever was going on with her sister, she deserves to know, especially in the circumstances.'

'I'd say ten grand is fairly significant,' Maisie says.

Someone gasps. Caz.

'Jaysus!' Rex.

Janet's afraid to think of what must have been festering inside Maisie for so long to cause her to be such a bitch. She feels it for Eddie, sitting defeated beside her.

'Look, it happened,' Eddie says. 'I'm not going into details. I didn't mind giving the loan – Lucinda's granted me lots of favours over the years, plenty of free publicity. My business wouldn't have been what it was without her celebrity stamp of approval ...' His voice trails away, Janet guessing he realises he's wading into dark waters, with his business gone kaput.

'Did she pay you back, that weekend?' Stella asks.

'No,' Eddie says.

A taut silence. Janet can't help thinking of the lavish way

they'd partied, each of them contributing a sizeable amount to the kitty.

'And then your business went belly-up,' Maisie says.

Trust Maisie to stick in the knife.

'Hey,' Eddie says, 'I know what you're all thinking, but I'd nothing to do with Lucinda's accident. I know it looks like I could have had a row with her that got out of hand, quite possible after the way Maisie spiked our drinks ...'

Janet swallows hard. Exactly the kind of scenario she'd been imagining, but with Aaron.

'But I didn't,' he says. 'Soon after that weekend, the insurance for my business was due to be renewed. The cost of it had gone through the roof, and with the lack of cash flow, the bank wouldn't extend any further credit. The running costs were fast becoming ridiculous anyway, and I decided to cut my losses. Whichever way the figures fell, my dockland apartment is gone, as is my motor. I feel such a failure. But why would I have hurt Lucinda? At least while she was alive, I had some chance of getting the money back.'

Eddie's voice cracks and there's a sheen of tears in his eyes. He looks and sounds like a broken man.

Caz speaks. 'Eddie,' she says quietly, 'you're not a failure. Anything but. It's unfortunate, but a fact of life, that many independent businesses have gone bust in the last year because of ridiculously high running costs.'

Eddie glances at her in grateful surprise, as though he'd been drowning and she's thrown him a life raft.

Caz continues, 'I don't think anyone here would imagine for one moment that you'd have it in you to harm a hair of Lucinda's head. We all know how much you loved her. How much we all loved her, even if it doesn't look quite like that right now.' Caz glances around the group, nodding to Stella, finishing with a meaningful look at Maisie.

Janet relaxes momentarily. No more than Eddie, surely Aaron wouldn't have had it in him to harm Lucinda in any way? How could she even think such a thing? But whatever is eating Maisie, she hasn't finished.

'We all loved her, for sure,' Maisie says. 'But if you ask me,' she goes on recklessly, 'she seems to have had every one of us under her thumb for one reason or another.'

'Under her thumb?' Stella picks up her words. 'What do you mean?'

CHAPTER THIRTY-ONE

Maisie

'Yes, Maisie, what's all this about?' Janet asks.

Both Stella and Janet are challenging her. Maisie knows she should be keeping her mouth shut. She came out of that little skirmish with Eddie on the wrong side. The main thing was to divert everyone away from the reason she'd messed with the drinks. But was the fact that Lucinda had seduced her then boyfriend any more humiliating than the way she was getting old aggravations off her chest? If anything, she's proved how small-minded she is.

'It's obvious Eddie was infatuated with her,' she says, needing to justify her words. She turns to Janet. 'And you always fell in with her plans, whatever they involved. Even going back long before the party, you were always available for whatever she wanted to do, nights out, partying, even cancelling your own plans to suit her ... I saw it in the messages on our WhatsApp group.'

Janet shakes her head as though Maisie is talking nonsense.

Maisie goes on, anxious to save face, 'Even Caz didn't escape her net, did you, Caz?'

'What – *me*?'

'You put your life on hold for her.'

Caz gives a short laugh. 'I don't know where you're getting that idea from.'

'You passed up on opportunities that didn't come again.'

'What opportunities?'

'When you dropped out of college, at the same time as Lucinda? Going off to London with her to seek your fortunes?'

'That was years ago.'

Maisie is on a roll. 'You could have been anything, Caz. Look at how hard you studied when you got that college course. You were determined to get on in life but you blew it by walking away because Lucinda wanted you to hold her hand.'

'No, she didn't. I made my own decision to go and we had a ball.'

'I'd like to have gone too, but you wouldn't wait for me to finish my exams. Then you came home after a few months with your future hanging in mid-air. What's the betting that was Lucinda's decision?'

'For Christ's sake, Maisie,' Caz says, clearly exasperated, 'that was years ago. We've all moved on since then. Who knows? I might have dropped out of that college course anyway. I went on to something more suited to me and I don't think I'm doing that badly for myself. You mightn't know this, but I'm quite successful in my field.'

'But when your golden opportunity to go to Hollywood arrived, you passed on that too.'

'Hollywood? When was this?' Stella asks.

'Earlier last year,' Maisie says. 'Caz passed up on an offer to work on a rom-com movie in Hollywood because she would have missed Lucinda's party. That was a huge price to pay.'

'So? Work will always come around again, but I don't see the purpose in all this,' Caz snaps.

'I'm pointing out that Lucinda had you in the palm of her hand as well,' Maisie says, 'which you must have resented at times.'

Caz is frowning at her.

'This seems to be turning into a right bitching session,' Stella says.

'I'm sorry, Stella.' Maisie summons the grace to apologise. 'I didn't mean to upset you or veer off the agenda.'

'I'm not making excuses for anyone, but I think we're all totally mega-stressed with the weekend,' Caz says. 'Lucinda ...' She blinks back sudden tears. 'Oh, gosh, she was a huge part of our lives, and we're all still in bits after her accident. We can only imagine how tough it's been on you, Stella. I loved Lucinda,' she says. 'I loved her since we were thirteen years old. Let's move on from the unpleasant words.' She gulps. 'I'd like everyone to see another side to Lucinda.'

Caz waits a few moments, pulling herself together. 'Lucinda saved me,' she says. 'I was a misfit, an unhappy teenager. I hated myself and I hated this strange new big school I found myself in, I felt on the outside of the gangs in the classroom. And then Lucinda sat beside me for French class and we got chatting. I couldn't believe it when she seemed to like me. Lucinda was her own self, flitting over all the cliques, taking me with her, under her wing. I found I could talk to her ...' Caz hesitates before continuing. 'See,

I was being … abused by my adoptive father, and I'd begun to self-harm, and Lucinda saw that and guessed something was wrong. When I told her what was happening, she went around to see him straight away. I don't know what she said to him, or what she threatened him with, but he never came near me after that.'

'Oh, Caz, I had no idea …' Eddie says, as though he can't believe her words.

'Nor me,' Janet says. 'Jesus, that must have been dreadful for you.'

Maisie doesn't know what to say. Caz's words have rattled her to the core.

Caz gives them a small smile, then goes on: 'So you see, Stella, you can imagine how I've always felt about … this angel who rescued me. Even later, it was her help and connections that made my career the success it was.'

'You're very brave to speak up, Caz,' Eddie says.

'I dunno about that.' She grins at him. 'Sometimes I think I'm still there, the thirteen-year-old who hero-worshipped Lucinda, and I never moved on. I don't care if it looks like she had me in the palm of her hand. Whenever Lucinda needed anything at all, I was always ready to drop everything for her.'

'Thank you so much, Caz,' Stella says. 'What happened to you was absolutely appalling but thanks for being able to open up about it. I'm always glad to hear stories about the good side of Lucinda. I know you were very close and she was lucky to have a good friend like you.'

There is a long silence, interrupted eventually by Rex. 'I think we all need fresh drinks after that,' he says, getting to his feet.

Maisie accepts another gin and tonic, hoping it will smooth over her acute discomfort. In view of Caz's shock words, she feels like a right bloody eejit, getting her petty aggravations out into the open. At her age she should have more sense. Why can't she be bigger than this? And why has she always set such store at being validated by the group? If she didn't feel valued by them, why has she always hung around, clutching at crumbs? Why has she always tried to fit in anyway? Why can't she be herself? Problem is, she realises in a sudden flash of clarity, she doesn't much like herself, if at all.

But that's a problem for another day.

'I'm off to bed,' Stella says, to the group at large, as she stands up. 'I'll check in with the guards after breakfast and then I'm heading home to Dublin. I'm sure you're all anxious to get back to your lives. I appreciate the trouble you all took to be here. We'll talk more in the morning. And thanks again, Caz, we'll chat soon.'

'Night, Stella, I won't be long after you,' Caz says.

'I think we'll all be hitting the sack shortly,' Eddie says.

'I hope you're not too upset about the way this evening panned out?' Rex asks her, catching her hand before she moves off.

'I'm not going to think about anything at all until tomorrow,' Stella says, with a sad smile.

He stands up and hugs her. 'Good idea. Sleep well.'

Maisie wonders how any of them will have a restful night. Despite Caz changing the conversation, the atmosphere in The Lookout is charged, as though Maisie has unleashed something dark and menacing, and they are no closer to filling in the gaps of Lucinda's last day.

ONE DAY EARLIER
SUNDAY, 29 JANUARY

CHAPTER THIRTY-TWO

Stella

The Lookout is still and silent when she awakes the following morning. The sky is beginning to lighten in the east with the approach of sunrise. She realises it's Sunday.

She still feels emotionally spent and drained, her mind constantly whirring, trying to work out what had happened to Lucinda, or who was behind the stupid pranks. Last night, when Maisie and Eddie had been talking, she felt that the conversation had jumped tracks without her noticing and that they were veering around a strange and chilling bend. As for Eddie – Stella had been shocked by his revelation. Why had Lucinda borrowed so much money from him? How come she hadn't known about it? She feels the urge to move, to get outside and inhale long gulps of fresh air.

She dresses quickly: a pair of warm jeans, a blue sweater, a long cardigan. She slips downstairs quietly, the house hushed around her. In the hall, as she lifts her coat out of the cloakroom, she realises she has no key to the hall door. She moves through the downstairs rooms, shadowy in the winter morning, heading for the utility room where all the spare keys are hanging up – and there she spots a key in the door to the side of the house. She lets herself out into the calm of the thin morning light, locking it behind her.

She passes the sheds and goes around to the front of the house.

Walking briskly in the freezing cold, her breath coming in white puffs, instinct guides her towards Wolf Head. Her own personal vigil, her private goodbye to Lucinda before the next round of sad formalities kicks in. She feels weirdly blank, as though everything inside her has been cut away, all fears, anxieties, and concerns about Lucinda. She no longer has to worry about her being lost in the thunderous, unpredictable sea. Lucinda has been restored to her, out of that broiling, restless water, thanks to all the service personnel and volunteers who worked together to make it happen. And Hugh – ensuring everything was as dignified as possible. Going, no doubt, above and beyond the remit of his job. There will be more to come, arrangements to make, more acres of red tape and form-filling. For now, that's all out of her hands.

There are no straight answers to Lucinda's accident. Her sister was an enigma. She'd led a life of which large parts Stella knew nothing about. She now knows that Lucinda only showed what she chose to show; she was a chameleon – a different person to everyone in her life. Whatever issues her friends might have had with her, she'd chosen to leave Stella in blissful ignorance. Next week, when she has recovered a little, she will hand it all over to Hugh. Tell him everything that has happened this weekend, everything that has been said, and let him look at it dispassionately and decide if anything is a matter for the guards.

For now, she gathers up all her good memories of Lucinda. They spin in front of her, streaming through her mind's eye, like a movie on fast forward. She thinks of the soft tilt of her sister's chin when she was suggesting something mischievous, the way her sparkling eyes smiled into hers whenever she told her she loved her, the feeling of her warm hugs all through her life. She needs only to remember that Lucinda will always be the sister who spun her around by a blue swimming pool under azure summer skies, dressed in white cotton, singing a Beyoncé song.

She doesn't go all the way to Wolf Head. She turns and walks back slowly, knowing she can't stay out much longer: people will be getting up, wondering where she is, and it'll be a busy morning in The Lookout, everyone leaving after breakfast. They have lives to go back to, and in Caz's case, a plane to catch.

She's coming down the final incline towards The Lookout when she hears a car in the distance, coming in her direction. Tadhg, probably, arriving with food from The Pier. Just as she reaches the gate, the car draws alongside her. Hugh Connell steps out and motions to the driver to continue up the driveway. A second car is now coming slowly up the laneway towards The Lookout. A garda car.

Hugh walks over to her and when she sees the look in his eyes whatever bubble she's been in that morning explodes into the air.

'What are you doing here?' she asks. 'You can't have news already?'

Her head is crawling with anxiety, her gabbled words rushing out like a torrent. She wants to keep talking, asking questions, keeping his words at bay, especially to stop him explaining the look she sees in his eyes. It chills her to the bone.

'I'm sorry, Stella,' he says, 'but I wanted to be the one to tell you.'

'Tell me what?' Every molecule in her head is silently screaming.

He puts his hand on her arm. She begins to shake.

'I'm so sorry to upset you like this, Stella,' he says, the sound of his voice advancing and receding in her ears. 'It's about the human remains found in the car. They aren't Lucinda's.'

Britt puts another mug of hot, sweet tea on the table in front of Stella. She's in the library with Hugh and Britt, aware of voices echoing around the house, people getting breakfast, others starting to pack. Someone is looking for their phone charger. She doesn't think any of them are aware of the reason for the drama unfolding in the library, although they know Hugh is in here speaking to her.

From where she is sitting, she can see out through a small arched window above a seating alcove. His car is parked outside, slewed right across the driveway, hemming in everyone else's. Behind that is the garda car, the two uniformed gardaí standing out in the chilly morning. She recognises them from the vigil of the night before and she guesses they are awaiting orders from Hugh. She tries to make sense of his words. They don't know the identity of the remains found in the car, which has been confirmed as the one registered to Lucinda. The process will take a while, but it appears to be a male, approximately six feet in height. The body was in the front passenger seat, secured by a seat belt.

Through the pall of her shock, she asks, 'Does that mean Lucinda must have escaped? Into the water?'

Hugh looks almost white-faced, and it frightens her, but his eyes are as gentle as his voice as he says, 'No, Stella. They don't think anyone else was in the car when it went into the water.'

'But she must have been ...'

'The car was damaged from the impact,' he says. 'They're starting their examination but they have confirmed that the doors were jammed closed thanks to the electrics giving out. The windscreen was shattered but is still intact. The evidence would suggest that no one escaped from the car after it went over the edge. Hopefully the examination will provide some indication as to how the car hit the sea. That could have a bearing on things.'

'Could she ... could Lucinda have been in the boot?' she asks. 'Did they check that?'

Hugh nods. 'There were no remains found in the boot, although articles including a couple of mobile phones and personal effects were recovered, which will be forensically examined.'

Something thin, like a needle-point laser, pierces her heart.

'This changes everything,' she says.

'Yes,' he agrees. 'Unfortunately, Stella, we could be looking at a murder investigation,' he says heavily. 'The death of the male passenger is suspicious. We need to establish the cause and timing of his death.'

Murder. It gives her no satisfaction to think she's been right in the sense that a crime has been committed. Lucinda's car hadn't toppled over the edge of Wolf Head through some accidental fluke. It had been deliberately positioned that way. But nothing makes sense, including the man in the passenger seat. And what makes everything so sickeningly terrible is that she doesn't know where Lucinda is now, or what has happened to her. From what Hugh is saying, she couldn't have been in the car after it hit the water. Had she jumped out of it in the nick of time? Slammed shut the driver's door? But surely if she'd escaped some terrible accident, she would have arrived back into The Lookout to raise the alarm?

She hears Hugh talking to Britt, whose face is creased with anguish. Stella gathers from what he is saying that Lucinda's friends will have to be told she wasn't in the car after all, and they will have to reconsider the original statements they made to the guards in light of this new information. There might be some small detail they have missed, some piece of information that could now be crucial to the investigation. Stella sees him go to the window and make a gesture. A third vehicle has pulled in behind the garda car, and she watches as Brendan and Imelda get out. The uniformed guards move to the side of the house.

'These things don't just happen.' She hears Hugh's voice as if from far away. 'Somebody has to know something.'

Remembering those days in the aftermath of the tragedy, the shock and horror reverberating around The Lookout in Lucinda's inexplicable absence, the party atmosphere suddenly changed into one of grief and horror, Stella feels suffocated. They're not back there again. They're somewhere far worse. Only one thing is clear: the man who was in the passenger seat had been sent to his death. In Lucinda's car.

CHAPTER THIRTY-THREE

Caz

It's past midday and Caz still hasn't managed to speak with Stella, who's in the library with Britt. Imelda has said they're not to be disturbed. Caz can't imagine the state Stella must be in. Even she is finding it impossible to stop shaking and crying, unable to believe the shocking turn of events.

Caz had been in the hallway when Stella and Hugh had come through the door and he'd ushered her straight into the library, calling for Britt. Then Imelda had arrived in, speaking to Caz urgently, telling her that Lucinda's body hadn't been recovered after all, asking her to gather Lucinda's friends in the living area so that they could be told of the latest development. Nothing was to go out on social media for now as it might impede the investigation. The guards were setting up a desk in the games room and going over everyone's statement again. Caz knew she wouldn't be getting her Sunday-evening flight back to London.

Rex had looked so agitated when she'd told him about the latest development that Caz wondered if he and Stella meant a lot more to each other than they were letting on. He'd been at the coffee machine in the kitchen and he'd been so startled with her shock news that he'd almost upended his freshly poured coffee. Had Stella been keeping him and their relationship at arm's length over the weekend to avoid any complications with the nature of the vigil?

'Are the guards here?' he'd asked.

'Well, of course. They're going to go over our statements.'

'I'll make myself scarce, so,' he'd said, 'stay in my room out of the way. Let them get on with their job. They won't need to talk to me – I wasn't here at the time.'

'Aren't you worried about Stella?' she'd asked, swiftly changing her mind about how much Stella meant to him, not bothering to add that, apart from Britt, who was family, Stella didn't want to see anyone at the moment.

'Of course, I'm concerned,' he'd said. 'No way am I heading home to Dublin, not while Stella is dealing with this shock. Have the guards any idea what might have happened to Lucinda?'

'I don't know,' she'd said.

'It's dreadful for Stella – I hope for her sake that if someone knows something, they'll tell the guards.' His eyes had bored into hers as though he'd suspected her of withholding vital information. It had taken an effort for her to look away. She'd been relieved when he'd gone upstairs with his coffee.

Hugh had come out of the library, and joined Imelda and Brendan in the games room, where they'd set out their paperwork across the covered pool table, their makeshift desk. Caz had been first in, an informal chat, they had said, but no matter how they put it, she knew it was a full-scale investigation.

Caz had found Hugh's presence unnerving. He'd said nothing, sitting to one side while Brendan and Imelda had gone through her statement, but there had been something in the needle-sharp, laser gaze of his eyes that had rattled her.

Nobody had mentioned the word 'murder', but if Lucinda wasn't in the car, where had she been all this time? And the possibility that she'd met with some misadventure was there in the attention to detail as Brendan and Imelda posed their questions. Was there anything new she wanted to add? Any other details she remembered, no matter how minor or irrelevant they might seem? Could she tell them everything she recalled about that day in her own words, and take them back to include the days prior to the accident.

She's not surprised that she's come out of the room weeping quietly at the deluge of memories the interview has evoked. Maisie has now gone into the games room, but Janet is hovering in the hall and ushers Caz into the shadowy media room. She closes the door and switches on the overhead light.

'What the hell does all this mean?' she says.

Caz is struck by how pale Janet looks. The drapes covering the windows are closed and the harsh, overhead light doesn't do her any favours, throwing into prominence the shadows under her eyes and the hollows in her cheeks. Janet – once the sleekest, most groomed, most healthy and body aware of them all – looks haggard.

'You're in a bad way,' Caz says.

'I can't believe this news. What do you think happened to Lucinda?' She looks at Caz closely, grabbing her arm. 'Do you think there's any chance she's still alive somewhere?'

'Do you?' Caz says, backing away so that Janet releases her grip. She can't cope with Janet's nerves when her own are shot to pieces.

'I don't know what to think,' Janet says, pacing the floor. 'Is there any chance Lucinda could have pulled this off to cover a disappearing trick?'

'Are you for real? What makes you think she'd want to disappear anyway?'

'Wouldn't we all love to start a new life, somewhere new, somewhere different, given the chance?'

'You don't have to disappear to do that. You can start over any time if you have the right attitude.' Oh, yeah? Caz sighs. She might have moved to London in search of new beginnings and a clean break from the past, but she has brought all of herself along, worries, fears, grief and regrets. There is no getting away from them.

'That's crap,' Janet says. 'All that mumbo-jumbo positive thinking drives me mad. We're all trapped in our lives and entanglements. It's impossible to break free. Did they give you any idea who the remains belong to?'

'Remains?' Caz shivers. 'The guards never mentioned those. All we know for sure is that Lucinda wasn't in the car. Other than that, they're not releasing any information.'

'Yeah, but didn't Stella say last night that Hugh confirmed remains were found? We all assumed it was Lucinda. The remains must belong to someone else. And how come they knew it wasn't Lucinda so quickly? Unless it was a male body. Do you think it was a man?'

Caz's head pulses with anxiety. This hasn't occurred to her – she's been so shocked that Lucinda wasn't in the car. Janet is right, of course, and the grim implications of this begin to pound inside her.

'Janet, calm down,' she says, more for her sake than Janet's. 'These things take time to confirm.'

'That's my point. God knows what state the body is in. If they knew so soon that it couldn't be Lucinda, it has to have been a man. And there were we, all this time, imagining Lucinda ...' Janet's eyes are flinty with stress. 'I don't know what I'm going to say to the guards.'

'Whatever you told them last time is fine. It's no big deal. This is part of the process – they have to ask us in case we remember something new. That's their job.'

'I can't remember what I told them. I was up to high doh.'

'Weren't we all? Take it easy. Once you start thinking about it, you'll remember.'

'That's the problem. I told them a few little white lies the last time, and I'm not sure what I said exactly.'

'Jesus – you didn't.'

'I was afraid, you see.'

'Afraid of what?'

'Afraid that Aaron might have had something to do with Lucinda's accident.'

'*Aaron?*'

'I wasn't sure. I don't know what to think. He was missing for a couple of hours that evening ... before Lucinda disappeared. He fobbed me off when I asked him where he'd got to.'

'Ah, Jaysus, Janet, you can't mean that! *Your* Aaron? Don't be ludicrous.'

'I know it sounds mad but you don't know what he'd be capable of if push came to shove. And, you see, we were all high as kites, especially Aaron. He hasn't a clue how much he was drinking that weekend. He was in tatters. I don't know what the hell Maisie thought she was doing ... Well, sort of I do ...'

Caz feels lost, unable to follow the thread of Janet's jumbled thinking. 'Listen to yourself! This is ridiculous. I can't even believe we're having this conversation.'

'Will the guards want to talk to Aaron again, do you think?'

'That'll probably depend on the investigation.'

'That's the thing … I'm afraid I might blurt out something to put him in the frame.'

'What frame? You're talking nonsense.'

'I wish I was.'

'Calm down, Janet. We were all in bits that weekend. I'm sure the guards took account of that when it came to our statements. You heard what Stella had to say, that the weekend was a big fog. She can't remember all the details, and we understood that. Nobody thought she had an ulterior motive or was covering up for something. That's all you have to say. You were upset at the time, and you can't remember the finer details.'

'Apart from I covered for Aaron, gave him an alibi. I know that much.'

'Why, though?'

Janet is shaking. 'I was afraid he'd found out what really happened in Santorini.'

'What are you talking about?'

'Did Lucinda ever tell you?'

'Tell me what?'

'I can't say it – oh God, it's so awful.' Janet shakes her head, puts a hand to her mouth, and rushes out of the room, leaving Caz staring after her.

CHAPTER THIRTY-FOUR

Eddie

Eddie sits on a stool in the home bar, propping his elbows on the polished wood of the counter, sipping chilled water in the hope of clearing his head. He sits so that he's facing out into the hallway and can see all the goings-on through the open door. When Caz had come out of the games room mopping her tears, he'd wanted to hug her, but he was afraid she'd shrug him away, and then Janet intercepted her in the hallway, both of them going into the media room.

Britt and Stella are still in the library, not to be disturbed, and he doesn't like to think what horrors Stella must be going through right now.

On top of his visceral shock about Lucinda, one part of his brain is under no illusion but that it's an investigative interview no matter how softly-softly the guards are presenting it as a chat. A glance through the side window when he came in here reminded him that gardaí are stationed outside in the grey January morning.

Making sure none of them does a runner.

Now Maisie has gone in to be interrogated. He's up next for the inquisition. God knows what Maisie is saying, but if she admits the part she played in ensuring that he, Aaron and

Lucinda were rightly sozzled that weekend, it might help his case. Then again she might let slip about the money he'd loaned to Lucinda. He hoped not. It would take the questioning in an entirely new direction. Like, for example, that he hadn't been repaid, and that he'd concealed this material fact last July, and since then, his business has gone to the wall. No, thanks.

'You're the only one I can talk to about this, Eddie,' Lucinda had said, her blue eyes appealing for understanding. 'The only one I can fully confide in. I can't bring myself to mention it to Caz, even though she's helped me out in the past ...'

He'd felt special that Lucinda, the great manipulator in some ways, had opened up to him and trusted him in a way she hadn't trusted anyone else. Although knowing then why she needed the loan, he'd fully understood her reticence.

Eddie racks his brains, trying to remember what he's already told the guards about Lucinda's last day. He remembers being sea sick on the boat, Tadhg giving him yet another shot of something that would 'cure' him. He has a vague memory of a slow, unsteady walk back up to The Lookout, the harbour, the dry-stone walls, the blue sky, the rutted laneway weaving in and out of his vision. All he has to do is to big up the idea that they'd all been having such a wild party and so much alcohol had been consumed that a lot of details are a little hazy. He's grateful in a funny kind of way that, thanks to the general conversation in The Lookout over the previous two nights, he should be able to sing from the same hymn sheet as everyone else where the timeline of events is concerned.

But something odd is nibbling at the edge of his mind, slithering out of reach, like the way the feeling persists that he did something major to upset Caz somewhere along the line. Was it something he'd seen? Or something he'd done? Did he do something to upset Lucinda on that last day? What had possessed him to get so drunk that afternoon? Or the previous night? Maisie hadn't helped matters, but that was no excuse. To his prickling embarrassment, being in The Lookout this weekend is reminding him of how much of an arse he'd made of himself in front of everyone, especially Caz. In fairness, since that weekend he's made an effort to cut back on the booze, but in the grip of grief, it's been tough.

He hears a door opening and freezes, but it's Janet, rushing out of the media room and heading upstairs. Caz comes out, following her more slowly. Neither of them has noticed him sitting there.

He'd been so glad to pack up his stuff that morning, relieved at the thought of getting away from here, even if it meant going home to the headache of winding up the last threads of his business. Since he arrived on Friday afternoon, everything about Wolf Head, The Lookout and the party weekend has been haunting him, and he can't wait to escape. Even Rex, when he'd joined Eddie for a quick beer yesterday evening, had admitted that he thought it was a spooky place. He hadn't wanted to ask Stella outright, he'd said, but what had possessed Lucinda to come down here? How had she even known it existed? It must have been a nightmare after her accident. It was weird how no one had seen her for hours. Had anyone else been hanging around The Lookout, apart from the friends?

Eddie had barely answered, irritated with Rex's invasive line of questioning. Although at least Rex had had the sense not to annoy Stella with his questions.

Then last night he'd lain awake for hours, his body rigid and alert, unable to relax, despite his exhaustion. At about two in the morning, he'd decided that a swig or two of brandy might help him sleep. All he had to do was ignore his ghosts and make his way down to the ground floor. He wasn't the only one unable to sleep. Up here on the second-floor landing, all was silent except for the whine of the wind, which had picked up again, but there was a faint crack of light coming from under Rex's door. Stella had told them that Rex might have to disappear upstairs now and again, for work. He didn't like the guy, but at least he was here for Stella, even if that meant he had to work into the small hours.

Eddie had paused at the top of the staircase, listening to the wind, images of Lucinda coming at him in the shadows. Suddenly it had seemed a nightmarish journey down all those open stair treads to the vast territory of the dark, silent living area and the bottle of brandy. Feeling stupid and hating himself for his cowardice, he'd slunk back into bed.

But now this morning the shock news flashed around like wildfire. He'd been looking forward to making a quick getaway, and then the guards had arrived in, saying they'd need to talk to everyone. Except Rex, of course. He'd heard him say something about getting out of everyone's hair and that he'd be ready to support Stella as soon as she needed him. Condescending bastard. Getting away from it all *and* relaxing in a luxurious suite while the others faced the interrogation squad.

Eddie pours a fresh glass of water, takes a gulp, and suddenly remembers what had been nagging him about

Lucinda's last day.

Janet had told everyone that Aaron had taken a lift back to The Lookout with Tadhg straight after the boat journey to the Skelligs. But he hadn't. In spite of being wasted, Eddie knew this, because halfway up the hill, he'd changed his mind about a lift and would have cadged one from Tadhg, smelly fish or no smelly fish. But at no point had Tadhg's van passed him, either on its way up to The Lookout, or on the way back down again, having dropped Aaron off. Then later, before anyone realised Lucinda was missing, Eddie had come downstairs at half past seven, and despite the wind gathering strength he'd gone out to the terrace for a beer to get away from the catering crew, who had just arrived. He'd been out sitting by the drinks hut when Aaron had appeared, slipping around the corner from the front of the house, clearly just arriving back and not wanting anyone to spot him returning. Without noticing Eddie, he'd paused for a moment as though gathering himself, before strolling in through the bi-fold doors looking as though he was coming in from spending time on the terrace. But he'd been wearing the same Rory Gallagher T-shirt and khaki shorts he'd worn on the boat trip, giving Eddie the impression that he'd just arrived home from Wolf Cove. He'd thought it was a bit odd that Aaron hadn't gone in through the front door, besides being back so late, but in the grief of Lucinda's disappearance, all this had gone out of Eddie's head. Hadn't Janet stated the other evening that they'd been in the Jacuzzi together?

What the fuck was that all about?

He hears the door to the games room opening. He jumps. It's his turn to face the grilling.

CHAPTER THIRTY-FIVE

Stella

In spite of her deep shock, Stella can't help but see there is something wrong with Britt over and above the alarming events of the morning. She seems to be barely holding it together, her eyes wide with unshed tears, her face contorted with emotion as she fidgets with her sleeves, the neckline of her jumper, the cups and saucers on the tray she had brought in earlier. They are still in the library but Hugh has left, wanting to sit in as the others are being questioned in light of the shock developments.

'Britt, what is it?'

A long silence. Britt stares at her, her eyes now haunted as she wrings her hands together.

Stella reaches towards her. 'Britt – what's wrong?'

'It's Lucinda. I'm heartbroken, and I can't hide it any more.' She breaks into a storm of weeping, her face buried in her hands.

Stella gets up to hold her but she pushes her away.

'I don't deserve your kindness, Stella,' she says, her voice ragged, 'considering what I've kept from you.'

Prickles run up and down her spine. 'What are you talking about?'

Britt dabs her eyes with a tissue plucked from her sleeve. There is something about her apart from her new fragility that puts Stella on edge. Britt's hands flutter to her throat and fiddle with the neck of her jumper. She is silent for what seems like a long time.

'Are you not well?' Stella asks, thinking of how thin she has become.

She shakes her head, but Stella has the gut feeling she's not necessarily denying she's sick. It's more that her tears spring from somewhere else deep inside her.

And then a breath of premonition stirs, and she wonders how she has been blind for so long. Everything comes together in her head in a flash of clarity and makes perfect sense ... all those trips to Kerry, the parcels that had arrived regularly to the house in Dublin bearing toys, books or clothes, the regular postcards from abroad, the warm love with which she had always enclosed her and Lucinda.

'Lucinda was your daughter,' Stella says.

'Yes,' Britt says hoarsely, her eyes brimming with tears. 'My daughter, my child, my beautiful baby. It's my fault that I wanted it all covered up, so it's my fault she went off the rails as a teenager. My baby, whom I loved with all my heart for a short while before I gave her up.'

'There was no phone-box,' Stella says, her head dizzy with this revelation.

Britt shakes her head. 'No, there wasn't. Your parents, Marie and Bernard, had no intention of telling Lucinda she'd been adopted – I had begged them not to. The afternoon Lucinda suddenly started asking questions, Marie got such a shock that she panicked and blurted out something stupid about her being found in a phone-box. That way there'd be nowhere for Lucinda to start looking, no trail to follow. But it all backfired. I heard how Lucinda had been horrified with her so-called shabby beginnings and her abandonment. Marie was trying to save me and she was hoping that the love and care she and Bernard gave Lucinda would make up for it, and help her see she was as much a cherished part of the family as you were. But the damage was done.'

Stella's stomach flutters with a dreadful anticipation. 'What exactly happened, Britt?'

'The old story.' Britt smiles through her tears. 'Pregnant at twenty-one, at the beginning of my teaching career, following an unfortunate incident after a village dance with the son of the local doctor. Unsolicited and most unwelcome to say the least. When I told him I was pregnant he laughed. He and his parents threatened me, and warned me that if I went around crying rape, I wouldn't stand a chance against the eminent doctor's son, who was a legend on and off the GAA pitch. They would see to it that my name would be dragged through the mud. Although things had improved for crisis pregnancies compared to earlier decades, we weren't far off the stigma of unmarried motherhood, and in my circumstances, my career would have been effectively over.'

Stella feels a huge heartache building up inside her. 'But, Britt – oh, my God, I can't believe this. It's so shocking. How on earth did you cope?'

'I hid it as best I could, working right up to the end of April when his father, in his official capacity, signed me off work due to a chest infection. I hated asking him for that, but there was no question of going to anyone else. I went to Dublin, and that was where I gave birth, your parents arranging to adopt Lucinda. I'll never forget the day I said goodbye to her. I held her tightly to me, as though I wanted her to absorb every single molecule of my love into her pores. I told her over and over how much I loved her, hoping somehow it would filter through into the very bones of her ...' Britt's voice breaks. After a moment she composes herself. 'Of course I had regrets, and giving her away even to the loving care of your parents was a heartbreak for me, but I felt I was doing my best for Lucinda by ensuring she had a safe, secure and loving childhood.'

Stella feels her heart cracking open. 'Jesus, Britt, I had no idea. It must have been horrendous for you.'

Britt shrugs. 'I got on with it, as most of us did in those days. The one good thing that came out of it was Lucinda. But when Lucinda was three,' Britt continues, 'I had a bit of a breakdown and took a sabbatical, going to America to get away from it all. By now, the doctor's son had completed his medical studies and had gone to work in a posh clinic in London. I missed Ireland and Kerry, though, and I came back home a few years after you were born, getting a teaching post in a school in Kenmare. I made the best of things as the years went on.'

'You couldn't have been more loving towards us,' Stella says, a rainbow of emotions coursing through her. Love, sorrow and regret for Britt and the trials she'd endured. 'Did Lucinda find out?' she asks gently, trying to piece things together.

'Yes, I had to tell her.'

'That weekend?'

'Yes.' Britt reaches for her tissues again before composing herself. Stella waits, afraid to imagine how angry Lucinda might have been with Britt. Was this a missing piece of her sister's last day?

'When she came to see me that Saturday ...' Britt's eyes are heavy with sadness.

'You can tell me, Britt, whatever it is.'

'The thing about Lucinda that day – I need to say this first – I sensed she was full of something I couldn't pinpoint, a mixture of disappointment in herself, but also a spark of fresh resolve.'

'I know what you mean.' Stella, too, had sensed that about Lucinda, that time she'd met her before the party, a new determination in her sister that she hadn't seen before. Although during those crazy, madcap days in The Lookout, she'd thought her new-found resolve had gone straight out the window. Seemingly not, according to Britt.

'This might come as a surprise to you, after all her protestations,' Britt says, 'but she told me she'd been doing some digging around, looking at adoption practices in the early 1980s, mother and baby homes, and all that sad history. She was trying to figure out a few things, like her own start in life.'

'You're joking.'

'I'm not, Stella. She told me she'd begun to look for records – she'd even gone into the national library looking at archived newspapers – but she'd found nothing so far about a baby abandoned in a phone-box. She wanted to know if I'd any information at all, like any idea of where the adoption had taken place. Had Marie told me anything at all? Could I point Lucinda in any direction?'

'And did you?'

Britt sighs. 'I did. I told her everything. And I feared the worst. I expected her to be angry, to shout, to blame, for keeping the truth hidden from her.'

Stella could well imagine her sister, hurt and horrified that Britt had kept this secret from her all her life. Was this what had precipitated Lucinda's accident? Blind anger at Britt?

'But there was none of that,' Britt says. 'That was the surprising part. Lucinda actually thanked me for telling her. I was in shock at her response, to be honest. I'd wanted to tell her the truth at various times over the years, especially after your parents died, but I was afraid she'd break the thin connection we had, and never speak to me again, so I stayed silent, settling for what I had with her. Anything was better than being frozen out of her life.'

'Sorry, Britt, go back a bit. Let me get this straight – she *thanked* you for telling her?'

'Yes. She said she could understand what it had been like for me at that time, and I couldn't have given her better parents. She had some terrible words to say about her biological father – he was the person who truly abandoned her besides violating me. I'd done the very best I could, she said, given the circumstances at the time. She asked me if it was okay to let you know, so of course I said it was fine. But, then, she never got talking to you, that Saturday evening.'

Was this the announcement Lucinda had been about to make that weekend? That she was off on a quest to discover her true parents?

Stella asks gently, 'Was there any reason you didn't tell me all this after her accident?'

'How could I?' Britt says. 'How could I throw such a grenade at you that weekend when you were in deep shock and needed every support you could get? I was afraid *you*'d never talk to me again. And I wanted to be there to help you as much as possible, without landing another shock on you, or casting myself in the role of bereaved parent. I was afraid you'd push me away for staying silent all these years. I did try afterwards. I wanted to come to Dublin to see you, to talk to you, but it didn't happen ...'

'I didn't give you much of a chance, did I?' Stella acknowledges, an undercurrent of grief coursing through her.

Britt had suggested meeting Stella in Dublin two or three times after Lucinda's accident, but she'd cold-shouldered each one of her approaches, not knowing she was in mourning just as much as Stella, caught up in the bitter and eviscerating grief of losing a child.

'My one consolation is that Lucinda made her peace with me, and I with her.' Britt shivers in spite of the warmth of the room. 'Dear God, in the space of a few hours I gained a daughter and lost her.'

Stella gives her a warm hug, saying nothing about her frisson of alarm. Lucinda's calm acceptance of Britt's confession and the way she made peace with her over an issue that had brought her great heartache for many years went against everything Stella would have expected. What had been going on in Lucinda's life?

And where is she now?

CHAPTER THIRTY-SIX

Caz

Caz is not the least bit surprised to see Maisie in tears after her interview. She's finishing off her packing when Maisie arrives in the bedroom looking for tissues to dab her streaming eyes.

'I told them,' she says, 'about what I did to the drinks. You should have seen the way they looked at me, especially that Hugh guy – I wouldn't like to cross him. I asked if they thought it had contributed to Lucinda's accident in some way, but they said they were keeping an open mind. Oh, Caz, I felt so ashamed of what I did.'

Too right, Caz decides sourly, an image flashing into her head of Eddie acting the eejit, fuelled by Maisie's concoctions. 'Look, Maisie, we're all upset,' she says. 'Why don't you go down to the kitchen and have a nice cup of coffee? There's apple pie in the fridge left over from last night and you might as well help yourself, I'm not sure what time we're going to get out of here.'

'Good idea,' Maisie says. 'It'll help me calm down a little.'

Caz is relieved to hear the door closing behind her. She hasn't the energy to listen to a self-reproachful Maisie who wants to get everything off her chest and thus solicit some kind of absolution from Caz.

After the shock of this awful morning has somewhat abated, Caz realises she is feeling let down. She'd thought that she and Lucinda had a special closeness in their friendship, but apparently not. Pulsing through her head is the knowledge that, over this weekend, everything she'd thought she'd meant to Lucinda has been blown away like feathers in the wind. Last night, when she'd heard that Lucinda owed Eddie a sizeable amount of money, she'd felt as though someone had punched her in the gut.

Why the hell had Lucinda needed that kind of money? Caz hadn't been aware of any financial problem she might have had, or been taken into her confidence. Why not? Why had she gone to Eddie? Entrusting him with her secrets rather than her best friend?

And from what Maisie had said when they'd been unpacking on Friday night, Lucinda had known something had happened in Santorini involving Maisie, which she hadn't shared with Caz. That had felt like a slight of some kind.

But the last straw had been Janet that morning. Santorini was the holiday that kept on giving, something going so wrong there with Janet that the memory of it terrified her. Lucinda had known about it all those years but never confided in Caz.

Then again Caz had always sensed that Lucinda had been far more important to her than she to Lucinda. She'd clutched onto their friendship, afraid not to fall in with Lucinda's plans at any time in case it sent the effervescent, vivacious Lucinda spiralling away. Trailing in Lucinda's brilliant slipstream, and thanks to the way she'd sent plenty of work in Caz's direction, she'd been able to adopt a more confident persona. Although she'd considered Lucinda to be her closest friend, it's clear she hadn't held that special ranking with Lucinda.

Caz realises with fresh clarity that she is entertaining ridiculous and petty thoughts, especially considering the sad circumstances. Proof, if anything, of what she's feared for years, that there is something inherently wrong with her, some terrible flaw. She glares at herself in the bedroom mirror, at her pale, unadorned face – how plain she looks without the benefit of enhancing cosmetics.

But as she stares at her reflection, she can't help seeing a spark of something in her eyes. At least she's still alive and breathing. Surely Caz Costello has a life worth rescuing. She'll need to take a long, hard look at herself when she gets back to London. Sort out her head. Weed out old, outworn beliefs. Stop the awful practice of pretending she's Lucinda during her casual sexual encounters. Stop having those encounters in the first place. She knows she's punishing herself with them, considering how empty and hollowed out she always feels afterwards. Surely she's worth more than that.

In the meantime, Lucinda is still missing. She needs to put herself to one side for now and find out why Janet is so terrified that Aaron could have been involved in Lucinda's disappearance.

Then, even if it's coming at a bad time for Stella, she needs to unburden herself of the secret about Lucinda she's been carrying for far too long.

CHAPTER THIRTY-SEVEN

Janet

Lying on her bed, Janet tries to rid her mind of a churning anxiety and forces herself to recall exactly what she said in her original statement to the guards about that last day. She can't escape being questioned – they'll be looking for her shortly. She has to be careful to stick to her earlier script and not drop Aaron in it.

Hand on heart, does she seriously think her husband could have it in him to be responsible for anything as harrowing as Lucinda's disappearance? Then again, who knows what dreadful things someone can be impelled to do in certain circumstances?

There is a soft knock at the door. She tenses.

'Janet? Are you in there?'

It's Caz. 'Come in.'

'Sorry if I'm disturbing you,' Caz says, 'but I'm concerned about you and what you said earlier.'

'You mean Aaron?'

'Yes. What's really going on?' Caz asks, worry wreathing her face as she sits at the end of the bed. 'You went home with Aaron after that weekend. You've been living with him ever since. Come on, you hardly think he's capable of anything nasty? Especially where Lucinda's concerned?'

Janet sits up and props a pillow behind her. 'That's the thing,' she says, biting her lip. 'We haven't talked properly since ... since the night of the Jacuzzi, actually.' It would be a relief to talk to Caz, she decides. She can't keep this bottled up much longer, and Caz is safe – she's always been there, staunchly loyal, a solid and reliable friend to Lucinda and everyone else.

Caz gives her a look of understanding.

'I know, it was a stupid carry-on,' Janet says, rolling her eyes heavenwards. 'Aaron was beyond pissed. But since then, we've been avoiding each other, sleeping in separate rooms, living separate lives. It's a perfect bloody sham. You've no idea. Thing is, Caz, the silence, the rift between us has suited me, because I'm afraid ...'

'Afraid of what?'

'To talk about that weekend at all. If Aaron found out about Santorini ... and he could have that weekend ...'

'Sorry – you've lost me. What's it got to do with Santorini?'

'You see,' Janet's eyes fill with tears and something gives way inside her, 'a dreadful thing happened the evening after Aaron and I got engaged. Maisie's boyfriend, Dean ...' She's shaking and shivering.

All of a sudden, she's back there again. Coming up from the pool in her flip-flops and swimwear, having run back down to pick up her sunglasses left on a lounger. The heat of the evening, the golden sunshine, the flowering scents coming from the hotel's beautiful gardens swirl around her as she takes a shortcut through the back of the gardens, heading for a side door in the apartment block, feeling on top of the world after her engagement to Aaron.

She tells Caz in fits and starts, her words trailing away from time to time as she struggles to breathe.

Dean is there in front of her. She knows immediately by his leering eyes what he wants and tries to dodge, but he blocks her way. He clamps a hand across her mouth and drags her off the curving pathway into the thick of the foliage. The horror of her helplessness as she struggles in vain when he presses her over a low wall encircling a palm tree, the stone surround digging into her tummy, the shock of his body invading hers as he pulls down her bikini bottoms and forces himself into her, sweating, grunting and drilling his way into her softness, laughing at her outrage, mocking her, telling her that her loved-up, romantic, sickly-sweet celebration of her engagement to Aaron has nauseated him. He needs to get the taste of it out of his mouth. By giving her a good seeing-to.

By the time Janet has finished, Caz has her arms around her, rubbing her back. Janet leans into her shoulder, still feeling flayed.

'Oh, my God, Janet, I don't believe this! It's horrific. I don't know what to say … that fucker! How *dare* he!'

Janet shivers and wraps her arms around her tummy. 'From the time Dean arrived, I knew he found me attractive,' she says. 'Then when Aaron and I got engaged, everyone was happy, but I saw how he was looking at me, sour and supercilious.'

'Why didn't you report him to the police?'

'And then what? Drag myself through soul-destroying invasive procedures and interviews? And what were the chances he'd get off scot-free? I'd been drinking and I was in a small bikini. In the meantime, my engagement to Aaron would have been spoiled for good. This would always have come between us. Besides everyone's holiday being ruined, our future together would have been shattered.'

It was as if he'd known she'd stay quiet about his assault – his *rape* – as if he'd known she couldn't bear to ruin the perfect occasion for Aaron and herself, that it would break her heart to soil this special time by damaging it with his vile behaviour.

'Dean said I'd been asking for it,' she tells Caz. 'He even slapped my face when he was finished. It would be his word against mine, he'd said. How was that for an engagement present?'

'For fuck's sake—'

'I had a choice,' Janet says. 'And I had to make up my mind almost instantly. If I called the police and spoke up, I knew Aaron and I would find it difficult, if not impossible, to claw our way back from it. Our lovely engagement – look at the way Aaron had planned it to the last detail – it would be ruined for ever, and the horrible aftertaste would last for much longer than the attack, which had been over in minutes. And I couldn't bear people looking at me differently, knowing what he'd done to me.'

'God, Janet, I had no idea.'

'Then, as I was heading into the apartment block, Lucinda came along and knew something was wrong by my face.'

'So you told her.'

'Yes, she forced it out of me in that vulnerable moment. She was great, though. We had a good talk. I explained to her that I had decided to forget it had happened. Pretend it had never taken place. Refuse to give it any energy. I was going to hold on to my dignity, tattered or otherwise. I was going back to Aaron with my head high and would act as if everything was still perfect and wonderful, plan our dream wedding and honeymoon, and set out on married life with nothing to tarnish it. I swore Lucinda to secrecy and, although she was outraged on my behalf, she promised to keep it to herself.'

'She never breathed a word to me,' Caz says.

'Dean cleared off home the next day, and I was so relieved, even though Maisie was upset.'

'He was an arrogant dick. I was delighted he was gone.'

'That was thanks to Lucinda …'

She doesn't get a chance to elaborate when Caz says, 'I wonder if Maisie ever found out?'

'Why?'

'Funnily enough she's mentioned Santorini to me a couple of times this weekend.'

'She has?'

'But wait …'

Janet can see by Caz's face that she is making connections, her immediate shock abating long enough for her to join a few dots.

'But what has this got to do with your worry about Aaron being involved in Lucinda's disappearance?'

Janet sighs. 'If Aaron found out what had happened, he'd be furious with Lucinda for the part she played in covering it up, disgusted she knew and he didn't. Look at how hammered he was that weekend. He could well have lashed out. Thing is …' Janet pauses '… he deliberately lied to the guards about that last afternoon.'

'I see.' Caz's face is grave.

Janet swallows. 'I went up to our room just before six o'clock to get ready and heard Eddie coming back into the room next door. He must have crashed because I could hear the sound of him snoring almost immediately. I thought Aaron would be arriving upstairs any moment but he didn't appear until after half past seven, looking much the worse for wear. I asked him where the hell he'd been, but he wouldn't answer me and walked straight into the shower. I went downstairs to get a drink, and then a while after he arrived down, we realised Lucinda was missing. Then he told the guards he'd got into the Jacuzzi with me when he came back from the boat trip. Of all things to say, Caz, the bloody Jacuzzi! He can't have been thinking straight. And why the lies in the first place? I was so gobsmacked I went along with him, and I've been afraid to mention it to him since. So, for me, it's convenient that we haven't been talking.'

Caz looks puzzled. 'But I still don't get … what makes you think Aaron might have found out? That particular weekend?'

'Two things,' Janet says. 'I've always been afraid Lucinda might have let something slip in the heat of the moment, especially with a few drinks on her, so I've always made sure to stay close to her and fall in with her plans, just in case, and she was pretty boisterous that weekend, but – oh, Caz, the thing is, I saw Dean, here in Wolf Cove.'

'Dean? You're joking.'

'I wish. After the trip to the Skelligs, when we were all sitting outside The Pier, I felt I was being watched and, oh, God, I saw the prick staring out at me from inside the bar with the exact same leer on his face.'

'Are you sure?'

'He was older and heavier, but I knew by the smirk on his face he was reliving what he'd done to me. And then the next night Lucinda went missing. *And* Aaron lied about where he'd been after the boat trip. Any minute now the guards will be looking for me.' Her voice thins out. 'What will I say?'

'Say nothing,' Caz urges. 'Do your deep breathing or whatever, but stick to your original statement. You'll have to talk to Aaron first. You can't drop him in it. I'd say he has a perfectly reasonable explanation. You could end up wrecking your marriage for good if he thought you suspected him of harming Lucinda.'

'But, Caz, the body in the car ...'

'Oh, shit. You don't think ...'

Janet's hands are shaking as she brings them up to her face. 'I don't know what to think. My head is on fire. I'm all over the place right now. You see ...' She pauses at the sound of her name being called. She grabs Caz's hands, squeezing them. 'Jesus. I'm up next.'

'You'll be fine. Slow breaths,' Caz says, as she guides her out the door.

CHAPTER THIRTY-EIGHT

Stella

There is a soft knock at the door before it opens slowly and Stella's heart jumps, wondering if it's Hugh with any developments. But it's Caz. Standing on the threshold, she looks in, her face creased with worry.

'Stella, I'm so sorry for what's happened,' she begins. 'It's absolutely dreadful, and I know you don't want to be disturbed ...'

She pauses.

'What is it, Caz?' Stella asks. 'Come on in.'

Caz steps into the room. 'I don't want to give you too much of a shock on top of the awful morning it is, Stella. You must be in bits. We all are. Janet's being interviewed now, she's the last, but before we all leave there's something you need to know about Lucinda. I can't keep it to myself any longer.'

Caz's eyes drift to Britt, who half rises to her feet.

'Please stay, Britt,' Stella says. 'Sit down, Caz. There's nothing you can say that will make things any worse.'

'I hate springing this on you now,' Caz says, looking anxious as she subsides into a chair. 'Lucinda didn't want anyone to know. She begged me to keep it to myself. I had to swear to tell no one. But then after the accident ...' Caz's face crumples.

'Just tell me.'

Caz takes a breath. 'That time Lucinda and I skipped out of college and went to London … well, it wasn't London, it was Belfast.'

'Why Belfast? What were you doing there?'

The answer is written all over Caz's face.

Stella says, 'Lucinda was pregnant?'

'Yes.' Caz replies, her voice almost a whisper. 'She gave birth to a little boy … I'm so sorry, Stella, this isn't exactly how I imagined telling you.'

'Oh, dear Lord.' Britt drops her head into her hands.

Stella feels so shaken it's as if a tidal wave has come crashing through the room, whipping her up in its path. Everything outside Caz's news has temporarily skidded to a stop inside her. Disparate things that have been floating around in her head come together. Lucinda's new resolve. Her visit to Britt. Most significantly, her calm acceptance of Britt's news about her parentage, a surprising turnabout from someone who had been incredibly angry to discover she'd been adopted, and determined never to look for her birth-parents.

'She was five months pregnant but hiding it well by the time she came to me for help,' Caz says, speaking softly. 'She felt I was the only one who'd understand, that we had a common bond. I had to help. That's why we dropped out of college. We went to Belfast for the final three months of her pregnancy.'

Something painful pulses through Stella's head.

'Sorry for landing it on top of you like this, today of all days,' Caz continues, 'and I'm so sorry for keeping it from you all these years. Lucinda never gave me any indication she wanted to talk about it.'

'I can't believe I had no idea,' Stella says. All she can remember from that time is the stubborn determination with which Lucinda had packed her case, ignoring their mother's distress, the way she'd tried to ease Stella's unhappiness, by giving her some of her favourite possessions. The way she'd come back up the garden path to give Stella a hug and tell her she loved her, when Stella had cried as she walked out the door.

'I know you probably thought we were living the high life in London. It was anything but,' Caz says. 'Lucinda invented that au pair job ... I got a job in a department store to support us and we lived quietly in a tiny flat. Then three weeks after the baby was born, we came back to Dublin. Lucinda carried on as if nothing had happened.'

But she hadn't, Stella recalls. She had changed. More restless, more short-tempered. Stella had put it down to withdrawal symptoms after leaving the bright lights of London and, angry after all the upset Lucinda had caused by dropping out of college on what seemed to be an unsuccessful whim, she had done her best to ignore her and her dramas, concentrating instead on her schoolwork. Lucinda had moved out of the family home soon after that.

'Have you any idea where her son is now?' Stella asks.

'No.' Caz shakes her head. 'I don't even know which Belfast agency she used. She said the less I knew, the better. He was born on the twenty-eighth of June and would have been twenty-one last year.'

'But she did use an agency?' Which meant there was a record somewhere.

'Yes.'

Thank God. 'And the father?'

'I don't know. Lucinda wouldn't tell me his name but I think it was someone she'd known for a while, she said something about being finally caught, that they should have been more careful. I know she felt ashamed of herself after the adoption. After all her outrage about her own birth-mother, she had gone and done the exact same thing. She had the baby adopted because she couldn't see any other way out, and she was furious with herself.'

'Our parents would have looked after her,' Stella says. 'I would have helped.'

'Lucinda didn't want to land her troubles on anyone, especially after all her carry-on. Your mother was rediscovering her life again after her first bout of cancer, your father had enough on his plate, and you were busy in school. She didn't want to put anyone out.'

Stella feels unravelled, her brain grasping the threads of this. Lucinda giving birth without telling any of them – how difficult it must have been for her to give up her baby.

'I'm glad you told me, Caz,' Stella says, struggling to pull herself together. 'And I'm so glad Lucinda had you around for support during that time. Thank you.' She takes a deep breath.

'You've no idea how much I've been torn in two these last few months,' Caz says. 'I didn't know whether it was best to honour the promise I made to Lucinda or break her trust.'

'This has been some morning,' Stella says, exchanging a glance with Britt, reassured by her nod of acquiescence. 'You might as well know, Caz, I found out earlier that Britt is Lucinda's birth-mother. Britt told Lucinda the truth about her birth on that last day. Unfortunately, we never got to talk about it.'

'Things were different forty years ago,' Britt says, her voice shaky. 'I wasn't in a position to keep her. I went through purgatory until I accepted that I'd made the best arrangements for her at that time. But I was lucky to be a small part of her life. Until' – her voice breaks – 'that awful Saturday.'

'Oh, Britt,' Caz says, going over to hug her, 'I can't believe you're Lucinda's mother but it's obvious in a way once you know, if that makes sense. I'm only sorry we found out in difficult circumstances. How did Lucinda feel about it when you told her?'

'She was quite happy,' Britt says. 'I'd been nervous of telling her because I knew how upset she'd been as a teenager when she'd discovered she was adopted. But when she told me she was finally getting her act together and had started to look for her parents, I couldn't stay silent any longer. And now,' she gives a small smile, 'what you've just told us means I have a grandson out there somewhere.'

'I think she might have intended looking for him,' Caz says. 'She'd been talking to me about reaching the big four-oh and getting her life on track. I wouldn't be surprised if that was the announcement she planned to make.'

'You could be right,' Stella says, pain ripping through her stomach at the realisation that she and Lucinda had never had the chance to share anything about the birth of her baby. Her sister a mother! How lonely her empty arms must have felt, how isolated and alone she must have been in keeping that secret from her family. Then, afterwards,

Lucinda imagining her child growing up, all those missed birthdays and Christmases – how she must have tortured herself. Suddenly she has a new perception of Lucinda: her devil-may-care attitude, her hectic lifestyle, was partly driven, no doubt, by a need to distance herself from the hurt she had self-inflicted in giving up her child.

CHAPTER THIRTY-NINE

Stella

There is the sound of voices in the hall, footsteps on the gravel outside, cars pulling away. Hugh comes back into the library. Britt takes one look at his face and heads out, mentioning something about the kitchen, Caz following her.

'Any news?' she asks him.

He sits down in the chair vacated by Britt. 'Sorry, Stella, there are no updates whatsoever on Lucinda's disappearance.'

She's tempted to tell Hugh about Lucinda's son and Britt's revelation but his face is so grim that her breath catches and pain slams into her heart. She has no room in her head to think about anything right now except her sister's disappearance.

'It's surreal. I can't seem to grasp any of this …' She shivers. 'I'd planned on going home today but I can't see that happening now.'

'As far as procedural matters are concerned, you don't have to stay. Neither does anyone else. We've finished talking to everyone for now. Brendan and Imelda have left. I have a car outside. You could come back to Dublin now, with me, if you like?'

'I can't. My car is here.'

'I could drive yours up for you, if you feel you can't do the journey alone?' he suggests, scanning her face with a kindness that almost shatters her.

She shakes her head. She's not prepared for that level of proximity with Hugh, but as well as that, going back to Dublin with Lucinda still missing is out of the question. There is a visceral ache in her heart telling her that Lucinda is still here, and she can't bear to leave her. Now that she hasn't been found with the car, in some ridiculous part of her head she can imagine her coming through the door, gliding down the stairs as if the past six months haven't happened.

'I'm not going home yet. I want to talk more to Britt, get my head around what's happened.' Think about where Lucinda might be. Had she any other reason for coming back to her roots, as she'd put it? Any motive, ulterior or otherwise, for returning to this place of her ancestors?

'Besides, I have Rex here with me,' Stella says, letting him know she wasn't totally alone in the world.

'Rex?'

'Rex O'Neill.'

Hugh frowns. 'We didn't talk to him.'

'There was no need. He never knew Lucinda. I met him afterwards and he only came down this weekend for moral support.'

'Right.' Hugh straightens, his soft demeanour vanished. 'I've a court case tomorrow morning and I have to be present, but I'll be in touch.'

'This isn't anywhere near over, is it?' she blurts out.

'No. I'm sure you understand that the picture has changed completely, Stella.'

'I thought this weekend would give me some kind of closure. Being able to put Lucinda to rest, properly, would have meant a lot.'

There is no such thing as closure in this life, she's beginning to realise. Life itself, of its very nature, constantly changes and evolves.

'We'll get to the bottom of it,' he says. 'Identifying the male passenger in the car is critical. We've no reports of any missing person in the vicinity around that time, but we'll be widening the net.'

'Lucinda's friends have no idea who it might be?'

'None at all. Nobody had anything new to offer that might throw some light on this situation.'

She thinks of the money Lucinda owed Eddie – had he mentioned that to the guards at any time? Or did it form part of the investigation? Yet what would it have to do with an unidentified man in Lucinda's car? She thinks of the way she'd sensed Lucinda's friends had closed ranks against her, that first night in The Lookout.

'We understand they're all upset,' Hugh is saying. 'We have everyone's details if we need any follow-up, and they're to contact us if they think of anything—'

'You'd tell me,' she interjects, 'wouldn't you, if there was anything I should know about Lucinda?'

There is a short silence.

'Of course,' he says smoothly.

But it's too smooth and a fraction of a second too late.

'Is there something to do with Lucinda I don't know about?' she asks.

She meets his eyes and holds them for what seems like an

eternity. Hugh Connell looks uncomfortable, and as though he'd rather be anywhere than here.

She feels cold all over. 'There is something,' she presses.

Hugh's gaze asks her for an understanding that she can't give.

'I'm not in a position to answer that right now,' Hugh says. He looks at her steadily with a mixture of concern and embarrassment.

'Fuck's sake.' She can't help the expletive.

'Look, Stella,' he says, 'I'm not in a position at the moment—'

'Go feck your position.' She shouldn't be talking like this. She knows he has a job to do but she's raw, exhausted, spun to nothingness. She can't even begin to think of what he might have on Lucinda.

'I have to return to Dublin now, but I'll talk to you as soon as I can.'

He stands there, appeal in his eyes.

She hugs herself, her arms in a self-protective gesture, which isn't lost on him. He merely tips his hand, briefly, to her upper arm before he leaves. She sits in the library, unable to move, long after the sound of his car fades away. She hears the voices of the others, footsteps on the stairwell. Presently the house seems deathly quiet.

She comes out of the library and goes down to the living area. The open-plan space is deserted. It's early afternoon, but the light outside is already fading, the January sky full of angry, low-lying clouds. She senses the mountain range towering behind the thick veil of murk that smothers them.

Has everyone bailed out and gone home without saying goodbye, thinking they were leaving her in peace? Or were they anxious to get away from this house of horrors? But they couldn't have gone anywhere without her hearing the sound of their departing cars, which had been blocked in by Hugh's until he left. She hasn't spoken to any of them since the bombshell dropped that morning.

Rex – she needs to talk to him before anyone else. She hopes he didn't feel excluded from the library that morning, but she couldn't bear for anyone to be around her apart from Britt in those first few shocking hours. Britt is nowhere to be seen either.

This is a bit weird, though, the house quiet and seemingly empty. Outside it begins to rain, the clouds opening and unleashing a torrent that drums down on the terrace and hurls long needles against the large expanse of glass. Out in the hall, all is quiet save for the sound of the hammering rain. The library door is open, likewise the door to the games room. She can see the rooms are empty. But the door to the media room is closed.

Something – a strange kind of apprehension – sends shivers down her spine. She opens the door.

At first she can't make sense of what's happening. Her mind refuses to compute the scene in front of her. The drapes are closed, the lamps are on, as is the large screen to her left where Lucinda had pranced around only the other night. This time it shows something different – a grid of images, like a security desk screening of CCTV footage obtained from multiple cameras. But it's The Lookout – small images of the ground-floor rooms, the hallway and stairwell.

Stella's mind is still curiously blank, her brain trying to grapple with what is in front of her eyes. Eddie, Caz, Janet and Maisie are all sitting in the front row of the plush armchairs facing the screen. Sitting on an upholstered chair between them and the screen is Britt. Beside her stands Rex, holding a gun loosely by his side.

Stella walks in, an icy chill running down her back. 'What the hell is going on?'

Rex smiles, as though she's asked him if he'd like a cup of tea. 'Ah, Stella, at last. You're a little late to the party, but no worries. Come in and join your friends.'

CHAPTER FORTY

Eddie

Eddie thinks he is hallucinating or that he's on the set of a television crime drama.

They'd all been in the kitchen, exchanging subdued small-talk, grabbing coffee or tea and a bite to eat before their respective journeys home. When he'd heard Hugh leaving, his car crunching down the driveway, he'd been aware of a lift of relief despite the shock of the morning. The guards were gone. They were finally free to leave, and he couldn't wait to get out of here.

Then Rex had come downstairs, his laptop in his hands.

'Stella asked if everyone would gather in the media room,' he said. 'A quick chat before you all head home.'

Eddie was surprised Stella hadn't simply joined them all in the kitchen, why did they need to have a formal meeting? And why was Rex strutting around with his laptop, as if impressing on them all how busy and important his job was that he couldn't bear to let it down for a moment? But Eddie was so focused on the idea of leaving that everything else was easily dismissed.

They'd all complied, heading into the room, where the drapes were already pulled. Rex closed the door, suggesting they make themselves comfortable, that Stella would join them in a minute. He even pulled over a velour-upholstered chair for Britt, more comfortable for her, he said, than those deep squashy leather armchairs. He placed his laptop on top of the floor cabinet running along under the wall-mounted screen and hooked up a cable between them. The screen sprang to life, and Eddie realised he was looking at images of various downstairs rooms in The Lookout, including Stella in the library.

'You weren't sitting around sipping wine when we were down at the harbour last evening, were you?' Eddie asked.

'Have you been spying on us?' Caz said, half rising to her feet.

'Sit. Down.' Rex stood behind Britt, took a gun out of his pocket, and pushed the muzzle against the back of Britt's head.

'What's happening?' Eddie asked.

'No one is to say a word,' Rex instructed. 'Right?'

It was the equivalent of a sucker punch to the gut. He heard Maisie's gasp, the sound of Caz's sharp, indrawn breath, Janet softly breathing 'Oh, fuck.' On the screen, they were all watching Stella's progress from the library to the open-plan area, and Eddie wanted to beam her a message somehow, urging her to pick up her phone and call for help.

'Sit in the front row,' Rex said. 'Where I can keep an eye on you.'

He managed to squeeze Caz's hand as they moved around, and he made sure to sit beside her. He wanted to tell her that he'd give anything to have her away from here, somewhere safe. On the screen in front of them, they all saw Stella coming out into the hallway, and approaching the door. He wanted to yell at her to get away and save herself, but it's too late.

Now she's here, waves of alarm shooting across her face as she joins them in the front row.

'What are you doing? What's going on?' Stella asks.

'Can't you guess?' Rex drawls lazily. He appears relaxed, but Eddie sees the glint in his eye that says he's ready and able to intercept anyone who tries to make a run for it. Although the gun trained on Britt is enough of a deterrent.

'Is this about Lucinda?'

'Good try.'

'Do you know where my sister is?' Stella asks.

'Do you?'

'Have you done something to her? Is that what this is about?'

'Ah, Stella, if you want to act the innocent, you'll have to do better than that.'

A pause. 'What's going on?' Stella's voice wobbles.

Rex looks bored at Stella's display of emotion.

Eddie can't breathe for a moment. Lucinda had been in trouble, hadn't she, when she came to him looking for the loan? Trouble? More like deep shit. If this Rex guy had anything to do with that, Eddie is probably the only one of them who appreciates that their lives are in serious danger. Say nothing, he warns himself. Do nothing to antagonise Rex. Wait and see. Then he realises that, thanks to Maisie's bitchy outpouring last night, Rex knows full well about the loan. Oh, fuck. A stab of fear punches him in the chest.

CHAPTER FORTY-ONE

Caz

Her head thumps. Blood has turned to water in her veins at this sudden new threat coming from, of all people, friendly Rex. She'd got that one wrong for sure. On top of all the crap that this unhappy weekend has brought, he's pulling a terrifying stunt. It seems to be an actual, real gun that he has, not a fake one. And this isn't a stupid prank, like Lucinda's ghostly singing, or her shredded scarf hanging on the door.

Stella is talking. 'I gather you didn't come down here just to give me support,' she asks.

'Correct.'

'You've been pretending to befriend me, but it was all about Lucinda, wasn't it?'

'Now we're getting somewhere,' he says, in bland tones.

'The mugging – it was rigged?'

'Oh, you are clever.'

Caz closes her eyes. You'd have to be a particularly cruel human being to take advantage of Stella at her lowest ebb. Rex doesn't seem to give a shit.

'You were using me,' Stella says, her voice ringing with hostility, 'to find out about Lucinda? And the investigation into her accident? What have you done with her? Do you know where she is?'

'That's the problem, Stella, I don't. But I think you do, and either you've been clever in keeping her whereabouts from me or I wasn't clever enough to wangle the truth out of you. Maybe I should have fucked you. That might have loosened you up.'

'Where is she? *Tell* me.'

'The fun and games are over,' Rex says, in a bored voice that chills Caz more than anything. 'No one is leaving this room until I find out where Lucinda is. Even if it takes until tomorrow. And if anyone has any stupid ideas, please apologise to Britt for your actions in advance for they will harm her. You won't get out of this house easily. I've collected all the keys, except for the one in the front door. Maisie, you might be kind enough to fetch it.'

'Me?' Maisie asks, in a wobbly voice.

'Yes, you. You're going to make sure the hall door is locked. I'll be watching you. After that, you're going to lock the door of this room also and give me both keys.' He reaches over and presses something on his laptop, and the screen changes to show a full-sized view of the area around the hall door.

Caz tries to breathe slowly through her mounting alarm. She hopes Maisie doesn't let her panic get the better of her and make her do something silly. But the other woman is clearly as shell-shocked as she is. She moves like a stiff puppet, going out into the hallway, checking the door, and coming in, she locks the door of the media room, giving Rex both keys, recoiling at the brief touch of his flesh as their hands meet.

They are the proverbial fish in a barrel, Caz realises.

'And by the way,' Rex says, 'in case you have them on you, your mobiles won't be much use because I've jammed the signal.'

'What the hell is going on?' Stella rises to her feet. 'I want to know what you did with my sister and where she is. *Now*.'

'I'd advise you to sit down,' Rex says. Something in the way he looks at Britt compels Stella to do as she is told immediately.

'It was you setting up those pranks trying to intimidate us,' Stella says.

'Not all of them,' he says.

'Yeah, right. You're probably the one who's been trolling me all along.'

'Trolling you, Stella?' Caz asks.

'Whatever lowlife is posting vile comments on the Instagram page set up to remember Lucinda has also been sending them to my personal mobile. Either the same person, or some copycat wanting to drag me down. Was it you, Rex, trying to make my life hell?'

'I've no time for social media,' he says, 'but I had help in that regard.'

A frisson of tension flares around. 'What kind of help? Who?' Stella asks.

Caz sees the way Stella swiftly scans the group of them sitting there. Does she think one of them could be helping Rex?

'Go figure that for yourself,' he says.

'Where's my sister?' Stella asks.

'Guess what, Stella,' Rex says, the dangerous glint in his eye at odds with his relaxed body language, 'I don't know where Lucinda is but I'm going to find out because you're going to tell me. One way or another.'

Sheer panic surges through Caz. Whatever had gone wrong in Lucinda's life is far more serious than anything she could have imagined.

CHAPTER FORTY-TWO

Stella

Her head is about to explode. She doesn't understand what's going on. What has Rex got to do with Lucinda? She'd never heard her sister mention his name. She doesn't recognise him as the man who brought her out for drinks and to the movies. From his controlled behaviour, appearing restrained and a little bored in the way he is standing, yet giving off the aura that he is totally in command of himself and the situation, she is in no doubt that he is cold-blooded and dangerous. The chair Britt is sitting in is placed midway between the cabinet with his laptop, and the front row of seats, so he has easy control of everything.

'I still don't get this,' Stella says. 'I don't get your connection to Lucinda. Or why you're so concerned about her accident, unless this is a devious way of covering up that you caused it.'

'You're good, Stella, you're almost convincing,' Rex says. 'I have unfinished business with Lucinda.'

'What kind?' Stella asks, terrified of something dark coming into the room. She senses it swirling around her, a menace, something raw and dangerous emanating from this man.

'I thought it was all too convenient,' he says. 'Wolf Head, about as remote as you can get, a weekend party with a select group of close friends, the way her car went over a cliff in time for a storm to suck it out to sea, and when it was too dangerous to attempt a recovery. Well planned. Perfectly orchestrated. A foolproof way of faking your own death.'

'You hardly think …' Stella begins, fear shooting around her insides at the implication of his words. The edges of something sharpen in her head, words Lucinda had uttered two weeks before her party – past sins not catching up with her, getting her act together. She's afraid to look too closely.

'I never heard such bullshit,' she says.

'It's bullshit that Lucinda, who feasts slavishly off social media, chose to have a significant party in such an inaccessible location in the first place, and you all agreed to refrain from posting anything about it. Did that not strike you as odd?'

Stella remains silent. How did he know about that? Unless, like the help he had with social media, he had an accomplice among them?

'But of course it didn't,' Rex says, 'because you knew what she was up to. And precisely why she wanted to be off the radar. She wanted no one outside her loyal circle to know she was here until her plan was executed. She wanted nothing and no one to get in her way or interfere with staging it. She knew she'd make enough headlines when her car disappeared. As for you, Stella, I thought that if anyone knew where Lucinda was, it was bound to be her sister. But in your case my patience wasn't rewarded.'

'You have it all wrong,' Stella says, a wave of defeat washing over her.

'I don't think so.'

'No.' Stella pauses, something in what he has said snagging the edge of her brain despite feeling crushed. 'If Lucinda had wanted to made headlines faking her own death, how could she be sure her car would be seen going over the edge? It was purely by chance.'

Rex raises his eyebrows. 'Was it? Old Seamus Dillon not only walks his dog up to the base of Wolf Head regular as clockwork most evenings, but he rarely brings his mobile and couldn't call for immediate help. There you have the perfect set-up.'

Stella feels cold inside. How does he know this? She didn't think it had been covered to that detail in the media. One of their group has to have been feeding him information.

'The facts are self-evident,' Rex says. 'She's not in her car.'

'She could have escaped from the car before it hit the water.'

He smiles thinly. 'Ah, but the guards don't think that's possible, do they, Stella?'

'You've been listening to our conversations,' she says.

'Some of them,' Rex says.

He obviously has the ground-floor rooms bugged for sound as well as images. God knows how many conversations he's been listening to this morning through his laptop software while pretending to work.

'I didn't think we were going to be that important to you,' she says.

'You're not. But I am curious as to why you all legged it down here at short notice. Were you anxious to cover your own backs, because you knew Lucinda wasn't going to be in the car when it was raised?'

'This is absurd,' Stella says. 'Lucinda didn't fake her own death. No one here helped her. You're talking nonsense and it's upsetting.'

'I'll tell you what's upsetting – someone trying to double-cross me.'

'But you've been here with us all weekend,' Caz says. 'You've heard us talking. It must be obvious that we're as much in the dark as you are about the accident.'

'Not if you agreed a conspiracy of silence. But you have a point. From listening to your goings-on, maybe one or two of you were involved, as opposed to the group.'

'Good luck with trying to figure that one out,' Caz says, seemingly unperturbed. 'You're forgetting something,' she goes on. 'The guards are bound to come back here, looking for us. What then?'

'I doubt it,' Rex says, in that deadpan voice. 'You heard them. You're all free to leave. As far as they're concerned, you'll be heading home today. They have your contact details if they need to talk to you again. But none of you are moving out of this room until I find out where Lucinda is. And I don't care how long it takes.'

Stella breathes shallowly, trying to visualise what would happen if they all rushed at Rex. Even if three of them attempted to launch themselves simultaneously at him, he'd still have ample time to put a bullet or two into Britt, or any one of them. They can't even make a dash for the door, because it's locked, the key in his pocket. She notices his glance drifting now and then to his own mobile, as if he's waiting on something or someone to come through. He must have some connectivity on it.

Surely Hugh will check in with her at some stage. But if he can't contact her, he might assume she's switched off her mobile while having a rest.

'I have two small children,' Maisie says, in a tremulous voice. 'Finn is only a baby. I'm supposed to be home this afternoon. They'll be missing me.'

'You should have thought of that before you got involved in this set-up.'

'How dare you!' Maisie says. 'You can't do this. Our families will be looking for us. They'll know something is wrong when we don't arrive home.'

'Do you think that bothers me?' Rex says.

'If anything happens to us,' Caz says, 'the guards know you're here … You won't get away with anything.'

'The guards don't know I'm here.'

An icy chill grips Stella. He's right in the sense that at no point over the weekend had Hugh or any of the guards met Rex, which probably isn't his real name. What has happened to cause this man to think Lucinda might go to such drastic lengths to fake her own death? Is this what Hugh has known about? Is this why a person of his rank was assigned as Stella's liaison officer? Whatever it was, it must have been something gravely serious and it's scaring her to bits.

That's without thinking of who might have been in Lucinda's car when it went into the sea. Whatever is going on must be scaring Janet to bits also because she gives a funny little cry that she quickly smothers.

'What's the matter, Janet?' Rex asks. 'Guilty conscience troubling you? You sounded very nervous when the guards were interviewing you this morning.'

'It's all this … I can't stick it any more,' she says. 'Oh, God, especially now.'

'Why not now?' Rex says impatiently, turning slightly away from Britt so that his gun is pointed at Janet.

'Please don't do that,' she says, half sobbing. 'You don't understand …'

'Understand what?'

'I'm pregnant.'

CHAPTER FORTY-THREE

Stella

Stella's heart somersaults. Everyone talks at once.

'Gosh, Janet!'

'Oh, Jesus.'

'Feck's sake.'

'What difference does that make?' Rex says.

'You have to let Janet go,' Stella tells him. 'She needs care and attention. Not this frightening level of stress.'

'I agree,' Britt says. 'Let Janet go.'

'Good try, Janet,' Rex says, a curl of amusement on his lips. 'But no one is getting out of here until I find out where Lucinda is.'

'Do you think I'd make this up?' Janet says.

'Nothing would surprise me with you lot.'

'Can't someone get Janet a glass of water?' Eddie asks.

Rex ignores him.

'At least let Janet get a bit more comfortable,' Stella says. Eddie reaches behind him and plucks throws from a couple of seats, passing them to Janet.

'I said no one is to move,' Rex says.

'You're a heartless fucker.' Stella shakes her head.

'Psycho,' Eddie says, half under his breath.

'Watch your mouth.'

'It's okay, everyone,' Janet says. 'I'll manage. It's just – we'd been trying for ages but the timing couldn't be worse.'

'And why is that, Janet?' Rex asks, in a silky tone.

'None of your business,' Janet says.

'We'll see about that,' he says. 'We've a lot to discuss, you and I.'

'Leave her alone,' Britt says. 'This kind of carry-on is not good for anyone in early pregnancy. Or at any stage of pregnancy.'

'And, of course, you'd know all about that,' Rex says.

There is a peculiar silence in the room. Stella realises he was listening to Britt talking to her in the library. She hopes Rex hasn't heard Caz's conversation about Lucinda's baby, but hadn't he mentioned something about listening to Janet's interview? It had been taking place at the same time as Caz was talking to Stella. She wants to keep the existence of Lucinda's son well away from this dangerous thug. She wants to hold the knowledge of him safely in her heart until they get out of here.

Britt seems to grasp this at the same time as Stella. She smiles reassuringly at her before glaring at Rex. 'I guess you overheard our private conversation.' Her gaze scans the group. 'No time like the present, even if it does hold some challenges. Lucinda was my daughter.' She pauses momentarily to let that news sink in. She has everyone's attention. Rex looks bored. 'I arranged for her to be adopted soon after birth by my cousin, Stella's mum,' Britt says.

'Interesting,' Rex says, in a bland voice. He looks relaxed, but Stella senses that he's ready to spring at a moment's notice. 'You do realise that you're at the top of the list. Which is why you're sitting in the hot seat. If anyone had a reason for helping Lucinda to hide somewhere it was surely you.'

'I wish it had been me,' Britt says spiritedly. 'I can't bear to think of her lost out there somewhere. But if I knew where she was, do you think I'd tell you after the stunt you've pulled? Not in a million years.'

'That's what you think.'

Stella sees the glances that Caz, Maisie and Janet are sending Britt, silently applauding her display of bravado, but Stella can't prevent waves of alarm from coursing through her body. Britt is no match for the likes of menacing Rex. Eddie must realise this too, because he asks, as if to dissipate the tension, 'Did Lucinda find out you were her birth-mother?'

'Yes, Eddie,' Britt says. 'She came to me the day of her party to talk about searching for her birth-parents. She was getting her life on track, she said, and that was when I told her the truth.'

'She said more or less the same to me,' Eddie says. 'About getting her act together. A few months before the party.'

'And that was why you loaned her the money,' Rex says.

'Yes.' Eddie looks startled, as though he has forgotten where he is and has admitted more than he meant to.

CHAPTER FORTY-FOUR

Eddie

'The money she never paid back?' Rex says softly.

Eddie tries to hold a wave of fear at bay. How has he allowed himself to be caught up in this terrifying situation? Fuck Rex to hell and back. And his friggin' gun. How are they going to get out of here in one piece? If any opportunity to escape arises, he has figured out that sad bastard Eddie has the least to lose. But it's Britt who's in the immediate firing line.

And sad bastard Eddie had better say as little as possible in front of Rex, and make out he knew sweet feck-all about Lucinda's affairs and the trouble she was in. He can't afford to give away anything or add to the tension in the room, or send anxiety levels off the scale, or risk an injury to Britt. He turns to Stella.

'Lucinda loved you, Stella,' he says, deciding it is the first and most important thing that Stella needs to hear. 'She begged me not to say anything to you about the money she was borrowing from me. She didn't want to be a problem to you. She cared about what you thought, and didn't want to cause you any grief.'

'If she was in trouble in any way, I would have helped her,' Stella says.

'She knew that,' Eddie says, 'but I'm not sure to what extent she was in trouble,' he fibs, almost afraid to glance at Rex, in case his face gives away what he knows, including the reason why Rex might be looking for her. Like, for example, a little matter of her drug problem, her drug debt, her rehab programme. Some of these were quite possibly linked to Rex and his unfinished business. And Rex seems quite comfortable with that gun, as though he's well used to handling one. The less everyone knows, the better for their own sakes.

'All I know is she didn't want to upset you or compromise your career in any way,' Eddie says. 'She told me that being able to keep up a normal front with you gave her back some of her self-respect.'

'I would have helped her out too,' Caz says, in a small voice.

'Oh, Caz,' Eddie smiles at her with as much reassurance as he can muster, 'she told me you'd helped her out before, big-time, and she didn't want to be bothering you again.'

Caz bites her lip.

'The next time I saw her was here, at the party,' Eddie tells Stella. 'She was supposed to talk to me then about arranging to pay me back but, well, the weekend veered off on a track of its own. We didn't have the chance to talk properly. Then ...' he drops his head into his hands '... she was gone. Lucinda was gone.'

Eddie pushes back a wave of sadness that threatens to engulf him in spite of the fraught situation. He still sees Lucinda sitting across from him in a Dublin city restaurant, telling him she was determined to turn her life around, her eyes bright with resolve. Something inside him crumples.

'I loved her,' he says hoarsely, 'from the first moment I saw her. She was so full of fun. I knew we'd never work as a couple, though. Lucinda wasn't someone you could ever pin down and I never wanted to clip her wings. She drove me mad sometimes. I knew she had issues with her parents, but there was something inside her, an energy that was contagious. There were times when she hurt me and I was sorry our paths had crossed at all. But on balance, I'd far rather have known her than not, and I would have done anything at all to help her out.'

'Can we move the narrative along, please?' Rex says. 'These revelations are getting us nowhere. All the same, I think you replace Britt's position on the top of the list of whoever helped Lucinda fake her own death.'

'You can put me at the top of your list as well,' Caz says.

Eddie flashes her a warning glance. If this is what he thinks it is, Rex is not to be trifled with. Caz gives a tiny shake of the head.

'You are very high on my list, Caz,' Rex says, 'in view of what you said last night. If I recall correctly, whenever Lucinda needed anything at all, you were ready to drop everything for her … If anyone knows where Lucinda is, you surely do.'

'As if I'd tell you.'

Eddie doesn't like the way Caz is squaring up to him. Or the way Rex is looking at Caz with a glint in his eye. He feels compelled to say something, anything, to distract Rex, to break the tension he sees escalating between them. His good-natured Caz hasn't got it in her to imagine someone like Rex could be a killer.

'Look, Rex,' he says desperately, 'if this is about money, I'm sure we can come to some arrangement.'

'Can we?' Rex looks amused. 'I'd love to know what gives you that idea.'

Eddie shrugs. Caz shoots him a quizzical look. He tries to give her a brief warning glance, but he's not sure how effective it is. 'As I said to Stella, I don't know what trouble, if any, Lucinda was in, but maybe money has something to do with why you're looking for her.'

'Why do I think you know more than you're letting on?' Rex asks.

'I dunno.'

'Good try. But unfortunately, Eddie, it has nothing to do with money. And the amount you said you gave Lucinda – I'd consider that small change.'

His eyes fasten on Eddie's in a gaze that sends alarm shooting through his veins.

Christ. How has this all gone so terribly wrong?

CHAPTER FORTY-FIVE

Maisie

'Right, you lot, someone had better start talking, and soon,' Rex says, regarding them all with a look of haughty insolence.

'I don't for one minute believe that Lucinda faked her own death or engineered a disappearing trick,' Caz says. 'She'd been talking to us about getting her act together. You heard all that.'

'Maybe getting her act together meant keeping her loved ones safe,' he sneers.

Maisie shivers. What kind of danger could Lucinda have been in that Rex thought she'd need to keep her loved ones safe? Sheer, unalloyed terror grips her.

'Why?' Caz asks, blindly ploughing on. 'Why on earth would Lucinda have to go to such extraordinary lengths?'

'Someone in the room must know the answer to that,' Rex says, his gaze scanning around, resting on each one of them in turn. 'I want to find out who it is.'

'For God's sake,' Maisie can't help spitting out, 'if anyone knows anything, *tell* him. I want to get out of here and back to my family. Caz, Eddie, stop trying to protect Lucinda. She wasn't that much of a saint. She was well able to hurt people as she saw fit.'

'Did she hurt you, Maisie?' The question from Rex is rapid fire.

'Of course she did.'

'Do tell.' He gives Maisie a chilling glance and inches the gun closer to Britt. 'I'm waiting, Maisie, or would you prefer me to put a bullet into Britt?'

'It was on that holiday in Santorini,' Maisie says, in a subdued voice. 'I saw Lucinda's other side.'

'What other side?' Rex asks.

'I don't think she ever told anyone about it,' Maisie says, 'but she snagged my boyfriend for herself. She didn't seem to care we were an item.'

Caz says. 'You mean Dean? Dean Fallon? Is that why he left early?'

A new and urgent tension slams into the room.

It's coming from Rex.

Jesus, what just happened? The threat emanating from Rex has escalated. She feels it in the air, like the shocking vacuum in the immediate aftermath of an exploded bomb. Something to do with Dean? Maisie folds in on herself, shrinking as far as she can into the seat, wishing she could disappear.

'Tell me about Dean,' Rex says, his voice icily calm.

'There's nothing to say.' Maisie shrugs.

'The guy was an asshole,' Eddie mutters.

Rex lifts the gun and positions it to the side of Britt's eye socket. 'Tell. Me. About. Dean.'

Looking at his stony eyes Maisie knows he is quite capable of doing Britt a fatal injury. He's killed before, she guesses, the idea chilling her. He won't hesitate to kill again. Oh, dear God.

There is nothing for it but to admit what happened, the ugly scene that stayed with her for a long time afterwards, eating away at her self-esteem, confirming what she'd thought about herself all along: she was no match for even a pale version of the beautiful Lucinda. And, if she was honest with herself, it had subsequently sent her into the arms of Keith, grateful for any kind of love, knowing he'd be the dull, reliable type who'd never dream of cheating on his wife.

Not dull at all, she realises, but safe, secure and, above all, kind. Grateful, too, for his small children, whom he loved to bits and looked after so well. No phone calls from him, asking where the clean vests were kept, or how Freya preferred her porridge, or that they had run out of baby wipes. He had all that covered.

Keith, I need you. I love you. All of a sudden, Maisie longs to feel one of his comforting hugs, to feel Freya's warm, chubby arms around her legs, her sticky fingers on her face, to cuddle Finn and soothe his crying with a feed of milk. To be up to her neck with a ton of wet laundry. To have wet laundry. The contrast between her noisy, chaotic home with its oceans of safe, reliable love, and this menacing room in The Lookout cuts her in two.

'Speak up, Maisie,' Rex says. 'I can't hear you.'

'We were an item for a short while, years ago,' Maisie says, her voice catching. 'We got together a month before we all went to Santorini and I asked him to join us. He came out on a later flight. I don't think the rest of the gang were too happy with him.'

'He was an overbearing prick,' Eddie mutters, in a tight voice.

Rex turns to Eddie. 'You had a problem with him?'

'Big-time. He was loud, aggressive. We all knew he spelled trouble, except Maisie.'

'Eddie, stay quiet,' Caz says.

'We were only in Santorini three nights when I saw Dean and Lucinda, together, on the beach walking off towards the rocks,' Maisie says on a sob. 'I followed them. I nearly lost them around by the caves, until I saw their footprints going into one of them … They were … his shorts were down … I knew what was going on.'

She takes a deep breath, the memory of that image still filling her with shame and humiliation. Shame that she hadn't been enough. Humiliation that Lucinda had enticed him away from her so easily. Her dash back to the apartment complex, feeling her heart was about to burst.

'When I tackled him about it later, we ended up having a big row … He – he … was furious with me … He packed his bags and left.'

A long silence.

'Is that it?' Rex asks.

Then, 'You don't know the full story, Maisie,' Janet says quietly, sitting up and pushing aside her blanket.

'I know what I saw.'

'You got the wrong impression,' Janet says. 'If you'd hung around long enough you would have seen what really happened. We kept it from you. My decision. Lucinda agreed to stay quiet for my sake.'

'Kept what quiet from me?' Maisie says.

Janet hesitates.

Rex says, 'Speak up, Janet.'

'Dean raped me the night before,' Janet says.

'I don't believe you,' Maisie says.

'Good for him,' Rex says, looking at Janet with such derision that Maisie shivers.

'I'd left my sunglasses down by the pool,' Janet says, ignoring him. 'I was hurrying back through the gardens when he pounced ...' She pauses. 'He said we made him sick, me and Aaron with our loved-up carry-on. He said he wanted to show me what a real man was like.'

Rex snorts.

Maisie's stomach flutters with anxiety. She recalls Dean's mocking remarks about Janet and Aaron's engagement – vomit-inducing, he'd said. Janet was getting on his wick, he'd said, the way she walked around flaunting those tits and ass, as if she was looking for a good ride.

They were words that had sat awkwardly with her but it had been easier to ignore them and go with the exciting flow of the holiday. Until she'd seen him with Lucinda.

'Stop.' Maisie shudders. 'This is terrible, Janet. I'm so, so sorry.' Recalling his exciting, bad-boy image, she could see him being brazen enough to grab exactly what he wanted, heedless of anyone else. Why hadn't she recognised his brash swagger for what it was?

'Shut up, Maisie. Keep going, Janet. This is all very interesting,' Rex drawls.

Janet continues, her voice thin and jerky, 'Afterwards, I was heading back to the apartment when I met Lucinda and found myself confiding in her, begging her to keep it to herself. I didn't want anyone else to know, especially Aaron. I knew he'd go in all guns blazing and I didn't want to wreck the rest of our lives.'

'Jesus.'

'We planned a little revenge,' Janet continues, her words searing Maisie.

'What kind of revenge?' Rex asks.

Janet shakes her head as if to dismiss him and looks across at Maisie. 'We needed to get him off your back, make sure he wouldn't wreck your life too. Lucinda pretended to Dean she fancied him, and the prick believed her! Talk about ego. The next evening, she lured him down to the caves, but when his shorts were down, she injured him where it hurt most. She even got Andreas and Christos in on the act.'

'Who were they?' Rex asks.

'The couple who managed our apartment complex,' Janet says. 'Lucinda didn't tell them what Dean had done to me, but she made out he'd assaulted her and needed to be taught a lesson. They were already waiting in the cave and they roughed him up and promised him they'd get him alone one night and give him a taste of his own medicine if he didn't get the first flight home. So Bully Boy ran off with his tail between his legs.'

Maisie is appalled. She'd got it all wrong. Far from seducing her boyfriend, Lucinda had been protecting her and Janet, making sure he'd get out of her life for good.

Only he hadn't. Not quite.

'Lucinda told me afterwards that Dean went ballistic when he realised he'd been set up,' Janet says. 'He swore he'd get his own back on her one day. I was a bit worried but Lucinda laughed it off. I kept the show on the road and over time I shoved it to the back of my mind, but it's something you never forget. I was always fearful of Lucinda letting something slip, but I don't think she ever broke my confidence.'

'She never said a word to me,' Caz says.

'Or me,' Eddie agrees.

'But then here, last July ...' Janet gulps '... when we were all together again, Lucinda was so wasted at times I was afraid she might let something drop. And then, oh, God, after all this time ...' Janet pauses, takes a few deep breaths '... I saw Dean down in Wolf Cove one evening.'

'Did you now?' Rex asks.

'When?' Maisie asks, sharp panic rising inside her.

'The Friday evening we were sitting outside The Pier. I nearly got sick on the spot. I couldn't understand how Dean happened to arrive down to such a remote place at the same time as us.'

Waves of panic crash over Maisie's head, squeezing her breath, making her heart pound. She has to come clean. Even if it means alienating her friends.

'It could have been Dean,' she says, with a sob, 'down here that weekend. And it would have been my fault. I told him we were all going to be here for Lucinda's party.'

Caz turns on Maisie. 'You didn't!'

'Holy shit, Maisie,' Eddie snaps, jerking forward in his seat.

Maisie recoils at his tone. 'Look, I didn't mean anything by it,' she says, half sobbing, 'and I didn't know about him and Janet.'

'Shut up everyone,' Rex says, something on the screen grabbing his attention.

Maisie follows his gaze, as does everyone else. One of the CCTV cameras is trained on the front garden, and something is coming up the driveway, twin headlights blazing in the gloomy afternoon.

CHAPTER FORTY-SIX

Stella

Up at the top of the driveway, the headlights sweep around in an arc before the vehicle comes to a stop.

'It's that gobshite Tadhg in his clapped-out van,' Rex says. 'What's he doing here?'

Stella had been holding her breath but now she feels it escaping. She'd half thought it might be Hugh, but he was en route back to Dublin.

'I expect Tricia has sent him up to see if we need anything,' Britt says. 'She has probably been calling my mobile.'

'Get rid of him,' Rex says.

'How am I supposed to do that?'

'You open the door and tell him calmly you don't need anything.'

'I don't think I can do that.'

'You have to.'

'He'll know by my face something is wrong.'

'You'll keep your face blank if you know I have a gun trained on Stella, ready to shatter her spine. Stand up, Stella. Out onto the floor.'

Stella stands up and moves away from her seat, still thinking that this is not happening for real. It's some kind of dream sequence, or more like a nightmare. Rex moves behind her, the gun pressed into her lower back. With his free hand, he flicks a button on his laptop and the screen is filled with an image of the hallway, just inside the door.

'I'll be watching you, listening to every word you say. Don't give me another headache in the shape of Tadhg. I'll use this gun if I have to, Stella first, then that whiny mother-of-two, as well as the mother-to-be.'

From behind her, Stella can hear Janet crying softly.

The doorbell echoes faintly through the soundproofing.

'Let me go,' Stella suggests, hating the thought of Britt undergoing this nerve-racking mission.

Rex ignores her. 'The keys,' he says, handing them to Britt. 'Bring them back safely.'

Stella is filled with a wave of emotion as Britt squares her shoulders and leaves the room.

They're all silent, hearing Britt's footsteps crossing the hall, imagining her lonely walk. On the screen in front of her, Stella sees Britt opening the hall door to Tadhg, who is standing outside, within camera range.

Britt's voice comes through surround sound, slightly disembodied. 'Hi, Tadhg, everything okay?' Rex presses a button to lower the volume and prevent it from swirling out through the half-open door.

'Tricia asked me to drop by,' he says. 'You're not answering your mobile. Do you need anything for this evening?'

'No, thanks, we're fine.'

'I see everyone's still here?' A question in his voice.

'Not for much longer,' Britt says. 'We'll be heading away soon.'

'Including Stella? I'd like to say goodbye to her.'

Stella's stomach flips.

'She's having a lie-down at the moment,' Britt says. 'It's been exhausting for her. She's coming to Dunmullen with me so you can catch her there tomorrow.'

'Grand so, I'll do that,' says Tadhg, his voice fainter as he moves away. Then, 'You're sure you're okay?'

'As well as can be expected, in the sad circumstances.'

'Of course. Sorry. I'll tell Tricia you don't need anything.'

'Thanks.'

Stella's heart squeezes. Dear Britt, pulling herself together as best she could to send Tadhg off on his oblivious way and keep them safe. Tadhg wouldn't know yet that the body found in the car is not Lucinda's, as the guards haven't released that information, and won't until they find out its identity. He wouldn't have a clue of the menacing twist the weekend has taken. The sound of the hall door closing echoes throughout the house, as though Britt is determined to let them know that she has safely dispatched the unsuspecting Tadhg.

She pauses for a few moments before coming back down the hall.

Don't do anything stupid, Britt, Stella urges. *Don't act the hero. We'll all end up getting hurt.*

CHAPTER FORTY-SEVEN

Britt

Turning from the door, Britt hesitates. She hears the sound of Tadhg's van rattling down the driveway, pausing at the entrance gates, then accelerating out onto the road, leaving them all alone again. It has killed her to have to do as she was told and send Tadhg away, blissfully unaware. Despite the knife-edge situation, she's had time to think, sitting on that chair.

She is the one with the least to lose – she's already lost the touchstone of her life, her beautiful Lucinda. Stella, Caz and the rest of the friends still have full lives before them – sure in some ways you're only getting started at forty years of age. Even at sixty-one, there are usually a couple of decent decades ahead, only she's had confirmation from her doctor recently that hers aren't going to be all that decent. They're not going to happen at all.

Lucinda's accident had been a massive shock to her system, coming so close on the heels of the morning she'd finally opened up to her daughter, revealing the truth to her. All her years of misgivings, and the anxiety of keeping secrets, of having to love Lucinda from afar, of being fearful of breaking even that tenuous connection, had fallen away in the face of the radiant smile and warm hugs Lucinda had given her when she'd finally revealed her true identity to her. For a glorious, sunshiny, wonderful interlude, they'd sat at her table as mother and daughter while Lucinda had chatted about her party, and Britt's heart had overflowed, her world transformed into a different place – a sparkling world full of warm, reciprocated love. The forty years since she'd given birth had collapsed into nothingness. All that mattered was the here and now, the sun shining through the window, Lucinda, her daughter, sitting at her table in a floaty yellow dress.

And then – just as she had begun to marvel at and give gratitude for the wonderful new trajectory her life had taken – it had all been whipped away, her heart pulverised, her spirit blindsided with sorrow. In those weeks after the accident, she'd felt the shift at a physical level inside her, like a peeling away from her usual moorings as though the wellspring of life itself had tilted into shadowlands far beyond her grasp. She didn't need the doctor or any CT or MRI scan to tell her what was wrong. The cancer that had taken her cousin Marie is now super-spreading around her, catching her unawares at times with the severity of the pain despite her regular medication. Medication that she had foolishly run out of that morning, expecting to be home in Dunmullen by now.

So she has nothing to lose in taking on Rex, and if anything happens to her, Stella will find out in due course that she'd been on borrowed time anyway. But can she risk something happening to her beautiful Stella? Never mind the rest of them. And somewhere out there, she has a grandson, another reason why she can't put Stella's life at risk. At the end of this, she's all he'll have of their family. A wave of sadness washes over her. Instinctively she knows she'll never meet him. Still, it gladdens her heart that the spark of Lucinda lives on somewhere.

Rex seems to have a dangerous agenda. Why is he looking for Lucinda? Or is he only too aware of her whereabouts and trying to determine who else might know? To what end, though? It doesn't bring her any comfort that the nightmare images she's held of Lucinda slipping down into the cold grey ocean, trapped in her car, weren't true. Something had gone wrong in her daughter's life and it involves Rex in some way. She's in no doubt from his demeanour that he's a professional gangster.

All the more reason why she can't risk doing something stupid.

She slowly retraces her steps back down the hall.

'Lock the door after you,' Rex says, when she comes into the room. He's standing facing her, Stella positioned in front of him, the gun presumably in the small of her back.

'Come back up here and hand me the keys,' he says.

Britt hesitates for a nano-second. She has an impulse to rush at Rex, but she knows it's futile to attempt anything. She feels gutted as she obeys his order. There is a loud ringing in her ears and when she reaches Stella, she tries to smile at her, but her face feels stuck. She drops the keys into Rex's outstretched hand, and he shoves Stella away, telling her to sit down, motioning to Britt to go back to her chair. This way, she knows, he stays in command of the group but can keep an eye on his mobile and the screen. She feels helpless and hopeless, her heart heavy. Then the new and all too increasingly frequent pain slices across her abdomen, causing her to double over with its crippling severity.

'No funny tricks,' Rex warns.

'Oh, for God's sake,' Britt says, breathing shallowly. She takes another step, clutching her stomach and she stumbles with the acute pain, her head cannoning forward into Rex's chest so that he loses his footing for a moment.

There is a snapping sound, then another. A second, much greater surge of pain explodes inside her, and she feels herself pitching forward as everything grows dim.

CHAPTER FORTY-EIGHT

Stella

Black panic overwhelms Stella at the sight of Britt crumpling to the floor, a spray of blood shooting in an arc out of her side. 'What have you done?' she cries.

'Silly woman,' Rex says casually. 'Let that be an example to anyone else who tries to do something stupid.'

'She tripped. She didn't do it on purpose. Now she could be dead.'

'She's not dead,' he says. 'Yet. Get her out of my way.'

'What – me?' Terror suffocates her.

'Yes. And you' – he jerks the gun at Eddie – 'give her a hand.'

'It'll be okay, Stella,' Eddie says calmly, meeting her eyes with a steady gaze. He crouches down to lift Britt's head and shoulders gently. Stella takes her legs and they carefully move her to the side of the floor cabinet, Eddie putting her in the recovery position, leaving a slick trail of blood on the wooden floor. Janet passes down a couple of throws and Eddie folds one, placing it behind Britt's head, wrapping another around her torso, packing it in as best he can where a trail of blood is seeping from her body.

'Britt will be fine,' he says quietly to Stella. 'She's a strong woman.'

'She was once, Eddie, but not so much now,' Stella says quietly, holding Britt's hand. Britt's face is already grey, her breath coming in short gasps.

'Hurry up, and get back to your seats,' Rex orders. 'Don't give me an excuse to use this again.'

Stella's chest is gripped with dread, as she reluctantly lets go of Britt's cold hand. She tastes the fear in the air. Maisie is weeping, Janet is white-faced, but Caz looks as though she's gearing up to do battle. Stella shakes her head at her, hoping she won't make the situation worse.

'If anyone else tries anything smart,' Rex says, 'you'll all regret it.'

'You won't get away with this,' Caz says.

Rex looks through her as though she's insignificant. His eyes alight on Maisie. 'Ah, Maisie. Come here.'

'Me?'

'Yes, you.' He crooks his finger at her and indicates the chair Britt had been sitting in.

'Does this mean I'm next?' Maisie asks querulously.

'That all depends. On you and your friends,' Rex says, with a grin.

Maisie gets up and gingerly sidesteps around the bloodied streak on the floor, casting a worried glance at Britt. 'I can't do this,' she cries, taking a step back.

'You bloody fool,' Rex says, in a casual voice. 'Sit down.'

Stella's heart is beating so fast she can feel it hammering through the wall of her chest. Maisie sits down and Rex stands behind her, within easy reach of his mobile and laptop, as well as the group in the front row.

'You were talking about Dean,' he says. 'Tell me when you saw him.'

'I'm too scared,' Maisie says, her voice high and thin.

'So you should be,' Rex says, clamping a hand on her shoulder.

'Maisie,' Stella says, meeting her eyes, 'look at me. Just tell me what happened. Don't worry about anyone else.'

Maisie looks at her forlornly. 'Oh, Stella, I'd no idea what he'd done to Janet. I met him in the city centre by chance one day, about a month before the party. He told me he'd been working abroad for years. He insisted we had a drink for old time's sake and I would have refused only I was going through a bad patch with Keith, on top of post-natal depression. One drink led to another, we got talking, and he brought up Santorini. He said he was sorry for what had happened, that I'd got the wrong end of the stick, that Lucinda had been annoying him, forcing herself on him, and when I didn't believe him, he felt he'd no option but to leave. He asked if I was still friendly with the gang and I mentioned something about us all coming down here for her party.'

'So he knew we were all going to be here that weekend?' Caz says.

'I didn't think he'd be interested,' Maisie says, her voice wobbling. 'Santorini was so long ago, but meeting him upset me. I was back there again, furious with Lucinda for hijacking my guy and for the way my life turned out. I kept thinking how exciting Dean seemed to be compared with Keith, and I was horrified I still found him attractive. During the party I messed with the drinks, thinking I was getting my own back, hoping Lucinda would do something stupid … I wanted someone else to know what it felt like to have her mess with a relationship …'

'You silly bitch,' Rex says casually, then wheeling around and pointing the gun at Janet, 'Janet! Talk! Start with that business you don't want me to know about.'

'Me?' Janet is ashen-faced.

'Yes, you. You saw Dean in The Pier. Why is your husband not here this weekend?' Rex asks. 'The husband who lied to the guards about his movements? And whose lies you backed up. You were afraid you might blurt out something to put him in the frame. You were afraid he'd found out what happened with Dean.'

'I don't know what you're getting at,' Janet says.

'Let's recap, shall we?' Rex says. 'You saw Dean, here, in Wolf Cove. Did Aaron see him? Find out what he'd done? Aaron went missing for a while that Saturday evening, didn't he? You don't know where he went. You covered for him in your statement to the guards. Why? Because you were afraid he'd done something stupid? He'd be gunning for Dean if he knew he'd fucked you. Maybe he was afraid to show his face this weekend because he knew the game would be up as soon as Lucinda's car was recovered.'

'No way, not Aaron.'

'You said it yourself. I heard you talking in here earlier today. You don't know what your husband would be capable of if push came to shove. As for what Lucinda said to you – wouldn't we all love to start a new life, somewhere different, given the chance? What did that mean?'

Stella is trying to keep up. Janet has given Rex a prime reason for Aaron to have harmed Maisie's old boyfriend, Dean. Does Rex also think Aaron might have helped Lucinda to disappear? No way. Lucinda would never have done such a thing without putting Stella in the picture.

Unless she was trying to save Stella from something worse. For example, if knowing Lucinda's whereabouts would put her at risk. Of Rex? Coming after her? Or Dean? Who, according to Janet, promised to get his own back on Lucinda for setting him up against Andreas and Christos. And was down in Wolf Cove at the time of the party.

Where is Dean now?

Suddenly she knows ...

She lifts her chin and gives Rex a challenging look. 'This isn't about Lucinda, is it? This is about Dean.'

CHAPTER FORTY-NINE

Eddie

'Stella!' Eddie can't hide his alarm.

He's come to the same conclusion himself and it fills him with dread. Rex has been trying to find out Dean's whereabouts without alerting anyone unduly. The last thing they need is Rex being unmasked as the gangster he is. The more they know of him, the more of a danger they pose to him, and the more doubtful it is that they'll get out alive.

Rex gives him a chilly glance. 'You sound concerned, Eddie.'

Eddie shrugs.

'I have a feeling you know more than you're letting on.'

'I don't know what you mean.'

'I think you do. I want you to tell me exactly where Lucinda is and what she did to Dean.' Rex pushes his gun into the back of Maisie's neck.

'Tell him, Eddie, for fuck's sake,' Maisie cries. She's openly sobbing now, tears pouring down her cheeks.

'I can't because I don't know. Honestly,' Eddie says, the sight of Maisie in the chair and Britt on the floor filling him with a formless panic. 'I know she was trying to get away from Dean.'

'You knew this?' Rex says coldly.

'Yes,' Eddie says, with a clutch of fear. There was nothing for it but to come clean. 'He'd arrived back into her life again … she was … I'm sorry, so sorry, Stella, there's no easy way to say this, but she had a drug problem.'

'No!' Beside him, Stella recoils.

'I found out when she came to me for help,' Eddie explains, his heart heavy. 'She'd dabbled lightly in her early thirties, then got clean. But early last year she met a woman called Cheryl at a party who booked her to overhaul her wardrobe. She'd come into a lot of money, Cheryl said, and wanted an entire new wardrobe. She then invited Lucinda to extravagant parties in her fancy house in Foxrock. There was lots of cocaine, and unfortunately, after a couple of months, there was some heroin, but thankfully, Lucinda realised early on she was in danger of becoming hooked.' Eddie wonders if he'd get away with the short version of events.

But Rex isn't having it. 'Go on,' he says. 'You know there's more.'

'She told me she wanted to get out of the clutches of a drug habit and circumstances that she sensed were starting to become dangerous …' Eddie pauses.

'Dangerous?' Rex prompts.

Wrong word, Eddie!

Maisie cries, 'Tell him, Eddie!'

'Cheryl was Dean's cousin. Dean wasn't long back from working in Amsterdam and the whole thing had been a set-up – his idea to get her hooked and under his control. Dean told Lucinda she had run up a big drug debt. He suggested a little prostitution or money-laundering might sort it out. He warned Lucinda that if she went near the guards, he'd arrange to come after you, Stella. Given your job, she was terrified for your personal safety and your professional reputation. The loan I gave her helped her pay back some of her immediate debt as well as for a short stay in a Scottish detox centre.'

'Scottish?'

'She didn't want to be seen in an Irish centre, in case word got back to you. She was determined to turn her life around and was going to sort out the rest of her debt as soon as she could. In the meantime, she'd already booked the party down here, and that was why she asked for a social-media ban. She was going to lie low and stay out of Dean's sight until she had the rest of the money to pay him off.'

'Go on,' Rex says.

'Go on where?' Eddie asks him. 'That's all there is. At the time of the accident, I kept my mouth shut in case Dean posed a danger to you, Stella. Let sleeping dogs lie, I thought. You had enough crap to put up with. I'd no idea that Dean was in Wolf Cove. Until now.'

'I can't believe all this,' Stella says. 'I would have helped Lucinda. Why didn't she come to me?'

'She didn't want to let you down or involve you in any way. She was terrified of something leaking out that might damage your career.'

'Enough of the bullshit, what else did she tell you?' Rex snaps.

Eddie's insides somersault. 'I don't know any more.'

'Of course you do. You're just trying to save yourself.'

'I've told you everything I know,' Eddie says, his breath painful. 'What else is there?'

'Start talking – fast.' Rex raises the gun, aiming it at Eddie.

Eddie puts his hands up, a white mist of terror descending in front of him. 'What do you want me to say?'

To Eddie's horror, Caz intervenes. 'He doesn't know any more,' she says. 'You heard him.'

'Oh,' Rex looks mildly surprised. 'From the sound of that, maybe you do, Lucinda's best mate.'

Eddie freezes at the silky tone of his voice.

'Do you think any of us would be that foolish with a gun pointed at us?' Caz says. 'Britt's injured. We're not stupid. Read the room.'

'I think you need to be taught a lesson as to who's being stupid and who isn't,' Rex says, pointing the gun at her.

Caz lifts her chin defiantly.

Eddie sees Rex's gaze drop to her chest as if checking the target.

'No!' Eddie jumps up in front of Caz. A sharp crack, a moment's shock, then horrendous pain blooms in his shoulder. He pitches forward onto the floor, dazed and gasping for breath.

CHAPTER FIFTY

Caz

'Eddie!'

A flash of fear electrifies her whole body. Eddie lies on the floor, breathing shallowly, blood seeping out from under his shoulder, fanning in a crimson arc. His face is parchment white, twisted with the effort of containing his pain. He emits low groans through his clenched teeth.

Heedless of the fact that Rex is letting everyone know he means business, Caz jumps to her feet. 'What the hell have you done to Eddie?'

'Sit down,' he warns. 'Or you'll be next.'

'There are still four of us left. You can't shoot us all at once.'

'Is that a challenge?'

She subsides into her seat at the look in his face.

'Caz,' Eddie mutters, his voice edgy with pain, 'do yourself a favour. Shut the fuck up.'

'Why did you jump in front, you mad thing?'

'Dear old Caz,' Eddie says, 'I know I'm late saying this but when you have a bullet in your body it kinda makes you want to talk.'

'Late saying what?'

He pauses, gathers his breath. 'I love you ... but I don't deserve you.'

'No, too right you don't,' she retorts, tears springing from her eyes.

'You've always been the best thing in my life.'

'Shut up with the crap,' Rex says. 'This is not the time for a deep and meaningful while I'm still waiting for answers.'

'Caz,' Eddie says, 'listen to me. Remember when it was us, together, piss-taking our way through life? I took you for granted the way only good friends sometimes can, not appreciating what I had.'

Where was this coming from? All the years she had waited to hear it. Why now? And here in front of this monster Rex? In case he doesn't make it, Caz realises bleakly.

'Eddie! Don't talk. Save your strength.'

'No, I need you to hear this,' he goes on, his voice rough and hoarse. 'When your life flashes in front of you ... you see how much time you've wasted. You're special, my best friend. I love you, I always have. You're someone I can be myself with, that it's safe to be me. I know I did something to upset you somewhere along the line and I'm so sorry about that.'

Even though these are words she has waited a long time to hear, Caz is far more concerned with his pallor, his wheezing breath, and the sight of his blood staining the floor.

'Eddie, shut up. Just rest. We'll talk when we get out of here.'

'No, Eddie, talk now,' Rex says, giving him a kick in the stomach. 'Tell me what you know.'

Eddie groans. 'Look, let the others go. They don't know anything. I'm the only person Lucinda spoke to about Dean and her drug problem. Stella didn't know … Lucinda was determined to keep it all from her. Stella was only guessing that this is about Dean.'

Rex gives Stella a cold look that petrifies Caz.

'Maybe I should have Stella sitting up here instead of Maisie,' he says. 'She might be more tempted to … explain her guesswork.'

Rex jerks his gun at Maisie who is still weeping copiously. 'In there.' Rex indicates Eddie's vacant seat.

Maisie stands up and stumbles into the seat, sitting between Stella and Caz, with Janet next to Caz.

'I can talk from here,' Stella says. 'And you can keep an eye on the four of us together.'

Caz guesses that Stella wants to keep them all as physically close as possible, for some kind of strange comfort. Not that it will make much difference to their fate.

'What do you know?' Rex asks.

'Not much,' Stella says. 'But if this is not about money, you said yourself ten grand is nothing to you, I'm guessing it has to be about the supply of drugs. You want to find out what Lucinda knows, what she might have told us, where she is, and where Dean is. Or maybe you were down in Wolf Cove yourself that weekend. You've killed him off already and you're now afraid his body is going to be found in Lucinda's car and traced back to you.'

Caz swallows back a surge of fear.

'Well done on your powers of deduction,' Rex says, 'but it's a little more complicated.' He pauses for a moment. Caz holds her breath. If Rex is going to explain himself it means it's unlikely they'll get out of this room unscathed, if at all.

Knowing him, and his level of preparedness for this situation, he must have a contingency plan for that.

'About four months ago I heard we had a problem,' Rex says.

'We?' Caz says. Who else is involved?

Rex ignores her. 'Dean, as he is known to you, had been planning on settling a stupid old score with Lucinda Oliver before going to eastern Europe to lie low for a while. But no one had heard from him in two months. He hadn't surfaced anywhere. Cheryl told us, after a little friendly persuasion, that Dean had been saying things to Lucinda he shouldn't have been saying, boasting about his lucrative prostitution racket and the clever money-laundering enterprises he was helping to control, and the unfortunate fates other people who'd crossed the family had suffered. He was giving her inside information that the guards would love to get their hands on. God knows what information she had on her phone. I checked out Lucinda, discovering she'd disappeared last July along with her car. I assumed he'd done the business and was deep in hiding.'

'The family?' Caz speaks up again, instantly regrets her remark. She doesn't want to know any more: it all sounds so menacing.

'The Foleys,' Rex says.

Stella drops her head into her hands.

'Oh, fuck.' This was Janet. Maisie shrinks back further into her seat.

Caz swallows hard. Dean Fallon had obviously been a fake name. Everyone knew the Foleys and their extended family were a dangerous drug cartel and organised-crime syndicate, with links throughout Ireland, the United

Kingdom and across to eastern Europe. Working behind a number of false business fronts, Jason Foley is the patriarch of the criminal empire, controlling it with his two brothers, Patrick and Kieran. The empire includes tiers of sons, nephews, their wives and girlfriends, and various business associates, all living extravagant lifestyles on the continent and in Dubai. Several years ago, they had been involved in a particularly vicious feud with a rival gang, the Slatterys, which had resulted in a high body count, and a number of them spending time in prison in Ireland and the UK.

Rex would have no trouble arranging a contingency plan for their disposal.

'I gather that Dean was foolish enough to let his obsession to get even with that bitch interfere with his job,' Rex says. 'Lucinda knew too much. She seemed to have been silenced, but I didn't know who else she might have talked to. Hence, I managed to introduce myself to Stella ...'

'I'm amazed someone of your ...' Stella hesitates '... standing took such a roundabout way to look for information. Why didn't you just kidnap and torture me until I told you what I knew?'

'Would that have worked?' He crooks an eyebrow.

'Nope,' she says.

'I didn't think it would. Not with you. It's a method some of my, ah, family use but I don't like getting my hands dirty unless I have to.' He glares at Eddie. 'And I wanted to keep all this under the radar as much as possible. Dean was also in trouble with his uncle for being so careless with his tongue. I wanted to get to him first, effect some damage limitation. During our search for him, his car was eventually spotted in Rosslare by one of our operatives, parked near to the ferry terminal, but Dean remained untraceable. I came down here this weekend to make sure that bitch was dead and there were no loose ends. But, hello, there was no Lucinda in the car after all. Maybe she's already spoken to the guards and is hiding out somewhere in a witness-protection programme while they build their case.'

Stella shakes her head. 'No way.'

'And now this body in the passenger seat of her car,' Rex continues, 'that could be a complication. If Dean is identified as that person, and you've placed him right here that weekend, one of you must have been involved as well as Lucinda. She would have needed a bit of help, getting that car over the edge of the cliff, with him sitting in it. I don't think she would have been able to manage that single-handedly.'

A long, deep silence. Something freezing in the air around Caz. Fear. A collective cold fear spreading its tentacles around the group as the full horror of the situation becomes clear.

'I helped her,' Eddie says hoarsely. 'It was me. Let everyone else go and I'll tell you what happened.'

His voice sounds weaker, Caz thinks. 'Shut up, Eddie, it was me,' she says.

'Anyone else want to volunteer?' Rex asks, with a sneer.

'We all helped, we were all in it together, except for Stella,' Janet says.

Rex flicks his wrist so that his gun is aimed at Janet. 'Janet, your husband, he's fit and active. Someone like him would be well capable of sending a car over a cliff, wouldn't he? Where do you live?'

'That's none of your business.'

'It is now.'

'If Dean is identified as the person in the car,' Stella says, 'it will lead the guards straight to you. I don't know how you think you'll get away with this, because you won't.'

'I'm good at being invisible, Stella,' Rex says.

Caz feels strangely calm, as if she has accepted the inevitable. 'But you said yourself Dean was acting foolishly. Surely your organisation, for want of a better word, would be only too happy to be rid of him.'

'Yeah, who cares what happens to that slimy piece of shit?' Eddie says hoarsely.

'I care,' Rex says, aiming the gun at Eddie. 'Don't talk about my brother like that.'

There is the sound of two more cracks in quick succession. On the floor in front of her, Eddie's body jerks before becoming still. Caz is stricken silent, her whole world crumbling before her.

CHAPTER FIFTY-ONE

Stella

Nausea surges up to Stella's throat. She prays she won't vomit and antagonise Rex further. Eddie has done nothing to deserve this horror. As for Britt ... Chills sweep around Stella's body at the sight of her, lying inert. She is barely able to make out the shallow rise and fall of Britt's chest, the occasional flicker of an eyelid.

Rex says, 'Listen up, you bitches. Fun time is over. I want straight talking. If the body in the car is Dean's I'll know within a couple of days.'

Stella realises that the guards probably have Dean's full details, including DNA, on file already. 'A couple of days?' she says. 'There's no way you can keep us here that long. And how are you going to find out, if the mobile network is jammed?'

'Are you for real?' Rex says, in a tone that implies she's stupid to question his authority.

She thinks of the way his eyes have been drifting towards his own mobile. Waiting for news of some kind? That reinforcements are on the way? Rex probably thought they'd all be a pushover.

'The longer this takes, the longer your friends are going to wait for medical attention.' He deliberately pauses. 'If it's still warranted, of course. And there's always the risk that another of you might have the rest of your life changed for ever. Furthermore, if it's Dean in that car, word will get out and the family, not only me, will be out for revenge.'

The name of the Foley family had been like a boulder slamming into her chest. Dean Fallon and Rex O'Neill were surely aliases. Rex's hair had been more than likely cut tight and dyed to alter his appearance. Could Rex be Raymond Foley? Known as Flick Foley, because of his deadly skills with a knife? Then there was Richard Foley, a cousin of his. Stella closes her eyes and tries desperately to recall what Raymond and Richard look like. She remembers from media articles that Richard is in his mid-forties and suspected of being the mastermind behind the money-laundering transactions in the gangster corporation, preferring to stay away from the drug-importation side of the business. So far, he has managed to evade the authorities. Working mainly on the continent, he's reported to have a luxury hideaway in Dubai and an apartment in Istanbul. There's also a Dylan Foley, who has spent a few years in prison in Barcelona for drug-trafficking. Dean?

'I guess one of the family members was my troll,' she says. 'You said you had some help.' Rex, of course, had got her personal mobile number, but the vitriol about her argument with Lucinda had begun before she'd told him about it.

Rex's eyes flicker to Eddie.

Eddie. Had he been taken in by one of the family? A woman, perhaps, shoring up his heartbreak over Lucinda, and he innocently feeding her nuggets of information about the weekend?

'And the YouTube video – did you engineer that?' she presses.

'You're asking too many questions. Shut the hell up,' Rex says.

How had Lucinda managed to get mixed up with these cut-throat criminals? How had her beginnings in a pink frilly bedroom in Lucan led to this nightmare terror? Little by little, Stella guesses, one small fork in the road of life leading to another and another, and from the most innocuous of beginnings – an incident in a hotel garden in Santorini, Lucinda coming to the rescue and defending her friend. Then, later, a vindictive Dean whoever-he-was seizing his chance, primed and ready for the opportunity to entice her towards the long, dark and lonely laneway of drug dependency.

Lucinda, finding herself becoming enmeshed in a repulsive world she'd never thought she'd inhabit. Lucinda, wanting to claw her way back in the face of the raw, brute strength of these villains. Unable to turn to Stella for help. Afraid to ask for it. Afraid to be a failure in her eyes. Terrified she'd drag her successful sister down into her mire.

The knowledge that Lucinda had been sucked into the tentacles of this dangerous cartel – it would have been impossible for her to escape unscathed – fills Stella with knots of sadness and dread. A wave of cold, helpless dejection sweeps through her. Why hadn't she been there for her sister? Why hadn't she loved her enough to *see* her, to listen properly, to hear what was going on behind the silences and the pauses, to know something was wrong? Why hadn't she loved her enough to show her she'd be there for her anytime? No matter what. She was the one who had failed her sister, not the other way around. But she'll have to deal with this particular grief later. She can't think of it now, not when Britt is lying on the floor, clinging to life, as is Eddie. And not when she needs to find a way out of the desperate situation they're in.

She digs her nails into the palm of her hand and bites down hard on her bottom lip. No matter how much she wants to, she can't scream or shout, or drop to the floor to hold Britt, to tell her how much she loves her. She must stay calm for now. Eddie is in poor shape, his breathing quick and shallow. At least he's alive. Just about.

Then she sees something on the screen in front of her, her focused attention to it alerting Rex, who wheels around.

A garda car is coming slowly up the driveway, blue lights flashing in the darkening afternoon. The car comes to a halt. A door opens and an officer in a high-vis jacket gets out.

Caz breathes a sigh of relief. 'What's the betting they've been trying your mobile, Stella, and got no answer? People will be looking for us.'

'They said they'd check in on us, and keep us updated,' Stella says. 'You should have added that to your siege plans.'

'I have it covered,' Rex says, pointing the gun at her. 'You're going to get rid of him.'

'If we ignore him, he might go away,' Stella says desperately. She doesn't see how she can chat to a guard as though everything is fine.

'He'll be back. All our cars are still in the driveway,' Caz says darkly, more, Stella guesses, to wind up Rex, not appreciating her terror.

'How can I face him and look normal?'

'You have to. You've no choice,' Rex says. He hauls Stella to her feet and puts the nozzle of the gun under her chin. 'I'll be keeping a close watch on you and everything you say,' he says softly. 'One wrong word, one move out of place, and I'll blow somebody's brains out. That's a promise.' He shoves Stella away.

Glancing down along the row, Stella sees tears escape Janet's closed eyes and trickle down her deathly pale face. Maisie is struggling with her breathing. Caz looks dangerously stubborn. On the floor, Britt and Eddie seem to be unconscious. Somehow this officer has to be sent on his way. Especially as Rex is beginning to look impatient. Stella takes a deep breath, and holding up her hands as if in surrender, she says, 'Right, I'll do it.'

She starts to move towards the door.

'You forgot something,' Rex says.

'What?'

'The keys.'

As Stella leaves the media room, the doorbell peals. She goes up the hallway, conscious that her every movement is being monitored carefully. She fingers the keys in her hand, selecting the one for the hall door, something about the feel of it in her palm triggering a jot of memory, like déjà vu.

She has a sudden flash of awareness.

Nothing like fear to concentrate the mind.

She unlocks the door and opens it, ushering in a blast of freezing cold air. She recognises him as one of the guards from earlier that day, the guy who was driving Hugh's car.

'Oh, it's freezing,' she says, wrapping her cardi around herself and hugging herself with one arm, sticking her other hand into her jeans pocket.

'Hi, Stella,' he says. 'Sorry for disturbing you, I'm checking in to see if everything's okay?'

'It is,' she says, warning herself not to glance in the direction of where she guesses the small cameras must be, the image of Caz or Maisie having their brains blown out terrifying her. 'Well, as good as can be in the circumstances. Have you any news?'

'No, no news. Hugh Connell asked me to pop up and check on you. He couldn't reach you on your mobile.'

'I switched it off when I was having a lie-down. I needed to blank out for a while.'

'I wasn't expecting all the cars to be still here,' he says conversationally.

'Oh, we're all watching a YouTube video of Lucinda in the media room,' Stella says. 'They'll be going soon.' She looks out, letting her gaze focus on Rex's car, wondering if the guard will notice at all. 'You can tell Hugh everything is fine,' she says, keeping her voice as light as possible, 'I'll talk to him tomorrow.'

'Okay. Well, if you're sure you don't need anything ...'

'No, nothing at all,' she says. 'Thanks for coming out.'

She extends her hand, ready to shake his, every fibre in her body on high alert. If this goes wrong, one or all of Lucinda's friends could have their brains blown out. She sees the guard frown for a nanosecond, clearly not expecting a handshake, but he accepts hers, a gleam in his eye as their hands make contact and he feels the key she's been holding against the palm of her hand with her thumb.

The key to the side door of the utility room that had been in the pocket of her jeans since her early walk that morning. The key she had secreted in the palm of her hand when she'd plunged it into the pocket at the hall door. In a sudden flash of memory, as she'd walked up to the door, she'd recalled that she'd come back in by the front door that morning and the side-door key had been in her pocket ever since. Rex had obviously collected all the keys that were hanging on hooks in the utility room, not realising there was another spare.

The guard is good. When their eyes meet, she stares into his. The handclasp barely takes two seconds, but when she takes her hand away, the key is gone.

'Right so,' he says, stepping back. 'I'll be off and I'll let Hugh know everything is fine.'

'Thanks,' she says, closing the door against the cold night, before locking it, knowing that Rex will be listening for the click.

She's outside herself with shock and horror. What has she set in motion in passing over that key? If Hugh senses there's a problem, how might he respond? Arriving here all guns blazing is no good. He has no idea of the grave situation they are in or that Rex could wipe them all out in seconds.

She fervently prays she hasn't made things worse and her head buzzes with a peculiar lightness when she returns to the room.

Rex is showing signs of impatience, tapping his foot from time to time, his face taut as he glances at his mobile several times.

'Do you think Eddie is going to be okay?' Caz asks Stella quietly.

'He needs urgent help, same as Britt.'

Stella can't look at Britt without her stomach heaving. In spite of her fear, she feels herself beginning to tremble with rage but she has to control it. She has no idea what she has put in motion, passing out that key. Maybe nothing at all. Maybe she has put them into a more dangerous situation. Her mind grapples with thoughts and ideas, trying to figure out if there is any way the four of them could separate Rex from his gun without inflicting any damage on themselves. But her mind comes up blank.

She tries another tack.

'Look,' she says to Rex, desperate to sound as though she believes what she's saying, 'I don't know what's happened, but if Lucinda is alive and in hiding somewhere, there's a chance she'll try to contact me once the news of her car and its occupant gets out – which it will. Surely, of all of us, I'm the one she'll come running to? I'm her *sister*. I mean the most to her. So why don't you let the others go, let Eddie and Britt get to hospital, and I'll stay here, with you, as your hostage?'

Rex laughs. 'Well, Stella, the sacrificial lamb.'

He glances at his mobile and he must see something that satisfies him, because he looks more relaxed. He checks the screen, which shows a dark and quiet front garden. Satisfied that the guard has gone, he presses a button and the screen is back to showing images of the downstairs rooms. He twirls around the chair Britt and Maisie had been sitting on so that it's back to front and he sits astride it so that he's facing them, his forearms resting across the back, one hand holding the gun.

'You don't even have to keep me here,' Stella says desperately. 'You could take me somewhere I wouldn't be found, I'm sure you have plenty of safe houses. Use me as bait until Lucinda, if she is alive, makes contact.'

'I'm sorry to realise I made a mistake,' Rex says in a dry, measured voice. 'I credited you with more intelligence than that.'

'It might work,' Stella says. 'I'm the only one who's of any real use to you where Lucinda is concerned. Caz, Janet and Maisie could say The Lookout was broken into by an armed intruder and I ran out after them … or something. They'd stay quiet to protect me, wouldn't you?'

'I don't know why you're being deliberately obtuse,' Rex says. 'The longer you refuse to talk, the longer your friends are waiting for attention.'

'How can we save them when we don't know?' Janet suddenly cries out. 'We're all here because we wanted to honour our friend,' she goes on. 'We thought Lucinda was dead. *Dead!* We've been in mourning for the last six months, dealing with our grief in different ways. We know nothing about anyone else in that bloody car,' she says, practically sobbing. 'Do you think we'd have been able to show our faces down here if we did?' Her voice rises, quivering. 'Or act the innocent with each other if we'd had anything to do with it?

Fuck's sake. No way. If Eddie is dying, it's all your fault. Same for Britt – I'm so sorry, Stella.'

Janet slumps back as though exhausted, her head tilted against the back of her armchair, her eyes closed. Maisie, too, has put her chair in the reclined position, lying back with her eyes closed, trying to blot out Rex and everything else, Stella guesses.

Caz takes up the argument. 'Do you think we'd be sitting here, saying nothing, if we were able to save Eddie and Britt? You're going to have to think again.'

'You're running out of time,' Rex says. 'Or rather Eddie and Britt are.'

Then Stella notices something odd on the screen, which shows images of both ends of the open-plan area, the library, home bar, hallway, staircase. She sees activity in the kitchen. Dark shapes wearing helmets and combat clothes are moving about, looking minuscule in the small grid. Someone coming into the hall, another dark shape following, into the library, checking around before backing out.

All of them are armed.

Even if she yells for help, she's not sure what might be heard over the soundproofing. And Rex could quite easily shoot all of them before anyone manages to storm the door.

Dear God, anything could go wrong.

CHAPTER FIFTY-TWO

Stella

Stella flicks her eyes away from the screen, petrified that she might alert Rex to her sudden interest. He has only to turn around and it will be apparent they have company. For a chilling moment she wonders if this is his back-up plan, more of the cartel arriving, the reason he seemed satisfied when he checked his mobile. But surely they would have announced themselves at the hall door.

And these men must have entered the house through the utility-room door with the key she had passed out. But before Rex had changed the screen view, there hadn't been any sign of a vehicle in the garden. Which means this is a covert operation. They must have an idea of who they are up against. But they don't know the set-up in the room, or that Rex has all of them sitting in his sights.

Caz is talking. 'Supposing one of us had some information,' she says. 'How do we know Eddie and Britt would get the medical attention they need?'

'You're pointing that gun at the four of us,' Stella says. 'How do we know we'd be freed if we told you the truth?'

'You don't,' Rex says maliciously.

Caz glances down at Stella, shrugging her shoulders slightly as though to say she's all out of options. Then her gaze drifts across to the screen and Stella sees immediately by her tiny start that she realises what's happening. They exchange the briefest of looks above the slumped Maisie before she lowers her gaze. Caz knows she needs to prevent Rex from registering her interest. Stella is grateful that Maisie is slumped in the armchair with her eyes closed. Otherwise, she'd give everything away.

There's something about the way Maisie is lying back ... but the inchoate thought slips out of reach.

'That doesn't give us much incentive to speak out, does it?' Caz says, as bitterly as she can in an attempt to keep Rex's attention on her.

'Speak out about what?' Rex obligingly asks.

'So what you're implying is,' Caz begins, speaking slowly, as though she knows she needs to hold his attention for as long as possible, 'even if we tell you where Lucinda is, even if we tell you the truth about what happened to Dean, there are still no guarantees about having Eddie or Britt looked after. So where does that leave us?'

'I think, Caz,' Stella says, speaking as slowly as Caz, 'if you know anything, just tell him. I know I would. I'd do anything to save Lucinda.'

'Save Lucinda?' Rex says. 'Keep talking. It might save you getting a bullet in the head. Or Janet getting a bullet in the stomach.'

Stella holds her breath as Janet opens her eyes, but from where she is sitting, Rex is partly blocking her view of the screen.

Then the way Maisie is lying back snags a memory – Lucinda showing her around The Lookout that first evening. The media room with its home cinema, surround-sound, and state-of-the-art armchairs. For total convenience, and in addition to the separate console, everything in the room can be operated from a keypad embedded in the side of the arm of each chair. The drapes, the lights, the degree of the chair recline, all the screen functionality including volume and brightness.

In the bottom grid of the screen, she sees three dark figures standing in the hall, just outside the door into the media room. In an operation like this, surely there will be officers outside the house, covering all exits. She has to time this well. There will be no second chance. She lets her hand drift to the keypad integrated into the arm of the chair. She presses a button and the window drapes slowly part. Nothing for the people in the room to see, only sheer darkness on the far side of the glass, but thanks to the lamplight within, anyone outside in the garden will be able to see who's in the room. And their exact location.

'Maybe we do know,' Stella says, thinking rapidly, turning to Caz, trying to send her a silent message. 'Maybe you're right and we've known all along. Everything there is to know about Lucinda and her disappearance. It could have been a big conspiracy organised by your friends, the Slatterys.'

'We might even know all about Dean,' Caz says. 'And what kind of fate he really met.'

Caz and she now have the full focused attention of Rex.

Janet looks at her, frowning. Then her eyes stray to the window, where the drapes are now fully opened, and she sits up a little straighter.

Rex follows the direction of her gaze and jerks his head. 'The fuck.'

'Oops, I'm sorry,' Stella says, pressing another button. 'I must have hit the button by accident.' The other button, instead of closing the drapes, darkens the screen.

'You'd better find that button again and close those drapes,' Rex says, not realising the screen has gone dark behind him.

'Sorry, sorry,' Stella's hands flutter helplessly, 'I'm so bad with technology. I don't know what I'm doing.'

'I'll do it,' offers Caz. 'It'll be quicker to close them manually.' She goes to stand up.

Brave Caz.

'Stay where you are,' Rex snaps, getting up and marching across to the window, stepping around Britt and Eddie. As he goes to pull the drapes, the door bursts open and Stella makes a sharp, downward signal to Caz. She pulls Maisie down to the floor. Caz does the same with Janet. A shot rings out, then another. Scuffling sounds. Shouted expletives from Rex. Bent double on the floor, half shielding Maisie, Stella can hardly breathe. Her eyes are squeezed tightly shut, as though in doing so she can remove herself from what's happening around her. The four of them lie together in a heap for what seems like a lifetime, although in reality it's only a few seconds. Then, a hand on her shoulder – 'Hey, it's okay, it's all over now.'

Stella blinks hard, takes a ragged breath, looks up in time to see a handcuffed Rex being marched out of the room between two men in dark combat clothes. A man is bent over Eddie, another over Britt, speaking urgently into a microphone. Dazed and disbelieving, Stella gets to her feet, as do the other women. Caz hugs her as though she'll never let her go. Maisie and Janet also embrace her before being led, both weeping, from the room. Caz tries to get close to Eddie, but is held back. Stella can't get near Britt. There are now three men hunkered on the floor beside her.

'Which one of you is Stella?' Another man comes forward. With his helmet faceguard pushed up, she sees that he's young, late twenties.

'That's me.'

'Someone wants a word.' He thrusts a mobile into her hands.

'But the phones aren't working,' she says inanely, shaking so badly she can hardly speak.

'This one is.'

She's so disoriented she almost expects to hear Lucinda's voice.

'Stella! Tell me you're okay?'

Hugh. She can't reply for a moment.

'Stella, are you all right?'

'Yes,' she says, shivering. 'I guess I am.'

She hears his exhale of relief. 'I'm sorry I'm not there and that I had to go to Dublin,' he says. 'Sorry you had to go through that ordeal, but you're safe now and in good hands. The team will look after you.'

'How did you know?'

'We heard that articles recovered from the boot of Lucinda's car were traced to a guy called Dylan Foley, also known as Dean, Darren or Daniel, so we knew what we were up against. When I spoke to Imelda and Brendan, I found out none of them had actually met that guy Rex who was with you. A red flag in itself. I couldn't get through on your mobile or any of the other phones, so we raised the Kerry emergency response unit and drew in a unit from Cork.'

'You sent the guard around?'

'Yes, he was doing a quick recce, so I knew you were okay at that stage, but the last few minutes have been ... Jesus, I didn't know what to expect ... Well done on passing out that key by the way, and letting him know which room you were in, but it was a stroke of genius to open those drapes, otherwise ...' His voice sounds as though it's about to crack.

Dear God, if they had broken in ...

'Some of the Kerry unit also intercepted a couple of members of the Foley family in a Transit van outside Kenmare. On the way to The Lookout, no doubt.'

'Who were they?'

'I'll update you with everything when I see you.' A silence. 'Look, Stella, do exactly as the team says. They'll keep you safe. I'll call you later and see you tomorrow. I'll be with you by late afternoon.'

She hands the phone back to the young officer. Flat-lined with exhaustion and emotion, she tells herself she's safe now, but she doesn't feel anything at all.

TODAY
MONDAY, 30 JANUARY

CHAPTER FIFTY-THREE

Stella

Stella wakes suddenly, panic engulfing her. The room is dark, and she becomes aware that she's in bed, a warm and cosy duvet cocooning her. She remembers she's in The Pier. All is silent. No sound of a wind of any kind, no spatters of rain, just a slight chiming sound filtering through from the masts of fishing boats in the harbour. Images from the night before surge through her mind and her heart slices in two.

Britt didn't make it. She was already dead by the time they were rescued.

They had all been allowed to grab some overnight necessities before they were escorted out of The Lookout, moving carefully, stepping exactly where they were told as they were in the middle of a crime scene. The state pathologist and the Garda Technical Bureau would be there first thing next morning. Stella had walked out on legs that felt like jelly. The pain of leaving Britt behind seemed to be on the other side of an impenetrable fog of fatigue. Outside, the dark night was lit up with an eruption of blue strobe lights flashing off garda vehicles converged in front of The Lookout, people milling about, some zipping themselves into white overalls, and ambulances being directed through.

Eddie, on a trolley, his face covered with a mask, being rushed into its clinical interior, the doors slamming, the siren cranking up.

Caz had begged to go with Eddie in the ambulance, but she wasn't allowed to, although a uniformed driver brought her and Janet to the hospital, Janet for a check-up on account of her pregnancy. Bundled in blankets, Stella and Maisie insisted they didn't need any medical attention, that they were fine, apart from fright and exhaustion.

They were brought down to The Pier to stay the night, where a shocked and disbelieving Tricia swung into action, sending them upstairs for warm, reviving showers, then providing bowls of fragrant soup and omelettes, followed by hot whiskey. Maisie begged to be allowed home to Dublin to see her family, but she accepted that she had to wait until the following day. In any case she was in no fit state for a long drive home at that late hour of the evening. They both gave preliminary statements to the guards, knowing there would be a thorough in-depth account of the events of the last few days required from all of them. Hugh called her after that, expressing his deepest condolences about Britt.

As Stella's head hit the pillow, inconceivable thoughts of Britt, lying dead in the media room, hammered in her mind.

She reaches for her mobile on the bedside table. It's seven o'clock in the morning. News of the incident will be breaking soon, if it hasn't already, but she ignores all the news channels and social media, and checks her personal messages. She hadn't bothered to open them the previous night – it was too much effort.

A message from Hugh, sent last night after his phone call, hoping she'd have a good rest, reminding her not to move outside The Pier but to stay put until he was down later that day. Then a couple from Leona, Emily and other work colleagues, sent yesterday, asking how she was and how the weekend was going, oblivious so far to last night's turn of events. There was a kind message too from Megan, one of the group of friends she'd avoided after the split with Leo, telling her she'd heard the news about Lucinda's car and was thinking of her during this sad weekend. If she wanted to meet her or any of the gang for coffee or a drink at any time, she was to give her a call.

She was glad of the offer, having distanced herself from the group immediately after Leo's unfaithfulness with Davina, assuming they'd be in Davina's camp. She'd needed to hide and lick her wounds in private. But maybe she'd got things wrong, and she knows now that she's going to need all the support she can get when this weekend is over.

But it's not over yet, not by a long shot. She still doesn't know where Lucinda is, and she can't figure out what part Rex played in the course of that dreadful weekend.

Rex – how stupid she'd been to fall for him.

Not, of course, that he is Rex in reality.

He'd wanted to get to his brother first. A brother who was speaking too freely about the family business, sharing highly confidential trade secrets. She knows that having a loose cannon on board wouldn't sit too well with those tightly structured, lean, mean organised gangs. What kind of damage limitation had Rex wanted to effect? Had he wanted to save his brother? Or had he wanted him out of the way, using Lucinda's accident as some kind of camouflage, then inveigling himself into Stella's life and following her here to make sure no loose ends remained?

Yet this morning, her conjectures seem off – surely Rex would have known that the car might be recovered and the body of Dean/Dylan discovered. Possibly, even, in the immediate aftermath of the incident. Which it might have been, but for the tide being so full and the winds particularly strong and high that evening. Hugh had said Dylan's belongings were found in the boot, so there was a strong chance it was indeed him. If Rex had engineered the incident, he would have known Dylan might be readily identified. He would also know where Lucinda was. In coming down to The Lookout this weekend, had Rex been trying to deflect away from himself any suspicions other Foley family members might have about Dylan's death? Testing Stella and Lucinda's friends to make sure they knew nothing?

All she knew for certain was that none of the party group had seen Lucinda after half past two that afternoon, when she had dropped Aaron and Eddie down to the harbour. Lucinda couldn't have managed the Herculean feat of pushing her car off the edge of the cliff, never mind with Dylan sitting docilely inside it. And he had to have been sitting docilely because his seatbelt had still been fastened when they found him.

Nothing adds up.

It's now half past seven. She can hear muted noises from downstairs: Tricia, up and about her day, moving quietly so as not to disturb them. The avalanche of visitors to Wolf Cove had departed in the aftermath of the recovery, and as far as

Stella knows, just Maisie and she are staying here, along with two gardaí.

Stella gets out of bed, pads across to the window and opens the drapes. It's dark out, the still harbour waters mirroring the indigo sky, a chain of lights around the pier reflecting on the surface, like jewels on a thread. Lights are on here and there, spilling onto the quayside. It's beautifully calm, but also, she guesses, bitingly cold. The Pier faces south along this part of the Kerry peninsula, and as she watches, she senses the sky lightening over to the east, heralded by a slight gradation in the thickness of the clouds. They are still an hour off sunrise, but it's on the way. Somewhere out there she has a nephew, waiting to be found, but it's sunrise to a day Britt will not wake to see.

Stella thinks of her still lying in The Lookout, the crime-scene tape being rolled around the perimeter and on the laneway leading up to it as they were leaving last night, the uniformed guards on duty outside The Lookout and at the entrance to the laneway, ensuring only authorised personnel were admitted. All of a sudden, she needs to breathe in cold, fresh air. After being cooped up in a state of terror for so long yesterday, and with the sadness of Britt's senseless murder heavy in her heart, she needs to move, to put one foot in front of the other, to be out in the stinging chilliness of the pre-dawn, to feel alive in some way.

Stay put, Hugh said. But Rex is now in custody, the guards on duty by The Lookout. A walk around the harbour as the dawn is breaking will be fine.

She hears Tricia moving about in the kitchen as she comes downstairs quietly, wearing jeans and a jumper under her quilted coat and thick scarf. Her mobile is in her pocket. As soon as she returns, she'll have a warming shower. She lets herself out the side door.

The salty air is freezing, hitting her face like nails, but it tastes like nectar. She draws in deep gulps of it, letting it fill her lungs, feeling it all the way down to her toes. She strolls across the cobbled quayside to the edge of the horseshoe-shaped harbour where there is nothing between her and deep water. Several fishing boats are moored to the right, along one side of the harbour wall, others out at sea, and from here she can see tiny glimmers of light bobbing on the horizon.

She continues walking, pausing by the spot where Lucinda's car had been recovered from the water, disturbing a flock of gulls feasting on some scraps. They scatter into the air with a beat of wings and screams of annoyance. She walks further down, beyond the locked gate to the jetty that allows access to the fishing boats, and up past the end of the curving wall that runs along the eastern perimeter of the harbour. Beyond this there is nothing but the inky sea, calm and still in the early morning, the edge of white foamy waves slapping lightly against a narrow shingle beach. In the near distance, the promontory of Wolf Head rears into the sky, its dark bulk visible against the now separating bands of indigo cloud. The shingle beach runs along the half-mile or so stretch up to the thick, rocky base of the Head – the route Tricia's father, Seamus, had taken the evening he'd seen Lucinda's car.

Stella looks up at the jagged bastion of the cliff edge, towering high above her. For six months her black thoughts have run around the same dark, never-ending spiral, imagining Lucinda's car toppling over the edge with her in it, wondering how it had happened and why. Now everything has changed, has become darker, more charged with fear, horror and terrifying uncertainties.

She hears footsteps crunching behind her and quickens her pace, sliding a little on the damp shingle. The footsteps also quicken in tempo. Something detaches itself from her jangled mind, a sliver of thought that had occurred to her late last night. She knew Rex had not been acting alone this weekend. Hugh had told her last night that other members of the Foley family had been arrested in Kenmare, but could more have arrived down to Wolf Cove undetected to keep an eye on proceedings? By now she is far closer to the base of Wolf Head than to the harbour. The likelihood is, she wouldn't be visible from the quays. She wouldn't be heard if she screamed. And no one at The Pier knows she has slipped out for some fresh air.

Stay put, Hugh had said. Why? Did he know something she didn't?

With the sea to her left and the looming bulk of Wolf Head rising on her right, the incoming tide washing over the serrated base of the rock face, there is no escape. She whirls around ready to face whoever is behind her.

No need to worry.

It's Tadhg.

CHAPTER FIFTY-FOUR

Stella

'Tadhg! Were you following me?' She attempts to sound light, but her fear is ebbing away so slowly that her voice shakes.

'Hey, what's happening?' he asks. 'There were guards crawling all over the place last night and rumours that someone's been killed.'

Tadhg probably knows nothing beyond his innocent visit to The Lookout yesterday evening. Fresh pain explodes in Stella's chest. She should have stayed in the privacy of her room at The Pier. Not that she's in any danger, but she can't handle this. Her breathing becomes erratic as she struggles to draw air into her lungs.

She tries to put him off. 'Were you following me?' she repeats.

'I was sitting in my van on the quays and saw you coming out of The Pier.'

'What were you doing there?'

'I'd come in off a fishing trip.'

She stands there, wondering what to say. 'I … It's … You won't believe it …'

'Jaysus, Stella, what is it?'

'Something terrible has happened. In The Lookout. Rex – he's not who we thought he was ...' She stops to gather more breath. 'He's part of some criminal cartel. Lucinda owed them money, and she had inside information on the gang that put her in danger. The cartel thought she had died in the accident, Rex came down here to make sure she had, but then everything went wrong ...'

'Went wrong how?'

They have started to walk back slowly towards the harbour and the quays, away from Wolf Head. Back to people, civilisation and Tricia at The Pier, the two guards.

'Rex thought she must have faked her own death ... Now Britt is dead and Eddie,' she gulps, 'Eddie is in a bad way.'

'Hey, hang on a minute. Take your time. Breathe in slowly. When you're ready, go back a bit. What happened to Britt? And Eddie? Jesus, what's been going on?'

'That's what I'm trying to explain. Rex is a gangster. He held us hostage in the media room yesterday ... He had a gun. When Britt was talking to you at the door, he was watching on a CCTV camera and had a gun trained on Maisie, ready to shoot.'

'What the fuck?'

'Then coming back into the room, Britt stumbled against Rex and he shot her. She was dead by the time we were rescued.'

'And Eddie?'

'Eddie tried to be a hero ... He threw himself in front of Caz when Rex tried to shoot her.' Stella stops on the spot, a flare of pain cutting through her tummy. She leans over, gripping her abdomen. 'Rex shot him twice. He's critical and – oh, God, Tadhg, it's a nightmare.'

'Sweet Jesus!' He takes something silver out of his pocket and Stella jumps.

'Hey, chill,' he says. 'It's a hip flask, with a small tipple of poitín. Have a drop. It'll ease your anxiety a little.' He unscrews the lid of the small flask, wiping the top with a tissue.

Stella can't believe she's necking a drop of poitín by the harbour before eight o'clock in the morning. It's a surreal moment – still dark, barely a glimmer of light along the eastern horizon, the sea quiet as if holding its breath until daybreak, the frilly edge of the waves curling gently up onto the shingle.

The poitín burns her mouth, sets fire down her body. They walk along slowly and come to the end of the beach, where the curving arm of the harbour wall begins, past the locked gate to the wooden jetty, the fishing boats at anchor, masts clanging gently in the air. The car park on her left, empty and silent.

Something snags her attention – something Tadhg had said – or, rather, not said. 'How did you know about Lucinda?'

'Know what about Lucinda?'

'About her not being in the car?'

'Did I say that?'

'No, but ...' Stella tries to unravel the thread of conversation. 'When I spoke about her faking her own death you never asked me what I meant by that. You didn't seem surprised.'

'I already knew,' he says. 'Word got out. You can't keep something like that a secret in a village like Wolf Cove.'

She shivers uncontrollably. Everyone around here probably knows. They were probably picking the bones of her sister's disappearance over their nightcaps, conjecturing across their breakfast tables, trying to figure out where she was or what she had done.

'If anyone has any idea where she is, it has to be you,' he says.

'I don't.'

'Somebody who was at the party must know.'

Stella sighs. 'We've gone over that more times this weekend. Around and around in circles. We've pulled apart everyone's memories of that last day but no one remembers seeing Lucinda after half past two that afternoon, when she dropped Aaron and Eddie down here for their boat trip. Even all the threats and questions from Rex couldn't find any answers.'

'Christ. Here—'

Without Stella realising it, they have veered into the car park where Tadhg's fish van is parked.

He pulls a key out of his pocket and deactivates the alarm.

'Jump in,' he says. 'I'll drop you up.'

She shakes her head. 'Not at all. It's only a few minutes' walk.'

'You're freezing,' he says. 'At least it'll get you in out of the cold.'

Despite her scarf, gloves and thick coat, the cold has seeped right through into her bones, and she's tired from trembling. She gets into the passenger seat, glad of the screen between the front seats and the stench of fish curling through from the back of the van. She looks behind her but whatever is there is covered with a large tarpaulin. Tadhg starts the engine, turning on the warm air.

'Do you think Lucinda had planned it all?' he asks. 'Was she trying to get away from this drug gang?'

'Did I say it was drugs?'

'Yes, you mentioned a cartel. They're always involved in drugs.'

'Are they?' She can't think straight. The air in the van is warming up and she's overcome with exhaustion. 'I don't know what Lucinda had planned,' she says. 'But I don't think she intended to disappear.'

'It sounds to me like she had every intention of disappearing,' Tadhg says. 'I feel sorry for the people she didn't bother telling, like you. I mean, what kind of a sister would pull that stunt?'

'No,' Stella protests. 'Lucinda wouldn't do that. Something went wrong. She was talking about getting her life back on track, getting her act together.'

'Maybe she meant she was getting the hell out of this crappy country.'

'No.' Stella jumps to her sister's defence. 'I think she was going to look for her son.'

'Her *son*?'

'She had a son, years ago.'

'Who told you that?'

'Caz. She spent months with her in Belfast when Lucinda was pregnant. Lucinda had the baby adopted and came home to Dublin. She didn't want anyone to know, but I'm so sorry she never told me about it. I would have helped her somehow. It must have killed her, handing the baby up. I knew how she felt about being adopted herself, but she couldn't see any other way out. The father didn't want to know.'

'And who's the father?'

'I don't know, but somewhere out there I have a nephew, and as soon as I get back home I'm going to find him, and try to trace his father. Caz thinks Lucinda was going to tell us all about it that weekend. I knew she had an announcement she wanted to make but she was keeping it for the birthday celebration.'

'I didn't realise Caz was involved.' His voice is a hard monotone. 'Lucinda never told me when—'

'When what?' When had he been talking to Lucinda?

He doesn't answer her. Something has seeped into the van, something cold, hard and virulent. Her stomach heaves. Cold realisation slowly dawns on her that she may have sleep-walked into imminent danger.

'Did you know?' Stella asks. 'About Lucinda's child?'

'Aye, yes, I've known since the beginning. Since she told Daithí he'd knocked her up.'

'What are you saying? What are you telling me?'

'Daithí was the father of her child.'

'*Daithí?*'

Of course. That makes sense. His older brother, Lucinda's summer romance, killed in a crash soon after Dad had died. Someone she'd known for a while, Caz said.

'I've known all along,' Tadhg says. 'Daithí wanted nothing to do with it. He told her she'd get no support from him, and he'd deny it. He didn't want to be saddled with a baby, so Lucinda decided to have it adopted and swore him to secrecy. That suited him fine. Then ...' Tadhg pauses '... he was gone anyway.'

'Why didn't you tell me?'

'It could have stayed a secret,' Tadhg continues, 'and it would have, only Lucinda decided to spill the beans. She told me she'd been in trouble with a drug cartel. They'd been threatening her and she said it made her realise what was important in life. She was determined to sort it out with them and make a clean break but she wanted you to know she had a son, in case something happened to her. She wanted to leave you with some hope for the future, someone to love, family ... so she said.'

'You seem to know an awful lot about Lucinda that I didn't know.'

'We had a good chat that weekend.'

'When was this?'

'The Friday night. After our boat trip she asked me to come up to The Lookout later that night. She had something to tell me in private. I met her in one of the changing huts after everyone had gone into the games room.'

The lights she had seen out the back – it had been Lucinda after all, but with Tadhg.

'Why didn't you tell me all this before now?' Lightheaded and fatigued, Stella tries to absorb everything Tadhg is saying, but her brain feels fuzzy. 'The cartel must have got to her in the end,' she says. 'Only why was Rex ...'

Still looking for her? Her voice trails away. This doesn't add up. Unless Rex is trying to fool everyone. There are missed connections. There are false paths she is running down, looking for the truth. She takes a deep breath, regroups her thoughts, follows the trail back ... the trail back to Tadhg. She takes a steadying breath. She feels for her mobile in the pocket of her coat. All she has to do is whip it out and send a quick message to Hugh.

'If Rex is still looking for Lucinda, as he claims, it has to mean the cartel didn't get to her, doesn't it?' she says. 'Did someone else have a hand in her disappearance? Do you know anything, Tadhg? Anything at all?'

Tadhg remains silent. He looks straight ahead, his profile set and rigid. He will not meet her eyes. The monster that's stealing its way around the van grows darker and darker. Every cell in her body prickles with alarm. Fear rushes into her throat.

'Do you know where she is? Tadhg? Or what happened to her?'

She sees a nerve twitch in the side of his face.

'I was hoping it wouldn't come to this,' he says eventually.

She grabs the door handle. It's locked. She jabs the button to open the window. Nothing happens. She pulls out her mobile and unlocks it but he is too quick for her, plucking it from her shaky fingers, dropping it down by the far side of his seat.

'Let me out,' she says. In the shadowy morning the quays are still dark, a grainy kind of darkness, the early shaft of light now disappeared behind a sky oppressive with clouds. She's on her own, locked in the van. Nobody is coming to help her. There is no cavalry. No Hugh. She pictures him back in Dublin, getting ready for his morning in court. Thinking she is safely tucked up in The Pier. Two guards in adjacent rooms, keeping her safe.

Oh, Hugh.

Tadhg puts the van into gear but instead of reversing out onto the quayside cobbles, he accelerates towards the back of the car park. Tucked away behind a crumbling wall, there is a narrow track on the left that looks more like an abandoned hiking trail looping up towards Wolf Head. It's overgrown and there's a makeshift sign hanging drunkenly from a post surrounded by a tangle of torn barbed wire. 'Dangerous cliff. Keep out. Loose rocks and shale.'

Tadhg ignores the sign, turns the van onto the track and surges up towards the first bend, the engine emitting a protesting whine, the side of the van scratching against the barbed wire and the thick undergrowth.

At the top of the bend, the overgrown track veers round to the right, climbing higher again, and to her left, in the distance beyond the headland, she can see the inky-silk expanse of the sea.

It's too dangerous to try to pull the wheel off him.

'What happened, Tadhg?'

'Lucinda happened. That's what. Lucinda, with her selfish decision to split the past wide open, to find the boy, to have my parents know about Daithí's little brat. Have you any idea what that would have done?'

'I'd have thought it would be an occasion of joy, once they got over the initial shock.'

'It would also have split my inheritance. If not done away with it altogether.'

She sees it now, the deep, dark threat of it leaping towards her, a potentially disinherited Tadhg, thanks to Lucinda's decision to get her act together, and Tadhg determined to stop it happening.

'My parents adored Daithí,' he says. 'The sun shone out of his arse. I never got a look in. Especially not after he died and the house was turned into a fuckin' shrine to him. They would have adored his son even more. They would have welcomed him with open arms and made sure he was included in their precious will. Some brat barging in on what's rightfully mine.'

'You don't know that for sure.'

'Oh, I do. Any time I fell the least bit short, it was always Daithí would have done this the right way, Daithí would have sorted this out, what a pity we haven't got him to depend on. What a pity we haven't got him to hand over the fishing trawler to, to make sure … The good Lord took the wrong one … If I heard that once, I heard it a thousand times. Can you imagine how a child of his would have been welcomed? I couldn't be having that now, not after all the crap I've put up with all these godforsaken years down in this backwater. I'm not sharing my inheritance with any blow-in, especially Daithí and Lucinda's ugly brat.'

'Do you know where he is?'

'No. Lucinda hadn't started to look for him yet. What's the betting she was going to enlist you to do some of the donkey work?'

She wouldn't have cared if Lucinda had looked for her help. It would have been gladly given. But the way he has answered her question sends fresh fear thumping into her chest.

'Do you know where Lucinda is?'

Silence. His mouth is drawn in a thin line.

'You do know where she is. She didn't go over the cliff.'

Still he says nothing. But his silence is proof of his knowledge. Her skin crawls. The inside of her head explodes into smithereens, but she has to keep talking, get him to talk, and use this time to try to figure out how she might save herself.

CHAPTER FIFTY-FIVE

Stella

'Who was in the car? Do you know?'

'It was Dean somebody or other.'

'Dean. How did he end up in her car?'

'I told him I was bringing him to Lucinda. He wanted to sort her out once and for all.'

'Oh, gosh.' Her heart thuds but something outside her helps her to encourage him to talk. 'Sounds like you sorted Dean out instead.'

'I did,' he says, in a boastful tone.

They are still rattling and grinding up towards the summit, the looping trail they are on running between high furrows and ridges in the terrain, which means the van won't be clearly visible to anyone taking a casual glance up the Head.

'How?'

'I met him in the car park down on the quays on Saturday evening, and I brought him up here, like this, only in Lucinda's car.'

Lucinda's car. From what he's saying, he'd been driving it. Had she also been in the car at that time? From under his seat comes the sound of her mobile ringing. Hugh? If she doesn't answer he'll think she's still sleeping. She can't believe he's the touch of a button away yet totally unreachable.

'He was only too happy to come,' Tadhg says, ignoring the mobile, sounding boastful. 'And he enjoyed a deep tipple of my poitín. Only I had a little extra ingredient mixed in and it made him kinda sleepy.' Tadhg laughs, a high-pitched, honking laugh that curdles her stomach.

'So when you got to the summit, you pushed the car over the edge, with Dean in it, and he hadn't a clue what was going on because you'd knocked him out with your special concoction?'

Gangster or no, what a horrible way to end his life.

Her mobile stops ringing.

'Yes.' Tadhg laughs his honking laugh again. 'But it all went a little bit wrong.'

'How?' She finds it hard to focus on his terrible words, but they will, she hopes, lead her to Lucinda.

'I'd worked out the timings the night before. I knew when the storm-force winds were due to reach Wolf Head, and when the tide would be swelling and the car most likely to be swept away, but it was supposed to look like Lucinda was in it as well.'

She hadn't been with him. Dear God, she can't bear to listen to this. How is Tadhg even talking as though they are having a normal conversation? If he murdered Dean, a stranger to him, so evilly and callously, what has he done to Lucinda, whose plans were anathema to him?

'What went wrong?' she asks, bile rising inside her.

'I was going to open all the car doors before I pushed it over the edge, but I misjudged the incline and in my hurry I mustn't have secured the handbrake properly. It rolled away from me too quickly and next thing it was gone, over the cliff. Bastard of a car. I was raging about that. It spoiled my plan. It was supposed to look as though Lucinda had been in the car and somehow freed herself before it hit the water. But people might still think that because when they checked the boot, they'd find Dean's backpack in it, along with a bag belonging to Lucinda that included her mobile and a burner phone.'

'Burner phone?'

'She used that for Dean – that was how she knew he was in Wolf Cove. He rang her when she was talking to me in the hut on Friday night. Apparently he told her she'd never get out of his clutches, and she was so shaken that she ended up telling me about him and the cartel. I didn't tell her Dean and I had already got chatting in The Pier on Friday night after your gang had left.'

'And all this time you must have been hoping the car would never be recovered, and Lucinda assumed to be the victim of a sad accident.'

'Only for my dad seeing it, the sighting would never have been reported.'

'That must have pissed you off.'

'Big-time, especially when the body has never been spotted. I've kept looking out for her, but there was never a sign.'

'Looking for her where?'

He stares at her as though she's stupid. 'In the sea, of course.'

In the sea? How? What did he do to her?

'Stupid bitch. She deserved what she got, planning to wreck my life and look for Liam.'

'Liam?'

'Her bastard of a son. That's what she called him.'

Even in the midst of fear, fright and menace, the name blooms into her consciousness. Liam. Somewhere out there she has a nephew, Lucinda's son. She has to hold onto that sweet, bright hope for dear life.

'It's mad that you knew about him and I didn't,' she says, trying to draw him out.

'She was going to tell you that Saturday at the party. I knew I had to stop her.'

A deep, dark sorrow engulfs her.

'Your parents are wrong,' she says.

'Oh?'

'I think you're far cleverer and brainier than Daithí ever was. I think you're able to do things he would never have dreamed of.'

'Why is that?'

'Up until now, everyone has thought Lucinda died in her car. What's the betting everyone will now assume she went over the cliff herself? Just after her car? Especially when her bag and mobiles are found in the boot? I can't think of any cleverer way of getting away with murder. Daithí would never have managed that.'

He doesn't answer.

'Or,' she continues, baiting him a little, 'is there any chance she has fooled us all and gone into hiding somewhere to get away from the drug cartel? Rex is convinced she has.'

What did he do to you, Lucinda? How did you feel? Did you know what was happening? I can't bear to think of how frightened you must have been, while we were all getting ready for the party, oblivious to your sheer terror.

'She didn't fool me,' he says, puffing out his chest, reacting much as she anticipated. 'Do you want to know how clever I've been?'

Once he tells her, there will be no going back. No more pretending, no more fencing around each other. Once she knows the truth, she will be in as much danger as her sister was. If she's not already. Her faint hope that someone in The Pier might notice her missing and raise the alarm is just that. Faint. Flimsy. Feeble.

'I think you're going to show me anyway,' she says.

Her mobile rings again.

'Fuck that,' he says. 'It's getting on me nerves.' He stalls the car, bends down, and fishes around by his seat. Then, as soon as he has retrieved it, he opens the window on his side and lobs her mobile out.

He turns and smiles at her. 'No more stupid interruptions.'

Then he puts the van into a high rev and, the engine screaming, he drives it around another looping bend. Suddenly the scrub and shale bordering the track fall away and, in spite of the still shadowy morning, she can see where they are. Up on Wolf Head, but on the far side from the viewing point and the laneway leading down to The Lookout. Here the terrain is rockier, full of outcrops and boulders and crumbling stones. Dolmens and cairns. Standing stones. A desolate, lonely spot, with nothing but the roaring wind, the far-off tumbling sea and occasional screaming seagull for company.

'Lucinda is here,' he says.

379

'She was supposed to be sucked out to sea by the tide,' Tadhg says.

'Was that the plan?' she asks, determined to keep him talking. The more he talks, the less attention he's giving her. She knows she can't rely on her unanswered mobile to alert anyone – whoever has called probably thinks she's still asleep, tucked up safely in bed at The Pier. How long will it take for anyone to realise she's not there? Then again with Rex, the recognised criminal, in garda custody, it would be no cause for alarm.

'Yes, but it didn't happen. She got stuck.'

'Stuck?'

'It was a great escape route years ago,' he says, making no move yet to get out of the van. 'An ancient site, a sort of holy well, that dates back to Celtic times. Over the hundreds of years, part of the base crumbled so that it formed a sea cave. People escaped down through the well and waited in the back of the cave for a boat to come in to bring them to America. That's if they were lucky. If the boat was late arriving, or if the timing was wrong, they drowned when the sea water came in at high tide. Locals think this place is haunted, saying you can hear the spirits of the dead and unburied screaming for help, but it's really the wind shrieking up through the caves.'

He turns to her, his face full of manic excitement. 'I thought I might have got rid of Daithí up here but he wouldn't play ball, scaredy-cat.'

'Get rid of Daithí?'

'Said he hated the place. It creeped him out. Wouldn't come near it. Still, I got him drunk enough to crash the bike.'

'Your extra-strength poitín?'

'He never suspected a thing. I was goading him about Lucinda and the brat, and he gulped it back. Didn't realise his alcohol levels were so high when he got on the bike.'

Dear God. If he'd killed his own brother for his inheritance, Lucinda hadn't stood a chance.

'That didn't work out the way I wanted it to either. I didn't know my parents were going to spend the rest of their lives idolising his memory so that I'd never come close to him in their eyes. So yeah,' he looks at her, 'I'm clever all right, but sometimes life is horse-shite.'

The morning is finally beginning to break. Clouds pushed away by the keening wind leave pale grey skies tinged with pink in their wake. 'You said Lucinda is here,' she reminds him, her insides gripped with cold, hard nausea at the thought of Lucinda being in this desolate place. 'How did you manage that?'

'She thought we were meeting Dean. We arranged that when she rang me on Saturday morning because I said I'd help to scare him away, make sure he didn't get up to any funny business with her. I didn't have much time. I was bringing your friends out on the boat, so I couldn't delay.'

'Hold on, was this *before* Aaron and Eddie went out with you?'

'Yeah. I met Lucinda in the car park at half past two, I had it all planned. I told her to park behind the big skip so her car was out of sight. I wanted it there so no one would notice me and Dean getting into it later that evening. I brought Lucinda up here in the van—'

'At half past *two*?'

The time Lucinda had dropped off Aaron and Eddie outside The Pier. No one had seen her after that. Because she had parked her car as instructed by Tadhg, and gone off in his van, up the twisty track, expecting she was heading off to meet Dean. Not realising she was going to her death.

Half past two: hours before she'd been noticed missing. Had she called her that afternoon to apologise, there would have been no answer and Stella would have thought she was ignoring her.

Oh, sweet Jesus.

'I had to give her a few scoops to quieten her. But she was a dead weight, I can tell you. I didn't mean for her to be out of it so much that she was so floppy. Still, it was easier to help myself to her things. I needed her car keys for myself, and her bag and mobiles to put in the boot of her car. That was a good trick with her scarf, wasn't it?'

'Her *scarf*?'

'Yes. I had it kept as a souvenir but then I dumped it back in The Lookout when the car was spotted. That time I called up with the food. Bet you never noticed.'

'What happened, Tadhg? What did you *do* to her?'

He looks at her reproachfully. 'There's no need to get cross with me. I don't like it when people get cross.'

'Just tell me where she is.'

'See over there.' He points through the windscreen. 'There are three standing stones – well, they were standing but they've fallen over a bit. They mark the way down to what was the holy well. I had to shift some of the smaller stones that cover it, and that was a right bugger.'

Beyond the rocky landscape of boulders and crumbling stone walls, she sees three slabs of stones, looking as though they are swaying drunkenly together.

'I pushed her down into the well,' he says. 'It was awkward. I thought when the high tide came in later that evening it might suck her out of the cave to the sea, but that didn't happen. I took the boat into the cave at low tide a couple of weeks later to check. I climbed up through to the back of the cave and when I shone up the torch, I saw her caught on a ledge up high. I knew by the piece of yellow material it was her. Too far for me to reach. Too high for the tide to get her. My bad luck. There's always something goes wrong, no matter what I do or how hard I try.'

She can't talk. Images in her head spin and collide.

'You're going to join her,' he says. 'Only you'll need a few more scoops of this poitín. You haven't taken enough and I'm afraid you might try to run away when I open the van door.' He presses his hip flask to her mouth and she wrenches her head away.

'Don't be bold,' he says. He flips down the visor in his van and pulls out a knife. A thin, sharp knife, the kind used to fillet a fish. She recoils.

'Lucinda didn't like this bit either,' he says.

Sweat pours down her face. Her mouth fills with water. The pain in her stomach swells and roars. It comes boiling up through her oesophagus, up through her throat, into her mouth and she pukes all over, spattering herself, the seat and the front of the van with vile yellow vomit.

'You stupid bitch! How am I supposed to clean that up?'

He jumps out of the van, and, rushing around, he pulls open the passenger door and hauls her out of the seat, the knife clutched in his free hand. After the stale heat of the van, the air is pure and free. She has nothing to lose. She pretends she's falling but instead she bends down and picks up a large stone, and with all the force she can muster, she whirls around and drives it up into his face. He staggers back but rights himself quickly. He dives towards her, blood dripping from his nose, the knife flashing. She bends down again and pulls out another rock, aiming for his balls this time, gathering the last vestiges of energy, putting her whole weight behind her thrust. On impact, he yells and bends double over his crotch.

'You'll pay for that,' he says, rushing at her, slashing the knife through the air.

She twists behind him, praying she won't trip on the uneven surface, but he grabs her arm and pulls her towards him. She tumbles down, her head crashing into the stony ground. He sits on her legs, pinning her with his weight, the knife raised in the air. Her left hand reaches up to clench the soft inner skin of his upper arm through his jacket as tightly as she can, holding the knife at bay momentarily, while her right hand scrabbles about in the scree around her, searching for a handy rock, fury lending her a frenzied adrenaline, fury that he was to blame for cutting Lucinda's life so short, rage that he thinks he can do the same to her.

There is no rock within her reach. Nothing between her and the knife save for the stretch of her left arm, which is beginning to tremble with effort. Their eyes lock. He looks at her, his gaze blank. There is a pause, a peculiar stillness. Life itself flashes in front of her. Was this the last thing Lucinda had known? Her left hand is wobbling. He cocks his head and looks at her dispassionately as though he knows he's won but he's in no rush to decide what part of her he'll aim for. She deliberately exhales, as though she has given up. Then as her left hand wobbles for the last time, she brings up her right hand, fingers outstretched, and drives them with all her might straight into his eyes.

He springs back, away from her, dropping the knife as he puts his hands to his eyes. She rolls out from under him and grabs it, slashing him in the thighs wherever she can reach, the knife slicing through his jeans. He is momentarily dazed with pain, and, her breath hard in her chest, she frantically looks around for another rock, grabbing one, raising it as high as she can before bringing it down with all her might on the top of his head.

She doesn't wait for anything. She's running and scrambling, dodging the worst of the loose scree and the outcrops, the scrawny gorse, praying she won't trip, her breath heaving, running away from where Lucinda is buried in this place of desolate beauty, aiming for the other side of Wolf Head, the track to The Lookout, the guards on duty. Screaming as she runs, hoping the noise will carry through the calm, still morning air.

EPILOGUE

Maisie

She awakes to the enticing aroma of frying bacon wafting up from the kitchen at The Pier. She fires off a text to Stella to see when she's heading down to breakfast – no reply. If it was anyone else, it wouldn't bother her, but she knows from her time in The Lookout that Stella is an early bird.

Stella's obviously blanking her after the part she'd played in unintentionally drawing Dean down to Wolf Cove. And who could blame her? Maisie's heart is heavy with sadness this morning. To think she'd wrongfully accused Lucinda of seducing Dean. How could she have been so blind to his violent nature? Full of remorse, she knows there is no one to talk this through with, no one to unburden herself to, not now, given the far graver events that have overtaken them all.

Britt.

And Eddie.

Lucinda still missing.

She can't wait to get home. She's been told it will be at least the afternoon before she can leave Wolf Cove. She doesn't care if it'll be a long drive by herself. She wants that time: she wants to feel, on every level, the almost five-hour journey home because it will tell her exactly how far away she is from all this horror. It has to stay far away from her precious babies, who love her unconditionally, and kind, reliable Keith, who also loves her completely and would never cause her a moment's anxiety.

He'd called her twice last night, full of concern, and she knows she doesn't deserve his loyal devotion. Her mum had been on the phone too, actually crying, making Maisie's heart contract when she told Maisie how much she meant to her, as well as the two precious grandchildren she'd brought into her life. She doesn't deserve that either.

She has a shower, dresses, and checks her phone again. Still no reply from Stella. Maisie knows she's lucky she can walk away from all of this horror relatively unscathed. She thinks of Lucinda, telling her how cute and adorable her small children were, who'd never known her son. Stella had told her late last night all about Lucinda's baby and Maisie had been stunned. Contrary to enjoying the high life in London as Maisie had enviously imagined, Lucinda and Caz had been living quietly in Belfast. She thinks of Janet, not finding it easy to become pregnant. Her heart splinters all over again. She's not surprised if Stella is pissed off with her and ignoring her this morning.

Maisie opens the curtains onto a grey January morning and pulls herself up sharply. Hang on a minute. Stop seeing everything in relation to yourself. Stop composing imaginary, self-centred narratives that could be far from reality. Look how wrong she'd been about Lucinda and Janet. Lucinda is still missing. How must Stella be feeling? She puts herself and her heartache to one side and focuses on Stella. The conscientious, heartbroken Stella is nowhere near as small-minded as Maisie, and she wouldn't be ignoring calls while her sister is still missing. She calls Stella's mobile. No answer.

Maisie leaves her room and, standing outside the door of Stella's room, she calls her again. There is no sound of a ringtone from inside. Maisie takes a deep breath. Even if Stella's gone out for a run, she'd have her phone with her, switched on, anxious for any news whatsoever, no matter what time of the day or night it was. She thinks of Rex – still insisting as he'd been led away that he'd had nothing to do with Lucinda's disappearance.

She hurries downstairs, immensely relieved to see the two guards in the dining room, having breakfast. She tells them Stella is not answering her mobile and both are instantly on their feet. Tricia is called with the master key.

Stella's room is empty. Maisie can do nothing but wait, helplessly, while they rush out of The Pier, both of them shouting into mobiles.

'Sit down and have some tea,' Tricia says. 'There's fresh bacon as well.' Her kindly face is wreathed with concern as she looks at Maisie, and it does something to the part of her that feels broken. She bawls like a baby.

It's an hour later when a garda car draws up outside. One of them opens the rear passenger door. A pale-faced Stella emerges, wrapped in a blanket. Maisie's heart jumps into her throat as she rushes out to her. There, on the cobblestones outside The Pier, Stella puts her arms around her and thanks her for saving her life.

Maisie hears afterwards that, due to her alerting the guards when she did, a search was hastily organised and a car went up to Wolf Head on the off-chance Stella might be there.

Stella had been spotted scrambling across the headland with a bloodied Tadhg in pursuit. He'd been gaining on her by the second. The outcome could have been far different, and no one any the wiser.

She hopes she has redeemed herself in some way.

Janet

'Are you going to tell me where you were?' Janet asks, on Monday afternoon, her stomach clenching as she finally voices what has been troubling her for six long months. 'That day – the day Lucinda disappeared,' she clarifies.

Sitting on a chair in a hospital cubicle, surrounded by thin blue hospital-grade curtains, Aaron sighs and rubs his face.

Janet sits back against the pillows, fidgeting with the coverlet, feeling as if the rest of her life depends on his reply. They are keeping her in for one more night on account of her blood pressure being a little elevated. If it's okay in the morning she'll be discharged into the care of a Dublin maternity hospital. She is seven weeks pregnant. Still early days, they've said, in cautious tones.

Still, a scrap of life the size of a blueberry is tucked up inside her, complete with a heartbeat of its own, growing and swelling as tiny buds and miniature eyes form, and she feels as though she's performed a miracle – or, rather, she and Aaron have, sometime during that passionate night at the wedding. How amazing to think that together they've made the beginnings of a whole new tiny, tiny person.

Life is crazy, she decides, birth and death going hand in hand in the continuum of life.

Asking Aaron to account for his movements during a two-hour period six months ago seems frivolous, not least after the overall horror of the terrifying things that have occurred. Her heart clutches as the roll-call of victims freshly roars into her head: Eddie, in intensive care, Britt dead – *dead*! – and Lucinda's body finally recovered from Wolf Head, brought down from her mountain grave where she has lain all that time. Both Rex and Tadhg are in custody, Tadhg arrested as soon as the wounds Stella had inflicted on him had been treated – the evil part he'd played in the tragedy, something none of them could ever have imagined.

Aaron had flown down to Kerry earlier, booking the flight as soon as Janet had called him the night before, words spilling out of her.

'There's no need to come down,' she had said. 'I expect to be home on Tuesday.'

'I'm not waiting that long,' he'd said. 'No way. I need to see you as soon as possible. I can't believe what you've been through.'

He'd been still in shock when he'd arrived, unable to grasp the reality of it all any more than Janet could get her head around it. He'd hugged her tight and kissed her, holding her close, the rift between them melting away in the face of the threatening situation Janet had been in.

'I never found out where you were,' she says. 'I feel it's been sitting between us for six months. When I covered for you with the guards – not that that part matters any more. We know Tadhg—'

'You never thought I …' He looks at her in shock.

'What was I supposed to think? You lied about being with me. You never spoke of it. We've been like strangers in our own home.'

'I didn't want you to know I knew …'

'Knew what?'

He stares at her, a mixture of compassion, sadness, regret, love.

She knows what he's going to say. It's as though they have developed their own unique brand of shorthand after more than ten years together. That has to count for something.

'I was talking to Tadhg,' he says, 'during that boat trip. On the way back from the Skelligs. Eddie was out of it, already sozzled.'

Something cold creeps around her heart.

'Tadhg told me there was a certain person hanging around Wolf Cove that I should be interested in. He'd got chatting to him in The Pier on Friday night after you left, and this guy was spewing a story about Santorini.'

'Dean,' she says, anxiety flooding her.

'The guy was boasting to Tadhg about …' Aaron pauses '… a girl he'd seen earlier in the bar. He'd been in Santorini with her at the time she'd got engaged, and he was boasting about what he'd done to her to help celebrate her engagement to a stuck-up prick called Aaron. Then he told Tadhg that he'd be hanging around for a couple of days and hoping for a repeat performance.'

It comes back to her again, the raw, outrageous sensation of him invading her body. It always comes back to that harrowing moment in the garden, no matter how much she pretends to have forgotten it, no matter how much she pretends it hadn't happened. Squashing it down, out of sight, out of voice, is never going to get rid of it. But taking it out in the clear light of day, and talking to Aaron about it, lancing it as you would a boil, might help the start of some healing, no matter how difficult it might be.

Aaron gives her a soul-searching look, part love, part sorrow. 'All these years, Janet, why didn't you tell me?'

'I was so ashamed,' Janet says, her fingers kneading the coverlet, 'I thought I had done something to invite it. I didn't want to spoil our lovely engagement, or have it overshadow the rest of our lives, not have you looking at me and thinking about it. I wanted to forget it had ever happened. Wipe it from my mind. Lucinda knew, though, and she carried out a little revenge on my behalf.'

'Not half as good as the revenge I would have dealt him, I bet.'

'I was afraid of that too, that you might have tackled him about it, and soured everything for all of us.' Her hand flutters to her neck. 'You didn't, Aaron. Say you didn't have anything to do with ... with ...'

'Shush, of course not. I did give him a couple of digs, though.'

'When?'

'When I came back in off the boat that Saturday evening. Tadhg had told me he was bound to be hanging around the quays, having a few scoops. That if I kept an eye out, I'd be sure to see him. I didn't get a lift up to The Lookout with Tadhg. He offered Eddie a lift but Eddie refused.

Said he'd rather walk. I made out I was taking a lift and Eddie was too pissed to notice that I hung back instead. I got a coffee and waited around the quays and, right enough, I saw Dean coming by, or should I say I recognised his lumbering walk. The years hadn't been too good to him. I waited until he had a couple of drinks under his belt and then I strolled up to him and said we had unfinished business. He scarpered pretty quickly when he recognised me, but I cornered him in the alleyway behind The Pier and socked him a few.'

'What time was this at?'

'After seven sometime. I left him there, bent double, and got back to The Lookout, straight up into the shower, and then … you know the rest …'

'Yes, I do.' Janet feels shattered all over again. 'I didn't know what to think when you lied about being in the Jacuzzi with me. I was so numbed and shocked over Lucinda that I went along with it. I'd seen Dean in the bar that night, and I was afraid you might have somehow found out about Santorini and the part Lucinda had played in covering it up … that maybe you'd been angry with her and she'd stormed off in her car, or something …'

Aaron shakes his head. 'If I'd known Lucinda had unsavoury history with Dean, that would have changed the picture completely and I'd have come clean. Tadhg implied that Dean was in Wolf Cove because he was sniffing around you again.'

'Trying to make trouble for Dean, maybe even trying to land you in it, if and when Dean went missing.'

'I don't understand why Tadhg had to get rid of him so callously.'

'From what I gather he was hoping to implicate him in Lucinda's death, making it look like she'd gone over the edge with Dean, according to what Stella told Maisie, but something went wrong.'

'How is Stella? This must be dreadful for her.'

'It is. I haven't been talking to her yet, just Maisie and Caz. Maisie's on her way home now and Caz is in the ICU, waiting for Eddie to wake up.'

Aaron blinks slowly. 'Jesus. I still can't get my head around all this. But,' he searches her face, 'if Maisie's on her way home and Caz is with Eddie, how come you're being kept in here? That bastard Rex didn't hurt you, did he? I hope there's nothing else you're keeping from me?'

She smiles. 'There is, actually, but before I tell you can we agree on something?'

'Sure. What?'

'That when we walk out of this hospital, we put everything behind us as best we can, Santorini, Wolf Cove, The Lookout. We'll always hold Lucinda in our heart of hearts, but there's no point in agonising over the bad stuff, not when we have good things to look forward to – small things,' she says, tears forming in her eyes, 'tiny, beautiful things, actually, and lots and lots of love.'

When she tells him their baby is the size of a blueberry, but she's already heard the heartbeat, his cry of delight echoes out onto the corridor and she wonders if Caz can hear it, all the way down in ICU.

Caz

She has plenty of time to think as she sits by Eddie's bed. There is no family member urgently demanding that she relinquish her post to facilitate them with the one-visitor-per-patient permit in ICU. The two of them are in the same boat in that regard, and in lots of other ways, including how they had put Lucinda, their imperfect, laughing and lovable friend, on such an exalted pedestal.

It will be a long haul, the consultant has said. Eddie's shoulder injury is in an awkward location, but physio, in time, will help bring it back to near normal function. The bullets in his abdomen have caused damage, and he is minus his spleen, but luckily one bullet missed his abdominal aorta by millimetres. He is expected to make a good recovery in time and could be out of ICU before the end of the week.

These are the crumbs of hope she is holding on to. Plus the way he'd spoken to her as he'd lain on the floor in The Lookout, in desperate pain. His only thought had been for her, using the last of his valuable energy to tell her he loved her. It has to count for something. It has to go some way towards wiping the slate clean of an incident in Santorini, when he'd called the wrong name in the heat of the moment. An incident that had happened years ago, when Eddie had been dazed after a bevy of lunchtime cocktails. Her idea that Eddie had needed the tranquillising effect of vodka and gin before she'd risk unleashing herself on him had been all wrong too. She deserved better than that.

And what had been equally wrong was the way she'd been using her friend's name for casual hook-ups after she'd moved to London, getting some kind of gratuitous kick out of pretending she was Lucinda. As well as being in denial over her friend's death, she'd been trying in a ridiculous way to paper over the memory of Eddie whispering Lucinda's name in her ear.

That had all started by chance.

Caz's mind flies back to The Lookout and that last day, the quiet of the house as she'd slipped downstairs in her dressing-gown to answer the doorbell for the drinks delivery. Lucinda had texted her shortly beforehand to say it was on the way but she was heading out, could Caz let Tadhg in? As he brought through a case of wine, more champagne, a couple of bags of ice, something had bloomed in Caz's head, following the scene on the boat the day before – the heat, the sultriness of it all reminiscent of Santorini, Lucinda flirting with Tadhg – so that Caz offered him coffee. Only it hadn't been coffee, had it? It had been fast and furious sex. In Lucinda's room. On Lucinda's bed. Caz fantasising that she was her friend, giving it everything she'd got. Using an incident that had happened ten years ago as an excuse to behave so bizarrely.

But what made it more grotesque was discovering the truth about Tadhg earlier today when she'd spoken to Stella. She had been racked with grief all over again. How could she ever forgive herself for having sex in that manner with that low-life? She'd admitted it to Stella straight away, Stella generously saying it was best forgotten: it had been part and parcel of the madcap weekend in The Lookout, it should stay in the past, and Caz wasn't to beat herself up over anything connected with Tadhg – he didn't deserve that head space.

When the grieving for Lucinda is less sharp and painful, she needs to get real about herself and recalibrate her life from the inside out. Find the real Catherine who's there somewhere behind all the junk. Shore up her self-belief. But she knows there is only one person who might fully understand where she's coming from.

Eddie, you messer, you'd better wake up.

She studies Eddie's defenceless face on the pillow, his slightly matted hair pushed back from his brow, his pale, high forehead, his eyelashes fanning across his cheeks, a mask covering his mouth and nose, drips routing in and out from various directions. She wonders how 'Catherine' might sound on his lips.

There is a muted flurry of movement from the desk stationed in the centre of the ward. The nurses are changing shift, the Monday-evening crew coming on. Ursula has looked after Eddie all day, checking dials and changing drips, making notes on a clipboard attached to the end of his bed, Caz finding her calm competence reassuring. Now another nurse comes. He introduces himself as Christian.

'I'll be looking after Eddie as we go through the night,' he says. Mid-thirties, she guesses, and attractive, the kind of guy the old Caz might have flirted with.

'And you are?' he asks.

'I'm Catherine Costello,' she says, reaching across to hold Eddie's hand. 'I'm Eddie's next of kin.'

Next of kin. It's a label that seems so right, something that can encapsulate caring, kindness, friendship and love. Nourished properly, it can expand like a pulsing ocean capable of supporting two people, allowing space to accommodate their flaws and hurts, as well as their togetherness and loving potential.

It is their truth, Eddie and hers. It is hope.

Stella

When she comes down from Wolf Head and in through the door of The Pier, swaddled in a warm blanket, Tricia looks after her, shooing the guards away to her sitting room, telling them they needn't dream of attempting to talk to Stella until she's at least had something to eat. Ushering her into the small dining room, she throws fresh logs into the stove before going out to the kitchen, then putting a light breakfast and a basket of fresh granary bread in front of her. Stella is glad of Maisie for company and some kind of solidarity, Maisie refilling the teapot, replenishing her cup, keeping any questions at bay, sensing Stella is far too shocked and overwrought to talk.

She asks for Maisie to be with her alongside Imelda when she's making her initial statement to the guards in Tricia's first-floor sitting room, stumbling over the words to put to the horrific images of her sister spinning in her head. Maisie and, later, Tricia when she is told are horrified at the part Tadhg has played in Lucinda's disappearance and Stella's attack, Tricia particularly gutted that an employee of hers and a valued member of their local community has behaved so viciously.

After lunch, Maisie leaves for Dublin, her car having been brought down from The Lookout.

Stella hugs her at the door. 'Drive safely, Maisie, and text me when you reach home.'

'I will.'

'Maybe we could meet for coffee soon,' Stella says.

'I'd love that, Stella, but I don't deserve it. I'm really sorry for messing with …'

Stella sees tears forming in Maisie's eyes. 'That's all in the past, Maisie. It's over. We should go along with Lucinda's wishes about what happened in The Lookout. It stays there, remember? Now go home to your lovely family. Maybe I could meet them someday.'

Maisie smiles. 'Yes, hopefully, Stella, I'd love that,' and thank you again.'

Imelda joins Stella in the sitting room. Tadhg has already spilled his guts out to the guards, she says, whimpering in pain at his flesh wounds, terrified he is going to die. In some distant place inside her, she's surprised by this squeamishness for someone who regularly fillets fish for a living. She'd inflicted no more than a couple of light wounds, enough to give her the opportunity to run clear. Tadhg would have gained on her and dragged her to the ground, finishing her off, dumping her where Lucinda lay, no doubt, had the garda car not arrived in time, thanks to Maisie's alert.

Tadhg was acting alone, Imelda says. No one else was involved. Dylan, as Dean, had told him of his plan to take out Lucinda – his words – and drive to Rosslare, getting a boat to France, and on to eastern Europe from there, lying low for a while. To cover all possibilities, Tadhg helped himself to Dylan's car keys and drove his car to Rosslare, leaving it in a large car park before returning to Kerry on the bus.

The intelligence the guards were gathering up to then had indicated that Dylan was becoming a bit of a loose cannon, and they surmised he had dropped out of sight for his own safety.

The evening draws in early and Imelda stays with Stella, keeping her company. Or, rather, she finds out later, keeping a watchful eye on her under Hugh's express orders, making sure she doesn't go off on any kind of dangerous wild-goose chase again. As if she has the energy. She sits on a sofa facing the stove, staring at orange flames licking the glowing logs and feels she has crashed full tilt into a high wall, unable to budge even an inch if the house caught fire. Beyond that exhaustion, waiting to pounce, there is a river of tears waiting to be shed.

Nonetheless, when Imelda alerts her to the updated news bulletin, Stella finds herself scrolling to the news site.

The Kerry Herald
Monday, 30 January 2023, 4.45 p.m.

UPDATE
Gardaí are continuing to investigate all the circumstances surrounding the serious incident in Kerry last night involving members of the Garda Emergency Response Unit. The body of the woman (61), who was pronounced dead at the scene, has been removed to the mortuary at University Hospital Kerry and the man (40) who was injured is in a critical but stable condition in University Hospital Kerry. A man (44) was arrested last night at the scene of the incident on suspicion of murder, attempted murder, false imprisonment and possession of a firearm.

He is currently detained at a garda station in Kerry under Section 4 of the Criminal Justice Act, 1984.

A garda spokesperson said that the suspect, who has links to the Foley criminal group, operates at a significant level within the world of organised crime, and members of the Garda National Drugs and Organised Crime Bureau are preparing to question him for various offences under the Criminal Justice (Drug Trafficking) Act, 1996 in addition to money-laundering offences. A man and a woman, also with links to the Foley group, were arrested in Kenmare last night and are being held for questioning at a garda station in Kerry.

A man (35) arrested on Wolf Head this morning is being questioned under Section 4 of the Criminal Justice Act, 1984 in relation to various offences including manslaughter, the kidnap and attempted murder of a woman (35), and two counts of murder including that of Lucinda Oliver (40), whose remains were recovered from Wolf Head this afternoon.

Gardaí believe they know the identity of the person whose remains were found in the submerged vehicle that was recovered off Wolf Head on Saturday afternoon and are satisfied that this will be confirmed on the conclusion of forensic and DNA analysis.

It reads like a horror story. Frozen to the core, Stella is relieved when Tricia comes in with fresh tea, switching on soft lamps, and through the un-curtained window she sees the chain of bright lights that encircle the harbour spring on. There are few people about, save for the guards on this dull January late afternoon. It is almost dark outside when she hears the door open quietly behind her, and she knows Hugh has arrived by the prickling in her neck, even before Imelda gets to her feet and leaves the room, prompted no doubt by his silent request.

He sits to the side of the stove, in the armchair Imelda has vacated. His hair is tossed and sticking up in places as if he's been running his fingers erratically through it. He hasn't bothered to take off his bulky jacket. It's open, showing his navy jumper underneath. His face is pale and drawn.

Her mind flies back to three weeks ago, when she woke up in bed beside him that morning, her body still glowing, nothing covering them but a thin, twisted sheet, and she remembers that she had been first to call it a mistake. She wonders if his pride had made him agree with her, or if there is any way she can salvage words she had uttered in alarm.

'How are you?' he asks. His gaze roves over her slowly and thoughtfully. In spite of her fatigue and her heavy heart, a little warmth begins to creep through her ice-cold bones.

'I don't know,' she answers truthfully.

'That was some escapade this morning,' he says.

'Yes.'

'I'm glad I didn't know about it until afterwards, when you were safely back here. Otherwise ...' He shakes his head. 'I told Imelda not to let you out of her sight under any circumstances.'

'It wasn't her fault. I slipped out without telling anyone.'

'Not that there's any danger for you out there now,' he said. 'You can be sure of that. Tadhg is under lock and key, as is the man you knew as Rex O'Neill, otherwise known to us as Richard Foley.'

'I was such a fool.' The words burst out of Stella.

'Please don't think that, Stella. Richard Foley is a clever criminal mastermind, who inhabits a lawless, subversive underworld. He's been running rings around the investigative forces of Ireland and Europe for some time, operating out of Dubai and eastern Europe. We've been keeping tabs on him, waiting for him to put a foot wrong, but somehow he managed to evade us and get into the country undetected. He changed his appearance completely and used an alias and fake passport he hasn't used before. He's heavily involved in the money-laundering arm of the Foley cartel, but he dislikes getting his own hands dirty, which is why he looked for help when he realised there was a body found in Lucinda's car. He came to the conclusion it might be Dylan. His cousins, Raymond and Adrienne, were coming out of Kenmare in a Transit van when one of our patrols intercepted them speeding. They found enough in the back of the van to haul them in for questioning. There was a burner phone also with your mobile number and Eddie's on the contact list as well as interesting texts and activity on Instagram.' He gives her a keen glance.

'My troll.'

'You should have told me you were being harassed.'

'I know. And there were a couple of incidents in The Lookout I should have mentioned earlier but I wanted to get through the weekend first. I'd say Eddie is entirely innocent, that he was also set up.'

'The content of the texts would bear that out. From what we have gleaned it seems Adrienne was behind Lucinda's Instagram tribute page and unsavoury messages to you, although in texts to Eddie, she was using the alias Arianna. Eddie's still in ICU and he's stable, but we won't be talking to him for a few days. Anyhow, Richard Foley has put a foot wrong at last and we're throwing the book at him.' Hugh pauses for a moment, before looking at her steadily.

'Jesus, Stella,' he says, 'it's dreadful about Britt, and you have my deepest condolences, but things could have ended a hell of a lot worse.'

Stella feels the hard weight of grief in the pit of her stomach. 'Britt was …' She grapples with the past tense, still unable to believe that Britt is dead. 'She was Lucinda's birthmother. She told me yesterday. I think I kind of had an idea, somewhere deep down inside. But all that wasted time …' Stella sighs. 'All those words left unsaid.'

'I know, Stella, I know,' Hugh says gently. He reaches over and holds her hand.

'But then I heard … God …' Stella gulps and tries to pull the frayed edges of herself together. 'Caz told me that years ago, when she was nineteen, Lucinda had a baby son and gave him up for adoption. I'm still in shock about it, but after all this, I'm going to find him.'

'I'll help you with that in whatever way I can,' Hugh says. His gaze lingers over every inch of her face as if he is studying it by heart. It rekindles a spark inside her. A ray of hope leaps. Beyond all this horror and heartbreak, there could be a life waiting for her. For them.

Needing to be satisfied she has the full picture, she says, 'You knew about Lucinda's involvement with drugs.'

'She was on our list as a person of interest whose name had come to our attention last year in connection with our investigation of Dylan. Then he disappeared off our radar.

We'd heard Jason Foley had been unhappy with Dylan's indiscreet behaviour for some time, and it was thought Dylan had gone into hiding to get away from him.'

'But you couldn't tell me that.'

'Not at the time, no. And afterwards it didn't seem appropriate to burden you with it. I came to Wolf Head about a week after Lucinda's disappearance to see if we could eliminate her from our list of persons of interest. I checked out the accident site at first hand, and I couldn't find any evidence to support anyone else being involved in it. Although I kept an open mind, unfortunately it veered towards the wrong supposition. It was a mistake and I'm heartily sorry about that.'

Then he tells her, as gently as possible, that he'd made it his business to be there that afternoon when the rescue team brought up Lucinda's body and transported it down the mountain under garda escort. 'Rest assured,' he says, 'the recovery of your sister's body was conducted in as careful and dignified a manner as possible.'

Something rips apart inside her, pulling her from seam to seam, and she begins to cry in a way she never has before, unrestrained, noisy, uninhibited, her breath heaving, letting it all out. Through her tear-blurry gaze, she sees Hugh getting up, pulling off his jacket, coming closer to her. His arms gather her into the warmth of him, one hand holding her securely, the other rubbing her back. Eventually her tears subside. There is a taut silence. A log shifts in the stove, sending up a shower of sparks. Otherwise all is quiet, not even a sound coming from the ground floor below. Everything in the room is distilled to the way Hugh is holding her, watching her, waiting for her to speak. In the silence of the room, something unspoken leaps between them. She feels a sliver of calm certainty slip softly through her bloodstream.

'Thank you,' she says, her voice soft and thick. 'There's a lot to get my head around. It's all a nightmare and it'll take a while to work through it.'

'Take all the time you need, and call on me whenever you want to talk.'

'There's something I have to say first,' she says, wanting to set things straight. 'We all make mistakes. The night we were together, I called it a mistake the next morning, which was wrong of me. I was so scared of the way you made me feel,' she admits.

His eyebrows shoot up.

'In a good way,' she whispers hurriedly.

His gaze holds hers, his eyes sparking with something that renders her breathless. He gathers her close. 'Oh, Stella, I was wrong to agree with you,' he says. 'I loved what happened between us but it was so ... brilliant, it scared me too.'

They don't have the luxury of an evening to themselves to sit and talk, or do more than touch the surface of the weekend's traumatic events. In between coffees and teas and an evening meal, Hugh is called away to phone calls and meetings, and then to late-night interviewing of Richard and Tadhg. Even the following morning, there is a constant stream of uniformed guards and plain-clothes detectives in and out of The Pier and The Lookout, Hugh moving around in the centre of all this activity.

But she's aware all the time of his quiet, unhurried check-ins with her whenever the opportunity arises, be it a look, a gesture, a touch on her arm, a hand on her shoulder, a private glance across a room, a few words of warm reassurance.

over a cup of coffee. It's enough to tell her that, beyond the sad and sorry rituals immediately in front of her, a future is beckoning, like a precious gift to be slowly unwrapped and savoured.

Exactly what Lucinda would have wanted for her.

From time to time, her mind drifts back to those last fraught moments on Wolf Head.

As Tadhg brandishes the knife over her body, and life itself flashes before her eyes, the truth of what Hugh had been trying to make her understand the night they'd spent together flashes like a beacon: love is far greater than a few angry words. Then scrambling desperately away from Tadhg and across the rocky terrain, as she screams for help she senses Lucinda catching her by the hand, running side by side with her, her blonde hair flying in the breeze, her yellow dress floating in the wind currents, her voice urging her on.

Run, Stella, run. Just a little bit faster. You can do this.

I'll love you for ever, can't you feel it?

Stella stumbles when she sees the garda car cresting the Head, sensing Lucinda's withdrawal, caught for a millisecond in a thin veil between two worlds. Then Lucinda lets go of her hand and her yellow dress twirls one last time before fading away, but Stella can still hear her voice:

Run, Stella, run into your future.

Find my son, tell him I love him.

Live every day to the absolute max. Squeeze out every ounce of joy you can.

Surround yourself with love.

Be happy.

ACKNOWLEDGEMENTS

Heartfelt thanks to my stellar agent, Sheila Crowley, who has looked after me throughout my writing career with her steadfast dedication, encouragement and friendship. Thanks also to Moi Lanne Wetzel-Liao for her help and support, and to all the hard-working team at Curtis Brown, UK.

I'm indebted to the immensely talented Ciara Doorley of Hachette Books Ireland, and the amazing Clare Pelly, who worked with me on earlier versions of this story. Their keen insight and sensitive guidance enabled me to bring the story to a whole new level. Thanks also to copy-editor extraordinaire Hazel Orme, and to Aonghus Meaney, the eagle-eyed proofreader.

Thanks to the dedicated team at Hachette for all the work behind the scenes, in particular the hugely supportive Joanna Smyth, also Breda, Jim, Ruth, Elaine, Siobhan, Ciara C, Stephen and Shauna.

Thanks to Mark Walsh and the team at Plunkett Communications for helping to spread the word about my books.

Thanks to the Irish writing community, including book-bloggers, booksellers, reviewers and our fantastic library service, and to my writer pals in the online and real world for lovely support, in particular Carolann Copland and Martina Murphy for regular check-ins and bolstering words.

I was lucky to spend a week in the inspirational ambience of the Tyrone Guthrie Centre, Annaghmakerrig while I was working on structural edits; thanks to all the hardworking team there and to the wonderful people I met.

A massive thank you to my family and friends, for your love and kindness and for always being there throughout the ups and downs of life, and special gratitude to my nearest and dearest, Michelle, Declan, Barbara, Dara, Louise and Colm, the infinitely precious Cruz, Tom, Lexi, J.P., Sophia, Éabha and Holly, and endless thanks to Derek – I wouldn't be where I am without your constant support.

Last but not least, a huge thanks to all my loyal readers for helping to keep me in my dream job. Your kind messages and words of support, on social media and through emails, mean everything to me and I am indebted to you all.